Geraldine

First published 2025 by
FREMANTLE PRESS

Fremantle Press Inc. trading as Fremantle Press
PO Box 158, North Fremantle, Western Australia, 6159
fremantlepress.com.au

Cover images by jakkapan / bigstockphoto.com
Designed by Design by Committee, designbycommittee.com.au
Printed by Everbest Printing Investment Limited, China

A catalogue record for this book is available from the National Library of Australia

ISBN 9781760993801 (paperback)
ISBN 9781760993818 (ebook)

Fremantle Press is supported by the State Government through the Department of Local Government, Sport and Cultural Industries.

Fremantle Press respectfully acknowledges the Whadjuk people of the Noongar nation as the Traditional Owners and Custodians of the land where we work in Walyalup.

100% Paper from well-managed forests FSC® C124385

Geraldine

ANDREA THOMPSON

FREMANTLE PRESS

Andrea Thompson is a music journalist, artist manager and promoter. Born in the north of England in the Swinging Sixties, Andrea has worked through a range of jobs including trades assistant in the north-west of Western Australia, factory worker, teacher and public servant, but her one constant is writing. Whenever the world makes her doubt herself, Andrea writes her way through the uncertainty. *Geraldine* began as a memoir. When Andrea discovered by accident that every other gender-diverse person in the world was also writing a memoir, she switched her focus and began writing for a central character who taught her the value and peace of the ordinary, and to never give up the fight.

For Matthew, Stuart and Garry, with love.

1

Geraldine was born in an entirely different hemisphere to the one she finally settled in. Younger than her brother by a full five years, she was a last-ditch attempt on Grace Sturmer's part to have a daughter. Frank wasn't really that fussed, in fact he was dead set against the idea, but Grace wore him down, eventually. After she was born, they named her Gerald and took her home wrapped in a blue blanket.

'Guess what?' That was Geraldine's oldest brother, Harry, fresh home from his first day of school.

'What?' said Grace.

'Pink snot.'

'Go outside and play,' said Grace.

Harry disappeared into the backyard, the darkening sky streaked with grey clouds, the air not quite cold enough that he could see his breath, but getting there. The yard was small, mostly concrete, boxed in between the pebbledash back wall of the house and the slatted wooden boundary fence. Through the fence Harry could see the neighbour's patch of lawn and loamy garden beds. He was over in an instant, though the fence was taller than him, and he picked his way through the thorny rose bushes, across the overgrown grass, down the side passage, forced his way around the edge of the rickety wooden gate into the neighbour's front garden and, in a few more steps, onto the road and across into the open fields on the other side. Once the five-year-old Harry had gotten over the audacity of his escape, he lost all sense of time, so immersed was he in the outdoors.

Back on their side of the street, Grace sat down and lit a cigarette, resting an ashtray on her distended belly and leaning back to luxuriate in the smoke. Grace had settled on her method of parenting quite early in the piece, and Harry had learned to disappear soon after he'd worked out what she was about. Geraldine could never remember if she knew these things from Harry's telling of tales or because she was always there, always watching.

One of Geraldine's earliest memories was of Grace from before Geraldine was born. Grace was sitting in a hospital room, just her on a chair, about dead centre. There was one more chair in the room, but no other furnishings. The curtains were drawn against the light that would otherwise have invaded the room's only window. The floor of the room was covered with worn, grey linoleum. The hospital was in the South Yorkshire town of Doncaster, after all. The walls were painted with dirty-cream lead paint – shiny, hard and thick. It was like they came in and slapped on another coat every time the bloodstains got too much.

Geraldine couldn't recall if Grace was sitting there voluntarily or if she was strapped to the chair. She couldn't see her closely enough. After a time, a man wearing a white coat came into the room. He had a beard and a lit cigarette. He took up a chair opposite Grace and they began talking, voices low so Geraldine couldn't hear them.

The man put out his cigarette in an ashtray that must have been on the surgical trolley next to Grace's chair. He picked up a syringe and proceeded to mainline Grace with whatever was in it. Before he had finished Grace had slumped in the chair, her head lolling to one side. The man put his hand to Grace's cheek and asked, 'Are you okay, Grace? Are you still with me?'

Grace began to rouse and as she raised her head, his hand still on her cheek, she opened her eyes and looked at the man with, what was it, love? Yes, love.

'I'm okay, thank you,' said Grace. 'Are you alright?'

Was she flirting with him? Her face was beaming.

The man lit them both a cigarette, movie-star style and, for an hour, maybe more, they sat and talked and smoked until Geraldine could almost see the nicotine dripping from the lead-lined walls of the hospital room. At this time, Geraldine was just a twist of cells, swimming around each other still wondering if they would join forces, what their potential could be. Jeez, but they loved that nicotine.

2

Geraldine pushed her way into the world on 16 May 1964. She was glad the pregnancy was over and, mostly, just wanted to sleep. She hated her father's beery breath as he leaned in close for a moment without actually touching her flesh. Then she caught a whiff of something else, the stale stench of burnt tobacco. Before she knew what existence was, where her body ended and the world began, what language was, Geraldine wanted nothing more than a cigarette.

Grace took one look at Geraldine's naked body, still streaked with blood and vernix and turned her head away once she'd ascertained that life had betrayed her again.

Mercifully, Geraldine had few memories of those first months and years of yearning, second-hand smoke and neglect. After a while, her cravings dissipated and she could observe herself and the world around her in a slightly more detached way.

'What do you want for your birthday?' asked her father, Frank, to a soon to be three-year-old Geraldine.

'I want to be a donkey,' said Geraldine.

The back room of the two-up, two-down on Bentley Road was brimming with family. Truth be told, even three people made the room feel crowded. It made Geraldine, the tiniest of tots, feel like she was holding back a tide of humanity.

'Yer what?' said Frank, a smirk already breaking across his face.

'I want to be a donkey,' repeated Geraldine, her resolve beginning to break as she read the play.

'Did you hear that?' said Frank to the room in general. 'Our Gerald wants to be a donkey.'

The adults laughed and chattered among themselves about our Gerald and his ways while Geraldine looked at them with a puzzled frown, knowing she'd made some sort of familial fuck-up, but not understanding quite what.

'Come 'ere, Gerald,' said Grandad from his chair parked by the fire, right in front of the telly, his outstretched arms already almost close enough to touch her.

Geraldine threaded her way through the crowd of relatives and reached her grandad, whereupon he wrapped her in his arms, picked her up and plonked her on his lap. There was a moment of stillness in which Geraldine knew she'd made a mistake. She shrank into herself just as Grandad's arms tightened, and he stiffened as he said, 'Gerout o' that wi'out moving.'

It was the first time Geraldine felt truly, suffocatingly trapped, but it wouldn't be the last.

3

Frank's presence hung heavy in their home. Last wisps of smoke gilded with sunlight that came through the lace curtains in the kitchen window as he left for work early in the morning. The growing worry as dinnertime approached and the daily lottery began of would he/wouldn't he be home in time. His mood and what would it be if/when he did come home. And, for Geraldine, would he remember to bring home the tomato crisps she'd asked for at breakfast? Geraldine knew this was a risky move because to get the crisps meant Frank had to stop at the pub on the way home. This opened up a whole cascade of potential cause and effect. If Frank didn't go to the pub there would be no crisps, but there was more chance that he'd be the affable man who occasionally made them queen of puddings. If he did go to the pub, there was a greater likelihood that he would forget the crisps, no matter how much he had to drink. And, the more drinks, the less likely it was to be a queen of puddings kind of night. Worst of all was if Frank stayed out late, came home with the staggers, all filled with grandiose goodwill to all men, women and others who crossed his path. On these nights, Grace became a variable in the family science experiment. If she didn't mention a single thing – the lateness, the missing dinnerness, the pissedness yet again – everyone in the house could breathe. If she mentioned even one thing, everything blew up, and the two adults of the house would be raging for hours, cupboards and drawers slamming as clothes and possessions were strewn across rooms in preparation for one or the other, or both, leaving. On these nights the kids huddled together in Harry's bedroom.

Geraldine lay on Harry's bed, pretending to be asleep, hoping her brother couldn't see her eyelids flutter with each raised voice, crack of furniture and *flumph* of stacks of clothes landing on the floor.

Harry took her arm and said, ostensibly to himself, but mostly to Geraldine, 'If he's asleep, his arm will stay up when I let it go.'

Harry held Geraldine's arm long enough for her to consider her choices – was Harry lying or telling the truth? It was hard to tell with her older brother, who'd once almost had her believing that tadpoles tasted like chocolate. Harry let go and Geraldine kept her arm upright and stiff. There was silence for a moment, a brief respite from the battle going on in the room over the hallway and then, with the slamming of a door and heavy footsteps on the stairs, it didn't matter anymore who was wrong and who was right. Geraldine let her arm go and the siblings held their positions in silence for what felt like hours. When Grace came in to check on them, her face still streaked and puffy with tears, they were both asleep, Harry holding Geraldine in his arms, cradling her head, her face perfectly round and pink.

For Geraldine, the worst nights were when Frank came home totally smashed, got past Grace, snuck noisily up the stairs and into Geraldine's room, packet of tomato crisps in one hand, cigarette in the other, and proceeded to sit on the edge of her bed. Frank spoke to his children in a singsong voice, whether he was pissed or otherwise. Geraldine hated it.

'Geeerald,' he'd say, thinking he was speaking softly and wafting his stench in eddies all around her room.

'Geeeeeerald, I've got yer crisps, son.' Then a bit shorter when she didn't stir. 'Gerald.'

Those nights Geraldine feigned sleep like an Olympic champion, rolling over and mewling like a little lost soul when Frank rested his hand on her leg. Some nights, if she was lucky, he simply fell asleep, chin resting on his neck, gently swaying in a breeze all of his own making, breath rumbling in his throat, then awaken after a few moments with a piggy snort. Geraldine worried that his burning fag would set fire to her bed and all that polyester would go up in one giant *whoof!* She imagined what the flames would be like, could feel their heat melting her flesh, smell hair burning and see bones cracked open, their marrow boiling. But still she didn't move.

After Frank left, Geraldine would eat her crisps, savouring the sweet tang of the tomato flavouring, using her saliva to melt the deep-fried, misshapen discs of potato rather than risk Frank's return with the sound of her chewing.

4

The Yorkshire market town of Beverley where the Sturmers lived was about as close to idyllic as you could get when your family had started out proper working class, consigned to the colliery and living in a mining village. Geraldine was two when her family made the move from Bentley, Frank having decided that working down't pit wasn't for him. In a way, it was a brave move, breaking away from family and generations of tradition, but it didn't stop Frank's father, uncles and male cousins from seeing him as something of a coward. For Geraldine, it meant that the freedoms she took from the increasingly exhausted and disengaged Grace were relatively safe. A four-year-old taking excursions on her own in the tightly wound streets of Bentley may not have lasted long, or even been able to find her way back home once she'd turned a corner or two. Beverley's streets were wide enough for cars to pass without pulling into the kerb and lined with front gardens scented with roses, apple blossom and hope.

Geraldine walked up and down the streets of Beverley speaking house numbers and car number plates under her breath.

'B – D – 5 – 1 – S – M – R,' she would whisper to herself, the random rhythms of the letters and numbers soothing the chatter in her mind, evening out her breathing.

Geraldine knew she wasn't meant to be here, but here she was, and if she kept her head down she knew no-one would pay her any mind. Later, Geraldine learned that this was called hiding in plain sight and, much later, that she was being mindful, staying in the moment as a means of coping with the world. How she learned to read the random numbers and letters on the car number plates up and down her street Geraldine never knew, but she soon knew which house and which people each car belonged to, and they got to know her, too.

'Hey up, Gerald,' said Mr Brooker from over the road and one up.

'Alright, duck?' asked Mr Gott, from two doors further on.

'Shouldn't you be home, love?' Mrs Thompson – who lived in the last house on their street before it met a T-junction – enquired nervily.

Geraldine never answered, just kept up her whisperings and continued on her way. People said she floated like a ghost, feet hardly touching the ground.

■□■

Geraldine had her brother to thank for her graduation to books. While Harry was absent at school she would forage in his room, leafing through readers he'd either lost or forgotten to return. Starting with *John and Janet*, Geraldine was able to match her knowledge of the shapes and sounds of individual letters with the pictures and form words. As she whispered to herself, 'See John run. See Janet run,' Geraldine was looking as far into the background of the illustrations as she could, wanting to know what was at the other end of the meadow John and Janet were running through. Were they running for the joy of it? Or were they running away? Geraldine wanted to know their story but these primers weren't giving it to her. She searched, tried to see over the horizon, but the pictures and text gave her no clue as to what John and Janet were really up to.

Geraldine first learned about stories when she discovered a copy of *Five Go Adventuring Again* wedged between Harry's bed and the rather grimy wall. Observing the marks on the wall and the predicament of the book, she wondered what he got up to while he was sleeping. When she first opened the book's pages, she felt the words rush towards her. There were books on a shelf downstairs that had only words on every single page. Geraldine had taken some of these down and handled them, turned their pages, but somehow they felt foreign, even forbidden to her. The copy of Enid Blyton's adventure felt a bit more forgiving with its illustrations and large print.

Geraldine worked her way through the letters, forming words under her breath with increasing confidence and, rather than leaning on the illustrations, began to see the story live in her mind. She could see, smell and almost touch the action and as her whisperings gained pace, the vividness and complexity of the pictures increased until they became almost unbearable. Geraldine had to pause for breath along the way or she felt the book would have her disappear into its world, but she read the whole thing in one sitting, moving only when she heard footfall on the stairs and realised Harry was home from school.

Five Go Adventuring Again was where Geraldine met George. It was the first time Geraldine knew something without knowing what it was. She tucked George away for later.

5

Death came to visit Geraldine late at night. She woke to the billowing of her curtains stippling the yellow glow coming from the streetlamp that stood resolute at the front of their house. There was an animal in Geraldine's bed. As she opened her eyes, it rushed along her torso, tickling her with its fur, and nestled in the crook of her neck, its tiny head resting under Geraldine's chin.

'Wake up, Geraldine,' the animal said.

'No, I'm sleepy. Let me rest.'

'Wake up!' the animal said, more urgently.

Geraldine rolled over, like she did when Frank came to visit, feeling the echoes of her body behind her as she moved, her torso taking a few moments to catch up with her head. The animal was still there.

'Wake up! Get up! You have to get up, Geraldine!'

Geraldine sat up, her head rushing, her mind floating, her breathing disturbed and her nose running. She could feel her strength flowing from her feet and disappearing into the chill of the room. Her hands felt like gloves. She swung her legs over the edge of the bed and stood up, swaying; the carpet under her feet feeling like that time they'd stopped off on the moors on a day trip to Whitby: spongy and difficult to navigate. As she pushed open her bedroom door, Geraldine had to gather herself and make a decision as to which door she would open next. She chose the one on her side of the hallway, hearing it creak as it swung open, and knelt by Harry's bed, shaking him with the last of her strength.

'Harry, wake up, I'm sick,' Geraldine said. 'Wake up, Harry. Please, Harry wake up.'

Geraldine stopped shaking Harry; her strength had run out and she couldn't tell whether she was actually saying her words out loud or just thinking them, like when she read. It took a lot to wake Harry after a day of bird nesting and generally disappearing into the countryside. When he finally stirred, Geraldine was lying on the floor at the side of his bed. As he sat up and swung his legs onto the floor he almost stood on her. Awake now, Harry yelled at the top of his lungs.

'Mum! Dad! Come quick, it's our Gerald.'

Frank was first across the hall and into Harry's room. He switched on the light and looked about him, trying to figure out if he should be mad or what was going on. When he saw Geraldine on the floor he scooped her up and began to fly with her down the stairs, calling out, 'Grace! Come quick!' over his shoulder.

Harry followed Frank and Grace down the stairs. Even at the age of nine, already experienced in the intimate dance of life and death from his time in the fields, he knew exactly what the limpness of Geraldine's limbs meant as their father carried her through the front door. He stood on the threshold of the house and rested his arm on the doorframe while he waved his parents off to the hospital. Harry had decided that he didn't need to see what would happen next, what had most likely already happened.

Frank had been an elite sportsman in his younger days – cricket and football. In his mind it was one more reason why he didn't want to blacken his lungs for a living, although his forty a day did a good enough job of that. All that aside, he'd never run as fast as he did when he carried Geraldine from the car and into the hospital.

'Help!' was all he could say.

Women in crisp white uniforms came rushing to take Geraldine from him. One of them wrapped Geraldine in a blanket and laid her shrunken body in a cot, placing her on her side to check for signs of life. Geraldine's breathing was shallow, her pulse was off the charts and rivers of sweat ran down her pasty, caved-in face.

Geraldine never forgot the moment of handover. She remembered thinking to herself, *I'm too old to be in a cot*. She was indignant, filled with rage at being mis-seen, waiting for Frank to rectify things, and disappointed that he never stepped in to make sure the hospital staff put her in a bed where, as a now four-year-old, she rightfully belonged. Geraldine didn't remember anything else about her brush with diphtheria until she was convalescing on a hospital ward sometime later. At least her mind didn't remember but her body did, and, for years afterwards her dreams, waking and sleeping, would remind her what death felt like.

■□■

Geraldine spent some to many weeks on the hospital ward, her mind not able to keep track of time. She would sit up in her bed, glad that the stupid nurses had finally got it right, and watch the comings and goings. Doctors did rounds in the morning and afternoons; otherwise it was just the kids and the nurses. Occasionally a bed and the child in it would be wheeled away by men in white uniforms who weren't doctors. After a time, the beds would return, but the children never did. Geraldine began to create her own stories about what happened to those kids lucky enough to get wheeled off the ward. She wanted nothing more than to join them.

During the nights, Geraldine would wake up sweating and gasping for breath, her chest heavy, her nostrils filled with the sharp smell of disinfectant and something else she couldn't place. In the dimness of her vision, before the light returned, she could see she was surrounded by intricate machinery, above her and on all sides; she could hear it whirring and see it moving.

As the dreams became less frequent, Geraldine was allowed to get up, putting on slippers and a dressing-gown to wander unsteadily around the ward. She visited the boy next door to her, and they took turns plucking out their eyelashes and placing them in the bed of the little yellow toy lorry the boy had with him. Geraldine watched them accumulate and stopped the game abruptly when she worried that her eyelashes might not grow back. One lunchtime, Geraldine was seated at a small table in the middle of the ward and ate lunch with a deaf girl who told her to eat the skin of her fish because it was good for her. No matter how earnest the girl's entreaties, Geraldine couldn't bring herself to do it.

'Would you like to go home, Gerald?' the doctor asked her one afternoon.

Geraldine thought for a good while, closing her eyes and trying to remember what home was like. She had no idea how long she'd been away for or if she wanted to go back.

'How about tomorrow?' the doctor said when he'd decided Geraldine was taking too long to reply.

6

Geraldine spent most of that summer convalescing in her bedroom. She read voraciously, churning through everything in the house that was even remotely written for children, including Harry's game and angling books, savouring their detailed illustrations and descriptions of knots and fishing, trapping and hunting techniques. She read encyclopedias, digesting the world from her second-floor bedroom, choosing random start points and then navigating from one bite of information to the next.

S is for *shaduf*, a device used in ancient Egypt to irrigate land in the Nile delta.

N is for Nile, the longest river in the world and considered to be the cradle of civilisation.

S is for John Hanning Speke, the British explorer credited with discovering Lake Victoria, the source of the Nile.

L is for Lake Victoria, the largest lake in Africa and bordered by Kenya, Uganda and Tanzania.

Geraldine would fall asleep surrounded by books in various states of disarray. She didn't care if she dog-eared or bent their pages, broke their spines and generally abused them. It was their contents she desired, not the paper and card. Oftentimes, she would spark out with a volume resting open on her chest and these were the nights when her dreams were most intense, the machinery of her death and survival coming to visit again. Geraldine would try to call out, but her voice wouldn't come; it was strangled in the mucus and constriction of her throat. The only thing that could bring her back was the touch of Bob's silky fur. The stink of disinfectant and – she'd figured it out now, read about it somewhere – anaesthetic, stayed in her room long after she woke each night, sweating and gasping for air.

At first, Geraldine didn't believe that Bob was part of her world. He'd woken her the night that death had made a close pass, but she'd put that down to what she'd come to call the crossover point, the space where the sky of life didn't quite touch the water of death, where all the rules of existence are different. When she saw him in her dreams, Geraldine could rationalise his existence or his belonging to the other world that she could see only in peripheral glimpses. But, when he appeared in her room in broad daylight and she'd checked she was awake by pinching herself on the neck right where it met her collarbone, she had to reassess.

'Bob?' asked Geraldine, never knowing where such a mundane name came from. Bob was small, so the name suited, she guessed.

Hearing the sound of her voice, Bob looked her way and approached along a ridge made by the cellular cotton blanket that was strewn across Geraldine's bed. The creature skittered right up to her face and rested in the lee of her neck, just as he had done the first night she saw him. This time, it didn't speak, just looked up at her, his deep black eyes teeming with life and intelligence. Geraldine looked back and felt like she was being pulled into another universe. She had to look away and, as she did, Bob turned around and settled with his furry little backside facing towards her, made a deep shuddering sigh and, Geraldine assumed, fell asleep. Geraldine studied the creature's furry rump and decided he was as entitled to share her world as anyone else. She thought no more of it, just enjoyed the companionship. Although there was a small part of her that recalled a section in one of Harry's books on preserving the skins of woodland creatures. It felt bad inside her chest to think about it, but the science of the process was attractive to her.

■□■

When she'd run out of books, Geraldine had to figure out what to do next. Going downstairs didn't feel like a viable option. Something about that single shelf of paperbacks in the living room didn't feel quite within Geraldine's reach just yet. Perhaps there was another way? In the evenings at what was officially bedtime for small children, while it was still plenty light outside, Geraldine had taken up interlocution with the two girls across the road. Not the house directly opposite, the one where Mr and Mrs Brooker lived. Geraldine had never met the girls, had never even seen them out on the street, but there they were in the window each evening, dressed in their nighties and waving at her. Starting by waving back, Geraldine soon tired of the limitations of this form of communication so, little by little, taught the girls something like a cross between semaphore and sign language. The signals she taught them were made up on the spot, but Geraldine had a knack for remembering and, each night, the three children built up a language all of their own.

It wasn't a massive leap for Geraldine to signal, 'Send books,' and using the covers of those she had in her room, she was able to show the girls what she'd already read and what sorts of things she'd like to read about. The first night she'd introduced the exchange of books into their conversation, Geraldine lay awake far beyond the dreaming hour, wondering if her invented language would result in any real-world outcome. The next morning, a brown paper parcel tied up with furry string and with the name 'GERALD' written on it in untidy capitals was sitting on the doorstep when Frank left for work. He was too busy huffing on a cigarette to pick it up.

'Grace!' he called, as he strode to his car. 'There's summat at the door,' and he was off.

Geraldine heard him. She hadn't really seen Frank since she came home from hospital, but she was glad to hear his voice this morning.

It was Harry who came up to her room, the small parcel in his hands.

'Where did this come from, our Gerald?' he asked.

'I don't know,' Geraldine said, with her hands outstretched.

'But what is it?' asked Harry. 'What's it for?'

'It's books,' said Geraldine.

Harry handed over the parcel and went back downstairs. Geraldine undid the string, untying the knots with ease, and pulled back the paper to reveal three books, each with lurid covers, the edges of the pages yellowed with age and, best of all from Geraldine's point of view, each of which she'd never read before. Geraldine opened the one on the top of the pile, *Finn the Wolfhound*, and was transported, with Finn, to Australia.

■□■

Books taught Geraldine about the entire world. Before she left Yorkshire she felt she knew the interiors of Africa and Australia as well as she knew Beverley. She longed to see these places, but first she had to go to school.

7

Geraldine's convalescence meant that she missed the beginning of the school year. When she turned up to class at the local nursery school – Frank standing behind her at the classroom door, one hand on her back, the other hanging on tightly to his lit cigarette –everyone turned to look. Geraldine stood and looked back, imagining her own face back to be round and pink, her eyes the brightest blue and her black leather satchel almost as big as she was.

The satchel was a gift from Frank and Grace, but gifts never came without a price in Geraldine's family. It was intended to be an inducement for her to go to school. They may not have been in the slightest bit interested in being parents, but Frank and Grace knew something about the human psyche, having learned that gifts could smooth over almost any disagreement or difficulty in times of scarcity. The problem was, they had no idea about school and what young girls were like.

'Here y'are, Gerald,' said Grace, as she passed her a brightly wrapped parcel the night before school was due to become part of her daily routine.

'What is it?' asked Geraldine before she took it from Grace's outstretched arms, knowing that accepting a gift was to accept indebtedness.

'Go on, open it, have a look,' said Grace, attempting encouragement.

Frank leaned forward in his chair, near the fire and directly in front of the telly. 'Take it, Gerald,' he said, finalising the transaction.

Geraldine took the parcel, feeling its weight, and sat on the floor to tear it open. When she had revealed the shiny black leather of the satchel inside she was impressed with its stiffness and smell, but it definitely wasn't for her. She thought for a while before rejoining negotiations.

'What's it for?' asked Geraldine, knowing full well its intended purpose.

'It's for school,' said Grace, 'for your books and pencils and things.'

'I don't want it,' said Geraldine.

'It cost a lot of money did that, Gerald,' said Frank. 'You're taking it to school. Tomorrow.'

▪▫▪

Geraldine lay awake that night working through her options. She'd never been to school a day in her life, not even to drop off or pick up Harry, but she understood that turning up with a massive black leather satchel wasn't going to endear her to anyone. Geraldine knew she could match any kid in any school when it came to knowing things, but she was far less certain about fitting in. She had a strong feeling that becoming part of the crowd was going to be hard for her. For starters, she didn't really need other people, but she'd read enough in the last few months to understand what capriciously antisocial places schools can be. Before she went to sleep, Geraldine made a plan. It wasn't much of a plan, but it was all she could muster given what she had to work with.

▪▫▪

In the morning, Frank drove Geraldine to school. Grace hardly ever left the house and, besides, she couldn't drive. It was a cold, drizzly September-almost-November morning. Geraldine sat in the front seat of the Morris Major, hoping it might break down as it so often did. Her satchel sat on her lap, empty, useless and dangerous. Its dull shine mocked her as Frank puttered through the morning traffic.

'Dad,' said Geraldine.

'What? What is it?'

'Dad, I have to go. I have to go to the toilet,' said Geraldine.

'What? No, we're nearly there, Gerald. Can't you hang on?'

'No, Dad, I need to go now.'

Frank pulled the car to the side of the road adjacent to a vacant lot, all rubble and overgrown with grass and the last of the summer's nettles. Geraldine hopped out and headed towards the red brick wall at one side of the empty space. When she came up alongside it and looked up it was dizzyingly tall and she feared it might collapse on her at any minute. Frank came and stood alongside her and offered some words of encouragement.

'Go on, hurry up.'

Geraldine silently pulled down her shorts and underpants and began to pee up against the wall. Frank stood alongside her, looking straight ahead. This was Geraldine's moment.

'Dad, I don't want to go to school.'.

'Yer have to, our Gerald. Everyone has to go to school.'

'But I can't go today. Can I stay home, just for one more day?'

Frank was caught off guard. He wanted nothing to do with what he was standing next to. It was broad daylight and he was stone cold sober. There was a pause and Geraldine stood facing the wall, ostensibly still peeing. Frank still looked straight ahead.

'Please?'

'Okay, just for today,' said Frank, letting them both off the hook.

■□■

The next day, there she was at the classroom door, that massive satchel strapped to her narrow shoulders and Frank's fag funking up the innocence of the classroom.

'Thank you, Mr Sturmer, I'll look after Gerald from here,' said Miss Kell.

Frank turned and walked away without a word, leaving Geraldine still standing in the doorway, her satchel blocking the watery sun.

'Come on in, Gerald,' said Miss Kell. 'Let's show you where to put that satchel.'

■□■

'Guess what?' asked the kid sitting next to Geraldine just before morning play.

'Pink snot,' Geraldine fired right back.

The kid stared at Geraldine like she was from another planet. Geraldine stared back at him, not helping at all. She watched his mouth move with no words coming out and felt the power of her silence.

At morning play Geraldine sat on the bench just outside the classroom, where the kids hung their coats. Technically children had to go outside and play – the corridors of the schoolhouse were meant to be kept clear of human traffic during breaks. Geraldine sat there anyway, her nose in the latest book from over the road, the only thing she'd brought with her to school that morning. When the other kids came rushing in from outside, Geraldine stood up and went to the classroom door. She soon realised she was at the front of the line and then further realised she wasn't paired with another student. She stood out of line for a moment and spotted her goldfish desk-mate towards the back, partnerless, looking nervous. Geraldine went and joined him, but her presence didn't appear to make him any less worried.

So began Geraldine's career at school. Mostly people left her to her own devices; it was boredom that was her greatest enemy. Miss Kell did her best to engage Geraldine, but that was no easy task while leading the class in chanting, 'A is for apple, ah, ah, ah. B is for boy, buh, buh, buh …' Geraldine watched in amazement while her classmates joined in the chant, wondering what sort of lives they'd led that they didn't yet know the alphabet. But there was one thing Miss Kell imparted to her class that term that Geraldine hadn't yet twigged to. Handwriting accompanied the learning of the sounds of the alphabet. Miss Kell gave the students great fat pencils and looked over their shoulders while they formed the letters in sequence, starting by tracing over the dotted shapes on paper printed especially for the task and then moving on to form each letter freehand, trying to stay on the bottom line and touch the top line. Geraldine was terrible at staying inside the lines, her pencil work all spidery and smudged, but she took to the task of writing like she had reading. Having seen its rudiments, it seemed so obvious to Geraldine: if there were books for her to read there had to be people to write them. She'd understood that all along, ingesting names like Blyton, Dawson and Durrell and recognising their authorship, but she'd never joined the dots in such a way that she realised she could write as well. Authors were just names on dust covers and the words on the pages inside the books were fixed. Geraldine hadn't thought for a moment about how the words came to be in the books she read. Miss Kell's crude teaching of handwriting made the process of creating text come alive for Geraldine and turned authors into real people.

Every day of term Geraldine couldn't wait to finish school so she could go home to write, then read. Thankfully, her career at nursery school was short-lived.

8

For Frank and Grace, the forty miles they'd put between them and Bentley when they'd moved the family to Beverley weren't enough. True, it was far enough that people spoke an almost entirely different dialect, but it was still too close. Frank had gone to night school to learn how to be a surveyor as a way of avoiding the inevitability of spending his entire working life underground. Now his occupation gave Frank and his family the opportunity for a completely different existence.

Frank and Grace didn't talk to the kids about the move until after they'd put the house up for sale.

'What's the sign at the front of the house for?' Geraldine asked at dinner, after coming home to find it stuck in their scruffy front lawn. She understood the words, but not the concept.

'We're moving,' Frank told her.

'Moving? Where?' Geraldine wanted to know.

Harry joined in. 'We're moving? Why?'

'I got a new job,' Frank told them.

'Why do we have to move because you've a new job?' Geraldine asked.

'It's overseas,' Frank told her.

'Overseas?' said Geraldine, her eyes widening.

'Yes, in Zambia,' said Frank.

'In Zambia?' Harry repeated. 'Where's that?'

Geraldine didn't need to ask, she already knew where Zambia was. On the map, in words, in her mind. For the rest of dinner she was already there.

'Africa,' she said.

'That's right. We're going to live in Zambia, in Africa,' Frank told them.

■□■

Just before Christmas 1969, the Sturmers boarded a plane and flew to Zambia via Rome, leaving behind the cold of England, the grey skies, drizzle and slush, and their extended family. For the next seven years it would be just the four of them.

9

Zambia, a landlocked country in southern Africa, gained independence from the British in 1964 with Kenneth Kaunda becoming the inaugural president. There was more, and Geraldine read it all, although she wasn't allowed to bring her encyclopedias on the plane.

'They're too 'evee, our Gerald,' said Grace.

Geraldine said nothing as she prepared herself for almost a full day of flying time without her books. What Grace didn't tell Geraldine was that she'd decided that her collection of books was too heavy to come with the family at all. This was an eventuality Geraldine wouldn't be able to prepare herself for until they had arrived and unpacked, several days and 5,000 or so miles too late. At least Geraldine was able to write, but when she'd filled the only exercise book she'd been allowed to bring, somewhere over Algeria, Geraldine found herself at a loose end.

Adding to her disturbance and sense that this trip to Africa may not be as advertised, Geraldine also noted before they'd got in the taxi to the train station, leaving their house for the last time, that Bob had decided not to make the journey with her. In a way, Geraldine wasn't surprised and, as their train neared Heathrow, she was already beginning to question whether Bob had been real. By the time Geraldine boarded the Alitalia jet she'd let go of the idea of Bob altogether.

■□■

Upon arriving in the most foreign of places imaginable to them, the Sturmers did their best to maintain their Englishness, even doing things they'd never done at home. On their first Christmas Eve a week or so after arriving, their new home still not properly unpacked, the four of them went to the pictures in the centre of Kitwe. There was only one film showing, *Born Free*, but Grace guessed it would just have to do so they bought their tickets and settled into their seats. Apart from the air-conditioning keeping the Southern Hemisphere heat and ninety percent humidity at bay, it was just like being back 'ome, so a very satisfactory couple of hours. Every single member of the family shed a tear at the end of the film when Elsa, now back in the wild, brought her cubs to meet the Adamsons, but Geraldine was the only one caught out.

''Ave you been crying, our Gerald?' said Grace.

'Yes,' said Geraldine, looking down, remembering she wasn't supposed to show emotion.

'Look, Dad, our Gerald's been crying,' said Grace.

'Awww,' said Frank. 'Isn't he a funny little thing.'

■□■

By the time they got home and Frank pulled the car into their lengthy, unpaved driveway, Geraldine was drowsy, her head resting on Harry's shoulder. Harry got out of his side of the back of the car and Frank came around to pick up Geraldine and carry her up the steps up to the veranda and the front door. Frank noticed the door was ajar as he balanced Geraldine in one arm and reached for the keyhole with the other. Frank pushed open the door with a tentative 'Hello?'. There was no answer from inside.

■□■

Everything looked like it was still there until they reached the kitchen. There, the fridge door stood open, its light pooling on the polished green cement floor. The family gathered round the open fridge and Grace sat on the floor and did an inventory.

'The chicken's gone,' she said.

'And the beer,' said Frank, looking over Grace's shoulder.

'And the Cinzano bottles,' said Grace. 'They only 'ad water in 'em. They must've thought they were full of drink.'

'Stupid bastards,' said Frank.

Geraldine hadn't heard Frank swear before.

'They stole our water,' Harry chimed in. 'Stupid bastards.'

The whole family roared with laughter at the thought of whoever had broken into their house stealing bottles of boiled water, thinking it was alcohol.

'Looks like they've only taken food,' said Frank, as he looked around the house.

'There goes Christmas dinner,' said Grace.

'Hopefully the police will catch them,' said Harry, working himself up more than a little. He was holding a kitchen knife by now. 'They won't want to come across me,' he said, his hand trembling as he held the knife out in front of him and made tentative stabbing motions.

Harry still had the knife in his hand when the whole family settled into Frank and Grace's bed, Geraldine and Harry in the middle. The Sturmers didn't get much sleep that night and, the next morning, Christmas Day, they were at a loss what to do. They knew no-one, the shops were closed and, each in their own way, they were far from home and weighing up the viability of staying. Grace made sandwiches from bread in the freezer and a bit of cheese and potted meat that the burglars had missed, or passed over. As Christmases went, it wasn't the best of times and, for Geraldine, being the first Christmas she remembered, it set a bit of a precedent.

10

Until she was transported to Zambia, Geraldine had only experienced the world beyond the two-mile radius of her existence in Beverley through books and sometimes television, but an almost uninterrupted diet of *Coronation Street* and *Ken Dodd and the Diddymen* didn't give Geraldine much insight into the wider world. Once she got over the shock of their travel and arrival – shuffling on and off planes, airports with armed guards, the face slap of humidity, temporary accommodation in the transit flats, showers, moving into their house, a bungalow set on a full acre of roughly cultivated land, Christmas and getting broken into, and, most of all the people, speaking languages she couldn't understand, with accents she'd never heard and wearing clothes she'd never seen; such a lot! – Geraldine felt ready to explore her new world.

■□■

Christmas over, Harry took his leave of the house via the front gate and began to walk the streets of their new home town. Grace and Harry made it clear that Geraldine was too young to join him.

'He'll slow me down,' said Harry.

'It might be dangerous,' said Grace, standing on the veranda looking more worried than usual.

Grace looked at Harry as if weighing up trying to get him to stay put as well. Harry turned and began walking up the driveway, conversation over before it began.

'Don't forget to be home for dinner,' Grace called to Harry as he opened and closed the five-bar gate enveloped in chicken wire.

'You stay here, our Gerald,' were Grace's parting words as she turned and went back inside, leaving Geraldine alone at the top of the driveway.

Geraldine stood for a long time sniffing the air. That was the one thing books couldn't give her, or her dreams, which were still drenched in disinfectant and anaesthetic – the scent of a place. Zambia smelled rich and earthy. The heat and the humidity created a sense of closeness, and Geraldine felt like she was wearing the air over her skin. She could feel its oversized molecules as she breathed it in and out, in and out, noting how it moved differently to English air. Somehow it was more alive. Geraldine winced as she felt a sharp sting at the side of her left foot. She looked down to see a massive red-and-black ant, fully an inch long, chomping on her flesh.

'Get off!' yelled Geraldine as she brushed it away, noticing the redness at the site where its pincers had tasted her flesh.

Geraldine stood still for a while longer, her eyes looking down at her bare feet and then sweeping the ground and the plants in the garden in widening arcs. Everywhere she looked, she saw movement. Trails of ants marched across the sandy driveway and disappeared into the thick, wiry grass of what she supposed was the front lawn. A lizard skittered through the sand in the opposite direction, finding a hiding spot on the other side of the fence dividing Geraldine's house from the one next door. A little grey dove took wing from the branches of the guava tree around five feet from where she was standing, its wing beats making high-pitched music. Then, closer to the front fence, where the tall grass merged into a hedgerow of large, bright-green leaves interspersed with massive orange flowers, Geraldine saw movement that she thought looked like a snake. She stood very still for a moment until another ant bite confirmed for her that lack of motion was not the best strategy. Life here would overwhelm anything that stood still for too long. Geraldine looked over to the hedge but she didn't see any more movement. Perhaps the snake had gone. Perhaps it was never there in the first place. Geraldine began to walk carefully across the lawn to take a closer look.

As she neared the hedge a group of five women approached from the street side.

'Little gel,' one of them said. 'Little gel, are you a madam or a *bwana*?'

'I—I don't know,' said Geraldine. She'd meant to say, 'I don't know what you mean', but it didn't matter.

'Little gel, can we pick in your bushes?'

'What?'

The woman took a step closer, reaching into the hedge and pulling out the biggest, greenest grasshopper Geraldine had ever seen.

'Look! Look!' the woman said, waving the struggling insect towards Geraldine. 'Look! Can we pick your bush?'

'Yes, yes, yes, you can,' nodded Geraldine, relieved that she was beginning to understand and hoping the woman would take the grasshopper out of her face.

The women moved in and began picking out the fat grasshoppers infesting the dense bushes along the fence, dropping them into brown sacks. Geraldine watched them in fascination as they settled into their work, talking to each other in a language that she later learned was Bemba. Right now she had no idea what was being said, just that words were flying around the hedgerow at a frantic pace and, occasionally, the women would look knowingly in her direction.

'What do you want them for?' Geraldine asked after watching and listening for a time.

'We eat,' said the woman. 'Here,' she offered Geraldine the fat green grasshopper in her hand, her face already creased with a giveaway smile.

Geraldine screwed up her nose, much to the delight of the women, who cackled with laughter.

'It's okay,' the woman said to Geraldine, dropping the grasshopper in her sack. 'We cook first.'

Geraldine smiled, happy that she was in on the joke.

'See you tomorrow, little gel,' the woman said as she and her companions swung their sacks onto their heads and continued walking up the street.

'Bye,' said Geraldine, watching the women until they were out of sight.

The piercing sting, this time on her right foot, told Geraldine she'd been standing still for too long. She turned towards the house just as a clap of thunder broke so close to her that she could feel the air rushing past her face. Immediately after there was a drenching downpour, great fat drops of water, warm like a bath, falling straight down from the darkest most imposing of thunderheads in all imagination. Geraldine looked up to try to get a better view of them, but her eyes filled with water. After around ten minutes, the rain stopped as abruptly as it had started and the clouds were nowhere to be seen. In Africa, things can happen in a great rush.

Geraldine watched the ground begin to steam as the sun took over again. Life that had scattered to find shelter from the rain, unlike Geraldine, began to return to the business of hunting and cultivation. A praying mantis flew right past Geraldine's ear – she could hear the whirring of its flight before she saw it – and landed on an exposed tree root, spreading its wings as it looked for dryness and warmth before going about the rest of its day. A frog travelled across the lawn, picking its way on all fours through the thickest of the roots and grass stems. Geraldine approached and reached out her hand to touch it, but it made a great leap away from her and, as she took her next step, another one, disappearing from her sight. The next time she saw it, just a moment later, a sleek black crow had the frog in its beak and was taking off again to eat its meal in one of the seemingly hundreds of trees that surrounded the edges of the garden. Geraldine paused for a moment to take stock, but was careful not to stand still.

■□■

That evening, Grace put calamine lotion on Geraldine's ant bites and warned her to be careful because it could be dangerous out there. Then she followed up with, ''Oo were those women you were talking to?'

'They came to catch grasshoppers,' said Geraldine.

'Grass'oppers? What for?'

'They wanted to eat them.'

'Eat them? That's disgusting. Are yer sure, our Gerald? They weren't pulling yer leg, were they?'

Geraldine was as sure as she could be, and the next afternoon, around three, she made sure she was in the front garden, waiting for the women to come by. It wasn't long before they were standing on the other side of the fence, plucking grasshoppers that were still invisible to Geraldine from among the leaves and flowers.

'What's your name?' Geraldine asked the woman she'd spoken to yesterday. 'My name is Geraldine.'

'Hello, Geraldine. My name is Susan.'

'What do you call a grasshopper in your language?'

'Hn?'

'This one,' said Geraldine, pointing to the grasshopper in Susan's hand. 'What's it called?'

'Ah, this one,' said Susan. 'This one we call, *kapaaso*.'

'*Kapaaso*?' Geraldine tried out the pronunciation.

'Yes, yes, *kapaaso*,' said Susan. 'Good to eat.'

Geraldine screwed up her face again and Susan laughed at her horror.

'You come with us,' said Susan. 'We show you. It tastes good.'

Geraldine looked over her shoulder to the house where she knew Grace would be watching.

'Not today,' said Geraldine. 'Maybe another?'

'Yes, yes, another day,' said Susan, her eyes looking off into the distance as if counting off the age before she thought Geraldine would be ready to step around to the other side of the fence.

'Yes, another day,' agreed Geraldine, still looking over her shoulder.

The thunder broke their impasse and the women hurried off while Geraldine stood under the cloudburst, getting deliciously drenched before drying herself off among the steaming plants and the busyness of the animals.

11

That evening, Frank came home with a dog, a little black mongrel.

'It's to guard the house,' he said. 'Make sure we don't have any more break-ins.'

'What's it called?' asked Harry.

'She's called Lass,' Frank told him. 'Now, yer not to go stroking her or nothing, she's a proper guard dog. Feller at the mine told me feed her once a day, raw meat and scraps and make sure she's outside all the time. He told me that's why all the houses have six-foot fences around them, keep the guard dogs in.'

The other three looked at the scraggly little mutt that was sitting under their dining table currently being handfed by Harry. Frank could see the doubt in their eyes.

'It's true, yer know, she's a proper guard dog,' said Frank. 'Gorn, geroutside,' he told the poor little thing, holding the back door open.

Lass slunk out, tail between her legs, belly low to the floor. Two kids followed soon after.

■□■

Two days later, Frank came home with another dog. It looked a bit like Lass although it was clear it had some other strain mixed in. Frank pulled the dog on a leash and choker chain from the back seat of his car while it barked and snarled as the family stood on the porch and watched.

'This is Brandy,' said Frank. 'He's a proper guard dog.'

At which he let Brandy go. The dog proceeded to run straight at Lass, bowling her over and putting his jaws around her neck, giving off a low, threatening growl. Lass froze, as did the Sturmers. It felt like not even the sky was breathing until Brandy decided to let go and Lass ran off to hide at the back of the house.

'See, a proper guard dog,' said Frank.

▪▫▪

When Susan and her compatriots came to visit the next day, Geraldine was waiting for them, looking forward to continuing their conversation in Bemba.

'*Muli shani*, Susan,' said Geraldine.

'*Bwino*, Geraldine.'

Brandy came rushing towards the fence, barking with a ferocity he seemed to reserve only for black people. Lass was a few paces behind, yapping in her high-pitched way. Brandy was in full attack mode, barking, snarling and throwing himself at the hedge, hard up against the fence hidden in its dense foliage. A cloud of grasshoppers made a hasty exit. Meanwhile, Susan stood impassive on the other side.

'You have a dog,' said Susan over Brandy's barking and snapping.

'Yes,' said Geraldine, embarrassed by the noise and disruption. 'Dad brought it home yesterday.'

Susan brought herself up to her full height, stood the way she would if she was carrying a heavy load on her head and stared over the hedge at Brandy, making eye contact. The dog quietened and they were left with Lass still yapping, a bit slow to catch up with what was happening. Brandy lay down, head on his paws and Lass wandered away, obviously with something more important to do.

'You people and your dogs,' said Susan. She turned to the other women. 'Come, let us go.'

Neither Brandy nor Geraldine moved until the women were out of sight. When the rain came, Geraldine soaked up its warmth while Brandy headed for shelter. Geraldine knew she had some ground to make up with Susan and the other women next time they met.

12

Geraldine lifted the latch to the gate, looking behind her to make sure Brandy and Lass didn't try to slip through the gap before she made it to the other side. The women were still picking grasshoppers from the hedge, chatting among themselves like nothing out of the ordinary was happening, while Geraldine felt like she would faint at any moment. Susan had invited her out again and this time, after the encounter with the dogs, Geraldine's sense of curiosity and obligation got the better of her. She kept looking behind her as they sauntered down the road, but Grace was nowhere to be seen.

The walk to the village took them between the mountainous white dunes of tailings from the copper mine, and cane fields that looked to Geraldine like they stretched on forever. Eventually the dirt path took a turn, and before them was a clearing where a mix of tin shanties and mud huts with grass roofs stood in the shade of a grove of mango trees. Dogs yapped at their arrival, but none rushed to greet them and bark like Brandy had. There was smoke rising from fires in front of some of the residences, where women sat on stools and stirred cooking pots. As they entered the village, the women went their separate ways and Geraldine was left at Susan's side.

'Come, Geraldine,' said Susan. 'Come meet my family.'

Geraldine followed her shyly to one of the huts towards the middle of the clearing. An old woman was sitting, stirring the contents of what looked like a kerosene tin resting on a mesh frame that straddled the embers of a fire.

'Come. Sit,' said Susan, gesturing to a stool on the other side of the fire.

Geraldine skirted the people sitting or crouched around the outdoor kitchen, the smoke burning her eyes as she passed through it. Once she was seated, Susan made the introductions.

'This is my mother, Damson,' she said, gesturing to the grey-haired cook. 'This is my husband, Bernard,' she said as she walked towards a man, holding out her hands for the baby he was holding. 'And this is our daughter, Rose,' said Susan, taking a seat and laying the baby across her chest, unwrapping her *chitenge* to expose her breast and, once she was satisfied Rose was settled, rewrapping her garment so it held the infant snugly.

'Hello Geraldine. Welcome to our home,' said Damson. 'Would you like something to eat?'

'Yes, please,' said Geraldine, hoping that grasshoppers weren't on the menu today.

'Here,' said Damson, holding out the wooden spatula she'd been using to stir her pot.

On the spatula's end was a thick white paste. Geraldine leaned forward to have a taste and then hesitated.

'What is it?' she asked.

'It's *nshima*,' said Damson. 'Made from maize.'

Satisfied it probably wasn't anything too new for her, Geraldine had a taste of the sticky white substance. Mostly it tasted of nothing, just clagged up her mouth.

'That's nice, *natotela*,' said Geraldine.

'Ah, good,' said Damson, 'you like it. Stay, and eat with us. Bernard, fetch the *kapenta*.'

Bernard set a wooden bowl on the table next to the fire. Geraldine peered into it and saw that it was filled with tiny silver fish. Damson dolloped some *nshima* into an enamelled dish next to the *kapenta* and Geraldine watched as the family began to eat. Taking it in turns, Damson, Susan and then Bernard each picked up a pinch of *nshima* between their finger and thumb, rolled it into a ball in the palm of their hand and then took a tiny fish, laid it on the ball of *nshima* and popped it into their mouth. They'd taken a few turns each before anyone noticed that Geraldine wasn't joining in.

'Come, Geraldine, eat some food,' Damson said, gesturing for her to come closer to the table.

Geraldine shifted her stool and, when she was settled again, took a pinch of *nshima* and started rolling it in the palm of her hand. The starchy substance was sticky and surprisingly resistant to her touch, but she soon got the hang of it and, by the time she reached out for a fish, had a pretty decent sphere resting in her palm. She laid the fish on top and brought it to her mouth, popping it straight in and beginning to chew. The *kapenta* was salty and spiky, its flavour and texture sharply offsetting the blandness of the *nshima*. Geraldine tried to swallow too quickly and gagged as the fish stuck in the back of her mouth. She began to cough and worried she might vomit.

'Here, Bernard, get the girl a drink,' said Susan, gesturing with her free hand.

'*Chibuku*,' said Bernard, holding out a plastic cup to Geraldine.

'No, husband, not that,' said Susan, holding her hand up towards Bernard. 'Get the girl some water.'

Bernard filled another cup from a jug at the side of his chair and handed it to Geraldine. Geraldine drank the water, gulping down the remnants of the fish and then swishing it around her mouth to clear the rest of the *nshima*, taking a final gulp and then a deep breath.

'Do you not like our food?' asked Damson.

'No, I do,' said Geraldine.

'Then eat some more,' said Damson.

Susan leaned forward, Rose now asleep at her breast. '*Mayo*, let the little girl be. She will eat if she wants to. And, Bernard, *chibuku*! It smells like sick. I don't know how you can drink that evil brew, but don't give it to little girls!'

Bernard giggled, his head bowed.

'This is not funny,' said Susan. 'Geraldine is our guest. Would you like some more water, Geraldine?

'No, thank you. I'm going to have some more *nshima* and *kapenta*,' Geraldine said, taking another pinch from the enamel bowl and rolling it in her hand. This time she was ready for the tastes and textures in her mouth. She chewed up the fish, feeling its tiny bones crunch against her teeth, and swallowed it down with an ostentatious smile and no water chaser.

■□■

The meal over, Geraldine began to feel the pull of home, wondering if Grace had noticed her missing.

'I'd better go,' said Geraldine, when she felt she'd waited long enough for her departure not to be impolite.

'Bernard,' said Susan, 'walk with Geraldine, see that she finds her way home.'

'Of course, *Mayo*,' said Bernard, putting down his cup of *chibuku*.

The two walked back to Geraldine's house mostly in silence, Bernard speaking only as they walked alongside the tailings dam.

'Look, this side, the earth is dead, this side we can still grow crops,' he said, sweeping an arm in the direction of the cane field. 'We cannot eat from the mine.'

Geraldine looked around her.

'I'm sorry,' she said.

■□■

When they got to Geraldine's gate, she saw Frank's car in the driveway and her stomach dropped.

'Thank you, Bernard, I'll be okay now.'

Geraldine wanted to tell him to go immediately, but she knew that wouldn't be polite. Bernard knew what was what, immediately turning on his bare pink heel when he heard Brandy arc up. He was gone before the dogs reached the gate, and Frank and Grace were at the open door on the green cement porch. Geraldine opened the gate, careful not to let the dogs out, and started the long walk to the house, made even longer by her parents' silence.

'Get inside,' was all Frank said, as Geraldine put a foot on the bottom step up to the veranda.

Geraldine walked silently past Frank and Grace and stood in the middle of the lounge room, waiting while they followed her inside.

'Who was that man?' Frank demanded to know once they were stood facing each other.

'That was Bernard,' said Geraldine.

'And just who is Bernard?' said Frank.

'He's Susan's husband,' said Geraldine.

'And who is Susan?' said Frank.

Geraldine felt it unlikely she would be able to give Frank a satisfactory explanation, so she said nothing.

'Do you know how worried we've been?' said Frank, raising his voice.

'Your mum called me at work and said you'd gone missing. We didn't know where you were, if you were dead or alive. We've been worried sick.'

'I'm sorry,' said Geraldine.

'Sorry isn't good enough,' said Frank. 'You can't go off with those people. It's dangerous here. They're dangerous, God knows what could have happened to you.'

'Nothing happened,' said Geraldine. 'I'm okay.'

'Don't talk back to me like that,' Frank yelled.

Geraldine had never heard Frank raise his voice to anyone but Grace. Frightened now, she stood her ground but had nothing more to say.

'It's dangerous. We were worried about you,' said Frank, lowering his voice and aiming for a more loving tone.

Grace maintained her position, but did not speak.

'Alright, go to your room,' said Frank, his voice now reduced to an almost whisper.

'What are we going to do?' Geraldine heard Grace say as she walked through to her room.

'I don't know,' said Frank. 'We need to get him to school, away from these people.'

13

Geraldine's dreams were still largely of machinery, death and hospital stench from which she would wake out of breath in a lather. Lately, though, Africa had begun to creep into her night-time excursions. Having always dreamed in monochrome, colours began to change Geraldine's world. Vivid green, blue, deep chocolatey brown, red, orange, and swirling purple, magenta and violet. The colours carried Geraldine along until she realised she could fly. When the darkness and machinery began to grip her, she could rise above her hospital bed and look down at the shrunken girl dwarfed by an expanse of white linen, cables and tubes. She could roll over on her back and look at the sky, so wide that she could see the curve of the troposphere and, below her, every plant, animal and spirit that ever lived. Sometimes it made her so dizzy that she could feel herself falling back to earth, waking just before she hit the ground. Other times, she was still flying when she opened her eyes to find it was morning instead of the middle of the night, another day in Zambia ahead of her.

■□■

Early January 1970, the six-year-old Geraldine was again faced with the prospect of school. After her previous experience she had mixed feelings. Mostly it was the anticipation of boredom that made her question what seemed to her to be another very late decision on the part of Frank and Grace.

'But, why do I have to go to school?' asked Geraldine.

'Because you have to go,' said Grace. 'Kids have to go to school. All kids do.'

If Grace thought her last statement was definitive, an end to the discussion, she was quite wrong.

'But I already know everything,' said Geraldine.

'You've barely been to school for five minutes, our Gerald,' said Frank. 'You don't know owt just yet.'

'I do,' said Geraldine. 'You don't know the things I know.'

This stumped Frank and Grace for a moment. As parents, they were both acutely aware that they had very little knowledge of their children. They'd married in their late teens. When asked by Frank's parents, they hotly disputed that Grace was already pregnant, but their chosen wedding date of 11 October suggested another truth. In Frank and Grace's world, people got married and had kids. They'd never thought about it much further than that.

'You're going. On Monday,' said Frank. 'Whether you like it or not.'

They were at the dinner table. It was Saturday evening. Frank and Grace were smoking. Geraldine's stomach churned with the stench. She couldn't bear the smell of cigarettes so close to food. Every night she asked if they could wait until she'd finished eating, and every night they lit up straight after finishing their own meals, making a show of blowing their smoke to the side. Geraldine didn't have much knowledge of her parents' lives, either.

■□■

School in Kitwe was somewhat different to the nursery school Geraldine had briefly attended in Beverley. For starters, there was no black satchel, it having been lost in transit along with all of Geraldine's books. The school sat two streets over from the Sturmers' house, taking up a full block and surrounded with the same six-foot fencing as all the houses up and down the streets of Kitwe. Geraldine wondered, as she walked towards the compound with Frank, if that was to keep the school's guard dogs in. The school buildings were gathered together in the centre of the block and surrounded by bare earth, trees and patches of grass. Milling around the buildings were what looked to Geraldine like hundreds of kids, dressed in all variety of clothes, very little evidence of a school uniform. Their movement, forming and reforming of groups, reminded Geraldine of a flock of birds. There was a sense of giddy freedom about these kids and, as she approached the open gate in the school fence, Geraldine felt an eagerness to join them.

If the content of the lessons started out much the same as with Miss Kell all the way back in Beverley, the delivery was startlingly different. Geraldine's new teacher, Mr Nkozi, took great delight in chanting through the alphabet with his class and the kids joined in with a musicality that swept Geraldine out of her boredom and soon had her singing along. It didn't matter that she knew all the letters, sounds and words, Geraldine was caught up in the rhythmic repetition, the cadence of her classmates' accents and Mr Nkozi's enthusiasm. When he spoke, his eyes would widen as if they were about to pop out of his head, his teeth flashing white and his gums the most delicate of pinks, as he wiped the sweat that dripped from his brow with the handkerchief that was perpetually in his left hand like it was stitched into his palm. Geraldine was mesmerised.

And then there was Jesus. Geraldine had never heard of Jesus before she went to school in Kitwe. She'd never come across him in any of the books she'd read, Frank and Grace had never mentioned him and yet here he was in class, the man who saved humankind from … Geraldine couldn't quite figure out what just yet. Mr Nkozi told stories from the Bible about Jesus, about God and the Holy Trinity, and Geraldine was intrigued. From the stories Mr Nkozi shared with his class, she divined that Jesus' life was somewhat complex. As a small baby he was hunted down and only just avoided being killed by the king of his birth country. His mum and dad were, in Mr Nkozi's words, common people, like us, but Geraldine understood his use of the word 'common' to mean something quite different to her parents' usage. In Mr Nkozi's world there was something dignified about being common that had nothing to do with going to the shops in your rollers. Jesus died for all humanity, Mr Nkozi told his class. He was crucified by the Romans. Jesus was the first freedom fighter.

■□■

A few weeks into term, Geraldine came home from school and asked for a Bible. They were at the dinner table, Frank and Grace smoking, Frank onto his third glass of wine, filled to the brim.

'Mr Nkozi's teaching us about Jesus,' Geraldine announced, squinting in the haze of smoke, the last mouthfuls of dinner sitting on her plate uneaten.

'Is he?' said Grace, hardly registering what Geraldine had said.

'Yes. He says Jesus saved humanity and that the story is in the Bible. Can I have a Bible?'

Frank and Grace were both paying attention now. Harry turned over his mash with his fork.

'What do yer want a Bible for, Gerald?' Grace said.

Frank stayed quiet, but watchful, picking up his glass and taking a long snifter.

'I want to learn about Jesus,' Geraldine said. 'Mr Nkozi said he was a freedom fighter. What's a freedom fighter?'

Frank decided this was the moment to do some fathering.

'Yer what, Gerald?' said Frank. 'He said what?'

'He said Jesus was a freedom fighter,' Geraldine repeated.

'We'll see about that,' Frank said. 'And, no, yer can't 'ave a Bible.'

■□■

When one of her classmates, Moses, invited Geraldine to come back home with him to play after school. Geraldine thought about Susan and her family, but she said yes, anyway, her heart skipping in her chest like a fish flapping on a jetty as she did so.

Moses' house was on the same street as the school, one block past where Geraldine would normally take a left, walk two blocks over and then turn right to her home three down from the intersection. Passing the left turn also made Geraldine's heart flollop as she considered the rights and wrongs of what she was about to do. Still, she kept going, chatting with Moses as if nothing was wrong. When they got to his house, Moses' family greeted him in Bemba; Geraldine able to pick out a word here and there. Moses returned their greetings and then turned to Geraldine, who was standing just a pace behind him, wondering what sort of welcome she might get. She thought she'd heard Moses say her name and then she was certain of it.

'Hello, Geraldine,' said the woman standing closest to the front porch.

The porch was made of red cement, as opposed to the green of Geraldine's. The colour was deep and the shine was lustrous, like it had been polished by a million feet over thousands of years.

'Hello,' Geraldine said and then, shyly, '*muli shani*.'

The woman's eyes lit up as her smile broadened her face.

'Moses! Moses! This one can speak Bemba!' she said. 'Ah, Moses, you are a good boy!' And then, to Geraldine, 'Welcome, you are most welcome to our house. I am Mrs Wilson. It is a pleasure to have you come to visit.'

■□■

Geraldine stayed only half an hour that day, estimating that this was the longest she could say she'd been held back from school without Frank and Grace suspecting she was in some sort of trouble. She needn't have worried.

'Yer home, are yer?' said Grace as she opened the kitchen door, Brandy and Lass jumping around her in the least guard-dog-like of ways.

Geraldine waited, but the missing time wasn't mentioned.

■□■

Most days after that, Geraldine would stop by Moses' house on the way home. They would often talk about Jesus and, in Mr and Mrs Wilson's home, Jesus didn't seem like a stranger. They would also talk about their day at school, the games of tag played on the hardened earth that circled the school like a racetrack, Mr Nkozi's bulging eyes and Mr Banda, the deputy principal, who stalked the school grounds at playtimes, looking for troublemakers to take to the principal's office for the cane. The principal, Mr Chola, rarely seen but always a presence, was a person to avoid for sure. Whenever he and his cane got a mention, Moses and Geraldine would roar with laughter about the fate of whichever poor kids had been on the receiving end that day, their laughter covering a tinge of fear.

14

The end of Geraldine's second school career came with a series of events at the beginning of the dry season. When Mr Banda escorted Geraldine and Moses to the principal's office one lunchtime they knew it was their turn to receive the cane. Their crime? That day's lunchtime game of chasey had ended with Geraldine and Moses, who were 'it', corralling a group of kids who galloped noisily into one of the school's toilet blocks. The pair were prowling outside the outhouse like lions waiting for a warthog to emerge from its den when Mr Banda rounded the corner.

'What is happening here?' Mr Banda said, closing in on Geraldine and Moses.

'Nothing,' they said simultaneously, making to walk off while the screams and shouts of the kids in the toilet block echoed off its walls.

'Wait here!' Mr Banda told them as he poked his head into the toilets to see what was happening inside. 'Come with me,' he said to Geraldine and Moses, once he was satisfied he had established what their crime was.

The pair walked behind Mr Banda to the school's inner circle of buildings – a place they rarely visited as it was where the older kids' classrooms were, the staffroom and the offices, including Mr Chola's. Mr Banda ushered Geraldine and Moses into Mr Chola's office where the principal, greying hair and thick glasses atop his wiry frame, sat behind a dark wooden desk.

'Mr Chola,' Mr Banda began without preamble, 'these two were playing kiss chasey. They had nearly one hundred children trapped in the junior toilets.'

Geraldine bristled at the injustice and the lies. They were playing chasey, yes, but no kissing was involved. As for the number of kids she and Moses had bailed up, it couldn't have been more than ten. She opened her mouth to say something but thought the better of it.

Mr Chola raised himself up to his full height of five-foot-seven and came around from behind his desk, bamboo cane already in his hand.

'Bend over,' Mr Chola said to Moses.

Geraldine heard the whoosh of the cane and the thwack as it impacted Moses' shorts. She took in Moses' gulp of pain. Then it was her turn. Mr Chola's cane missed her shorts altogether and caught her across the top of her left thigh, stinging like a snake bite. Tears flooded Geraldine's eyes. While she was still bent over in front of the principal's desk, she took three short sharp breaths in and out to stem the flow. When she was ready, she stood up.

'Go now,' said Mr Banda. 'Back to class.'

Mr Chola didn't say a word.

■□■

Geraldine took herself into the shade of a tree and pulled up the leg of her shorts, bending around to see the deep welt that Mr Chola's cane had left on her soft pale flesh. It was already red and angry, and Geraldine knew that it would bruise all the colours of the rainbow.

'Are you okay?' Geraldine asked Moses.

'Yes, I am okay,' he replied. 'Are you?'

'Yes.'

After school Geraldine went back to Moses' house, where they recounted the day's events to Mr and Mrs Wilson.

'Are you sure?' Mrs Wilson asked. 'Are you sure you didn't do anything wrong?'

'No, *Mayo*, we were just playing,' said Moses.

'Be more careful in future, next time you might get six,' said Mrs Wilson.

■□■

Geraldine stayed at the Wilsons until well after dinnertime and, as she was walking home, the streets darkening with the sunset, brilliant orange on the horizon, shadows getting longer and the sounds of cicadas starting up in the trees, she knew she'd have some explaining to do.

'Where have you been?' asked Frank. 'We've been worried sick, Gerald.'

Frank led the conversation only when things were very serious.

'I've been at Moses' house,' said Geraldine.

'And 'oo is Moses?' said Frank.

'He's my friend,' said Geraldine. 'From school.'

'We didn't know you 'ad any friends,' said Grace. 'You've never mentioned anyone.'

'Well, I do,' said Geraldine. 'I have Moses.'

'Where does he live?' asked Frank.

'In Kantanta Street.'

Frank then asked the question that was most pressing for him and Grace.

'Is he black?'

'Yes,' said Geraldine.

'Go to your room,' said Frank.

■□■

The next morning Grace saw the stripe of red just below Geraldine's shorts.

'What's that?' she said.

'Nothing,' said Geraldine.

'C'mere, let me have a look.'

Geraldine reluctantly stood while Grace came to her, lifted the leg of her shorts and ran a finger across the welt, her touch bringing back the pain and heat.

'Tell me what 'appened, our Gerald,' said Grace.

Geraldine told her.

'That's it,' said Grace, 'you're staying home today, I'm not having you go to school with those kids anymore.'

15

Frank and Grace sold the trip as a holiday, but the siblings were wise to their ways. Geraldine: just turned six and at the beginning of her understanding; Harry, at eleven years old, had just about left home already. They were to go to boarding school in Rhodesia. On the way, the family was to take a holiday road trip. The longest road trips the Sturmers had taken until now had been very English affairs, day trips to the seaside. For some reason they always involved being up at four in the morning, ostensibly to beat the bank holiday traffic, although every time they hit the motorway they rediscovered the truth that every other person in Britain was attempting the same as them. On the way, time was often spent at the side of the road, Frank doing his best to fix whatever fault had brought to a halt whatever old banger he'd bought on the cheap. While the car was moving, or even just sitting in traffic, the family would sing.

Geraldine loved the togetherness of the family singalongs that they only ever felt free enough to do in the car.

There was Frank, Frank, working in the stores, in the stores / There was Frank, Frank, working in the stores / In the quartermasters' stores, the family would sing together.

My eyes are dim, I cannot see / I have not brought my specs with me / I have not brought my specs with meeeeeee, Frank would sing back.

They would go through each family member in order of age, Grace next, then Harry, then finally Geraldine. No-one had a song sheet, the songs were never rehearsed, they were passed along, Geraldine surmised later, through generations. Besides, Geraldine's name didn't scan, so she had to improvise.

There was me, me, waiting in the stars, in the stars / There was me, me, waiting in the stars / In the quartermasters' stars, Geraldine would sing, the rest of the family okay with her lyric change, but laughing uproariously when they heard her sing 'stars' instead of 'stores'. Geraldine could cope with that, but she could never work out what she was singing wrong, so she stuck with her version whenever they were in the car. She much preferred 'Roll Over'.

There were four in the bed and the little one said / Roll over, roll over.

Geraldine loved her starring role in this one, because much of the rest of Sturmer family life privileged age.

There was one in the bed and the little one said / Good night.

Then she would ask, 'Let's sing it again. Can we, can we please?'

Geraldine could usually get one or two repeats of 'Roll Over' out of her family, but then that was it, singing time was over. On this trip, however, the music didn't stop. At Harry's instruction, Frank tuned the radio according to which locality they were driving through, picking up Zam Rock, a fusion of traditional African music and the hard and psychedelic rock that was beginning to take over the airwaves in Europe and the US – arpeggiated guitar lines layered in with fuzzed-out blues rock and vocals, often sung in English, that mapped out the blueprint for Zambia's emancipation. Geraldine closed her eyes and drank in mile after mile of African rock music interspersed with the odd Jimi Hendrix song, soaked up the words and the sense that change and liberation were on the way.

When she opened her eyes and looked out of the car window, she could remind herself that she was actually there in the middle of the revolution, right as it was happening. Her mind had a sense of it, the exhilaration and the importance. The flashing scenery, mostly low-lying grasslands, sparsely treed with the occasional rocky outcrop surrounded by dense foliage, gave her the immediacy of being there. But, for Geraldine, her age had her one step away from its epicentre, whereas Harry had obviously spent time immersed in the scene. Before the radio announcer could back announce, Harry would say things like, 'Oh! Listen to this! This is the Peace. They played at Nkana last week.'

Harry knew them all and already had an encyclopedic knowledge of their free-rolling evolution, although Geraldine was sure that her encyclopedias had never once mentioned a thriving contemporary music scene in Zambia. Geraldine spent the hours of that trip on the back seat of the Ford Zephyr, its shot suspension making the ride feel like they were on a low-flying rollercoaster, pumping Harry for everything he knew, soaking up his murmured stories of sneaking out at night to go to shows in the local neighbourhood. The entire journey they saw not one single wild animal.

■□■

Before spending a day in Salisbury, Rhodesia's capital city, the Sturmers stopped off at Mermaids Pool, where they goaded each other into more and more stupidly daring acts on the natural rockslide that streamed down into the lake below, ate steak, chops and boerewors cooked on a *braai* and, not long after sundown on each of their two nights there, slept exhaustedly in the mud huts that surrounded the resort's swimming pool. Geraldine dreamed of the passing landscape and seeing the Peace supporting Jimi Hendrix at Kitwe football stadium. She flew over the crowd, taking in the smell of reefers, and hovered side of stage feeling the intensity of the performers. These were not human beings: they transcended their flesh as they joined together to make music, their energy transmitted via sonic waves into the ears and souls of their audience. It was something like a human sacrifice and it felt too good to leave, but daylight called Geraldine once again to join her family on the rockslide.

The stopover in Salisbury was to buy school uniforms. The outfitters was in a three-storey building of sprawling dimensions. Communication across and between the floors was via an elaborate set of vacuum tubes into which staff would insert capsules containing their handwritten notes and instructions. Geraldine wondered how they knew where their messages would end up, but the whole system seemed to work and, in the space of an hour or so, the Sturmer children were kitted out for school: everyday uniforms, Sunday uniforms, sports and gymnastics gear, even casual clothes. When they left the outfitters, the two siblings were dressed in their Sunday best uniforms, their black tin trunks containing everything else that was to be sent on to their final destination.

■□■

Geraldine experienced some new feelings when it came time for them to be left at the entry to Barthouse Boys School, which had come highly recommended by one of Frank's workmates. The first, she later learned, was anxiety. This feeling gripped her bowels and made her want to go very urgently. It tightened her chest and squeezed at her lungs and heart, making it difficult to speak or catch her breath. It turned the bones in her legs to jelly, making her feel like she would sink to the ground at any moment. It made her sweat and, most of all, it made her want to run. Actually, correct that: it made her want to evacuate her bowels and run.

'You'll have Harry to look after yer, our Gerald,' said Grace.

Geraldine could barely hear her. She just wanted Frank and Grace to be gone so this moment, these feelings, could be over. When the headmaster called time on the parting, Geraldine didn't look back.

'Come, Harry, Gerald, let's get you settled,' said Mr Caan, as he turned and walked towards the school's entrance.

Geraldine followed Mr Caan, with Harry a few steps behind. Once they were inside the door, standing in a high, vaulted passageway that seemed to travel forever in both directions, they were greeted by Matron Johannes.

'Gerald, you'll go with Matron to the junior school and Harry, you come with me to the seniors,' said Mr Caan.

'Come along, Sturmer,' said Matron, already moving to their right at a purposeful pace.

Geraldine hesitated, taking a while to work out who Matron was talking to, and then turned to hurry along behind her. This time she looked back and saw Harry following Mr Caan in the opposite direction, his head bowed. As she watched Harry get smaller, Geraldine felt loss for the first time. It was an itchy, quivering feeling in her chest that she did not like at all and it stayed there, twisting and turning inside her like she'd ingested a small animal. Geraldine fantasised about cutting her chest open and pulling out the animal, its fur slick with her blood, its body pulsing and thrashing in her fist, her chest open, the white of her bones showing beneath the deep red of her life force.

16

Geraldine quickly learned that boarding school was an institution of routines and rituals. Almost every moment of her life, from waking in the morning to returning to bed at night, was taken up with supervised activity. Boarders were taught how to make their beds on rising in the morning, given only minutes to shower, brush their teeth and make themselves look presentable. They and their beds were inspected, and any infractions were dealt with on the spot. Geraldine's bed neighbour was forever having his stubborn cowlick brushed into submission by Matron Johannes, his head pulled forward and springing back with every vigorous stroke. Until Kosie Thomas' hair was tamed, no-one in Geraldine's dorm was allowed to go to breakfast. The anticipation of their lateness made Geraldine's stomach turn airy loops just below her heart.

Arriving at the canteen even a few moments late for breakfast meant that Geraldine and her dorm mates would be at the back of the line for the porridge that started every day at Barthouse. The school cook, a man as wide as he was tall, served porridge from a large cooking pot, doling out a ladleful as each child presented their bowl held up in both hands. Watching from the back of the line, Geraldine couldn't help but feel that this was intended to be just as much a form of worship and supplication as the interminable church services boarders were forced to attend every Saturday morning. Geraldine was used to more processed fare, and just the sight of the seeds, husks and other detritus swimming in their watery mash of oats made her heave. The closer you were to the back of the line, the deeper Mr Sibanda had to dig into his pot and the greater the quantity of indigestible, teeth-separating, throat-scraping litter found its way into each bowl. Geraldine laboured over her porridge every morning. Taking tiny mouthfuls and leaving black seed pods stuck around the rim of her bowl, she would eventually feel that she was finished enough to be able to show one of the teachers who patrolled the canteen at every mealtime. Sometimes she was allowed to leave and head for her classroom with enough time to saunter across the grassed quadrangle, looking past the school buildings to the trees standing on the school's perimeter.

Other times, Geraldine was made to stay and finish her porridge, the watery scraps and sticky seed pods she had left in her bowl deemed by one of the more stringent teachers as too precious to waste. Those mornings when Geraldine hurried across the quadrangle, her only focus was on quelling her rebellious stomach. Breakfast at Barthouse always finished with toast, but in the half a term she attended, Geraldine never once tasted the smear of margarine on the white crusty bread that Mr Sibanda baked fresh every morning.

Considering he was the main cause of her morning lateness it was a surprise to Geraldine that she and Kosie Thomas became friends. Kosie was from a white Rhodesian farming family with a property in the north of the country, but too far away for him to be a day boy. For the boarders, day boys were ephemeral creatures. They arrived after breakfast in time for morning classes. They swelled numbers in the school's canteen at lunchtime but, by the time the boarders were allowed a few minutes of freedom between the end of afternoon classes and tea, they had disappeared again. They certainly never had to attend service in the school's chapel on Saturday mornings.

Kosie was tall with thick blond hair and long limbs. He was good at sport, handy with a cricket bat even at the age of six. He could run and frolic like a springbok and steamed with impatience at being held behind a desk in their classroom. Geraldine was, in almost every way, his opposite. Her pink face flushed red in the African sun, her stubby legs seemingly incapable of carrying her any distance at all and, as for cricket, she'd only ever seen it done on the telly. Kosie showed her his bat one afternoon, reverently touching the Gray-Nicolls decal that looked to Geraldine like it had been put there only to cover up the place where the handle and the blade of the bat were joined.

'This is the same bat they use in South Africa, *ja*,' Kosie told Geraldine.

Geraldine maintained her silence, hoping to understand the significance of this as Kosie kept talking.

'*Ja*,' Kosie continued, 'you have to put linseed oil on it to stop it cracking. Here, smell.'

Kosie proffered a dirty rag he'd just held over the top of an upended bottle of yellow liquid he'd pulled from his cricket bag. Geraldine tentatively leaned in to smell, her nose already crinkling, Harry's obsession with getting her to smell and taste all the bad things making her cautious. Given her experience, she was pleasantly surprised at the sweetish, nutty aroma.

'Smells good, *ja*?' said Kosie, seeing the look on Geraldine's face.

'*Ja*,' said Geraldine.

■□■

At night, after lights out, Geraldine and Kosie would talk across the narrow gap between their beds. Kosie told her about farm life in Rhodesia, his world ranging from his family's house, surrounded by wide verandas and ringed with acacia trees, across the scrubby bush where he and his older brothers would hunt anything that moved with homemade catapults. To Geraldine, Kosie's life felt improbably dangerous and, as she described her former life in Beverley, she was conflicted by her desire to embellish her world so that it would be something like the equal of Kosie's. For Geraldine, Kosie and his life were exotic fruit indeed.

Inevitably, Geraldine and Kosie got caught talking after lights out by one of the teachers who crept along the hallway that connected the school's dormitories, listening at every door for sounds of disobedient children. Kosie was part way through a story of hunting kudu with his father and uncle, with him standing the other side of their Land Cruiser's bonnet while Uncle Charles felled a bull with a single shot to the neck, the crack of the rifle echoing off the kopjes that dotted the landscape of the Thomases' farm.

'You two!' said the teacher in an urgent whisper. 'Come with me.'

Geraldine and Kosie didn't have to wait for their names to be called, they knew it was them Mr van der Walt was talking to. They climbed out of bed and followed the tall shadowy figure through their dorm towards the light cast by the partly open door. Outside in the hallway it was like the school had been floodlit. Geraldine and Kosie blinked owlishly as their eyes adjusted to the light and they awaited their fate.

'You, Thomas, stand here,' said Mr van der Walt, beckoning Kosie with a finger to the other side of the corridor. 'That's it, face the wall. Stand up straight and keep still.'

Geraldine watched, her mouth open a little as she wondered what would happen next.

'Sturmer, you this side,' said van der Walt, as he beckoned for her to stand facing the corridor's other wall, opposite Kosie. 'Right, you two, you can spend some time staring at the cracks in the paint and thinking about what you've done wrong,' Mr van der Walt told them. 'You're not to move and don't say a single word, or there'll be real trouble.'

With that, he walked off down the hallway, stopping to listen at doors until Geraldine could no longer see him out of the corner of her eye. It felt to her like it was forever before she even dared breathe again. Once she regained her breath she heard Kosie's muffled giggling behind her, the occasional stifled snort. Geraldine was mortified at first and then the mirth of having gotten away with it began to overtake her body. Her stomach shook, her chest and shoulders wobbled with the power of her contractions and the tears welled in her eyes as she stifled her laughter. Geraldine couldn't remember a time when she'd ever wanted to laugh so much and so hard. She felt a surprising freedom, caught up in the illicitness of it all as she and Kosie did their best to hold on to themselves.

■□■

Geraldine felt like she could endure the dullness of boarding school. She kept the magic of the music she'd soaked up on the trip to school with her always. Even in the silences that were a main feature of most of her days, Geraldine's head was thrumming with music. It got so she could hear a song and predict what note, what chord was coming next and, not long after, Geraldine was making up her own music, no instruments, no singers, all in her head.

After a while she began to question the role of Jesus in her life and in the wider world. Every Saturday morning after breakfast the boarders would be herded into the school chapel for the weekly service. Barthouse Boys School's version of the whole God story seemed more than a little bit unnecessarily harsh to Geraldine. There was no room for movement in the sermons given by the minister who, each week, hammered home God's power and glory and the need to prepare for Jesus' imminent return to earth. Having had access to the Bible in her daily classwork, Geraldine found herself disagreeing with the minister's views on Jesus, much preferring Mr Nkozi's version of the saviour.

Geraldine began to formulate a theory about religion which she put to the test one Saturday morning as she and her dorm mates were being ushered to church by their class teacher, Miss Johnson.

'Why do we have to go to church?' Geraldine asked.

'Because we have to,' said Miss Johnson, not anticipating Geraldine's sedition.

'But, why?' asked Geraldine. 'Why are we made to go to church? Why don't we get to choose?'

'Because God loves us,' said Miss Johnson.

'But God doesn't make us go,' said Geraldine. 'You're the one making us go.'

'Gerald, quiet down, or you'll be in trouble,' said Miss Johnson. 'Come, we must go.'

Geraldine quietly digested the look in Miss Johnson's eyes and felt clear in her mind that any trouble that might arise from her further refusal to go to church would have nothing to do with God and certainly not Jesus.

■□■

Early the next week Geraldine was seated in the canteen at teatime working her way through a plate of veggies, calculating the minimum amount she could eat before a teacher would pass her plate as cleared. She inspected her food with her fork, turning over the potatoes, carrots, greens (Geraldine had no idea what they were) and peas. The maggot she discovered as she ran her fork through the peas on her plate came as no surprise to Geraldine, but it did to her stomach, which threatened the kind of rebellion that would have had Geraldine washing up in the kitchen after meals for weeks. Quelling her urge to projectile vomit undigested vegetables over her fellow boarders, Geraldine put up her hand and waited. A deliberately long time later a teacher came over, one Geraldine didn't know and who obviously didn't know her.

'Yes?'

'There's a maggot in my peas,' said Geraldine.

The teacher ran his eyes over her plate and, finding no such creature among the shiny green globes grouped together in one corner said, 'Get on and eat your meal. You'll stay here until your plate is empty.'

Geraldine sat in front of her plate and contemplated what to do next. She searched with her fork, but the maggot was nowhere to be found. Even in the absence of any physical evidence, Geraldine knew she was right. She wanted to comply, but every time she mustered up the gumption to bring a forkful of food to her mouth, her stomach warned her of the consequences of following the teacher's instructions. Geraldine sat looking at her plate as the canteen emptied. Finally, she was the last student remaining in what now felt to her like a very large room. The teacher came back to inspect Geraldine's plate.

'You haven't eaten your food yet,' he said. 'You can't go until your plate is empty.'

'But there's a maggot in my peas,' Geraldine said, restating the facts of the matter.

'There isn't,' the teacher said. 'Now eat!'

The teacher's sharpness made Geraldine consider her predicament once more, but her stomach still wasn't willing to play along, so she sat, staring at her plate, willing the maggot to emerge from a pea so that she could show the teacher and put an end to her evening meal. While her stomach wouldn't settle, the pull of her impending lateness for everything that came after tea at Barthouse filled Geraldine's chest with a herd of galloping butterflies. She very much disliked being late. The next voice Geraldine heard was Miss Johnson's.

'What are you doing, Gerald?' she asked.

Geraldine looked up to find that she and her class teacher were the only two people remaining in the dining hall. She could hear the rattle and clank of pots, pans and plates being washed in the kitchen behind the partition at the back of the hall, the whoosh of water being sprayed over the dirty dishes from that evening's tea. The only plate remaining in the canteen was hers.

'A teacher told me I have to eat my food,' said Geraldine, 'but there's a maggot in my peas.' Geraldine looked around the room for the teacher, but he had obviously moved on from his canteen duties.

'Jesus wouldn't want you to waste your food,' said Miss Johnson.

Geraldine looked at her, asking without saying a single word if she believed this to be true.

'Okay, how about you just eat some of your carrots?' said Miss Johnson, changing tack.

The woman and the girl both knew that if she hadn't brought Jesus into it, their impasse would be over, the stone-cold veggies scraped into the compost bin and Jesus would be none the wiser.

'I don't think Jesus wants me to eat this food,' said Geraldine, 'otherwise he would have made me hungry. I don't feel hungry. I feel sick.'

Miss Johnson took a long while to calculate the odds.

'If you feel sick, Gerald, you should go see Matron,' she said. 'Go on, off you go.'

Geraldine got up and left the canteen. Outside it was darkening, and she could just see that last tinge of the sunset way beyond the school's boundaries. Children and teachers were nowhere in sight. For a moment, Geraldine thought about walking towards the sun.

17

At half-term every boarder at Barthouse Boys School went home for a week, except Geraldine and Harry. They hadn't really seen each other since Frank and Grace had left them at the school. The workings of the senior and junior schools were kept separate except at mealtimes and on Saturdays, when the older boys would file into the back of the chapel and take up their seats across the last two pews. From her place in the second row of hard, uncomfortable, high-backed wooden benches, Geraldine could turn around and catch the occasional glimpse of Harry, but she never waved to him or made eye contact and he never did either. There would be serious consequences if they were caught doing anything but seriously contemplating God.

The siblings were left, mostly, to their own devices, under the none-too-watchful eye of the headmaster, Mr Caan, and his wife, Mrs Caan. Mr Caan reminded Harry and Geraldine of the boundaries of the school and where they could and couldn't go. Meals were to be taken in the Caan's residence, a cottage that stood alone on the school grounds just far enough away from the cluster of classrooms and dormitories to afford some privacy. The cottage had a low stone wall around it and a single gate at the front that was resolutely closed.

Geraldine was allowed up to the senior end of the school to share a dormitory with her sibling. That night they talked for the first time in weeks.

'You alright, our Gerald?' Harry asked.

'*Ja*,' said Geraldine.

'What's that?' said Harry.

'*Ja*, I'm okay,' said Geraldine.

'Yer talking like an Afrikaner,' said Harry. 'Yev only bin 'ere five minutes,' he continued, laying his Yorkshire accent on thick.

Geraldine hadn't noticed. To her, she sounded normal, but, *ja*, there did seem to have been some changes.

'You alright, Harry?' Geraldine asked, moving the conversation along.

'They 'it us,' said Harry. 'Give us the cane even if you've done nothing wrong. I hate it here.'

Geraldine could neither see nor hear the tears, but she knew Harry was crying, giant, heaving silent sobs.

■□■

The next day at lunch, Harry and Geraldine met the headmaster's daughter, Jacqueline. Around Geraldine's age, she invited them to come to her room and play after lunch. All three children looked to Mr Caan for his assent before leaving the table and following Jacqueline through the living room and down a short passageway to her bedroom. She walked straight through the open door, but the two siblings hesitated on the threshold.

'Come,' said Jacqueline, 'let's play dolls.' She said this to no-one in particular, just happy to have some playmates.

Harry slunk into the bedroom and sat himself on one of the two single beds that stood against a wall each along the length of the room. Geraldine took up a spot opposite Jacqueline on the floor between the beds in what looked to her like a sea of dolls of varying sizes, parts of dolls and, covering every part of the floor, doll's clothes. Geraldine had never seen so many toys; she was overwhelmed by the variety and colours, and she was conscious that Harry was sitting over them, looking on in bored judgement. Jacqueline proceeded to show Geraldine her dolls, naming each one and showing her their outfits. When she finally got to her Barbie doll, she showed Geraldine her thick, blond hair, inviting Geraldine to stroke it. She showed her how Barbie's clothes could be buttoned and unbuttoned, just like real clothes, how her rather oddly shaped stilettos came off and on and – speaking like she was about to reveal the very secret of life itself – Jacqueline showed Geraldine Barbie's leopard-skin-print knickers.

Geraldine looked at the tiny underwear and the newest of feelings rushed through her veins. She had never coveted an object so much in her short life. In fact, she'd never coveted an object at all until she saw those perfectly formed doll knickers. She said nothing in the moment, but when Jacqueline left the bedroom to go elsewhere, Geraldine was moved to speak.

'I want those knickers,' she said.

'Well, tek 'em, then,' said Harry. 'She's got so much, she'll never miss 'em.'

Geraldine looked up at Harry. Then she picked up Barbie and removed her shoes and trousers, then the underwear, which she secreted in the pocket of her shorts. Geraldine was shaking with adrenaline-stoked fear as she redressed the Barbie doll, expecting to be caught at any moment with her trousers only half back up and her pink curve still exposed. No such thing eventuated.

'Let's go,' said Harry, after Jacqueline had been gone for what he considered to be long enough.

He got up and left Jacqueline's bedroom, walked back up the passage, through the living and dining areas and to the door that led to the short path and the gate. Geraldine followed, all the time expecting a voice or a hand on her shoulder that never came. As they passed through the gate, Geraldine carefully and quietly closed it behind them and kept following Harry.

When they were back on familiar ground, Harry said, 'Let's run away.'

18

Running away was easy. There was nothing to stop the two siblings at the boundary of the school, no fence or gate, no teachers or other staff. They'd decided to go the back way instead of past the school's main buildings and onto the road that was the shortest route back to the rest of the world. They thought they were sure to be stopped if they went that way. Instead, they walked in the opposite direction across the school's playing fields and picked up the dirt track that traversed the open farmland that stretched as far as they could see. The joining of the track and the school grounds was marked with two tall wooden fence posts and, to the right, a deep pit with a dead cow at the bottom. Such were the pit's dimensions that the cow looked tiny to Geraldine. She glanced at it as they walked by but decided not to get too caught up in thinking about how it had got there and why it was waiting to greet them as they crossed the school's boundary.

The siblings walked in silence for hours, seeing no other living thing except the occasional lizard sunning itself in the middle of the track. Harry was resolute, his head held high, looking for the next part of their route. Geraldine did her best to match his pace without asking for him to slow down, or to stop and rest too many times. She constantly looked back, wondering when Mr Caan would catch up with them. She wanted to ask Harry to go home, but she knew there was no possibility of that. They had brought with them no food or water, just the clothes they'd been wearing at lunch and, in Geraldine's pocket, the leopard-skin knickers she felt were somehow responsible for causing their current circumstance.

Cresting a rise in the track, Harry put up his hand for Geraldine to stop. Once she'd caught up, she stood at Harry's side, almost reaching his shoulder as they inspected the tarmacked road running perpendicular to the track a few hundred yards in front of them. The afternoon was still and silent and the road carried not a single vehicle.

'Which way should we go?' asked Harry.

Geraldine felt the flimsiness of her youth as she considered her answer. When Harry had suggested they run away, she'd done a quick confirmation of the facts before saying yes. Harry was almost twice her age and his advanced years gave her enough of a sense of safety that she could go along with his idea. She'd also remembered Harry's silent sobbing from the night before and felt a sense of responsibility for him and his hurt that, as a six-year-old, she couldn't yet explain but understood well. But she hadn't expected Harry to ask her what they should do.

'It's okay,' said Harry, seeing Geraldine pause. 'I know what we should do. We're close to the border at Chirundu, but we don't have passports. They'll catch us there and send us back. I think we should go the other way, towards Salisbury. They won't be expecting that.'

Geraldine nodded in agreement, relieved at not having to be in charge.

'See those bushes on the other side of the road?' he said. 'Let's go over there and hide, keep an eye on the traffic. When we see a car coming we can hitch a lift.'

They walked the last few hundred yards towards the T-junction, Geraldine all the while surveying the dense bushes, squinting to give her eyes more power to see into them. They were exactly the sort of place you'd find a lion or three. As they crossed the road and climbed through the low, wire-strand fence on the other side, Geraldine felt fear. It was something like she'd felt when she used to hear Frank trying to tread lightly on the stairs in Beverley, but at least in those moments she knew what she was up against.

They had good sight of the stretch of road bringing cars towards them from the north-east so Harry was able to assess whether he liked the look of them before deciding if he would try to flag one down. He let a few go, and Geraldine was starting to get impatient with him when he set his sights on a white sedan.

'This one,' he said. 'Let's try this one. I'll talk to them.'

They stood at the side of the road, Harry with his thumb out and Geraldine at his side trying to look, she didn't quite know what. Appealing? The car slowed and pulled to a stop alongside them, the wheels on the passenger side inches from their feet. The woman in the passenger seat wound down the window.

'Hello, children,' she said. 'What are you doing here?'

She was wearing a green-and-yellow sari with a bindi on her forehead. As well as her, there were four other adults in the car. Harry waved Geraldine back with his right hand.

'We're going to visit family in Salisbury,' said Harry. 'We're going to our uncle's for half-term. Can you give us a lift?'

The woman looked at Harry and Geraldine and then into the car.

'We have no room,' she said, 'but you look hungry.'

She turned to one of the men in the back of the car.

'Rudra, give me that bag of bread rolls and some of the bottles of cool drink.'

The man handed forward two white plastic bags to the woman, which she passed through the car window to Harry and Geraldine.

'Good luck, children,' she said. 'I hope you meet your family soon.'

As the car drove away, Harry took a bread roll out of the first bag and passed it over to Geraldine. When she looked inside, she saw it was filled with what looked like enough crusty rolls to feed the entire school at teatime. She took one and started eating fast and as savagely as she'd imagined a lioness would have done had it been waiting for them on the other side of the flimsy wire fence. Harry passed over a large glass bottle of lemonade, its outsides dripping with cool water and its insides just as deliciously icy. Once they'd pared back their hunger, Harry looked back down the road and decided they should return to the bushes. They sat hidden from the road and watched as the sun set, staining the horizon with surreal oranges, reds and pinks and, as it passed out of sight, bruising the earth purple and finally leaving behind only black. They hadn't seen another car since the white sedan.

■□■

There was no choice but for them to bed down for the night. Harry broke leafy branches from the bushes so they could make a kind of nest. With each crack of the supple offshoots, Geraldine pulled her head back into her neck, waiting for the corresponding crack of an animal's foot breaking a dry twig on the ground. But this night, in their tiny part of Rhodesia, cause and effect had taken a break. They slept while all around them nothing of any scale occurred. As the sun broke in the east, the only sign that they had been out in the bush were the ant bites that peppered their bare legs.

Harry decided to try to flag down the first car they saw that morning, a pick-up truck that was leaving behind it a plume of the fine dust deposited on the road overnight by the persistent north-easterly. The car pulled up alongside them and the driver, a man in his thirties, leaned over to wind down the passenger side window. Again, Harry did the talking while Geraldine clutched what remained of yesterday's bread rolls and cool drink.

'Where are you kids headed?' said the man.

'We're going to Salisbury to meet our uncle,' said Harry, continuing their lie from yesterday.

'*Ja*, you are, are you?' said the man.

'*Ja*,' said Geraldine, as she stepped forward. 'We have some food for the journey,' she said, holding up the white plastic bags. 'Our family gave it to us.'

The man looked at the two of them and the flies buzzing around their heads for a moment.

'Hop in,' he said. 'I can only take you to Sinoia. Is that okay?'

'Yes, thank you,' said Harry, looking back at Geraldine.

Geraldine nodded and climbed into the pick-up, planting herself in the middle of the bench seat as Harry got in beside her and shut the door.

'Better wind that window up,' said the man as he pulled back onto the road again, tyres skidding as they looked for purchase on the loose sand at the side of the road.

They found their driver had few words as he drove them towards Sinoia. Harry and Geraldine swayed with the motion of the pick-up, which soon left Geraldine asleep, head resting on her sibling's shoulder.

'Rough night?' said the driver, looking from Geraldine to Harry.

'Yes,' said Harry, hoping that would be the end of the questions. He shrugged his shoulder and roused Geraldine.

Nearing the city of Sinoia, their driver slowed as the traffic – vehicles and pedestrians – thickened. The outskirts of the city were marked by ramshackle outcrops of housing and light industrial buildings, corrugated iron being the building material of choice. Roadside vendors had their wares laid out on blankets or low tables right at the edge of the road. Here you could buy everything from ground nuts and heads of maize to local art sculpted from wood, malachite and ivory. Children ran up and down the edge of the road steering wire cars between the vendors and the edge of the tarmac. Adults shooed them away, unconcerned that they would get tangled with the traffic on the road.

'Where do you want me to drop you?' asked the driver.

'We're going to Salisbury,' said Harry, not knowing what else to say.

'Okay, I'll take you as far as I can.'

As far as he could was a junction on the other side of the city.

'This is my turn,' he said, as he pulled over to the side of the road. 'Salisbury is that way,' he told them, pointing to the road ahead to make sure Harry and Geraldine knew where they were going.

The siblings got out on the passenger side and stood in the powdery pinkish dirt at the side of the road.

'Thank you,' Harry said through the open window.

'Be careful,' said the man, as he drove away, taking the right turn to whatever was his destination.

Harry and Geraldine were alone again. They heard silence for the first time since that morning as they stood at the side of the road. Geraldine looked up at the sun and estimated it was well past lunchtime, news her stomach was also telegraphing with its cramps and moans.

'I need to go to the toilet,' said Geraldine.

'Let's get off the road for a bit,' said Harry, 'think about what to do.'

The pair ducked between the strands of the wire fence that still marked the side of the road and walked into the bush. This didn't look like cultivated ground, the earth was baked dry, wide cracks showing where water had once been. The land was open, irregularly peppered with low-growing trees, granite rocks of various sizes pushing their way through the iron-hard soil. Harry decided they should rest for a while in the shade of one of the bigger outcrops, and they sat with their backs leaning up against the warmth of the ancient stone, watching the traffic on the road a little way below them.

'Best not go too far,' said Harry. 'We don't want to get lost.'

'*Ja*,' said Geraldine. Then, 'What are we going to do, Harry?'

Harry didn't say anything, just sat watching the cars on the road.

'Harry?' said Geraldine, 'I'm scared. What are we going to do?'

Harry looked at her, saw the tear tracing dirt down her cheek.

'I don't know, our Gerald,' he said.

Geraldine sniffed, breathed in sharply and said, '*Ja*, okay.'

19

By the morning of day three, Harry and Geraldine were front page news across southern Africa, their grainy passport photos looking out across the continent under the headline *RUNAWAYS!* The police and army were searching for them but, concentrating their resources on the country between the school and the Chirundu border crossing, they were miles from the pair as they made their way back to the roadside from the lee of the rocky outcrop where they'd spent the night. Again, Africa had blessed Harry and Geraldine with its stoic silence, the only movement shooting stars that had Geraldine wondering for a moment if Jesus was looking out for them, a thought she discounted after having listened to Harry talk about the treatment he'd received from the teachers at Barthouse's senior school. Geraldine spent much of the night wanting to be home, but she was confused by the multiple images, thoughts and feelings her desire conjured.

They walked back to the roadside, and Harry tried to flag down the first car that approached, another pick-up truck. It slowed and pulled over to the side of the road, the driver winding down the window on Harry and Geraldine's side as he brought the car to a squealing stop.

'Where are you going?' he said.

'Salisbury,' said Harry, offering no further explanation.

'You'd better get in, then,' said the driver, as he leaned over and opened the passenger side door.

Harry and Geraldine stepped up onto the bench seat, Geraldine sitting closest to the driver, who patted the vinyl with his large, bony hand, skin hanging loosely from his knuckles like he'd draped it on before leaving the house that morning. His fingernails were broad and long, like animal horns and his fingers were stained yellow with nicotine. Geraldine looked at him before parking herself on the seat, waiting until she saw both of the man's hands on the steering wheel. His face was tanned, drooping at the eyes, his nose tracked with red and blue capillaries. His chin was covered in grey stubble and his hat was stained with years of sweat. The man's eyes were a worn-out blue, his pupils tiny black dots.

The man leaned forward to pull the cigarette lighter from the dashboard and lit his king-size, turning to Harry and Geraldine as he pulled away from the side of the road, the fuming cigarette still in his mouth, and said, 'I'm Wayne, pleased to meet you, *ja*?'

Wayne had lots of questions.

'What are you doing out here on your own?'

'We're travelling to visit our uncle,' said Harry.

'Are you now? Where does your uncle live?'

'In Salisbury.'

'Where in Salisbury?'

'We're going to call him when we get there,' said Geraldine, 'so he can come and pick us up.'

'Are you now?' said Wayne.

'*Ja*,' said Geraldine.

■□■

About an hour into their journey, Wayne pulled over at a roadside cafe, no more than a few wooden benches and tables shaded with a thatched roof.

'I'm guessing you two are hungry?' he said.

Wayne ordered sausage and egg rolls, looking at Harry and Geraldine as he took out his wallet to pay. The rolls were dripping with butter and tomato sauce, and they sluiced them down with bottles of ice-cold Coca-Cola. Geraldine thought it was the best breakfast she'd ever had. Back in the pick-up, their bellies full, Harry and Geraldine slept. Geraldine opened her eyes as she felt the motion of the car slow and elbowed Harry awake as she read the sign at the front of the building to their left: *Police Station*.

'C'mon, you two,' said Wayne as he got out of the truck. 'I think this is where you belong.'

Neither of the siblings thought to run, there was nothing much left in them.

■□■

While they were together, Harry and Geraldine stuck to their story, and the kindly woman police constable who chaperoned them past the counter at the front of the station, past the maze of offices and into the canteen, seemed willing to play along.

'You're visiting your uncle, you say?' she confirmed. 'For half-term?'

'Yes,' said Harry. 'He'll be waiting to pick us up soon, we just have to call him.'

'And what's this uncle's name?'

'Fred,' said Harry. 'Fred Sturmer.'

Harry and Geraldine did have a great-uncle Fred, but he was back in Doncaster as far as they knew.

'And you were allowed to go and see him for half-term?' asked the constable. 'You had your parents' permission?'

'Yes,' said Harry, 'we couldn't go home to Kitwe, it's too far, so they said to go and stay with Uncle Fred.'

'Okay, we need to check this out. We're waiting for your father to call and the headmaster of the school is on his way. Meantime, would you like a Coke?'

The constable left them at the table while she walked over to the machine to get their drinks.

'Keep to the story,' Harry told Geraldine. 'It's working.'

Geraldine nodded. Much to her surprise, they did seem to be getting away with it. Their parents and the school being out of touch was helping with the confusion.

'Here we are,' said the constable, putting a bottle of Coke in front of each of them.

She sat back in her chair and looked the children over for a moment as they drank thirstily from the thick glass bottles.

'Gerald, how about you come with me for a moment?' she said. 'I can show you the rest of the station. Would you like that?'

'Yes, please,' said Geraldine, always up for something new.

'C'mon then,' said the constable, 'bring your drink and let's go. We'll see you in a little while, Harry.'

Harry watched them go and, as Geraldine looked over her shoulder, he gave her a look, half defiance, half defeat.

The constable led Geraldine along a corridor, quiet rooms on each side, that led to a set of stairs.

'Come on down,' she said to Geraldine.

Geraldine followed and, as she saw the constable opening the steel door at the bottom of the stairs, she began to feel fear creep up from her feet, down from her head. As the door opened and she saw the cement floor and the row of barred cells on each side, it reached her stomach and she was almost sick.

'Come in,' said the constable, like she was inviting Geraldine into her home.

Geraldine took a step through the doorway and into the low-ceilinged passage. Thankfully all the cells were empty, but the smell of disinfectant that barely covered the stench of bodily fluids – vomit, piss, blood and shit – added to Geraldine's dread. The smells took her back to hospital and death. Geraldine's hearing and eyesight went on the wonk and her legs threatened to give way under her. It took a while before she heard the constable.

'This is where we keep the criminals,' she said. 'If you don't tell me what's really going on, this is where you'll spend the night.'

Geraldine cried, there was nothing else left to do.

The siblings had survived three days and two nights travelling across the untamed wilds of Africa, the whole world waiting to hear their fate in the jaws of some creature, but this was how their journey ended.

'We ran away,' said Geraldine, once she'd gotten hold of her tears. 'We just want to go home.'

Again, Geraldine's mind was filled with conflicting thoughts and feelings as she said the word 'home'.

■□■

Home wasn't where Harry and Geraldine ended up, not right away, anyway. It had felt good to be free of the lie, but Harry was filthy on her for coming clean.

'What'd d'yer go and do that for?' he'd said after the constable had brought Geraldine back up from the cells and told him she'd ratted them out.

Geraldine said nothing, she just wanted their little adventure to be over. An hour or so later, there was Mr Caan, talking to the constable in the doorway of the canteen where she'd left them sitting, knowing they had no more run left in them. He pointed in their direction and turned and spoke again to the constable. The two of them walked over to the table where the siblings were still seated, wondering what might happen next.

'Children, it's so good to see you,' said Mr Caan. 'We've all been so worried. Come, let's go.'

'Are you alright to go with the headmaster here?' the constable asked.

Harry and Geraldine nodded and the constable looked them over like she hoped they might say something, but they didn't.

'Okay, then, away with you,' she said, as she turned to escort the trio out of the police station.

Mr Caan had parked his dusty British racing green Jaguar right outside, almost exactly where Wayne had pulled up to drop them off. The long drive back to the school was completed in silence.

■□■

At bedtime, Mr Caan asked Harry to come with him for a moment while Geraldine got settled under the covers. It was dark when Harry returned and Geraldine was on the far side of wakeful, almost irreversibly asleep. She heard Mr Caan say, 'Your father will be here tomorrow to pick you up,' and fell asleep to the metronomic sound of Harry's sobs. The next morning Frank arrived in his Ford Zephyr and drove the kids back to Zambia.

20

'I won't. I won't go,' said Geraldine.

'We'll get you something,' said Grace. 'Anything you like.'

'No. I won't. I can't.'

Frank and Grace were negotiating Geraldine's return to boarding school.

'You can't think of anything you'd like?' asked Grace. 'Anything?'

Geraldine gave the conundrum some thought.

'I want a kitten,' she said.

There was a giant freeze in the hot room. Even the flies stopped buzzing. Geraldine knew Grace was deathly afraid of cats, so if she was going to close this deal, that was her price, back to boarding school for a kitten. Geraldine smiled at Grace, blue eyes on blue, and waited, nothing more to be said. Grace looked at Frank, who lit a cigarette, just one for him, and blew out smoke but said nothing.

'Okay,' said Grace.

'What?' said Geraldine.

'Okay, you can have a kitten. But not until you get back at the end of term.'

Geraldine nodded. 'Okay then,' she said.

■□■

The new school was in England. Schools, that is, because Harry was headed to the senior school and Geraldine was off to prep school on her own. The three of them flew off, Zambia Airways to Lusaka, Alitalia to Rome and then London, reversing their journey of eighteen months ago. Frank stayed behind for work. Grace and Geraldine arrived at Havenhouse Preparatory School in a taxi, having first dropped Harry off at the senior school that straddled the main road of the small town twenty miles or so up the A303. He was to board in New House, est. 1543, and that's pretty much all Frank and Grace had been able to tell the siblings about King John's College and its feeder prep school.

Still, Grace seemed surprised that Havenhouse sat in its own grounds atop its own two-mile driveway, a sandstone country mansion that the school's prospectus boasted had been a hospital for wounded servicemen during World War Two. As the taxi crunched to a stop outside the school's enormous front door, Grace let out a Yorkshire 'Oh!'. As Geraldine got out and put her newly shod feet on the gravel driveway, dark sand to match the house's facade, she was concentrating only on her bowels. They were greeted by Mr Hassell, a tall man wearing a baggy blazer and camel-coloured slacks, casual clothes given they'd arrived the day before boarders were due back for the start of the school year. His hair was black and wiry, with a streak of grey on the left side near his irrepressible fringe, which he constantly swept back.

'Welcome, Gerald,' said Mr Hassell, holding out a massive hand.

Geraldine put her hand in his. He felt kindly, his eyes had comfort in them and a touch of humour.

'Now, let's get you settled,' said Mr Hassell. 'Come along, come along,' he urged as he turned to walk up the stairs and through the front door.

'Go on, our Gerald,' said Grace, turning back to look at the taxi.

'Come with me?' said Geraldine.

Reluctantly, Grace followed Geraldine up the front stairs and into the billiard room, a marble staircase to the right heading up to the house's next level, taking a turn to the left once it was halfway there, following the contours of the room. A full-sized snooker table stood on the stone floor in the centre of the room. Mr Hassell took a left around it and disappeared down a passage at the far end of the entry hall, not once looking back to see if anyone was following him. Geraldine hurried after him, with Grace coming along behind clutching a packet of cigarettes. They found themselves at the back of the house, outside Mr Hassell's office, a dark wooden door with *HEADMASTER* embossed at adult eye-level in gold lettering. Waiting outside the office was Matron, a slender woman, grey hair cropped close, sensible shoes, brown stockings and a white nurse's dress.

'Gerald, you go with Matron and I'll just have a word with your mother,' said Mr Hassell.

'Foller me,' said Matron, heading towards a rickety oak staircase, stained dark brown like it was made out of old country-pub roof beams. The treads were shiny and worn from hundreds of years of footfall.

Geraldine and Grace didn't get to say goodbye to each other. She ate in Matron's rooms that evening, soft-boiled eggs and soldiers with butter. When it was time for bed, Matron sat on the edge of the bare mattress next to Geraldine's and read to her from T*he House at Pooh Corner*. Geraldine rode gently into sleep on Matron's West Country accent and A.A. Milne's words. She didn't know when she'd spent a more pleasant evening.

▪▫▪

Havenhouse was where Geraldine got her first proper education. Not that she hadn't learned plenty from her three previous schools, but this was where she started to tap into the sort of rigour that enabled her, ultimately, to eschew the rules. Geraldine was in her element. Not at first, because they started her off in 3B, the lowest stream – not knowing anything about her past, Grace being a bit economical with the details – and Geraldine knew she should be with the kids over the corridor in 3A. It didn't take long before she was sent across.

The curriculum at Havenhouse took in maths, English, French, Latin, geography, history, religious education, current events, biology, physics, chemistry, art and, for balance, woodwork. Music was optional; singing in church on a Sunday morning, sometimes Sunday evening, was not. When she was handed a hockey stick during Saturday afternoon sport, she realised she'd found a game that complemented all the school's book learning. What Havenhouse was keen on producing were children who knew their stuff and could apply it, with a bruising brutality, if that's what it took to win. Geraldine soon learned when and how to wield her stick, just the same way she learned how to wield language and logic.

Her days were fuller than they ever had been, but Geraldine still found time to walk the aisles of the school's library, touching the spines of the books on the shelves and storing away a for-later reading list in her mind while borrowing every week her limit of three books. The library was also where Havenhouse's only communal television was located, and every Thursday after tea kids crammed around it to watch *Top of the Pops*. Geraldine drank it all in like it was part of the school curriculum, remembering, comparing and judging everything. She preferred Smokey Robinson to Deep Purple, loved the white soul of Dusty Springfield and was mesmerised by Pans People. Jimmy Savile confused her. He smoked cigars, which was a big minus for Geraldine, and his way of speaking sounded contrived. Even in 1970 he looked too old to be involved with kids.

■□■

There were six students in Geraldine's dorm, including her. Their sleeping quarters were called Achilles after Her Majesty's warship. It made no sense to Geraldine to name a warship after a figure with such an obvious weakness. Three of her dorm mates were from England, one from Ireland and one from Australia, although, like Geraldine, Mark Turvey was originally from England. As they were getting ready for lights out they were allowed a precious half hour to chatter with each other, play games and get up to mischief. Turvey's dad did something in the army, and for the new school year Turvey had brought with him some little white pills that he claimed could purify water.

'Let's try them,' said Corrigan, the Irish kid with no discernible Irish accent, just the brash nature some people from small places carry with them.

'What are we going to do?' asked Thatcher. 'We need something, not the water from the tap. What can we try them with?'

'I've got some ink in my pen,' said Geraldine. 'Let's see if they can purify that.'

'What about some pee?' said Sprague.

'Oh, yes! Let's try that,' said Corrigan, now very excited.

Turvey started to look overwhelmed, uncertain that the pills he'd purloined were up to the challenges his roommates had thrown down, but he couldn't back out now. Geraldine looked at him and could immediately see his dilemma. Turvey's bid for leadership of the group had gotten away from him, but boarding school isn't about backing down, it's about holding out until you fall from the greatest height possible and break bones. Two glasses were taken down from the dresser at the farthest end of the dorm. Corrigan took one to the toilet on the other side of the passageway while Geraldine squirted ink from her fountain pen into the other. It was deep blue, almost black.

'Here,' she said, holding out the glass to Turvey, 'put one in.'

'Let's wait until Corrigan comes back,' said Turvey. 'Do them both at once.'

Geraldine knew he was stalling but didn't press the point. Corrigan returned with a glass half full of yellow piss. It smelled sweet and pungent and the kids all did a collective 'Eugh!' as they saw and smelled it.

'Okay, let's go,' said Corrigan. 'Put one in here.'

Corrigan and Geraldine held out their glasses and Turvey dropped a white pill in each. Nothing immediate happened and, after much shaking of the liquid inside and checking to see if the pills were dissolved, still nothing discernible had happened. It was time to test if they worked.

'Who's going to drink them?' asked Hooper, his only contribution to the show so far.

'I think Turvey should,' said Geraldine. 'They're his pills.'

Not even Turvey could argue with her logic. Geraldine offered him the glass of ink and he looked at her, begging for release. She held the glass out with a steady hand and waited for him to take it. Very eventually he raised the glass to his lips, five kids watching and willing him on like he was about to drink poison. They couldn't wait to see what happened. Turvey lowered the glass, his lips stained blue with ink.

'Here, it tastes fine,' he said to Geraldine, offering her the glass back. 'Drink some.'

'No,' she said, 'not until you've tried the other one.'

Again, no arguing with that logic. Turvey turned to Corrigan who had been pretending to drink from his glass. He handed it over. Turvey raised it to his mouth with a show of confidence, the rim touched his blue-stained lips. He held the glass there for a moment and then pulled it away with enough momentum to spray Corrigan and Sprague with drops of Corrigan's piss.

'Eurghhhh!' they all chorused and then fell about in fits of giggles.

'Shhhh! Quiet!' Hooper said in a stage whisper. 'Matron will hear us.'

The kids giggled some more and then moved off to their beds so they would be ready for lights out, leaving Turvey to clean up the mess.

21

As Christmas and the end of her first term approached, Geraldine began to think about home. She'd not given much thought to Frank and Grace over the last three months, though she missed Harry fiercely. Walking the corridors of Havenhouse, she'd sometimes hear Mr Moore's smoker's cough from around a corner and think Frank was there with her. Every time she heard the gravelly hack, Geraldine's chest would swell with anticipation and deflate immediately when she saw the little man rounding the corner, his woolly hair flopping up and down with every step. In those moments there was a tinge of sadness in Geraldine for a call she no longer knew how to answer.

Christmas term ended with a special meal – roast chicken just like they'd almost had in Zambia – and Christmas pud. Mr Hassell stood up from his seat at the high table on the stage at the centre left of the dining hall to say a few words. He spoke about how much the staff would miss all their children and wished them safe travels and safe return in the New Year. Dinner was followed by a service in the school's chapel, where they sang carols and closed with 'God Be With You Till We Meet Again', a turgid hymn that had Geraldine in tears. That night in Achilles, the six dorm mates talked long after lights out, knowing that any indiscretions would be forgiven on their last night together.

'How long does it take to fly to Australia?' Geraldine asked Turvey.

'Twenty-four hours. What about you? To Zambia. How long does it take?'

'About a day,' said Geraldine.

She couldn't imagine the distance to Australia. Nowhere could be that far away.

■□■

The siblings were flying home on Lufthansa, with a stopover in Frankfurt. Harry took their tickets to the check-in desk, he being fifteen now and fully in charge. The uniformed man behind the counter examined their tickets minutely and frowned, looking at the pair and then back at the tickets.

'I'm sorry,' he said to Harry, 'but your flights haven't been confirmed. There are no seats for you for the next leg of your journey.'

'What?' said Harry.

'You have to confirm your bookings twenty-four hours before your flight leaves. There are no seats for you on the aircraft.'

'Yer what?' said Harry.

'Allow me to call someone.'

The man picked up the phone at his desk and spoke for a few minutes.

'Someone will be with you soon,' he said. 'Please step aside now. Next, please.'

The siblings stepped to the side of the line. Geraldine could feel her stomach knotting, her legs disappearing from under her.

'What's going on?' she asked.

'I don't know,' said Harry. 'Something to do with our tickets. Someone's coming, it'll be alright.'

The 'someone' arrived wearing the same uniform as the man at the check-in desk. He spoke to his colleague, who handed him the siblings' tickets, which he looked over closely before turning to talk to them.

'Children!' he said in his brightest voice.

The two stood staring at him.

'Children, my name is Walter. There is a problem with your tickets. We can't get you on tonight's flight to Lusaka, but we can get you on one tomorrow. Tonight, we will look after you here, put you in a hotel and then we can get you home.'

'Tomorrow?' said Geraldine.

'Yes?' said Walter. 'Tomorrow.'

'No,' said Geraldine, 'I need to go home tonight. Mum and Dad are waiting for us.'

'It'll be alright, our Gerald,' said Harry. 'We're still going home.'

Harry's face had turned from worry to excitement at Walter's mention of staying in a hotel.

'No, I need to go home tonight,' said Geraldine.

Walter decided that movement would help.

'Come, children, come with me,' he said, as he started walking away from the check-in desk with their tickets in hand.

The further they moved from the check-in desk, the louder Geraldine wailed, until Walter felt he had to bring their caravan to a halt. They were in the middle of the airport's duty-free shops.

'Here, I will buy you something,' said Walter, pointing to the window of the nearest shop. It was stacked with toys, model cars, board games and stuffed animals. 'What about this fire engine?'

Geraldine eyed the shiny red diecast model. It looked expensive. For a moment she was tempted, but she decided there would be no deals tonight.

'No!' said Geraldine. 'I want to go home.'

'Are you sure?' said Walter. 'You can have anything you like.'

'I want to go home,' Geraldine repeated, her tears set for the long haul.

'Come then, let's go,' said Walter.

For a second Geraldine thought they would head back to the check-in desk and stopped crying. She started up again when she saw Walter continuing in the direction they'd just been going.

The siblings had never stayed in a hotel before and Harry showed his excitement by calculating aloud the tales he could tell. Geraldine had quietened down, but she was in no mood to listen to her brother as he told her it would be okay. Eventually Harry left her to sit and stew, and got on with investigating the amenities, TV, minibar ('Don't touch,' Walter had said), and those little soaps and shampoos in the bathroom. Even something called shower gel. It smelled so nice that Harry had almost persuaded Geraldine to taste some when she was saved by a knock at the door. Walter had returned.

'Right,' he said, 'I've made some arrangements and got you on tonight's flight in first class. You are very fortunate. Quickly, you must come with me now, they are holding the plane for you.'

Harry's look made it clear to Geraldine he did not feel that this interruption to their international holiday was at all fortunate.

■□■

They arrived in Kitwe in the glare of the next morning's light and heat. The siblings were still in their school uniforms, Geraldine in shorts – the only one dressed for the weather – as you weren't allowed to wear long trousers in winter until sixth form at Havenhouse. They climbed down the steps at the front of the plane, and Geraldine looked for Frank and Grace behind the cyclone fence that separated the landing strip from the carpark. For a moment she couldn't see them and shit began to stir in her bowels, but they were there. For the big things, Frank and Grace were mostly reliable.

'We've got a surprise for you at home, our Gerald,' said Grace once they were in the car.

'What is it?' said Geraldine, forgetting the deal she'd made just three months earlier.

'You'll 'ave to wait and see,' said Grace, smiling.

Sitting in the lounge room, Geraldine couldn't see anything that looked like a surprise. Grace disappeared for a moment and then came back holding something in her hands. Geraldine couldn't quite see what it was until Grace was reaching out to hand it over to her. It was a tiny Siamese kitten, with the bluest of eyes and chocolate-coloured eyebrows and ear tips.

''Ere,' said Grace. 'Fair's fair.'

She handed the kitten to Geraldine and it scratched her outstretched hand, drawing blood.

'I don't want it,' she said, handing it back.

Geraldine noticed that Grace took the kitten from her willingly, stroking it gently and talking nonsense to it. It appeared that Grace had managed to get over her fear of cats. When she put the animal on the floor it skidded along, hardly being able to get any purchase on the shiny cement. Geraldine decided she'd changed her mind, she wanted the kitten after all. She got down off the sticky vinyl lounge chair and lay flat out on the cement, reaching out to the kitten. It skittered in and scratched her again.

▪▫▪

There were no movies and no break-ins that Christmas. The siblings opened their presents on Christmas morning to find that they'd both been given a cassette recorder. Father Christmas had definitely delivered this year.

Harry went to his room and returned with a case of cassettes, popped one in his player and there they were, listening to a tune Geraldine knew very well.

'Do you watch *Top of the Pops* at your school?' asked Geraldine.

'This is Led Zeppelin,' said Harry.

Geraldine looked at him, noticing for the first time that his hair was longer, below his ears. She learned a lot about music those few weeks they were home, as she went through Harry's cassette collection while he was out doing whatever older siblings did. She also learned the art of bootlegging as she used her cassette player's corded microphone to record the music she liked the most on the blank cassettes she'd asked Frank to bring home. There was a lot of atmosphere on the copies she made, sometimes barking and yapping as Brandy and Lass ran mad circles around the house, sometimes voices speaking indistinguishable words, but these just added to Geraldine's incorporation of the music into her being, helped her visualise where she'd first heard Zeppelin, Pink Floyd, Hawkwind and the Who.

■□■

When they returned to school for the new term, Frank checking and double-checking that all their flights were confirmed, Geraldine had given pride of place in her hand luggage to her cassette recorder, her cassettes and enough spare batteries to last her through to her teens. At the airport in Lusaka, just as they were about to board the Lufthansa jet to Frankfurt, Harry asked Geraldine if she'd like to swap bags and carry his one with the King John's College logo on it. Geraldine was reluctant to let her own bag out of her sight but finally agreed when Harry told her how grown-up it would make her look. As soon as they were through customs at Heathrow, Harry swapped back with her.

22

As well as her cassette recorder, Geraldine also brought a stuffed toy with her on her return to Havenhouse for the spring term. A soft toy was the only thing she'd lacked in her first term at her new school, the other kids in her dorm having at least one treasured teddy, Hooper had a whole herd that would take up most of the top half of his bed. Geraldine had noted well that, when her peers settled to sleep, occasionally to the sound of Matron's voice reading to them from a favourite book of English fantasy – by the end of autumn term they'd graduated to *The Lion, the Witch and the Wardrobe* – they clutched under their pink noses their favourite soft toy. Geraldine felt the lack, though she'd never had one before, and arranged a trip with Frank to downtown Kitwe one Saturday after Christmas to rectify things. She came home with a lion that Grace insisted she call Leo. He sat proud, back straight, his black mane expressing his youth, his amber eyes staring out across lands he'd never roam. The Sturmers still hadn't seen a lion in the wild, but Geraldine thought Leo represented her home country well enough, and he was soft and snuggly and, as it turns out, robust enough to stay with her until the end of her career at Havenhouse.

Sprague didn't make it back to school for spring term; he was replaced by a slight, dark-haired kid called Richard Porter. The first night, after lights out, the dorm mates whispered to each other across the beds, sharing stories about their holidays and trying to keep themselves occupied so they wouldn't have time to think about the stretch to half-term during which they'd see neither parents nor home. The trick was always to keep active, keep moving, keep talking, keep doing something until you found yourself waking up the next morning to the sound of Matron's handbell as she walked the corridors of the once stately house, waking her charges for breakfast.

Settling into the rhythms of boarding school life, Geraldine began to realise that, threaded through the packed days, there was time enough for independence and personal excursions. The teachers were watchful but they never actually counted heads; so as long as you turned up for lessons, sport, meals, evening study and bedtime, you could do much as you pleased. Also, though many places on the school grounds were out of bounds, unless you got caught in the act of going to or leaving them, they were the best sorts of places to find some solitude. In spring and autumn terms Geraldine loved nothing more than to take her cassette recorder and a book to the cricket pavilion on a Saturday afternoon after sport. The wooden building's double doors were never locked and there was an electric heater in one corner that made up for the gaps in the building's construction.

Lost one Saturday reading *Stig of the Dump* and listening to *Atom Heart Mother*, Geraldine froze as she saw the pavilion's door opening. She was lying on her front alongside the heater, close enough to stay warm, not close enough to singe. Every ten minutes or so she would turn to warm the other side. It just so happened that as the door began to open she was facing towards it. There was no point moving or calling out, she'd been caught and she'd just have to take whatever punishment was coming her way. Right then, Geraldine could have handled anything except restriction of her movements during what she now firmly considered to be her free time. With these thoughts rushing through her head, she was surprised when it was Porter's pasty face that looked at her around the door.

'Come in!' she hissed. 'Before anyone sees you.'

Geraldine was annoyed at having been discovered by another student. She intensely disliked sharing her secrets.

'I thought I saw you come in here,' said Porter. 'I didn't think we were allowed?'

'We're not,' said Geraldine. 'So you didn't see me and I didn't see you.'

By now, Porter had come in and closed the door behind him. He walked over to where Geraldine was now sitting on the floor. If he'd been an inch or two taller, she might have felt that he was standing over her, but he didn't have the height for intimidation. Still, Geraldine weighed up how best to handle this circumstance.

'What do you want?' she asked.

'I don't know,' Porter said. 'I was just bored and I saw you. What are you listening to?'

'It's Pink Floyd,' said Geraldine. 'You won't have heard of them. I have a brother.'

'So do I,' said Porter. 'Where's yours? Mine lives in London.'

This trumped Harry, still at King John's College, just up the A303.

'Away,' Geraldine said, keeping things vague.

'Ah, away,' said Porter, seeming to know what she meant. 'Can I have a listen?'

The two sat together in silence as they listened to the full thirteen minutes and two seconds of 'Alan's Psychedelic Breakfast' (parts I, II and III), saying nothing as the track dissolved into what sounded like an insistently leaky tap played over the distant noise of a toilet flushing. This was the first time Geraldine had shared her music with another person, other than Harry. They were startled back to earth by the click of the cassette recorder's play key as the tape ran out.

■□■

After that Saturday, Geraldine and Porter – or Ricky as she came to call him – became inseparable. Ricky's parents lived close enough to Havenhouse that they could deliver packages to him: tuck, cassettes, batteries and, when his brother came down from London, tattered copies of *Melody Maker* and *New Musical Express*. They had no idea what they were reading and as often as not they'd turn a page to find an article or picture torn out, but they soaked it all up, anyway.

On Sunday afternoons they'd sneak into the school's gym to watch Mr Shelley, the biology teacher, play his drums. Students and teacher never once acknowledged each other, but each knew who was in the room, and Mr Shelley always seemed spurred on to smash his drums with greater power when he knew he had an audience, even if it was, as the teachers at Havenhouse generally acknowledged, the two weirdest kids in the school. When he took a break, Geraldine would press play on the cassette recorder, hoping that just once Mr Shelley would comment on Jim Morrison and the Doors or Bread.

Sitting together at evening study one night, Geraldine and Ricky looked up to see Mr Shelley heading their way. Usually when a teacher approached it meant you'd done something wrong earlier that day, and now it was time to pay the price with anything from a black mark to the cane, although at Havenhouse the cane was reserved for really bad things, like being out of bounds, open defiance of the order of the school or fighting with another student. Geraldine tried to think what she might have done wrong as she watched Mr Shelley come closer, picking his way among the randomly placed tables of students, open books, pens and pencils scattered in front of them. He was a walking illustration of the Doppler effect as the hum of conversation that filled Big Hall quietened at each table when the teacher passed, and rose again in his wake.

'Sturmer, Porter,' said Mr Shelley, by way of getting their attention.

'Yes, sir?' they both replied, trying to sound anything but nervous.

'I hear the two of you like music,' said Mr Shelley.

Geraldine began to worry where this was going. No-one had told her it was wrong to like music other than the religious and classical that was standard fare in the curriculum, but it was possible. Havenhouse ran on unwritten rules.

'I want you to help me. I'm putting on a music quiz and I wondered if you'd like to write some questions for me?'

Geraldine looked at Ricky.

'Yes, sir,' she said. 'Yes please.'

'Right then,' said Mr Shelley. 'Come to my flat after lunch on Sunday. Don't forget and don't be late.'

'We won't,' said Geraldine.

When they thought Mr Shelley was far enough across Big Hall, Geraldine and Ricky dared to look at each other and burst out laughing, carried away with exuberance at the outlandish invitation they'd just received.

■□■

After lunch that Sunday, having been able to cram very little into their excited stomachs, the friends crossed the school quadrangle to one of the newer buildings away from the main house, climbed the stairs up to the first floor and knocked timidly at a blue door, a pane of frosted glass taking up most of its top half.

'Come in, boys,' said Mr Shelley, as he opened the door that led straight into his sitting room, a small dining table just to the right of the door and mismatched chairs over on the far side. As Geraldine looked into the room, she was surprised to see Mr Alcock, the chemistry teacher, sitting in an armchair on the opposite side.

'Come on in, children,' said Mr Alcock, holding up the glass in his right hand in greeting.

Mr Shelley sat Geraldine and Ricky down at the dining table and gave them each paper, a book to lean on and a biro. Students at Havenhouse were never allowed to write in biro.

'Let's see if you can do ten questions each,' said Mr Shelley. 'And don't forget the answers, just in case we don't know,' he said, giving Mr Alcock an as-if grin.

Geraldine's first question was, 'Who wrote the theme tune for *Top of the Pops*?' Answer: Page, Plant, Jones and Bonham (Led Zeppelin). Half an hour or so later, Mr Shelley came over to inspect their work.

'This is very good, Sturmer,' he said. 'Porter, you too.'

But Geraldine knew she'd done the best out of the two of them.

Then Mr Shelley noticed the marks on the cover of the book Geraldine had been leaning on. She had gripped the biro so hard in her eagerness, the unfamiliarity of the writing implement and wanting to control her untidy hand as best she could, that she had pressed almost through the paper and scored her questions into the glossy cover of Mr Shelley's book.

'You've ruined it,' Mr Shelley said, as he held it up to the light for a better look.

Geraldine looked down and said nothing, wishing she could disappear.

'Look, that's it, children,' said Mr Shelley, his book in his right hand, their work in his left. 'You can go now.'

'Bye kids,' said Mr Alcock from the other side of the room, taking a sip from his glass as he watched them leave.

They were never invited back, but Mr Shelley would make a point of asking Geraldine what she was listening to when they crossed paths as she wandered the corridors and halls of the school on evenings and weekends.

23

Across the world, 1976 was a year of change. Even in Zambia the grown-ups were talking about new bands where the singers would get sick on their audiences. They talked about it in hushed voices, smoking and drinking while they lamented the decay of society.

'The Beatles never did owt like that,' said Frank.

Geraldine listened with quiet interest, hoping she wouldn't be noticed and sent from the room. It was the Christmas holidays. This year it was only her at home, Harry having dropped out of King John's College when he got caught riding a motorbike with two of his mates riding pillion through the backstreets of town. He was advised by the headmaster that leaving would be preferable to being expelled and, being eighteen, he decided to stay on in England.

Frank and Grace were back to their loud disagreements, always precipitated by Frank coming home late and pissed, and ending with the two of them throwing wardrobes full of clothes and shoes across the room, each of them threatening to leave. Mornings after were always hushed, Frank hungover and contrite, Grace giving him and everyone else in the house the silent treatment. Still, Geraldine was surprised when Grace announced that she'd be coming back to England with them at the end of Christmas holidays.

'What for?' said Geraldine.

'I'm going to look for somewhere for us to live and, after, Dad's coming home an' all. We're going back to live in England.'

'Why?' said Geraldine.

'Because we are,' said Grace.

Frank kept out of it.

■□■

At the airport, Grace fiddled nervously with the wads of banknotes she had strapped around her waist. Taking foreign currency out of Zambia was illegal. She was wearing a loose polo-necked jumper in the humid heat of the wet season, but no-one seemed to notice. Geraldine kept the King John's College bag close to her – the one that Harry's friend Delilah had asked her to take to him. When they reached Charles de Gaulle Airport, Grace removed the cash but kept the jumper on against the winter cold. Once they'd cleared customs at Heathrow, Grace hailed a taxi and the two of them climbed in.

'Where to?' said the cabbie.

'Martock,' said Grace

'Where?' said the cabbie.

'Maar-TOCK,' said Grace in the way she spoke to the locals back in Zambia, like he was stupid.

'You know that's a hundred miles or more?' he said.

'Yes,' said Grace, feeling for the cash around her waist, forgetting for a moment she'd put it in her handbag. She looked inside, felt the bills. 'Yes,' she said, 'that'll be okay, thank you,' her tone a bit more conciliatory, but only a bit.

The two of them sat in the back seat of the taxi and hardly spoke for the entire two hours of their journey. Geraldine watched as the buildings thinned out, noticing landmarks and towns that she recognised from her train journeys between London and Havenhouse. Martock, and Harry – because that's where he was living now – weren't too far from school she surmised.

''Ow much?' Grace said when they'd arrived at their destination, behind a row of shops.

The cabbie repeated himself and Grace looked worriedly into her handbag.

Geraldine kept her smirk to herself.

■□■

Harry was living with two hairy friends, leather and denim being the preferred mode of dress. They vacated the flat that evening when Grace announced the two of them would be staying for a while, the exhausts of their motorbikes echoing between the back of the shops and the garages that stood in a row behind them. Geraldine was confused, because she was now living in Library Flat, Martock, with a library nowhere in sight, but mostly because Harry seemed none too pleased to see them.

'Did you bring my bag?' Harry asked Geraldine.

Geraldine handed over the white, vinyl shoulder bag with the King John's College crest on it. It was the first and only time she saw Harry smile that night and, as she went to sleep, she wondered what he needed it for now he was no longer at school.

■□■

The next morning Grace sent Geraldine off to school in a taxi for the start of spring term. As always, Geraldine was the first of the boarders to arrive at Havenhouse, and she was able to spend time with Matron before the other kids straggled in, subdued by the stretch of time that would keep them from home.

'Still got Leo, I see,' said Matron.

'Yes?' said Geraldine, wondering if Matron thought she was too old for teddies.

'And what are you reading at the moment?'

'I have this one,' Geraldine said, 'but I haven't started it yet.'

Geraldine pulled a copy of Alistair MacLean's *The Way to Dusty Death* from her bag and held it out for Matron.

'That's proper grown up,' she said.

Geraldine wondered what she meant and was about to ask when Porter wandered into the dorm, accompanied by his parents.

'Ah, Matron,' said Mr Porter, 'could I have a word?'

Geraldine and Porter were left alone. At first they had nothing to say to each other, the few weeks they'd spent apart in their different worlds making the resumption of their friendship a tenuous thing.

'Ricky!' Geraldine said eventually, a smile breaking out across her face.

'Geri!' said Porter.

They sat on their beds looking at each other and Geraldine felt like this term might just be okay.

'Have you heard of the Sex Pistols?' asked Porter.

'The what?' said Geraldine. The name didn't make any sense.

'The Sex Pistols,' Porter said again. 'They're from London. Here.'

He handed Geraldine a slip of newsprint which contained Neil Spencer's first piece on the band, written for *NME*. Geraldine read it, knowing as the words unfolded that this must be the band Frank and Grace had been talking about. Quite how they'd gotten wind of them, she didn't know, but the pictures she saw in her mind as she read Spencer's article made her need to know more. Geraldine kept the slip of paper.

'Have you got any of their music?' she asked.

'No,' said Porter.

It would be almost another two years before Geraldine heard what the Sex Pistols sounded like.

24

That school year Geraldine and her dorm mates were in Dreadnought, which meant they were close enough to get an occasional invitation from Mr Alcock to watch TV with him. The chemistry teacher's rooms were at the end of the corridor, the last door on the third storey of the house. He had two adjoining, one for sitting in, the other for sleeping in, the rest of his needs being met elsewhere in the school's buildings.

Geraldine's and her dorm mates' incursions to Mr Alcock's rooms were infrequent but memorable and highly, if tacitly, anticipated. It would work like this: as they were cleaning their teeth and getting ready for their half hour before lights out, Mr Alcock would appear at the door of their room and stand watching in silence until the dorm mates became aware of his presence. They might be laughing until snot bubbled from their noses at the knife they'd dared Corrigan to steal from the dining hall, smirking at the poem that Thatcher made up on the spot about his music teacher or crowding around the packet of biscuits that Porter had been delivered that day – chocolate digestives – asking him for just one more, one more, until the packet was empty and he had nowhere to put the distinctive wrapper that wouldn't find him guilty of the crime of eating in the dorm. Sometimes, on evenings of their highest spirits, Mr Alcock had to clear his throat before they noticed him and turned in his direction trying to look serious, innocent and sleepy all at the same time.

'Another delivery from home, Porter?' Mr Alcock might say, to let them know that nothing got past him.

Then, once he'd established his primacy, he'd invite them up to his room to watch telly before lights out, turning and walking away the moment he'd issued his invitation, leaving the dorm mates in some confusion about the invitation and whether or not they might just be in trouble. The six of them would creep along the dimly lit hallway to Mr Alcock's rooms, trying not to squeak a single floorboard or in any other way disturb Matron. It was well known among the students at Havenhouse that Matron and Mr Alcock didn't see eye to eye, and they'd been turned back before when she'd come across them heading in his direction.

Whoever arrived at Mr Alcock's closed door first, usually Corrigan, would knock quietly, tentatively, and Mr Alcock would say, 'Come.' They would find him always with his back to them, sitting dead centre of the couch that faced the TV, his bald patch just beginning to show at his crown, glass in hand, an armchair to one side, a dining chair to the other. Mr Alcock would call each of the dorm mates over by name and tell them where to sit, two either side of him on the couch, one on the armchair, the other on the stiff-backed dining chair. The pecking order changed sometimes, but Geraldine always coveted one of the two spots closest to Mr Alcock, without knowing why.

Occasionally, if there was something particularly distracting on telly he thought they should watch, Mr Alcock would detain the dorm mates after lights out. One night they watched a BBC *Play for Today,* about a proto rockstar. Geraldine couldn't remember her name, but her band was called Slagbag. In one scene, the lead and her boyfriend were zipped together in a pair of sleeping bags. It looked to Geraldine like they were dancing to the music, which was what really had her attention. When the scene switched, Mr Alcock asked her to come to the room next door for a moment so he could show her how to make his drinks.

'That way, I won't have to get up and down all evening and disturb all of you,' he said.

Next door there was a bed, double, tidily made, the Havenhouse way, a small dresser and a table with a tray of bottles and glasses on it.

'Come over here,' Mr Alcock said, as Geraldine lingered at the doorway.

She crossed the room and stood next to him as he poured gin and tonic, talking her through the measures.

'See, Gerald,' Mr Alcock said as he rubbed her thigh, 'it's a bit like chemistry, you have to get everything in the right proportion.'

'What's this?' asked Geraldine.

'Oh, that?' said Mr Alcock. 'That's just a bit of fun. Do you like it?'

In order to answer Mr Alcock's question, Geraldine had to take a closer look at the picture in the magazine, multiple conjoined people on a beach, gathered around a long table loaded with food.

'I don't know,' she said.

'Well, maybe you should come and visit me tomorrow night so we can have a chat about it,' said Mr Alcock.

Geraldine tried to calculate whether her need outweighed her fear and eventually said, 'Yes.'

25

Spring half-term was the first time at Havenhouse that Geraldine was able to go home. In terms past she'd spent half-terms with her grandparents up in Yorkshire or occasionally with the Porters at their rather lavish country house in a village close enough to the school that it made Geraldine wonder why Porter wasn't a day boy. Those were the best half-terms, the two of them free and unencumbered in the Somerset countryside, only going back to the house for meals and bedtime, no-one ever asking where they'd been and what they'd been doing.

Getting out of the taxi and climbing the stairs to Library Flat, Geraldine discovered that Harry had moved out and it was now just her and Grace.

'Alright, our Gerald? How was school?' said Grace, smoking in front of the telly.

'It was alright,' said Geraldine, as she passed through to her room and dropped her bag. She came back and sat at the other end of the settee.

'What's for dinner?' she said.

'I thought we'd get some fish and chips,' said Grace. 'The chippy's just round the other side. Do you want to go and get them, our Gerald?'

'Right,' said Geraldine.

After dinner, Geraldine and Grace settled in to watch TV. The next morning Martock was blanketed with snow. Geraldine had occasionally seen snow, but nothing on this scale. Every low-lying piece of ground, including the roads in and out of the village, was piled high with it. That morning, Geraldine walked the streets of her new home, feeling the silence that the snow brought, the atmosphere so close that it felt like her ears would pop. The snow was soft to touch and crunchy underfoot, and people all around the village were out building snowmen and throwing the stuff at each other.

Geraldine joined in a snowball fight with some kids across the road from the shops.

'Where are you from?' asked one of them, her accent thick like Matron's.

'I'm from ... I go to school ...' Geraldine didn't know how to explain herself. 'I live in the flat on the other side of the shops.'

'What? With the bikers?' the girl asked.

'No,' said Geraldine.

Geraldine wondered if she was talking about Harry and his friends. It didn't seem right to her.

'No,' said Geraldine, 'with my mum.'

'Oh? C'mon, let's go get them!' said the girl, raising her voice as she charged off in the direction of the other kids, a snowball in each hand.

Geraldine followed, happy that there seemed to be no more explaining to do.

■□■

The day after, Martock was still blanketed with snow, but the cold air had turned it mostly to ice. Where roads were cleared it lay hard and blackened at their edges. Geraldine had never imagined snow could be black, but here it was. It reminded her of the poster on the wall of the Chirundu border post, two elephants facing the camera, their backs a deep green. Geraldine had asked one of the border guards about it as she passed through the second time.

'They get stained green as they walk under trees and the leaves rub against their backs,' the man said.

Geraldine didn't know whether to believe him, but what other explanation could there be? Green elephants and now black snow. Coming home from checking out the conditions that morning, Geraldine learned from Grace that it could be another week before the roads out of Martock were cleared, so she'd be late getting back to school. She wouldn't be able to return Sunday evening as planned, it might be Monday or Tuesday. Geraldine's stomach churned at the thought of arriving back late. Every day, she went out to check the conditions, pushing her walks closer and closer to the edges of the village to see for herself what was holding things up.

Monday evening, while she should have been back at school, Geraldine settled on her side of the settee to watch the telly with Grace. BBC2 showed a documentary about a woman called Julia. Geraldine didn't really know what she was watching, but she sat there for the full hour, willing Grace not to notice what was on and turn over. At the end of the programme Julia was walking through a park and a little kid, much younger than Geraldine, maybe five, came up to her and said, 'You're a poof, in'tcha, mister?' Geraldine's sadness encompassed her entire world.

■□■

Geraldine's late return to school meant she missed the news that Mr Alcock had left over half-term, his replacement yet to be advised. The dorm was filled with chatter and speculation.

'I heard he was asked to leave by Mr Hassell,' said Thatcher.

'Why?' said Hooper.

'I don't know, that's just what I heard.'

'I heard it's because he had old boys come back and stay with him,' said Corrigan.

'What's wrong with that?' said Thatcher.

'They stayed with him,' said Corrigan, without any more words to explain himself any better.

The speculation went on until Matron came to the door of their dorm and said, 'It's time for sleep now, boys. You have to be up early tomorrow, remember. We don't want anyone sleeping in. Good night, now.'

'Good night, Matron,' the dorm mates chorused.

In the silence that followed Geraldine tried to unravel everything but without any success. Drifting off to sleep, she felt the echoes of the hospital and death, smelled again for the first time in years the disinfectant and anaesthetic. In her dreams she was searching for Frank and Grace. She could hear Frank praying; Grace was nowhere to be found. Geraldine woke in the early hours lathered with sweat; the heaviness in her chest felt like someone was sitting on her. When she opened her eyes, a figure was standing over her. She heard Mr Alcock say goodbye, saw him raise his glass. In the confusion of Matron's morning bell she was convinced that everything she'd experienced during the night had to have been a dream, but when she thought about

Mr Alcock's visit she felt her hackles rise, her chest began to separate from her body, and she had to breathe deep and long to bring herself back. She knew for certain that Mr Alcock was dead, but though he was a topic of conversation right across Havenhouse for the next few weeks, she never offered this knowledge to anyone.

26

Frank's return to England brought change. The Sturmers moved from Library Flat, Martock, to two Langport Road, Weston-super-Mare. Backed up against the railway line far from the seafront, St Austell was Frank and Grace's attempt to switch careers by running a boarding house. Geraldine's new school was over the humpy rail bridge, down the hill and on the edge of the Oldmixon council estate, very much on the wrong side of the tracks. She'd never worn corduroy trousers before. They were part of the Westland Comprehensive school uniform, brown, along with a white collared shirt and a brown jumper. As Geraldine walked to school for the first day of winter term, the *zzsh, zzsh, zzsh* of her trousers caused her something like confusion. Should they be making this noise?

Geraldine had grown tallish for a twelve-year-old, her face had lengthened, lost its pink, and her hair, once bleached blond in the sun, was deep brown and, now that she was no longer at boarding school, approaching her collar. Her eyes had taken on a deeper blue. As her cords telegraphed her every step, Geraldine worried that she might not fit in at this new school in this new town. She'd never been too concerned about fitting in before, but this September day it felt pressingly important. What if she got to the school gate and she was the only one wearing cords?

Westland Comprehensive was nothing like boarding school as far as Geraldine could see. The kids milled chaotically about the schoolyard and the grounds at the back of the buildings, forming clumps without any sense of order or cohesion. When the bell went, there was no quickening of pace among the student body, they sauntered towards their classrooms like they had all day. There were no teachers in the yard to chivvy them on, either. This lack of pace and focus made Geraldine anxious. She didn't know whether to hurry on to her form room or lag behind with the loose groups of assorted children. She was torn between the potential approbation of her form teacher or the first-day ridicule of her peers for breaking some unwritten rule of the playground. Did they call it a playground?, Geraldine wondered, as she decided to stick closer to the squabbling kids. She knew their forgiveness would come harder than any teacher's. Geraldine soon learned that lateness or even turning up at all wasn't a pressing issue at Westland Comprehensive.

■□■

At St Austell, Frank found an enthusiasm for home renovation as he prepared for the influx of guests the next summer. He and Grace papered and painted every wall and surface of the house's interior, enlisting Geraldine's assistance when she was home.

'Look, Gerald, you've left streaks in the paint. There's even a hair in it!' Frank told her on inspecting Geraldine's handiwork with the skirting boards along the hallway that led to the kitchen at the back of the house.

Geraldine quietly cleaned her brush and downed tools. When the Sturmers had first moved into the house, at the tail end of summer, Geraldine had been very taken with the cupboard under the stairs. She kept returning to it, opening the door and turning on the light, sizing it up. After a few days of inspections, she'd spoken to Grace.

'Can I sleep in the room under the stairs?' Geraldine asked.

'What?' said Grace.

'I've had a look. I think my bed will fit. Can I?'

'Away wi' yer,' said Grace. 'You can't sleep in the cupboard. What's wrong with you, our Gerald?'

Geraldine didn't know, but she had a rising feeling that something was. She'd always known how to feel unsettled, but this was something else. Grace didn't enquire further after asking Geraldine what was wrong with her, and Geraldine didn't offer up what she didn't have the words for. As she quit her job as a house painter, Geraldine walked past the cupboard and took one last look inside before she turned to climb the stairs to her bedroom above the kitchen, its window overlooking the railway line. She lay on her bed and read.

■□■

Frank built a fireplace in the living room out of irregular slabs of dark-grey stone. It extended beyond the hearth to the left of the room, taking up half the height of the wall, providing an extended mantlepiece and nooks for ornaments which Grace filled with little treasures from Zambia, wood carvings, ornaments made of malachite and ivory. In the far corner of the room stood a wooden giraffe, fully five feet tall. The Sturmers called him Bryn. If ever Geraldine felt her memories of living smack bang in the middle of Africa were fading, she'd stand by Bryn, touch his smooth wooden nose and rock him back and forth on his rather small base. He wasn't that well made, but he stood proud.

Frank's last renovation job was to make and install a kitchen cabinet. He spent days drawing up the diagrams, buying the materials and constructing what was to be a display piece that stretched the entire back wall of the kitchen. It had glass sliding doors and was divided into top and bottom storage areas by a shelf running along its length. When the gloss paint was dried, Frank fixed it to the wall and, job done, loaded it up with the family's crockery and glassware. Grace and Geraldine were in the living room watching *The Love Boat*. In the background they could hear Frank's activity at the other end of the house as he manhandled the plates and glasses into their new home.

'Come and have a look,' said Frank, standing at the door of the lounge room.

Grace and Geraldine got up, ready to troop down the hallway with Frank to admire his handiwork. They heard the crash before Geraldine had even left the lounge. Frank turned and ran down the passage towards the kitchen. The other two remained still for a moment, wondering if they should follow. When they arrived in the kitchen a few moments later and saw the carnage, splintered wood framing a sea of broken glass and various shades of china, Frank on his hands and knees rescuing the few pieces that weren't broken, they stopped dead, each of them looking to Frank for a cue as to what their reaction should be. He smiled, holding up a mug in one hand, a plate in the other.

'Looks like there's a few things left,' he said.

Grace and Geraldine smiled back and then the laughter started. It was tentative at first, but when Frank joined in, it swelled into an uproar from which they felt for a while they might never recover.

'It'll be alright, luv,' said Grace, kneeling to help Frank with his recovery mission.

'Look at the wall,' said Geraldine, pointing to the space where the cabinet had been only minutes ago.

They all looked up. There were eight craters where the wall plugs had been torn from the plaster, ripping away the wallpaper that Frank and Grace had put up only days earlier.

'Looks like I'm going to need bigger screws,' said Frank, grinning at his lack of DIY acumen.

The laughter started up all over again.

Once the mess was cleared, Grace and Geraldine returned to their seats in front of the telly. Frank went out. As the night progressed the two remaining Sturmers would look at each other and giggle. They were both in bed by the time Frank got home. Geraldine, still awake, listened for the noise, but there was none.

27

Each day of term, Geraldine presented herself at school, taking time to get used to the daily switch from home to life inside the gates of Westland Comprehensive. Though she'd created little freedoms for herself at Havenhouse, Geraldine was unused to the sort of independence that her new school offered. She would turn up to her classes and, at times, even her teachers seemed surprised.

'You're here, Gerald?' said Mr Potts at the beginning of English towards the end of her first term.

Geraldine looked around her. She was one of five students, the rest of the seats in the classroom were empty.

'Yes?' said Geraldine, wondering what would happen next.

'Good, good,' said Mr Potts. 'I just thought you might be … with the other kids?'

Geraldine looked around her again and sized up the other four students she was sharing the room with. There was Caroline with her plastic arm who sat behind Geraldine in geography and passed her notes. There was Graham, lanky and slight with a squiggle of blond hair and a squeaky voice. Other boys and some girls kept telling him his balls hadn't dropped yet. The other two she'd spent three months with, and she still didn't know their names. Geraldine realised she hadn't quite made it onto even the first rung of Westland's social ladder yet.

'Anyway, it's good you're here,' Mr Potts said. 'I've been meaning to talk to you. I used to think that people whose handwriting slopes backwards weren't that bright until I met you.'

He wandered away to the front of the class and sat at his desk, leaving Geraldine to wonder about his words. She struggled with the compliment and determined to work on her handwriting, to push it forward. That was her main takeaway from the conversation. When Geraldine realised Mr Potts had no intention of teaching them anything, she opened her exercise book and started writing, the biro still foreign in her hand. Geraldine had ditched her fountain pen on the first day of school when the kid sitting next to her in form had said just loud enough, 'What's that?' and she'd been surrounded by her classmates who all wanted to look at her olden-days pen. They weren't so much deriding Geraldine's difference as they were just plain curious, but she recognised that it wasn't the best of starts. When school broke for the Christmas holidays, Geraldine walked home alone, as she had every other day of the term.

28

Christmas 1977 brought the Sturmers' extended family to St Austell. Some of them, at least. Harry returned from wherever he'd been living, doing whatever he'd been doing, and Geraldine's grandparents arrived on Christmas Eve. Her grandfather, Bryn, was as tall and gangling as her grandmother, Flora, was short and stout. They'd spent the occasional day, never a night, with them on their sporadic returns to England and, of course, there were Geraldine's half-term breaks, of which her greatest memory was the noise of the traffic on Bentley Road while she was trying to get to sleep in the front room, and the chamber-pot under the bed, sometimes already half full of yellowy brown piss, that passed for a toilet, the only other one being situated halfway down the backyard. Occasionally they had visited Grace's side of the family, over the hill in Bentley, but not once since returning to live in England, and it didn't look like any of the Donkin aunties, uncles and cousins were invited to Christmas this year. When Bryn's brother Fred arrived, three had become four, then six, then seven, and the house started to feel to Geraldine rather full.

The family all assembled on Christmas Eve. Bryn, Frank, Fred and Harry went to the pub after dinner and didn't return until after Geraldine had long disappeared into sleep. Geraldine's rest that night was assisted by the two nips of Baileys that Grace had allowed her while the women waited at home by the fire. She enjoyed the subtle burn of the whisky wrapped in the silky sweetness of the sugary cream and, after her second nip, Geraldine had considered asking for another one but thought better of it. She sat quietly on the orange-and-green Axminster carpet and licked her glass clean, hoping her hunger wouldn't be noticed. Geraldine woke the next morning remembering nothing of her dreams and feeling refreshed. She stepped lightly down the stairs to find the fire in the living room dead and cold, and the Christmas tree standing in the window surrounded by presents.

She took a seat on the settee and waited for the rest of the house to come to life. Grace was first down after Geraldine.

'Morning, luv,' said Grace. ''Appy Christmas!'

She gave Geraldine a hug then sat down and lit a cigarette.

'Make us a cup of coffee, will you?' she said.

Geraldine escaped into the kitchen and lit the cooker for the kettle, staying while she watched it boil. She carefully measured out a heaped teaspoon of Nescafé instant and poured in some milk, stirring with a teaspoon. Geraldine was on a hiding to nothing as she tried to get the freeze-dried granules to dissolve in the icy milk, but she still tried. Grace rarely asked her to make her a coffee, saying hers was the worst she'd ever tasted. Geraldine couldn't work out how – the ingredients were standard, the quantities barely changed. Mr Alcock and his exhortation to repeated trials taught her the result should be the same every time, but not for Geraldine. She felt like her reputation for making bad coffee was some sort of in-joke between Frank and Grace. Pouring in the boiling water and stirring, Geraldine finished by adding two teaspoons of sugar and hoped for the best.

'Here you are, Mum,' said Geraldine, holding the mug in front of her, handle out.

'Thanks, luv,' said Grace, as she set the mug down on the table at the side of her chair and lit another cigarette.

Frank came in next.

'Hello, luv, 'appy Christmas,' he said to Grace. ''Appy Christmas, our Gerald. Get the fire going, will you? It's bloody freezing in 'ere.'

Geraldine sat down in front of the fireplace and began to roll and scrunch sheets of newspaper into tight sticks, laying them on top of last night's coals. She then placed some smaller pieces of coal on the nest of newspaper and lit the paper with a match, watching intently as the flames began to work their way through the black and white, and gently lick around the lumps of coal, tentatively, like first-time lovers, then with greater urgency as the coal began to warm to their caress. Geraldine watched and waited until she saw the flames begin to turn from dirty yellow to blue – more learning from Mr Alcock's chemistry classes – and she then cautiously placed more coal on top of the pyre, careful not to deprive the flames of oxygen by putting on too much of the filthy black substance too quickly. Every additional piece of coal she added was timed to mitigate the risk of putting out the juvenile flames and leaving the lounge room a smoking mess and, worse still, having Frank move her aside and take over.

Geraldine was so lost in her task that, when she stood up to retake her seat, the fire burning well and throwing off heat already, she found the room was full. Everyone except Harry was downstairs, all with cups of coffee or, for Bryn and Flora, tea.

'Do you want yer presents, our Gerald?' said Frank.

'Yes, please,' said Geraldine, heading towards the tree.

'Better go fetch Harry, then,' said Frank with a laugh.

Geraldine ran up the stairs two at a time. She pushed open the door to Harry's room.

'Harry. Harry! Wake up, it's Christmas,' said Geraldine. 'Come on, Harry, wake up.'

'Fuck off, our Gerald,' said Harry.

Geraldine turned to leave.

'Alright, our Gerald, don't get yer knickers in a knot,' said Harry, 'I'm coming.'

Geraldine smiled but didn't turn around.

'There y'are, yer lazy bugger,' said Bryn as Harry opened the door to the lounge room.

''Appy Christmas,' said Frank. 'Now, let's open the presents. Gerald, give 'em out for us.'

Geraldine stepped over to the tree and sat down next to the pile of brightly wrapped parcels. She handed out each one as it came to hand, but left the largish rectangular parcel to the end, knowing it was for her because she'd checked the labels before anyone else had come down, hoping it was what she thought it was.

'Oh, this one's for me,' she said once she'd handed out all the other gifts, trying to sound surprised.

No-one in the room paid her any attention as she unwrapped the parcel. Inside was a box with the word 'Dansette' on the top and a picture of the contents.

'You got me a record player!' Geraldine said.

She rarely raised her voice, but she was properly excited looking at the box. It didn't matter to Geraldine that it was second-hand. Frank and Grace looked up and smiled.

'That's right, luv,' said Frank.

Geraldine opened the box to inspect the contents, hoping that all the parts were there or that it didn't need batteries or something that would stop her from being able to use the record player until the shops opened again. Based on past experience she wouldn't have been surprised. She finished unboxing and placed the maroon case to the right of the fire, out of the way of the heat and close enough to a plug that she could get power to it. She connected the power cable, plugged it in and clicked the switch to the right of the platter to the On position. A red light glowed above the On/Off switch and, as she picked up the tone arm, the platter started to spin. It worked! Only trouble was that Geraldine didn't have any records, all the music she owned was on cassette. That Christmas day they went through Frank and Grace's surprisingly eclectic record collection – Buddy Holly, the Beatles, Johnny Cash, Osibisa; but there was no Zeppelin, no Pink Floyd, no Hendrix, no Eagles, no Hawkwind, not even any Suzi Q, Geraldine's first proper rockstar crush. After lunch, when torpor and sleep hit the adults, Geraldine moved her most prized possession upstairs to her room, away from unsteady hands and careless feet.

29

Money became an obsession for Geraldine. In 1977 an LP cost anywhere between three pounds and four pounds fifty, depending on where you shopped. After Christmas was done and it was just the four of them again, Geraldine set to work thinking through how she could gain some income. Since she'd left boarding school, she'd been granted a pound a week pocket money. The last time she'd had pocket money before that was in Beverley, where she'd get an irregularly shaped, bronze-coloured thruppenny bit each week. Frank would drop it into her pudgy palm and she'd spend it on sweeties at the local newsagents. Now thirteen, Geraldine felt as if her needs were greater and more urgent. As she ate her Ready Brek one morning just before the New Year, Geraldine turned to Grace, who was sitting with her morning coffee and cigarette.

'Mum?' she said.

'Yes, luv?' said Grace.

'Mum, I was thinking. Could I get a rise in my pocket money?'

'I don't know, our Gerald,' said Grace. 'Money doesn't grow on trees, yer know. You'll have to ask your dad.'

Geraldine knew she'd have to ask Frank at some stage, but it was always best to start with Grace.

'Yer dad's not working at the moment,' said Grace. 'We 'aven't got a lot of money, you know.'

Frank and Grace always kept their plans to themselves, but Geraldine had figured out that they were living off whatever cash Grace had been able to smuggle back to England from Zambia and that Frank must've done the same when he came back. She knew that they were beginning to advertise their bed and breakfast ready for the coming summer season. She'd posted the envelopes addressed to papers in Birmingham, Manchester and even

Yorkshire in the red pillar box at the top of their street, the one she walked past every day on her way to school.

'Shall I ask Dad, then?' said Geraldine.

'Yes, ask yer father,' said Grace.

Conversation closed.

■□■

Later that morning, Frank was hanging pictures in the dining room, cigarette held between his lips so he could use both hands.

'Dad?' said Geraldine.

'What is it, our Gerald?' said Frank, the cigarette still in his mouth.

Geraldine noticed that Frank's hair was thinning. There was less at the front and sides, his bald patch was winning.

'Dad, I was thinking, could I get a rise in my pocket money?'

Frank put down his hammer on the dining table, sucked on his cigarette and took it from his mouth with his free hand.

'What for, Gerald?' he said, smoke coming out of his mouth with his words.

'I need to buy records,' said Geraldine. 'I'll work for it, help in the house. I can help in summer when you have people staying.'

The idea of a houseful of guests seemed to sway things for Frank. He was still high on the idea of earning money without ever having to leave home to go to work.

'Alright then,' said Frank. 'I'll tell you what. You can have fifty p more a week from next year and, if you help out when we've got people in, I'll think about making it more.'

It wasn't as much as Geraldine had hoped for, but from the look on his face Frank seemed to think that next year was still a way off. Geraldine decided not to remind him that tomorrow was New Year's Eve.

'Thanks, Dad,' said Geraldine, and left before he could change his mind or begin adding other conditions.

She went upstairs to look at the classifieds at the back of *NME*, marking the records she wanted to mail order and wondering if the packages would fit through the letterbox. Geraldine went downstairs to the front door, stopping by the lounge to pick up one of Frank and Grace's LPs. When she concluded the letterbox was too small, she started to worry and wonder how parcels got delivered to houses. In her recollection, the Sturmers had never received a parcel in the mail before, and it had suddenly become important to Geraldine to find out how the process worked.

'Can I go to the newsagents, Mum?' Geraldine asked.

'Don't go spending yer money before you've got it,' said Grace.

'I won't,' said Geraldine.

■□■

The air was crisp, the ground slippery. Geraldine stepped carefully on the cracked pavement as she headed towards the main road that joined the seafront with the other side of town over the railway bridge. Instead of turning right, she turned left towards the prom, some miles ahead. The newsagents was only a few minutes walk up the road. Arriving at her destination, Geraldine pushed open the white, half-glazed door and heard the bell ring as it separated inwards from its blue frame. Geraldine nodded to the man behind the counter and then looked into the shop to where the racks of papers and magazines were kept. She headed towards them so she could leaf through the latest issues of *NME* and *Melody Maker*. Blocking her way as he stood in the narrow aisle between shelves was John Stookes, from school. On seeing him, Geraldine didn't know what to do. John made her decision for her.

'It's Gerald, isn't it?' said John.

'Yes,' said Geraldine.

'Happy Christmas,' said John.

'Happy Christmas to you,' said Geraldine.

'What're you doing?' said John.

'Just come to look,' said Geraldine.

'What at?'

'I was hoping the new *NME* was in,' said Geraldine.

'Me too,' said John.

30

'Hey, wait on.'

Geraldine looked behind her. She'd just taken the right into Sunnyside Road, which angled down the hill behind the railway line towards school. There was John Stookes, shambling along like a bear in his light-brown afghan coat that nearly reached the pavement. Geraldine slowed her pace but didn't exactly stop. John pulled up to a walk alongside her and they travelled in silence for a moment. Geraldine wondered what would happen next.

'I got a new Bob Dylan album for Christmas,' said John. 'Want to come over and have a listen after school?'

'Er, yeah,' said Geraldine, not sure why she felt reluctant about the invitation but sensing something was astray.

During school, Geraldine thought about it. Best she could figure, it felt to her a bit like her friendship with Moses back in Zambia. Geraldine decided to take the risk; it felt minor compared to the enduring risk of being at home. At the end of the day, they met at the school gate and walked back up the hill, over the bridge and past the newsagents. John's house was just a few doors up. They went upstairs, to his bedroom, John making a quick detour into the lounge on the way through. He cued up side one of *Blood on the Tracks* and, as the acoustic guitar and piano of 'Tangled Up in Blue' broke through the crackle and hiss of the opening grooves of the record, he opened up the palm of his right hand and showed the contents to Geraldine.

'Do you want one?' asked John.

Geraldine looked for a long time; part of her, deep, distant and insistent, definitely did.

'No,' she said. 'No, thank you.'

John looked at her as he lit one of the cigarettes. He lay back on his bed and smoked while the album played on. Geraldine sat on the floor. She didn't care much for Bob Dylan, his music felt too empty and underproduced to her. For her, music was for getting lost in, and Dylan was already lost to her. After what she thought was long enough and John had smoked the second cigarette he'd filched from his mum's pack downstairs, she spoke over the music.

'What else have you got?' asked Geraldine.

'Mmm?' said John.

'What else have you got? What other records?'

'Don't you like Bob Dylan?' said John, like it could already be the end of their friendship.

'I do,' lied Geraldine. 'I just wondered what else you had.'

'Here,' said John, 'have a look.'

He handed Geraldine a slim pile of LPs and she leafed through them. Led Zeppelin, *Untitled*; Rush, *2112*; Steve Miller Band, *Fly Like an Eagle; The Dark Side of the Moon* and *Sabbath Bloody Sabbath*. On the bottom was an album by a band Geraldine had never heard of – Television. The album was called *Marquee Moon*, and its cover art was mostly taken up with a photo of what she guessed were the band members, although they looked like they might already be dead. The man standing slightly to the front and almost centre was holding out his right arm ever so slightly, the elbow just touching the palm of his left hand. It looked to Geraldine like he was quietly asking to be rescued. That picture alone was enough to make her want to listen.

'Can we put this one on?' Geraldine asked.

'That's my brother's,' said John. 'I don't really like it.'

John leaned down and turned Bob Dylan over, and they listened to side two in silence, John in quiet bliss and Geraldine trying to figure out how she could take *Marquee Moon* home with her. In the end, it was simple.

'Can I borrow this?' Geraldine said, as 'Buckets of Rain' ended with a crackling hiss, holding up the cover in her left hand while inspecting the spiral motif on the white inner sleeve in her right.

'Yeah, okay,' said John.

Geraldine left in a hurry before he could change his mind. Home just before dinnertime, Geraldine breezed in the front door and straight up the stairs to her bedroom. The growling guitar and bass that kicked off the opener, 'See No Evil', made her lean over from her bed, pick up the tone arm and start the track again so she could listen over. By the time she got to the shamelessly intricate guitars and time signatures of the title track 'Marquee Moon', Geraldine was gone. She'd never heard music like this before. The bit in the title track, close to the end, where they broke it all down and then built it back up again, thrilled Geraldine in a way that she couldn't even begin to describe.

■□■

The next morning, Geraldine waited on the near side of the bridge for John. When she saw him walking towards her, she ran to meet him.

'John. John!' she said as she ran towards him.

'What? What is it?'

'You've got to listen. You've got to listen to Television.'

'What?'

'You have to listen to them. Have a proper listen. Trust me.'

'Alright,' said John.

'This afternoon, after school?'

'Alright.'

■□■

'Have you got a cigarette?' John asked when they were upstairs in Geraldine's bedroom.

'No,' said Geraldine. 'Here, listen,' she said, cuing up track one, side one. This time it was her turn to lie back on the bed while John sat on the floor. They listened to the whole album in silence.

'What else have you got?' said John at the end of 'Guiding Light', not even making it to the end of side two.

Geraldine felt insulted, all she wanted to talk about was Television. Besides, she still had nothing else to show, no other records at all, only a case of cassettes.

'Nothing,' she said. 'I don't have any.'

'We'll have to do something about that, then,' said John, grinning at Geraldine. 'Let's go into town on Saturday, have a look at records.'

■□■

Exon's Records was in Dolphin Square, an example of municipal overreach if Geraldine had ever seen one. She couldn't imagine anything like a dolphin swimming through the slimy estuary mud that was the main feature of Weston-super-Mare's seafront. The shop was a small square of real estate, packed with row upon row of LPs. The man at the tiny counter seemed bigger than the entire space, but somehow he managed to fit behind his till. Over his shoulder was a noticeboard, index cards pinned to it with handwritten invitations to gigs in Weston and Bristol, an impossible twenty miles up the motorway. They flipped through the records, everything from A to Z, spending what felt like hours under the watchful eye of the shop's proprietor and namesake, Ken Exon. Geraldine kept going back to the brand-new copy of *Marquee Moon* filed under 'T'.

'Go and ask him to have a listen,' said John. 'He won't know you've already heard it.'

Geraldine stepped up to the counter and held out the LP.

'Not a bad choice for someone so young,' the shop owner said to Geraldine. 'Are we buying today?'

'Can I have a listen?' said Geraldine.

'Sure,' said the man, as he slid the inner sleeve out of the cover, expertly removed the black disc and placed it on one of the platters behind him. 'Number one, over there,' he said, pointing with his chin, his hands full of vinyl. The listening booth was a perspex hood that you had to duck under to get into; headphones hung on a hook on the wall, and next to them was a volume knob.

Geraldine put on the headphones and heard sounds she'd never heard before. The guitars were all around her, some outside and some inside her head. The drums were off in outer space and Geraldine was somewhere in between. She listened for as long as she dared and then took off the headphones and went back to the desk.

'Thank you,' she said.

'What?' said the man as he lifted his head out of the latest *Melody Maker*.

'Thank you,' Geraldine repeated, not quite knowing what else to say.

'That's okay,' said the man. 'Come back again, I think you'll be alright.'

Geraldine tripped out of the shop and found John pacing in the empty space of Dolphin Square. She'd forgotten he was with her until she saw him again.

'C'mon, let's go,' said John, turning for home.

As they walked through the laneway that joined Exeter Road with Ridgeway Avenue, bollards at either end denying access to cars, John felt safe enough to take his hand out from under his afghan. In it was a copy of Rainbow's *Rising*.

'Told you we'd do something about your record collection,' said John, laughing stupidly as he finished the words.

Geraldine didn't say anything. It was clear the record was for John's collection, not hers. They went back to his house and had a listen, but it just sounded old to Geraldine, all that guitar playing for the sake of it and not a single note that told her a story. John was in bliss, laying back smoking one of his mum's cigarettes.

'I'll see you later,' said Geraldine, halfway through side two, and left John to his reverie.

On her way home Geraldine stopped in at the newsagents and asked the man behind the counter to set aside a copy of *NME* and *Melody Maker* for her each week. She paid for the first week and left for home, already looking ahead to next Thursday. When the day came, staring at her from the cover of the first copy of *NME* she bought with her own money were the still unhealthy-looking members of Television. For Geraldine this couldn't have been a coincidence. Here was her new bible, Tom Verlaine her new Jesus, music her new religion and, like all zealots, she got stuck in like nothing else on earth mattered.

■□■

For Geraldine, the thing about discovering new music was that it was her own. There was something that she liked about the sense of freshness and the unknown, feeling like she was the first to something, throwing off the old and embracing the new. It made her feel whole, emboldened, like it was her job to be different. In 1978, *NME* was a visual battle of artists and bands with long hair and, increasingly, those with short. By the end of the year the battle was over, punk had won and Geraldine was pulled into its scrappy world of defiance. She may not have looked any different on the outside, but inside, her molecules were realigning, she was coming into her own. Week after week she would read *NME* from cover to cover every Thursday afternoon and evening. When she'd finished, she'd start again, reading the bits she'd skipped over in her hurry to come to grips with the more interesting articles. On her third run through she'd pore over the photos; most of them with silly captions that made her double take, catching her every time with their obscure humour. Towards the back of the paper there was a round-up of events from the previous week, little blurbs telling her what people had been doing in London mostly, sometimes Manchester, occasionally Birmingham. On her final run through, Geraldine took scissors from the kitchen and cut out photos to stick on her bedroom wall with Blu Tack. She was taken one week with a photo from the back of the paper of two girls kissing on a crowded dancefloor. Geraldine passed over the page more than twenty times before she cut out the image and stuck it up next to a photo of Bruce Foxton in full flight, his legs tucked under him, holding on to his Rickenbacker bass like it was his only way back to earth. Every night before she went to sleep, Geraldine looked at her growing collection of photos, always finishing with the young women. She wondered who they were and what they were doing now.

31

That summer was a disaster for Frank and Grace. The first guest at St Austell was Uncle Fred, who turned up to stay for a few days at the end of July. Sitting at the table for his cooked breakfast on the first morning of his stay, he picked up the bottle of HP Sauce and gave it a good shake, whereupon the lid came off and brown sauce covered every wall and picture in the dining room. A glob of it dripped down Grace's face. Geraldine had been standing in the doorway watching. She was torn between hating Fred for ruining Frank and Grace's hard work and the snorting urge to laugh as she saw the sauce dripping down Grace's face. Grace stood frozen for a moment, not knowing what to do.

'Sorry,' said Fred, not sounding like it at all.

Geraldine fumed at his lack of contrition.

'That's alright,' Grace said, 'It'll teach me to put the lid on properly. ''Ere, eat yer breakfast before it goes cold.'

Grace returned to the kitchen to bring Fred's tea and toast and then did her best to wipe down the walls. They were stained so badly Frank had to repaint the dining room after Fred had gone. This time, instead of cream he chose a dark blue.

'Like the sea,' said Frank.

It doesn't look like the sea anywhere near here, was Geraldine's assessment, but she kept her thoughts to herself. During the August school holidays, summer season proper, Frank and Grace hosted only two more couples at St Austell, one for a night and the other for two. And that was it, their idea of running a guest house had run aground. Almost a year of renovating and waiting had left them with an empty house and no income.

■□■

As had become the pattern in Geraldine's life, if not the expectation, the new school year brought change to the Sturmer household. Frank started a job selling double glazing door to door. He left the house every morning, returned every evening for dinner and then went to the pub. For a year there had been an air of mild optimism at St Austell, but now hush and uncertainty had returned.

Towards the end of September, Harry fetched up at St Austell. As with his last return at Christmas the previous year, Geraldine had no idea where he'd been or what he'd been doing, but it felt good to have him back. She was shy around him. They'd both changed in the months since they'd last seen each other and Harry now seemed to be immersed in a life that Geraldine coveted but had so far only experienced in words and pictures, and on black vinyl. Harry installed in the now empty downstairs bedroom a Marshall amplifier and speaker stack, a Fender guitar and a Fuzz Face pedal. She knew what the first two items were for, but she'd never seen an effects pedal before. While Harry was out, Geraldine would sit on the undressed bed over against the wall and look at Harry's gear, never daring to touch it, but fascinated by its possibilities. Until now, she'd never really played a musical instrument. The closest she'd come to making music was singing in the school choir at Havenhouse, an experience so conflicting that she'd packed away her voice.

■□■

A few weeks after his return, Harry woke Geraldine one night. She thought at first something must be wrong. The last time they'd had such a late-night encounter was when she'd woken Harry because she was in a fever and about to die of diphtheria.

'What is it?' said Geraldine as she sat up in her bed. 'What's the matter?'

Harry sat on the edge of her single bed and leaned over to touch her leg.

'It's okay, everything's alright,' he said, grinning and smelling of beer.

Geraldine's chest pounded with latent fear. She sat still and didn't say anything.

'Do any of your friends smoke pot?' asked Harry after a while.

Geraldine frowned. She knew a lot was riding on her answer to this question, but she had no idea what. The straight-up response was no. One afternoon after school at John's he'd pulled a bag of something green out of his drawer. He told Geraldine it was dried wild lettuce and that he'd read it could give you a high like smoking cannabis. Geraldine had watched while he rolled a cigarette, mixing the green leaf with tobacco from one of his mum's cigarettes. John had smoked the funny-smelling substance and, afterwards, they sat for a while, Geraldine having given her customary polite refusal.

'Anything?' she asked after a few minutes.

'Nope,' said John.

They both giggled, Geraldine with relief, John a bit embarrassed that his scheme hadn't gone as he'd read.

Finally, Geraldine replied, 'John up the road does. I don't think anyone else from school does.'

Her answer seemed to satisfy Harry. He waited a moment, digesting the information and thinking things through.

'Do you want to try some?' he said.

Her immediate response, 'Yes,' surprised Geraldine, but Harry was inhabiting a world she wanted to be part of and maybe this was the way in.

They went downstairs and sat in the darkened lounge room, door closed behind them, the grate still glowing with hot coals from the day's fire. Harry took a while to roll a joint, lit it and began to toke on it like it was a lover. Geraldine watched him, beginning to think she'd misunderstood, that she was only here to witness rather than partake. Satisfied that he was where he wanted to be again, Harry handed Geraldine the joint, his eyes blazing red in the darkened room.

'Watch out for it, it's a bit strong,' he warned her. 'Take a drag and hold it in as long as you can.'

That's just what Geraldine did. As she exhaled, after what seemed like an age of holding her breath, the world began to cant to the left and her body felt so heavy that it was essential to lean back against the settee in case she somehow fell off. Geraldine held out the joint for her brother and concentrated on the growing light. Colours became brighter and things in the periphery of her vision began to gently breathe in and out. Geraldine felt a sense of deep relaxation. Her face ached with smiling and the stillness went on forever. Finally, Geraldine heard her brother's voice.

'Are you okay?'

She turned to him and smiled, her head moving slightly more slowly than her eyes. Harry rolled another one and they smoked it in silence, this time Geraldine taking her share of the pungent smoke.

'Are you hungry?' said Harry.

The moment Geraldine heard his question, she realised she was consumed by a ravening desire to eat. She had never felt so hungry.

'Hold on a minute,' Harry said as he disappeared through to the kitchen at the other end of the house. Geraldine sat in the warmth of the room cocooned in her thoughts, her mind freewheeling and disordered. When Harry returned it was with a bowl of something he called halva. Geraldine never heard of it before and, given this was the person who'd told her that tadpoles tasted like chocolate some centuries ago, she was a bit wary.

'Go on, try it, it's good,' Harry said through a mouthful.

Geraldine took a taste and it was like nothing she'd ever eaten before, which of course was true, but it was more than that. The flavours and textures danced in her mouth. Once she'd started, she couldn't get enough of the stuff.

When the halva was gone, the siblings slipped into silence for a while until Harry decided the room was too hot. The coals in the grate were still glowing red and they decided they needed to do something to turn them down. Harry suggested putting some water on them, so Geraldine went to the kitchen and out the side door to the shed to fetch a bucket which she filled at the kitchen sink. She carried it back to the lounge room, careful not to spill the icy liquid along the hallway carpet. Once she got back the siblings sat and parleyed for what felt to Geraldine like a very long, intense time, figuring out the right way to get the job done.

'Just don't put it on too fast,' were Harry's last words of advice to Geraldine.

The eruption of steam and ash surprised them both. Geraldine didn't know why, they both should have known what was going to happen, but the mind is a wonderful thing. They both truly believed that they could defy the laws of chemistry and physics. So much for their posh public-school education. Geraldine looked back at her brother, ready to be in trouble, her body shifting towards anxiety. The racing of her heart moved from being a distant curiosity to an urgent warning. Harry was laughing, harder than

Geraldine had ever seen him laugh before. Geraldine put down the bucket and joined him back on the sofa so she could survey the damage. She was giggling uncontrollably. Great fat gulps of air shaking her entire body.

The ash was still settling as they looked around the room, floating down in lazy spirals of white and grey. It covered every single surface, including the siblings. After a while they managed to galvanise themselves enough to clean up the room, wiping down all the surfaces they could find and putting away the bucket. When they were satisfied they had restored order they went up the stairs to their bedrooms. Geraldine slept so well that night that Grace had to come and wake her in the morning.

'What did you do last night?' said Grace.

'What do you mean?' Geraldine said, playing for time while her mind calculated all the permutations, including what it would mean to get busted for smoking pot.

'There's ash all over the lounge room,' said Grace. 'Come downstairs and have a look.'

She turned and left Geraldine to get herself out of bed and come downstairs. Grace's madness – not anger – left a cloud behind her.

Geraldine came downstairs and tentatively stepped into the lounge room, at which point she saw clearly that she and Harry hadn't quite managed to finish their cleaning job from the previous night. She could see some smears on the mantle shelf over the fireplace where she'd tried to shift the ash with a cloth, but the rest of the room was still covered in a fine layer of it.

'What did you do?' repeated Grace.

Geraldine looked around the room, her mouth gaping, mind racing. Grace didn't ask Geraldine why she'd been downstairs after everyone had gone to bed, or who she'd been with. Geraldine instantly saw Grace's missed opportunity and her opening.

'I was talking to Harry after he came home last night,' said Geraldine. 'It was hot, so he asked me to put some water on the fire to cool it down, but it went all over. I'm sorry.'

Geraldine must have achieved just the right amount of blame shifting by mentioning her older sibling, long acknowledged as the potential family bank robber, because Grace began to soften.

'I thought it was volcanic ash from Mount Saint Helens come down the chimney,' she said, still looking a bit confused, like she knew she was missing something but having no idea what it was.

Geraldine stifled her laugh at the preposterousness of Grace's hypothesis.

'Sorry, Mum,' Geraldine said as she headed towards the kitchen, thinking it best to leave things there. Besides, she was starving.

32

That Saturday, Geraldine moved her record player into the downstairs room and plugged it in by the bed. She was lying back listening to one of Harry's records, a battered copy of Hawkwind's self-titled debut when he arrived downstairs around midday.

'Alright, Gerald?' said Harry when he noticed her over in the corner.

'Yes, thank you.'

'What you doing down here?'

'I thought I'd listen to some of your records,' said Geraldine. 'Hope you don't mind.'

'Nope. But I'm going to play for a bit so you'll have to switch it off now.'

'That's okay,' said Geraldine.

She'd got exactly what she'd come for.

Harry had gone away to King John's College one term and returned with a classical guitar. When he was home, he spent the entire holidays playing the arpeggios and chords to 'House of the Rising Sun'. To Geraldine, this musical transformation felt like magic – one moment Harry couldn't play, the next he could. When he was out one day, she picked up Harry's guitar and began to strum, mimicking what she'd seen him do. But, used to instant success, Geraldine couldn't emulate even one of the sounds she'd heard her sibling play. The nylon strings left deep welts in the fingers of her left hand and she felt like a failure. She'd given up but never stopped trying to figure out what it was that Harry had that she didn't. Today, she learned what that was.

Harry switched on the Marshall amplifier and strapped on his guitar, turning the volume-pot clockwise until the buzz coming from the speakers was just loud enough. He stood facing the speaker cabinet and played.

Geraldine didn't recognise a single song in the entire two hours that Harry practised. She lay on her side and watched while he moved through chord sequences and lead breaks, stopping and going back to the beginning of a run every time he made a mistake. His face was lined with concentration, his dark fringe hung over his eyes as he hunched forward, and every now and then he'd take his left hand from the fretboard and give it a shake. Harry's focus and intensity was something Geraldine had never seen in him before. She was daunted by her older sibling's accomplishment. Geraldine had always thought she was the smarter of the two of them, a pecking order that no-one spoke of directly, but everyone seemed to understand. Today she'd learned about a different kind of smart. And the day wasn't over yet.

'Do you want to come into town?' Harry asked, as he switched off the amp and took the guitar off his shoulder, resting its strings first against the speaker box, making minute adjustments as he did so to make sure it wouldn't slide to the floor the moment he let it go.

'Sure. Yes. Yes, please?' said Geraldine, unsure what a trip to town would entail.

Harry picked up his jacket, and Geraldine went to the hall and put on her school coat, not knowing if the weather outside warranted it, but wanting to be as much like her sibling as she could be.

'We're going out,' said Harry to anyone who might be listening and with that they were through the front door, up the short garden path to where Harry's Ford Escort van was parked on the road right outside the house.

Geraldine opened the passenger door and was hit by the pungent sweet smell of cannabis. The odour made her nervous.

'C'mon, it's alright,' said Harry, sensing her hesitation. 'We're just going to look at some records.'

With that, Geraldine was fully on board.

They drove up Clevedon Road and took a right at the seafront, a few tourists still walking along the prom, sitting in deckchairs and taking donkey rides on the sandy part of Weston's beach. The tide was out, so the muddy water that passed for the sea in this English resort town was just an occasional glint on the horizon as the pale sun intermittently broke through the low clouds. They took a right down Regent Street, opposite the pier, and

Harry weaved his way through side streets to the carpark at the back of the amusement arcades that lined both sides of Weston's main drag.

'This way,' said Harry, as they left the multistorey.

Geraldine followed him to Exon's Records. She hadn't been there since her visit with John Stookes. Worried that his shoplifting might become her responsibility, she'd stuck to the racks at the back of Woolworths in the High Street ever since. As Harry entered the shop, Geraldine hung back in the doorway.

'Hello, Harry,' said the man behind the counter.

'Hi, Ken,' said Harry.

'Who's that?' said Ken, pointing with his chin to Geraldine.

'That's our Gerald,' said Harry. 'C'mon, Gerald, don't be shy.'

Geraldine took a step inside.

'Do I know you?' said Ken, squinting at Geraldine, his eyelids hooded.

'I was here a while ago,' was all Geraldine offered, worried that too much detail might give her away.

Ken Exon looked at Geraldine for a long time.

'I know,' he said.

Geraldine, breathed in, getting ready to run.

'Television!' said Ken. 'You had a listen to *Marquee Moon*.'

'Yes,' said Geraldine.

'I thought you were alright then,' said Ken, 'but I didn't know you belonged with this one,' he continued, looking at Harry. 'Come in, come in.'

Geraldine stepped through the door and joined Harry, who was by now in a trance-like state, flipping through the shelves of LPs.

'Have you heard this?' he said, holding up an LP that had three tough-looking men standing in an alleyway on the cover.

Geraldine had read about the Clash. She desperately wanted to hear their music.

'No, not yet,' said Geraldine. 'I've read about them, they sound good.'

'Shall we get it?' said Harry.

'Really?'

'Yes, I think we should,' said Harry. 'I saw them just before I came back to Weston.'

Harry took the record to the counter and did the deal with Ken, who bagged the record while they exchanged pleasantries.

'You DJing tonight?' asked Harry.

'Yeah, I'll be on from around ten,' said Ken.

'Might see you there then,' said Harry.

'Alright, see you then.'

With that, they were ready to leave.

'Oh, Gerald,' said Ken, as she was just about through the door.

'Yes?' said Geraldine.

'Don't forget to tell your mate he still owes me for that Ritchie Blackmore album.'

Geraldine flushed bright red, her face so hot she thought it might catch fire. She opened and closed her mouth, frozen on the threshold.

'Go on,' said Ken. 'It's alright, you'll do.'

With that he turned his attention to whatever was on the counter in front of him and Geraldine was free to go.

'What was that all about?' Harry said as they walked across Dolphin Square.

'Nothing,' said Geraldine.

'Alright then,' Harry said. 'Let's go to the pub.'

Geraldine gulped.

'Aren't I too young?' she said.

'It's alright, kid,' said Harry. 'Stick with me and you'll be fine.'

■□■

The Three Queens took up a corner block far enough away from Regent Street that it was occupied mostly by locals. As they approached the glass-and-wood double doors, one standing open, the other permanently closed, Geraldine heard the music. When they stepped inside, there was a band playing in a corner of the front bar, thumping rock-and-roll covers, the singer doing everything he could to engage the thin audience intent on a pre-dinner beer.

'Sit over there,' Harry said pointing to an empty table with a curved bench seat on one side and a couple of chairs on the other.

Geraldine sat as far back in the bench seat as she could, hoping no-one would notice her. She kept her eyes down and her ears on the band. It was the first time she'd experienced live music other than in church or at school concerts. It felt wrong, which Geraldine put down to her being in a pub, but it moved her in ways she didn't expect. She tapped along with her foot, but it was the thrills she felt in her chest, all down her back and the raised hairs on her arms that surprised her. When she looked up and the singer made eye contact with her, Geraldine was back to blushing again. She couldn't contain her shyness and embarrassment.

'That's Richard,' said Harry, as he came from the bar with their drinks, a pint of bitter for him, in a straight glass, and a lemon, lime and bitters for Geraldine.

'Who?' said Geraldine.

'The singer,' said Harry.

'Do you know him?' said Geraldine.

'Yeah, of course,' said Harry. 'We've played together a bit.'

Harry sat back in his chair, picked up his pint and turned to face the band, watching them intently as they worked their way through their set. Geraldine picked up her drink and did likewise. When the band took a break, Richard walked over to their table.

'Alright, Harry?' he said. 'Who's this?'

'That's our Gerald.'

'Alright, Gerald?' said Richard.

Geraldine nodded and took a sip of her drink. Richard and Harry nattered on for a while, completely ignoring Geraldine, who went back to looking down at the table. When Richard left them to get a drink from the bar, Harry turned back to Geraldine.

'They'll be famous one day,' he said.

'Do you think so?' said Geraldine, having no idea what it took to be famous.

'Yes, I do,' said Harry.

'What're they called?' said Geraldine.

'Racey.'

Geraldine tucked the name away for future reference.

Harry and Geraldine finished their drinks before the band started their next set, so that ended up being the first and last time Geraldine got to see them play live.

'C'mon, let's get home for dinner,' said Harry, as he stood up checking his pockets for his wallet and keys. 'Don't forget your record.'

'My record?' said Geraldine, as she picked up the LP still in its brown paper bag.

'Yes, you can have it,' said Harry.

'Thank you!' she said, grinning and all red in the face again. Today had been quite the day for her autonomic nervous system.

When they pulled up outside St Austell, Geraldine rushed up the path to the front door, willing Harry to hurry up so he could let them in.

'We're home,' Harry said to anyone who was listening.

Geraldine rushed past the lounge room and into the next, pulling her new record from its sleeve and placing it side one upwards on the platter. The needle crackled as it caught on the grooves and the opening beats of 'Janie Jones', the drums, the staccato guitar and Joe Strummer's tuneful non-singing had her in a full-body reaction all over again.

■□■

After dinner Geraldine took her record player back up to her room and listened to *The Clash* over and over, the frenetic music, the barking instructions for living arousing her in a new way. That Saturday night she took control of her own sex for the very first time. She felt the power of her body unencumbered by the handsiness of others, their images of what love looked like, and revelled in the exhaustion that came afterwards. Geraldine sighed deeply as she crossed over into sleep. Often a tricky navigation for her, tonight's journey was different. She tried to figure out why in her dreams. She saw Bob for the first time in years, but only his sleek back as he scuttled up the same hill Janet and John were perpetually coming down. She tried again to see into the distance, but was trapped by the sharp, straight edges of the page. Geraldine looked behind her and saw the machinery that had saved her life but reminded her of death, smelled the bitterness of glycol. Grace sat in a chair smoking and Frank was somewhere, anywhere but home. When Geraldine opened her eyes the next morning, the first thing she saw was the array of photos on her bedroom wall. She studied their greyscale dots and decided they were not enough for her.

33

Early in the new year, Frank's days as a double-glazing salesman now behind him, he turned to the profession he had once learned at night school to escape colliery life, and found himself contract work in Libya. Geraldine was the only sibling home for this family announcement; Harry, his guitar, amplifier and van were elsewhere for the evening.

'Right, our Gerald,' said Frank. Once he was satisfied he had Geraldine's attention, he lit two cigarettes, handed one to Grace and took a deep draw. 'I have to go away. For work.'

'Ah,' said Geraldine.

She didn't ask where, just hung on Frank's use of 'I' instead of 'we' and hoped it wasn't just a slip of language. She wasn't planning on going anywhere new for a while, if ever.

'I'll be gone for three months,' said Frank.

'Okay,' said Geraldine, wondering when the announcement would be over and she could go up to her room.

'To Libya,' said Frank.

'Libya?' said Geraldine, finding some interest in the topic after all.

'Yes, I'll be working on oil exploration.'

'Ah,' said Geraldine, her interest assuaged.

'So, we've decided,' said Frank, 'to give you a bit more responsibility. We want you to have your own key to the house so you can come and go as you need to.'

'Okay, thank you,' said Geraldine, already calculating the possibilities associated with this new development.

Frank handed her a copy of the front door key, no ring, no tag.

'And you'll help your mum,' said Frank.

'Yes,' said Geraldine, although she'd known for a long time that Grace was beyond help.

Geraldine got up to leave the lounge room.

'I'm going to my room,' she said to Frank and Grace at the door. 'When are you leaving?'

'Tomorrow morning,' said Frank.

Geraldine turned and disappeared upstairs.

34

Next time they were at Exon's, Geraldine saw a notice on the pin-up board to the side of the counter. It was for tickets to see the Jam at Bristol Polytechnic. Geraldine stared at the notice until Ken noticed and turned to her.

'What's up, young 'un?' he said.

'Are you selling tickets for this?' asked Geraldine, pointing to the notice.

'I think I have some left,' said Ken, opening a drawer under his counter. 'Yes, here we are.' He held up a wad of strips of thin, dull-pink card held together with an elastic band.

Geraldine licked her lips.

'How much are they?' she asked.

'One pound fifty,' said Ken. 'Have you got the album?'

'No, I haven't,' said Geraldine.

Harry came over and joined the conversation.

'What's up, our kid?' he said to Geraldine.

'I was just looking at these tickets for the Jam,' said Geraldine, 'but it's in Bristol, at the polytechnic.'

'Think we should go?' said Harry.

'It's this Saturday,' said Geraldine. 'Your birthday.'

'Can't think of a better way to spend it,' said Harry. 'We'd better get some tickets now then, before they're all gone.'

'Two, is it?' said Ken, taking the elastic band off the wedge of tickets.

'Sounds about right,' said Harry.

'He hasn't got the record yet, either,' said Ken.

'Better get one of them, too,' said Harry.

This time, Geraldine didn't have to wait for Harry to get out of the driver's side, lock his door and saunter up the garden path. She had a key and she was upstairs in her room listening to her new record before he'd even got through the front door.

■□■

By the time Saturday came, Geraldine had learned every word to every song on *In the City*. She'd studied the pictures on her bedroom wall, looking for a clue as to what might be acceptable attire for a Jam concert. The band wore suits, white shirts and ties, but that wasn't going to work for Geraldine. Nothing in her wardrobe looked likely. She had a few white shirts for school, but these were the wrong cut and didn't have button-down collars. She had a pair of jeans, straight-leg Levi's that she'd managed to get Frank to buy her at the beginning of summer, but the rest of her wardrobe looked childish to Geraldine, and wrong. Geraldine woke Harry at nine, as early as she dared as he usually never rose before midday. She stood by Harry's bed for a long while, watching him sleep and then sat on the edge and gently shook his shoulder.

'Harry, wake up,' Geraldine said softly.

Harry sat bolt upright, swiping Geraldine's hand from his shoulder.

'What? What is it?' he said, before he was even properly awake. His eyes focused on Geraldine. 'What are you doing? What's wrong?'

'Nothing,' said Geraldine. 'I'm sorry.'

'Foof, alright then,' said Harry, making to lie down again.

'No,' said Geraldine. 'No, no. I need you. Can you take me to the markets this morning?'

'Er, yeah, alright,' said Harry. 'What for?'

'I need some clothes for tonight.'

'Have you got any money?' said Harry.

'Yeah, I have,' said Geraldine.

'Give me a minute then. I'll see you downstairs.'

When Harry came down, what felt to Geraldine to be many hours later, she was waiting in the hall, her house key in the left pocket of her Levi's and five pounds – two crinkled pound notes and change – in her right. It was all she had. Geraldine could have walked to the markets on her own, but she was hoping Harry might make up for any shortfall in the cost of whatever she could find to wear that night. The markets were already busy by the time they arrived. Geraldine walked ahead of Harry, eager to find something to wear and wanting to stay out of Harry's line of sight as long as possible. She was holding up an olive-green t-shirt with a V-neck and capped sleeves, slightly longer at the back than the front when Harry caught up with her.

'Isn't that a girl's shirt?' said Harry.

'I don't know,' said Geraldine. 'Is it? I think it might suit me.'

'If you think so,' said Harry, and drifted on.

Geraldine held the shirt up against herself one more time and paid the stallholder the two pounds fifty asking price, giving him most of her change. Next came the tricky part: Geraldine wanted a jacket. She walked slowly past the stalls looking for second-hand clothes, figuring this was the only way she'd be able to afford what she was looking for. The jacket she lit on was black, faded with age and slightly too small in the shoulders and arms. It had a stained cream satin lining and narrow lapels, single breasted with two buttons. Geraldine loved it from the moment she pulled it off the rack. She tried it on and then took it off so she could look at the price tag pinned to the inside pocket. It was four pounds fifty. Geraldine put the jacket back but kept her hand on the top of the hanger where it sat on the clothes rack. She looked around for the stallholder, who was giving change to someone else. When she'd finished, the woman turned to Geraldine.

'Can I help you, love?'

Geraldine pulled the jacket from the rack again and held it out to the stallholder.

'How much is this?' she asked, hoping that by asking she might be able to do a deal without haggling.

'That's four fifty, love,' the stallholder said without even looking at the price tag.

She must have seen the instant change in Geraldine's face, the shrinking of her shoulders.

'What about four quid?' the stallholder said.

'Can you hold it for me?' said Geraldine. 'Just for a while?'

'Alright, love,' said the stallholder.

■□■

Geraldine found Harry standing in the booze tent, half a pint of cider in his hand and talking to someone. When she saw him, Geraldine slowed her step as she approached, drew in her breath and then stood quietly at Harry's side waiting for him to notice her. It took him a while.

'What's up, our kid?' said Harry, looking down at Geraldine.

'Can I borrow one pound fifty?' said Geraldine.

'Borrow? Did you get yourself a job?'

'No,' said Geraldine, looking down at her feet.

'You're alright, our kid,' said Harry, giving her a boozy smile and rummaging around in his pocket. 'Here,' he said, handing her two pound notes. 'And make sure I get the change.'

Geraldine snatched the notes from his hand, turned and ran back to the second-hand stall. When she arrived, she was out of breath and red in the face.

'What's up, love?' said the stallholder as Geraldine came to a halt right at the place where she'd left the jacket on the rack.

'The jacket,' said Geraldine. 'You said you'd hold it for me. It's gone.'

'Settle, petal,' said the stall holder. 'I've got it here for you.'

She reached behind the table where she kept her money box and held the jacket out towards Geraldine.

'Four pounds?' said Geraldine, already sorting through her money.

'That's right, love.'

Geraldine handed over the money and took possession of the jacket, putting it on right away. When she got back to the booze tent and sidled up next to Harry again he noticed her straight away.

'Look at you, our kid,' he said, taking her in. 'Don't you look a treat.'

'Here's your fifty p,' said Geraldine.

'Keep it,' said Harry. 'I think you might need it more than me.' He smiled at Geraldine and put his arm around her shoulder, pulling her towards him.

'You're growing up, aren't you, our kid?' he said, with pride watering his eyes.

■□■

The closer the car got to Bristol, the more Geraldine's nerves began to get on top of her. She'd decided on white socks and her black school shoes to go with her Levi's, new jacket and t-shirt. As she sat looking down at her feet, her shoes looked too big at the bottom of her straight-leg jeans, and the inch or so of sock showing between the hem of her jeans and her shoes looked too white. She had her t-shirt untucked, and the rounded flap at the back went halfway down her bum, while the back of the jacket rode up over her waist. The vee of her t-shirt showed more chest than Geraldine had anticipated and the jacket was too tight to keep buttoned up. She wanted to ask Harry to turn the car around and take them home. Instead, Geraldine shrank back into the passenger seat and kept quiet. Harry didn't notice her anguish, he was too busy concentrating on driving and not bringing himself to the attention of the police patrolling the M5.

Their next obstacle was getting into the venue. The student union at Bristol Poly was licensed and Harry had already mentioned that Geraldine should stay close by him and let him answer any questions when they went in. At Geraldine's insistence, they'd arrived early, which, as they were walking up to the building, she thought could have been a mistake because people might pay more attention to them. They walked up to the door and past the bouncer who looked them over but said nothing. Harry handed over their tickets at the desk and the girl sitting behind said nothing either as she tore them in two and handed Harry the stubs. Harry put his arm on Geraldine's back and moved her along. They were in. The room was dark, a bar running the full length at one end and the stage at the other, equipment glinting in the white lights the roadies used to work by, but mostly in shadow. Harry headed straight for the bar and ordered a pint, asking Geraldine if she wanted anything. Geraldine shook her head and stood next to Harry, her back to the bar surveying the room. She knew exactly where she wanted to be, she just didn't know if she had the courage to get there. Harry seemed settled at the bar and, as Geraldine watched people filter into the room, she could feel her chance slipping. She went to say something four or five times before she found her voice.

'I'm going down the front.'

'Sure, kid,' said Harry, 'I'll be here. Have fun.'

Geraldine immediately set off, weaving her way through knots of people, the crowd getting thicker the closer she got to the stage. Sometimes being on the small side had its advantages, and Geraldine was able to slip and slide her way past the growing numbers until she was up against the crash barrier just to stage right. She rested her elbows on the steel bar in front of her, head resting on her left forearm, bum out holding space behind her, and waited.

As time went on, the crowd grew until it filled the room comfortably and then uncomfortably. The noise from the waiting punters grew from chatter between friends to a roar, to clapping in unison and, finally, chants of 'We want the Jam! We want the Jam!' When the houselights went down Geraldine was standing up straight, pressed against the security barrier, locked in at either side, no chance of her backside saving anything now. The roar from the crowd that accompanied the dimming of the lights was frightening. The four-piece that came on stage was greeted with a collective shove forward and an uptick then diminution of the crowd noise as people realised this was not the Jam at all. For half an hour the foursome went through a bunch of songs that no-one in the room had heard and no-one wanted to hear. The audience was here for one thing only. The boos and catcalls began halfway through the first song. When it was clear the band was going to attempt a second, its opening chords were greeted with a volley of half-empty beer cans, spraying foamy lager over the people at the front of the room as they spiralled towards the stage. The bass player, standing stage left, took a can to the chest and made to come over the security barrier and wade into the crowd. People surged forward to meet him and he thought the better of it. Geraldine held her spot, her jacket reeking of stale beer, her body turned sideways so she could see what was happening in front and behind simultaneously. The band kept their heads down and played fast and hard, and by the time they hit their fifth song, they had won over the sea of punters. Either that or the crowd had run out of projectiles. Either way, the mood of the room changed, and by the time the singer shouted, 'Thanks for nuffink,' into his microphone as his bandmates closed out their last song, they were greeted by ragged cheers. The lights went up and the audience turned as one and headed for the bar. Geraldine stayed in her spot and waited some more.

When the lights went down for a second time, Geraldine still wasn't ready for the crush. She had to stiffen her whole body just to stay standing, gripping onto the steel rail in front of her because her life depended on it.

The noise built and built as the stage stayed empty and, finally, as Paul, Bruce and Rick jogged into their spots, reached a level that turned from waves to slabs of solid air. The band broke into 'Art School', Weller ringing out the first four chords and then shouting out, 'One – two – three – four,' while the entire crowd shouted along with him as the band and audience began singing and moving as one. Geraldine hadn't expected this. The trio on stage moved, played and sang like this would be their last act. Everything they did was in fast motion and the energy they threw out was reflected back to them re-intensified by the crowd. It was one united, joyous, dangerous sing along as the Jam took them through a wringer of emotions from the standard heartbreak of lost love to the unassuageable anger of a generation of kids with no future.

■□■

That night changed Geraldine's life. Being part of the exchange of energy between musicians and audience felt like it had rewired her brain. Geraldine was addicted.

'What did you think?' said Geraldine, when she made her way back to Harry.

'Yeah, it was alright,' said Harry.

Geraldine felt a shock of disappointment and then let it go. Nothing could keep her down tonight.

'C'mon, let's go,' said Harry.

'Wait,' said Geraldine. 'Wait!'

She got in line at the merchandise desk and handed over her last fifty p to buy herself a button badge with the Jam logo on it, the graffiti design from the front cover of their album. Geraldine stood at the merch desk and pinned the badge to the right lapel of her jacket not caring that people behind her were pushing into her so they could take their turn.

'Thanks for coming, darling,' said the woman behind the desk.

Geraldine wandered behind Harry back to his van in a dream, her ears ringing, her body aching and her voice almost completely gone. She touched her badge all the way home and, when she finally got to bed, Geraldine lay there, eyes closed, and saw and heard the whole experience over and over again, savouring every scissor kick, every reverb, every 'Fuck!' remark Weller made as he spoke between songs.

'How you feeling?' Weller had said after they'd ripped through the 'Batman Theme'. 'Alright?'

'Yes, thank you, Paul,' Geraldine said to herself as she fell into sleep.

35

The next Monday at school Geraldine wore her new jacket and badge, beer stench and all, and caused quite a stir. It started when she met up with John on the corner near the railway bridge.

'What?' he said. 'You're a mod now, are you?'

'What do you mean?' said Geraldine.

'That jacket,' said John. 'And, who's that?' He leaned in to look at her badge. 'I thought so, the Jam. They're mods.'

'I don't care,' said Geraldine, 'I like them. I saw them on Saturday. In Bristol.'

'Really?' said John.

'Yeah, I did,' said Geraldine, smiling and going all mysterious. 'It was great!'

'You didn't,' said John. 'You never did.'

'Here,' said Geraldine, showing John her ticket stub.

Again, he leaned in to look, Geraldine was careful not to hand it over.

'Fuck me,' said John, finally acknowledging Geraldine's truth. 'What was it like?'

'It was great,' was all Geraldine could say. It didn't even come close to doing the night justice, but it was all Geraldine had right now.

'I've never been to a gig,' said John.

'We should do it,' said Geraldine.

The two friends walked the rest of the way to school in silence. As they entered the school gates Geraldine held her head high and stared back at the kids whose heads popped up to look at her. For a few moments she was top of the heap. Next minute she was in a heap on the cold, wet bitumen, the wind knocked out of her and a rip in the knee of her school cords, blood beginning to ooze through the material.

'Fucking mod,' said Patrick Burges as he swaggered towards the oval, a group of kids swarming around him to share his victory.

Geraldine got up and began to brush the dirt off herself while standing on one leg so she could test the movement of her bloody knee, nearly falling over again in the process. She heard a voice behind her.

'Hey, hello.'

Geraldine turned around to locate the source of the voice and saw up close for the first time someone she'd previously only seen from afar.

'My sister's a mod,' the girl said.

Geraldine looked at the girl, taking in her burgundy hair and eyes lined with thick kohl, her defiant take on the school uniform, which included a wide, black taffeta skirt and a white blouse with the collar turned up so that her shoulder-length locks sat variously inside and outside its edge.

'Is she?' was all Geraldine could think of to say.

'Yes, has been for ages,' said the girl. 'You should ask her about clothes and stuff. She wears these pencil skirts you can hardly walk in.'

'Who's your sister?' said Geraldine.

'Don't you want to know who I am, first?' said the girl.

'Oh, yes, of course,' said Geraldine.

Geraldine had wanted to know who this girl was since she'd first seen her but had never had the opportunity or courage to speak to her.

'I'm Sasha,' said the girl. 'I'll tell my sister you said hi.'

'Um, no, it's okay,' said Geraldine.

'You don't want to talk to her?'

'No. I mean, yes, but I'd rather talk to you.'

'We'll see about that,' said Sasha.

36

Geraldine sat downstairs with Harry next time he practised his guitar. She lay on the bed, observing and waiting for a break so she could speak to him. The moment Harry set down his guitar she cut straight into the silence.

'Do you play in a band?' she asked.

'Kind of,' said Harry, 'It's a bit loose at the moment. Adie, our drummer, is back in London for a bit and Bopay, our other guitarist is so good he won't stick around for long, but he's still okay to jam. And we don't have a singer.'

'Can I come with you to rehearsal next time you go?' said Geraldine.

'Yeah, of course,' said Harry. 'Do you want to have a go at singing for us?'

'Er, no, I don't think so,' said Geraldine.

With what she had in mind, Geraldine decided it would be much better if she didn't let on about her lack of musical talent too early.

■□■

Rehearsals were at the tech college in the centre of Weston. There were four soundproofed (almost) rooms on the first floor along one of the wings, fronted by glass so people passing by could see inside. Most evenings when lectures were over this was the most highly trafficked part of the college, where musicians brought up their gear in the lifts or carried guitar cases up the concrete staircase, and outside the four rooms a straggle of hangers-on, girlfriends, boyfriends, wannabe girlfriends, wannabe boyfriends, drug dealers, buyers and, occasionally, bookers from local venues scouted new acts for their pubs and clubs. Geraldine climbed the stairs a step behind Harry, wanting to stay close until she knew what she was in for.

'Who's this?' said Bopay, a tall, slim man with the shiniest and longest black hair Geraldine had ever seen. He already had his guitar strapped on and ready to go. To Geraldine, it looked too heavy for his slight frame, like the strap would slip off his narrow shoulders at any moment.

'This is our Gerald,' said Harry. 'It's alright.'

At which Bopay lifted his hands from his sides and returned to the task of rolling a joint, which he then lit, toked on and handed to Harry. Harry did the same and passed it over to Geraldine. Geraldine shook her head; the glass made her feel too exposed. Harry shrugged and handed the joint back to Bopay and returned to the task of setting up. By the time the joint was finished, both guitarists were ready to go and Geraldine sat back in a far corner of the rehearsal room and watched them do their stuff. Harry began, playing G, D and C over and again. It was the simplest Geraldine had seen him play and she wondered why, until Bopay joined in. He started with a few tentative notes, finding his way in between and around the chords, playing some repeating scales and then, after a pause for what Geraldine realised later was dramatic effect, he began to shred, up and down the fretboard. The sound and feel reminded her of David Gilmour with its fluency and smoothness, but then Bopay began to crunch out some fuzzy, distorted blues licks, transforming his sound onto the Jimmy Page side of the aisle. He ended with a massive two-note break, heavy on the wah, that reminded Geraldine of Gary Moore and Thin Lizzy. She took it all in and when they stopped to roll another joint, she decided she would join them. The hash hit Geraldine like a freight train. It scattered all her thoughts and made her look into the eyes of each person standing in the corridor outside the rehearsal room, searching for their reason for being here tonight. Harry saw her staring.

'Cool it, Gerald,' he said. 'The police aren't allowed in here, it's students only.'

'Are you a student here?' said Geraldine, tearing her eyes away from the glass wall.

'No,' said Harry.

That left Geraldine with too many questions. She began ordering and phrasing them in her mind, but decided it was too big a task for her to manage right now. Harry stepped over to her and put his hand on her shoulder.

'It's okay, Gerald,' he said. 'You're safe with me. Always.'

His words gave her a rush of lightness and she smiled back at her brother.

'Thank you,' she said, beaming at his face, haloed by the fluorescent behind him.

'Here,' said Harry, 'how about you try singing.' He handed her a microphone. 'Just follow me.'

Geraldine took the microphone and Harry and Bopay started playing again. Geraldine watched her sibling intently and, when he gave her a nod as Bopay's wailing died to a chunky, palm-dampened groove, she lifted the microphone to her mouth and started to sing whatever words and tune arrived in her head.

■□■

The next time Geraldine attended rehearsal with Harry, Bopay was already in the room again, skinning up a joint. A drum kit was set up at the far end of the room, and a few minutes later a man with a bass guitar came in and set up next to the drummer.

'Gerald, this is Adie,' Harry said, pointing to the drummer, 'And that's Marcus,' he said nodding in the bass player's direction.

'Where's Julia?' Harry asked no-one in particular.

'Don't sweat, she'll be here,' said Bopay, passing Harry the joint.

By the time they'd all shared it, Geraldine again passing, Julia had arrived. She was tall, wearing an afghan coat a little bit shorter than John Stookes', had sharp cheekbones and hair halfway down her back.

She looked around the room, introduced herself to Geraldine as the band's new singer, much to Geraldine's relief, and then turned to the assembled musicians and said, 'Alright, let's do this.'

They played through a passable version of Patti Smith's version of Them's 'Gloria'. The boys stopped and looked to Julia.

'Let's do it again,' she said.

By the time they'd finished for the night, they had it down, it was sounding good. While the musicians packed up their gear, Julia turned to Geraldine.

'What did you think?' she said. 'Did we do okay?'

'Yes,' said Geraldine.

'That's it?' said Julia. 'Nothing else?'

'You were great,' said Geraldine. 'By the time you finished, it was really tight.'

'Tight, eh?' said Julia. 'What do you mean by that?'

'It was good,' said Geraldine. 'Really good.'

Julia smiled at Geraldine.

'You're good, kid,' she said, 'I'm just giving you some. What are you doing here, anyway?'

'I'm with Harry,' said Geraldine.

'Yeah, I know that,' said Julia. 'But what're you here for?'

'I want to learn,' said Geraldine. 'I want to learn how to put on a show.' She'd never said those words to anyone else before.

'Ha!' said Julia, loud and theatrical enough that the males lifted their heads up from their gear. 'I told you we should be looking for management, and here it is.'

'That kid can't manage us,' said Marcus.

'Why not?' said Julia, giving him the evils, her shoulders back.

Marcus didn't reply and neither did any of the others.

'Here's the deal, Gerald,' said Julia, 'If you can book us a gig by next week, you can manage us.'

'Okay,' said Geraldine.

■□■

On the way home Harry was quiet. Geraldine worried that she might have done something wrong. Turns out he was just very high and having to concentrate hard to drive the van in a straight line anywhere near the speed limit. As they pulled up outside St Austell, Harry let out a whoop.

'You're going to manage us, our Gerald,' he said.

He stuck out his hand and shook Geraldine's very solemnly and then burst into raucous laughter.

'You're going to manage us, our kid! We might just get somewhere now. We sound alright, don't we? We've never played a gig, I don't think we even have a name.'

The words were tumbling out of Harry. He was as excited as Geraldine had even seen him. She smiled and let the words shower over her.

'I'll tell you what,' said Harry, 'let's go inside and celebrate.'

Once they'd ascertained that Frank and Grace were safely asleep, Harry rolled a joint, and they sat in front of the dead fire and smoked it.

'No need for any buckets of water tonight,' said Harry, giggling.

Geraldine sat back in silence, her mind turning over at a rapid rate, the hash helping her work through the permutations of what it might mean to be a band manager and how the hell she would get them a gig. Up in her room she lay in bed and listened to *In the City* on the highest volume she dared and achieved the most complete and colourful orgasm she'd ever experienced. She lay back depleted and replete and went to sleep knowing that she wanted more of this, more of everything. Her dreams had no boundaries, she flew over landscapes that teemed with every variety of life, flocks moving and merging into single entities and then deforming and reforming over and over again. Bob was nowhere to be seen.

37

Next day after school Geraldine walked with John up to the newsagents and invested forty p in a packet of twenty pieces of card, A4 sized, multi colours.

'Want to come over for a bit?' asked John.

'Can't. Busy,' said Geraldine, turning for home, leaving John standing outside the newsagents watching her go.

Geraldine unlocked the front door and without announcing her return home settled herself at the desk where she used to do her homework. She tore a page from one of her schoolbooks and, holding it in one hand, thumbed through the pages of the latest copy of *NME*. Each time she saw a likely looking image she placed the lined page from her exercise book over it and traced its outline with a felt-tipped pen. She did this five times, each time on a fresh page. Next she took out a piece of card from the cellophane packaging, rifling through the sheets until she was satisfied she had the right colour. She folded it in half on the horizontal, taking care to make a sharp line with all the edges meeting perfectly. Then she lay the card on her desk bookwise and looked at the space intently, her eyes going back and forth from the card to the five sheets of paper torn from her schoolbook. Geraldine then took each one of the lined sheets and cut around the outline of the images. When she had released them from the pages, Geraldine experimented with laying the outlines on the card until she was satisfied they were all in their right place. She stuck them down lightly with Blu Tack, hoping it wouldn't leave a mark on the card the same as it did on the wallpaper in her bedroom, and then traced around the outline of the combined images with the same black felt-tipped pen, taking care not to press too hard and ruin the tip right at the beginning of her work. Once she'd finished, Geraldine removed the paper and Blu Tack, concentrating so as not to damage the flimsy cut-outs or leave any marks, and held up the card to inspect her work.

Geraldine stopped for a while to consider how she would approach the rest of her task and more importantly to give some thought to a name for Harry's band. Her first thought was 'The Famous Five', but she dismissed it immediately. Geraldine considered this to be adult work. She then went through more names beginning with 'The', working her way through the alphabet, writing down the ones that sounded promising:

The Aardvarks

The Absent

The Abusers

The Ache

The Agenda

The Alarm

When she arrived at it, it sounded a bit dumb to Geraldine at first, but the more she turned it over in her mind, the more it made sense. It was one of those mildly abstract, ordinary-sounding names that could mean everything or nothing, or both at the same time. She decided it would do very nicely. Geraldine went to work with red, blue and black felt-tipped pens and wrote the band's name at the top of the card in tri-colour bubble letters. She held it up and had a look at her work.

THE DESK

Geraldine avoided an exclamation mark, not wanting to overload the name with too much drama. It sat nicely just above the silhouette of five band members, woman to the front, drummer to her right so you could see what he was doing, and twin guitars and bass arrayed in a line behind and to the left of the vocalist. Geraldine liked what she saw and opened the card up to start on the next page, which was when she saw that the markings on the front had seeped through. She put the card down, angry with herself for not checking earlier in the process. The next day after school she walked back to the newsagents with John and invested sixty p in a packet of thicker card. This time John didn't bother to ask if she wanted to come over. That night, Geraldine went through the whole process again, five times. She finished off her work by adding her name and phone number to every page of all five cards, something she had thought about but hesitated over for a few reasons, eventually deciding this was an important enough moment to throw caution to the wind.

FOR BOOKINGS CALL GERALDINE 416255

■□■

Geraldine decided not to show Harry her work just yet, but she did have some questions for him.

'Have you played in any pubs here before?' Geraldine asked Harry the next afternoon when she got home from school.

'Yeah, a few,' said Harry.

'Which ones?'

Harry reeled off some names, most of which Geraldine had heard of. Most of them were tourist bars along the seafront, well known to locals, but usually avoided in favour of more out-of-the-way places. Geraldine tucked the names away and then returned to her desk and spent the evening creating five more cards. When Saturday came around she felt ready, if a little bit nervous.

Geraldine's first stop, just after midday, was Exon's Records. Ken was busy behind his counter serving customers so she hung back among the shelves, thumbing through records with one hand while clutching her promotional brochures (that's what Geraldine had practised calling them to herself) in the other. When the shop only contained her, Ken and a biker type at the back of the shop going through the second-hand bins, Geraldine approached.

'Alright, young one?' said Ken.

'Yes,' said Geraldine, hesitating.

Ken looked across the counter at her, waiting. Shyly, Geraldine separated one of the brochures from the pack and put it on the counter.

'Can I put this on your noticeboard?'

Ken picked up the card and Geraldine began to feel self-conscious, like a child who's sat at the adult table for a moment too long. She watched him study it, squinting at the gatefold section where she'd written a biography for the Desk, making some claims about the band and its members that may or may not have been entirely true, and included a list of the songs they could play, again mostly true but some aspirational. On the back she'd written *Available for Exclusive Bookings Now in Weston-super-Mare.* Ken turned back to the front page and looked up at Geraldine.

'Geraldine?'

'Yes, that's my name,' Geraldine said, looking him straight in the eye.

'Okay,' said Ken.

'Okay?' asked Geraldine.

'Yes, okay. Go ahead and put it up.'

Ken handed her a drawing pin and she pinned it dead centre of the board, not minding at all that it covered over some of the other adverts.

'Any ideas on where else I should take it?' she asked.

Ken reeled off some names, most of them the same as the ones Harry had given her, with one exception.

'Oh, yeah,' said Ken, 'take one to the Three Queens. Tell Joe I sent you.'

■□■

Geraldine took her three remaining brochures to rehearsal with her the next Tuesday night. She settled into her corner while the band set up and played through some songs. When they stopped for a break, Julia stepped over to Geraldine, leaving the boys to their joints for a moment.

'So, how did we go, hotshot?' said Julia.

Geraldine looked at Julia and shook her head.

'Nothing?' said Julia.

'Not yet, but I've been working on it,' said Geraldine. 'Here.'

Geraldine held out one of her brochures. Julia took it and looked it over silently for a while.

'The Desk?' Julia said. 'I'm not sure I like that.'

Geraldine's heart sank.

'I dunno,' said Julia. 'Maybe. Maybe it could work?'

Julia laughed out loud when she read the band bio Geraldine had written, which caused Geraldine's heart to sink even further and palpitate all at the same time. It was a new and mighty uncomfortable feeling for her.

'You. You have a talent for this,' said Julia, smiling at Geraldine. 'I think you're worth another chance. Oh, and we need to talk later, Geraldine,' she said right before she turned back to the boys to carry the news, and Geraldine's brochure, to them.

The five bandmates talked quietly, passing a joint and the brochure from hand to hand. Julia sauntered back over to Geraldine, all of her motion in her hips.

'We're keeping you on,' said Julia, before turning back to the band and saying, 'Let's go, we have work to do.'

Geraldine sat quietly in the corner for the rest of the rehearsal, barely hearing the band, her mind a whirl of emotions and possibilities.

■□■

'Do I call you our Geraldine from now on then, our kid?' Harry asked as he was navigating them home.

'Yes, please,' said Geraldine, luxuriating in the thought.

'Alright, our kid,' said Harry. 'Will do.'

38

The call came on Thursday that week.

'Weston four one six two five five,' said Geraldine.

'Hello, is Geraldine there?'

'Speaking,' said Geraldine.

'Hello, Geraldine,' said the voice, 'it's Joe from the Queens.'

Geraldine held her breath.

'Is your band available this Saturday? I've had a cancellation.'

'Yes. Yes, they are,' said Geraldine, having no idea if they would all be free.

'Alright, good,' said Joe. 'It's three sets starting at eight-thirty. Fifty pounds for the night and all the beer they can drink.'

'Great,' said Geraldine.

'Tell them to be there by six to set up.'

Geraldine held the phone to her ear until the insistent beeps of the broken connection brought her back to the world. When she put it back on the cradle, she couldn't contain herself.

'Harry. HARRY!'

Harry scurried out of the lounge room where a few minutes before he, Geraldine and Grace had been watching telly after dinner. Loud noises and unexpected visits did seem to have a way of quickening his pace.

'What's up, our kid?' said Harry, looking from her to the front door and back again, worry lining his face.

'It's okay,' said Geraldine. 'I've just had a call.'

'A call? For you?' said Harry.

'Yes, for me,' said Geraldine, giving him the tone that said she got phone calls all the time, even though they both knew she didn't.

'So?'

'What?'

'Who was it?'

'Oh, yeah,' said Geraldine. 'The Desk is booked to play the Queens. This Saturday.'

'What?' said Harry. 'Saturday? That's Racey's night. They've played Saturdays there for ages.'

'Joe said they'd had a cancellation.'

'I'm going to the pub,' said Harry. 'See you when I get back.'

Geraldine went back into the lounge and sat in the chair next to Grace's.

'Everything alright, luv?' said Grace.

'Oh, yes,' said Geraldine.

■□■

Joe took Geraldine aside when the Desk had finished their last set.

'Here's your money,' said Joe. 'Tell them they can come back next Saturday, but they need to learn some more songs.'

The band had played the same eight songs in each of their three brackets, in a different order each time. The punters didn't seem to mind, but Joe seemed unhappy. Over time, Geraldine learned that this was his perpetual state, but it was early days in their relationship just now.

'And you,' Joe said, looking Geraldine over, 'how old are you? Tell me you're sixteen. I can't have kids in my pub on a Saturday, even if you're not drinking.'

'I'm sixteen,' she said, holding Joe's eye.

Right then the bell for last orders rang and Joe returned to his place behind the bar to deal with the final mad rush of the night. Julia came over to find out what Joe had been talking to Geraldine about. She nodded when Geraldine told her they'd been booked again for next Saturday, but needed to learn more songs.

'What about the money?' Julia asked.

Geraldine held out her hand containing five crumpled ten-pound notes. It was more money than she'd seen in one place in her life, not counting the time Grace smuggled the family's life savings back from Zambia and that didn't count because Geraldine had never actually seen the paper.

'Good girl,' said Julia. 'Now, we need to talk about your cut.'

'My cut?'

'Yes. As manager you get a percentage of everything we earn.'

Geraldine hadn't thought about this. She was doing it because she burned inside at the thought of being involved in something that could move people like live music moved her. She'd never considered money.

'I'll tell you what,' said Julia. 'Tell Joe that it's sixty from next week and that way you can keep a tenner for yourself. Try it, see what happens.'

Geraldine waited for the crowd at the bar to dissipate and walked over to Joe, full of hubris at this new development.

'We're on for next Saturday,' she said, 'but it'll be sixty quid. A bit extra for the new songs.'

Geraldine had never said the word 'quid' before in her life and it felt lumpy and misshapen in her mouth. Joe looked at her across the bar.

'Jesus! Alright, then,' he said. 'It's a good job you're only sixteen.'

Geraldine turned and walked away from the bar. She resolved never again to say the word quid.

■□■

With a residency at the Queens locked away, Geraldine updated the Desk's promotional brochures and took them back out to venues along the seafront. It wasn't long before the band was playing Thursdays and Fridays as well as Saturdays, and Geraldine was putting thirty pounds a week in her pocket. Once word got around, the phone at St Austell started ringing a lot more, the callers almost always wanting to talk to Geraldine. She kept a notepad by the phone, taking names and numbers, making dates for bookings and to go and see bands that were interested in her booking them. Most of them were rubbish. Geraldine also learned that she needed to like the people she worked with. She discovered that looking after a band, even as a part-time endeavour, is a very personal service. First up, Geraldine wouldn't take on anyone who couldn't reconcile her name with the person when they first met. They either got it or she wasn't bothered. Next, she'd size them up, see if any of them felt like they might have it, whatever the fuck it was. The third and final test was always the most interesting one for Geraldine and set a bar that later in life she almost regretted.

'Who's your favourite band?' Geraldine would ask.

Any responses that weren't on Geraldine's list meant instant dismissal.

If you said 'the Clash', you were in, if you said 'the Police', you were out. Conversely, if you said 'Curved Air', you were in, if you said 'Genesis' you were out. Go figure! Geraldine learned early on that rock-and-roll was a fickle business.

■□■

Not long after the Desk's Queens residency started up, Geraldine and Julia had That Talk.

'Who are you, Geraldine?' Julia asked, once they were seated in the airy room that was her ground floor bedsit.

'What do you mean?' Geraldine said, avoiding for a moment longer the conversation they'd both known for weeks they were going to have.

'C'mon, luv, you know what I mean,' said Julia.

The two of them, girl and woman, spoke for hours. Geraldine spilled everything, completely matter-of-fact because this was simply her life.

'Jeez, that's heavy,' said Julia, when Geraldine paused for a while, seeming to have come to the end of her narrative.

'Why?' said Geraldine.

'Well,' said Julia, pausing to gather her thoughts, 'I don't really know, actually. But it's not normal, is it?'

'What do you mean, "normal"?' said Geraldine.

'It's not very common,' said Julia. 'There aren't many people like you.'

'There's no-one like me,' said Geraldine.

Julia smiled, nodding her head. They sat in silence for a while as Julia rolled and lit a cigarette.

'Do you want one?' Julia asked.

'No, thank you,' said Geraldine.

'Have you been to see a doctor?' said Julia.

'What for?' said Geraldine.

'They might be able to help.'

Geraldine thought back to the BBC2 documentary, the one that had held her so transfixed, but that had ended so brutally.

'I saw a program on telly once about someone who had a sex change,' Geraldine said.

'Is that what you want?' Julia said.

'I don't know,' said Geraldine.

The idea that she couldn't just keep being herself without some sort of, something, she didn't know quite what – approval, intervention? That idea saddened Geraldine.

39

Come August, Geraldine had a problem. She hadn't considered the impact of autumn on Weston-super-Mare until the phone at St Austell stopped ringing as the bars and pubs on the seafront began to shut down for the winter. She still had the Desk at the Queens. The rumours were that Racey were in London having been signed by Mickie Most, and the Desk were a handy replacement. Since that first Saturday, they'd learned a whole bunch of new songs and they were tight as. It also didn't hurt that they had Julia out front. She copped a lot of shit from drunken blokes, especially as the nights wore on, but she was usually able to bring the oiks onside with a word or a look and, if someone overstepped the line she wasn't averse to coming off the stage and mixing it with them. She'd stood toe to toe with one bloke and invited him outside, an offer he declined before shutting up for the rest of the night. She'd poured countless pints over countless heads, most of them round and bald. Once, Julia kneed a very persistent and hands-on type square in the balls, a painful humiliation from which he failed to recover in any sort of a hurry. While she took her excursions, the band would improvise at whatever point of a song they happened to be, which is how the Desk became known for their extended wig-outs and the possibility of some choice crowd interaction. It was a combination that drew in punters from miles around.

Geraldine figured that, even in winter, there would be locals wanting to get in among some live music and, if the usual venues were locked up against the coming cold weather, she determined to find some new ones. She also figured that there'd be kids at school who'd go to see her bands if they had the opportunity. The best on offer was the occasional disco at the youth club and Blades, a nightclub on the Regent Street strip that opened on a Saturday afternoon once a month so underage punters could come to listen to the DJ and dance under the lights. Geraldine felt like she could do better, she just had to find a venue. Having walked the streets of Weston, Geraldine settled on the 3rd Weston-super-Mare Scout Group hall. She called and made a booking for the third Friday of autumn term and started preparing.

Geraldine had also been to the public library, a lonely-looking, red-brick building on the far side of town, her visit prompted by her heart-to-heart with Julia. So far in her life the only doctors Geraldine had seen were the doctors at the hospital in Beverley, who she only faintly remembered; the Havenhouse doctor who'd stuck his finger into her pelvic cavity while cupping her and telling her to turn her head and cough; the various doctors who delivered her six-monthly cholera vaccinations while the Sturmers were living in Zambia; and, here in Weston, the take-your-pick from the local NHS doctors clinic, the last time being when she'd had her ears syringed. Geraldine felt it unlikely that any of them could, as Julia had put it, help her. So, as she had done most of her life, she turned to books and reading for a solution. Building on what she had learned in biology at school, Geraldine wanted to find out more about the biology and chemistry of puberty and beyond. Now fifteen, Geraldine had discovered her orgasm, but so far was relatively undisturbed by any outward effects of her rising hormones and, instinctively, she knew it would be better for her to keep it that way. She had a shy desire to grow breasts. Geraldine was confused about this urge, as she had no consistent language to articulate what she knew, just the messaging from her body.

After an afternoon spent at one of the reading desks in the library, Geraldine set out for home, frowning and uncertain. When she arrived at St Austell, unlocked the door and let herself in, she took the first right into the lounge room instead of heading straight upstairs as she usually would. Grace was watching telly, Harry was nowhere to be seen.

'Alright, our Gerald?' said Grace.

'Yes,' said Geraldine as she settled into a seat.

She leaned forward to take off her shoes and tucked her legs up under her. Grace and Geraldine sat in silence while *Westward Diary* ran through the notable events of the day. Geraldine paid little attention, she was too busy thinking through the conversation she wanted to have with Grace. She was about to speak when the presenter moved to entertainment news.

'It's been confirmed that Weston-super-Mare group Racey have signed to Rak Records and are in London working on their first single,' the woman said, reading from the autocue.

'I guess we'll be seeing them on *Top of the Pops* soon?' ad-libbed her male companion.

The inset image was of the band wearing what looked to Geraldine like teddy-boy suits. She squinted at the TV to try to get a better look, but the presenters had moved on to the local weather before she could confirm.

'Huh!' said Geraldine, taking in the news.

'Yer what, luv?' said Grace.

'Oh, nothing,' said Geraldine, 'just the telly.'

Geraldine sat back in her chair. Now she'd have to wait a bit longer before she could start talking to Grace. Geraldine waited until the news proper was on, sat through the headlines and took her chance during the first advert break.

'Fresh cream cakes, naughty but nice,' said the television.

'Mum?' said Geraldine.

'Yes, luv?' said Grace, her eyes still on the telly.

'Mum,' said Geraldine, waiting for Grace to turn to look at her.

'Yes, luv?' said Grace, mild concern on her face.

Grace took a cigarette out of her packet and lit it, inhaling and then blowing smoke away from Geraldine.

'What is it, luv?' said Grace.

'I think I need to see the doctor,' said Geraldine.

'What for?' said Grace. 'Are you alright?' she asked, frowning.

'I'm alright, Mum, I just need to ask some questions,' said Geraldine.

Geraldine hoped this approach would curtail the conversation, but it didn't.

'What sort of questions, luv?' said Grace. 'Yer know you can talk to me, don't you?'

'I do, Mum,' lied Geraldine, 'but I think I need to ask the doctor.'

'Alright then, Gerald, I'll call them tomorrow and make an appointment for you.'

'Thank you,' said Geraldine.

They both turned back to the TV and Geraldine stayed with Grace for what she judged was long enough before getting up and going to her room.

'I'll call you when dinner's ready,' said Grace, as Geraldine closed the sliding door.

▪▫▪

The next afternoon Geraldine and Grace sat in the waiting room at the doctors' surgery, Geraldine, at Grace's insistence, in her school uniform and Grace in her Sunday best. The Sturmers had never attended church as a family, but the dress Grace had on that afternoon was exactly what she would have worn if they did. They waited almost an hour while a weary-looking man released one patient from his consulting room, walked over to the desk where his receptionist handed him a folder and then called out the name of his next patient. Geraldine looked at him, trying to remember if she'd been to see him before. She didn't think so. The longer the wait went on, the more anxious and fidgety Geraldine became. By the time she heard her name being called, she flinched at every syllable. Geraldine sat still for a while as the whole waiting room hesitated, those still in line hoping for a no-show, the doctor looking increasingly annoyed at the prospect.

'C'mon on, Gerald,' said Grace, giving her a gentle elbow. 'It's your turn.'

Geraldine stood up and followed Grace towards the doctor's room. He closed the door behind them and invited them to take a seat.

'What seems to be the problem, Gerald?' the doctor said while reading through Geraldine's almost non-existent notes.

There was a pause and after it had gone on for too long, the doctor lifted his head and turned to Geraldine.

'I don't have all day, young man. What are you here for?'

Geraldine blushed and her anxiety nearly got the better of her, but she'd rehearsed this moment, so she stuck with her plan.

'I've known since I was four that I'm different to my body. I've been trying to work out what to do, doing some reading in the library. I'm female and I want help ...'

Geraldine tailed off while the doctor and Grace held their breaths to see if there was any more. Once he'd finished waiting, the doctor paused and made Geraldine wait some more, then began to speak.

'Young man,' he said, 'I have a waiting room full of sick people who need my help. I don't know what you've been reading, but I don't appreciate you coming here and wasting my time and upsetting your mother like this.'

Geraldine looked at Grace. She didn't look at all upset. Her face was a mixture of confusion and the beginnings of holding back laughter, a bit like when Geraldine had said she wanted to be a donkey for her fourth birthday.

'Now, unless there is something else you want to talk to me about,' the doctor continued, 'you should go and let me get on with seeing people who need me.'

He stood up and opened the door of his room, stepping towards the reception desk without looking back to see if Grace and Geraldine were following. They left the consulting room and took a left towards the surgery's exit, Geraldine doing her best to keep out of the doctor's eyeline. The pair walked in silence for a while, Grace smoking a cigarette. When she'd finished, thrown the stub on the path in front of her and extinguished it with a twist of her right foot, a move she was so practised at she barely had to break step, Grace spoke.

'What was that our Gerald? What did you think you were doing?'

'Nothing,' said Geraldine, keeping her eyes on the path.

'Did you think it would be a joke or something?'

'No,' said Geraldine.

'Well, why did you do it?' said Grace.

Geraldine didn't reply. She was silently sobbing, her mouth open, eyes almost closed, saliva beginning to run down the side of her chin. When Grace saw her, she clucked and held out her arm to Geraldine. Geraldine dipped her shoulder away from Grace and kept walking.

'Have it your way,' said Grace, and lit another cigarette.

As soon as they got in the front door, Geraldine went up to her room and lay on the bed in silence. Until recently she'd happily revelled in her growing understanding of herself, not thinking for a moment that the world may not understand. It didn't matter to Geraldine if they did or not, but she'd never anticipated the sort of matter-of-fact rejection she'd just experienced.

40

Geraldine returned to school wearing new eight-hole oxblood Dr Martens boots, a new pair of camel-coloured straight-leg cords, a new slim-fit white shirt with a button-down collar, untucked, her trusty jacket now with its right lapel covered in button badges, a light covering of foundation and mascara. John looked her up and down when they met at the railway bridge but said nothing. Inside the school gate, heads raised like so many meerkats until, walking through the schoolyard with her schoolbag over one shoulder and John at her side, if now a half step behind her, Geraldine again came to the attention of Patrick Burges. He was shorter than Geraldine and most of the other kids at Westland Comprehensive, but he carried himself with an air that a certain type of English thug had perfected in the late seventies. He constantly boasted to anyone who'd listen about going to the Bristol Rovers to get into fights with the away team's fans, although Geraldine had never once seen him on the telly when *Westward Diary* reported on the antics of local football hooligans and she felt sure that his spiky blue hair, pale skin and mad eyes would make him easy to pick out from a crowd. Nevertheless, here he was approaching her across the tarmac playground, kids parting in front of him so as not to impede his progress.

Burges came to a stop in front of Geraldine, blocking her way. He looked her closely up and down.

'What are you now, Sturmer? A fucking poofter?'

'No,' said Geraldine, holding his stare, trying not to blink too much in case he noticed the curl she'd put in her lashes that morning.

They stood frozen for a good while. Geraldine didn't notice the kids forming a circle around them. By the time Burges made his move, it was three deep. He grabbed her by her lapels and swung her, legs in the air, to the ground where she landed with an *oooof*. Geraldine lay there for a moment, dizzy and disoriented, but feeling no pain. From her sideways perspective on the lumpy bitumen of the playground she could see Burges' Docs doing their work and for a second Geraldine smiled to herself because hers were so much newer and better looking than his. He wouldn't have seen it, but Burges wiped the smile from Geraldine's face by finding his way between her raised knees and clenched elbows, catching her right in the sweet spot where the chest and stomach meet. There was blackness behind Geraldine's eyes for a moment and she remembered what it felt like to die. It wasn't unpleasant, it allowed her to release herself from her protective ball, let the ache in her arms, legs and neck dissipate as she found a way to exist on the absence of air, while striations of the brightest reds and yellows chased the black from her eyes just in time for her to see Burges take one last shot, his face red with fury, his lips curled back, teeth bared like a scrapyard dog.

The last kick caught Geraldine on her left temple.

■□■

Geraldine spent the night in hospital, under observation with concussion, three cracked ribs on her left side, multiple grazes and bruises that bloomed on almost every part of her. Harry and Grace sat at the side of her bed until visiting hours were over.

'What did he do this for?' asked Grace.

Geraldine shook her head and refused eye contact.

'I'll send some people to your school to sort him out, if you like, our kid,' said Harry.

'Don't make me laugh,' said Geraldine, even her crinkling eyes causing her pain. 'Who you going to send, Bopay?'

Harry chuckled for a moment and then returned to his anger.

'I know people,' he said. 'Proper bikers. I'll get him sorted. If you want.'

Geraldine shook her head and held out her hand to Harry.

'It'll be alright,' she said, as they held on to each other.

■□■

Sitting up in bed at home the next afternoon reading *NME*, Geraldine heard a knock at the front door. She couldn't hear what the voices were saying, but after a few moments, she heard someone coming up the stairs. John put his head around her bedroom door.

'Is it okay if we come in?' said John.

'Yes, come in,' said Geraldine, paying no attention to what he might mean by 'we'.

In came John, and behind him a girl with burgundy hair.

'Hi, it's Sasha,' she said.

'Hi,' said Geraldine, wondering what was going on. 'Yeah, I remember.'

'Sasha asked if she could come over and see if you're okay,' said John.

'Oh. Oh,' said Geraldine. 'Yes, erm, yes, come in.'

Geraldine was wearing pyjamas. She began looking for a hole to climb into.

Sasha was wearing a black taffeta skirt and thick black eyeliner. As far as Geraldine was concerned, she was by far the most attractive girl in school.

'I wanted to see if you're okay,' confirmed Sasha.

'Yes, yes, I'm fine,' said Geraldine, wincing as she tried to sit up straighter. 'I will be.'

Sasha took a seat on Geraldine's bed and smiled at her.

'That's good, I'm glad you're going to be okay,' said Sasha. 'Maybe I can come back tomorrow and see how you're going?'

'Yes, okay,' said Geraldine.

'Alright,' said Sasha, 'see you then,' and she and John slipped out of Geraldine's bedroom, down the stairs and away.

Geraldine knew she wouldn't be back.

■□■

Sasha did come back. The next day, and the next. That Saturday, when Geraldine was recovered enough to take her first steps outside, Sasha was downstairs waiting for her. They headed up Clevedon Road towards the seafront and, once they were past John's house, Sasha slipped her hand into Geraldine's and they walked the mile or so to the prom in silence, Geraldine not wanting to break the spell with her chatter and Sasha, who knows what Sasha was thinking but Geraldine liked this, she liked it a lot. When they got to the prom the wind was blowing a gale. It punched through their clothing and by the time they'd crossed the roads heading west and east and the wide grassy strip that divided them, the pair were freezing, lips blue and teeth chattering. They found a bus shelter and sat as deep into its walled bench as they could, keeping off the worst of the wind coming straight up the Severn estuary. The tide was, as always, out.

'It's nice to see you, Geraldine,' said Sasha.

'It's nice to see you, too,' said Geraldine.

Sasha leaned in and they kissed. Geraldine closed her eyes and put her arms around Sasha's waist. When they finished they sat, arms around each other, Geraldine's head leaning on Sasha's shoulder. Again, Geraldine curbed her chatter, although there were so many things she wanted to say and some she felt she needed to say. She was afraid to put a foot out of place in case Sasha disappeared from her life as abruptly and unexpectedly as she'd come into it.

'Will you be coming back to school?' Sasha asked, eventually.

'Yeah,' said Geraldine. 'Next week. I've still got to give out the flyers for the show.'

'I've been talking to my friends, getting them to spread the word,' said Sasha. 'Loads of people have said they're going to come. But, do you think it'll be okay?'

'What do you mean?' said Geraldine, not following Sasha's switch of gears.

'You. At school,' said Sasha. 'Will you be okay?'

'I think so,' said Geraldine. 'I don't think he'll do that again.' Geraldine had a flash from the kicking. 'I don't think his Docs would be up to it,' she said.

They grinned at each other and Sasha leaned in for another kiss. This time Geraldine made sure to keep her teeth out of the way.

■□■

Geraldine's first all-ages show was a success. By the time the night was over and Julia had thanked the audience for coming out to see the Desk and, 'Oh yeah, those other two bands, whoever they were,' they'd had 187 people, most of them kids, through the door at 75 p each. Geraldine said to Sasha it must be something about being part of the in-crowd now as she was reckoning up at the end of the night, and Sasha punched her for being so stupid.

'Geraldine, you're the fucking in-crowd now,' said Sasha. 'Be careful what you do with it.'

The last two weeks at school Geraldine had stuck close to Sasha's side, but she needn't have worried. Patrick Burges was nowhere to be seen during her first week back, and Geraldine had a stream of kids straggling up to her during morning breaks and lunchtimes saying hi. Not much more, just acknowledging they were glad Geraldine was okay. When Burges did return, he gave Geraldine a look the first time he saw her and Geraldine's heart started to run like it was intent on breaking the hundred-metre world record. But that was it. If Geraldine saw him in the schoolyard he was always surrounded by his football terrace mates. Geraldine sometimes wondered when she saw them if they were talking about her, but then she told herself to get a grip – how could she possibly be more interesting to watch than men in shorts running around after a ball? – and she'd have a little chuckle to herself.

41

'My sister's on the pill, you know,' said Sasha one Saturday afternoon as they were walking to the Queens.

'What?' said Geraldine.

The two were arm in arm, but Geraldine was busy wondering what Joe wanted to see her for.

'My sister, Jacklin, she's on the pill,' said Sasha.

'Oh, okay,' said Geraldine.

'Do you want to try it?' said Sasha. 'I can pinch them for you, she can just get some more.'

'You'd do that for me?' said Geraldine.

'Well, yeah, of course,' said Sasha. 'Besides, it's not like it'd be a big thing or anything, she's always losing stuff.'

'I don't know if it would work,' said Geraldine. 'I've been doing a bit more reading and I don't know if it would be strong enough.'

'What are you going to do, then?' said Sasha.

'I've got an idea,' said Geraldine. 'I dunno, it might work, but I'm not sure.'

'What is it?'

'Let me talk to Joe first and I'll tell you all about it,' said Geraldine.

■□■

Joe wanted to talk about New Year's at the Queens.

'But it's only September,' said Geraldine.

'You know, for a smart kid you're a bit stupid sometimes,' said Joe. 'New Year's is our biggest night of the year and I want the Desk and another band to start early before them, get people in and keep them drinking. You can never lock in your New Year's bookings too early. Remember that, kid.'

'Um, yeah, okay, I'll sort it, Joe,' said Geraldine, her blush showing through her foundation.

'Alright, see you do,' said Joe. 'It'll be a big night and a big payday, so don't let me down.'

'I won't,' said Geraldine. 'Cheers, Joe.'

'Cheers' was another word Geraldine determined never to say again.

▪▫▪

'Tell me your plan,' said Sasha as they started the reverse journey, arm in arm again.

'I don't know if it's much of a plan,' said Geraldine, 'but it might work. There's this friend of Harry and Julia's ...'

'Are they a couple now?' said Sasha.

'No. No? I don't think so?' said Geraldine, 'I don't know. They just have this friend, they buy stuff off him sometimes.'

'What stuff?'

'Erm, stuff, drugs, speed, pills,' said Geraldine.

'Oh, stuff, right,' said Sasha.

'I was thinking about asking him.'

'Asking him what?' said Sasha.

'If he can get some for me.'

'Get some what for you?'

'Estrogen.'

'This friend of Harry and Julia's, where would he get estrogen from?'

'Where do you think he gets the pills from?'

'I don't know,' said Sasha, 'but they're not estrogen, are they? No-one gets high on that.'

'Yes, I know that,' said Geraldine, 'but he must get them from chemists somehow. Or someone does.'

'So?' said Sasha.

'So, I've been thinking maybe whoever does it could look out for some estrogen for me. I've got money.'

'Fuck! Really?' said Sasha.

'Yes, really,' said Geraldine.

'Who're you going to ask, then? Harry or Julia?'

'I think I'd be safer asking Julia about this one,' said Geraldine.

Geraldine arrived at Julia's at the appointed time and they sat down with a pot of tea and caught up with the latest gossip and news on the inner workings of the Desk while they waited. The windows of Julia's flat were closed against the cold and the dark, the net curtains hanging dead still. When her dealer, Marty, finally arrived a tick over three hours later they were sat in front of the ten o'clock news, their conversation long since exhausted. Marty's head was too big for his scrawny shoulders, even under the black leather biker jacket he always wore. His skin was white and almost translucent, and Geraldine thought she could just about see the bones of his skull. She could hardly look away from the pulse at his temple. Geraldine was nervous. She realised that, as an occasional dope smoker, she was now doing some serious levelling up in the world of illicit drugs. She'd weighed up her decision over and over since first talking to Julia, and every time the answer was the same. Yes, what she was doing was technically wrong, but she'd tried doing things the right way and she believed firmly that her need outweighed the wrongness of any illicit activity she might engage in.

Geraldine sat and watched while Julia and Marty engaged in the ritual of buying and selling drugs. First there was the small talk, the how are yous, what've you been up to's, hope life's treating you well's. Then there was the offer and refusal of a drink, Marty still standing, Julia seated where she'd been most of the evening. There was no mention of Marty's lateness, it was always understood that in this market the buyer had to wait and the seller would arrive when they were ready, if at all. There was a moment's silence before Marty led the next part of the conversation.

'Do you have the money?' he said.

Julia took some notes from her purse and held them out for Marty, folded and mostly hidden in her hand.

'Thank you,' said Marty, as he took the notes and flicked through them with the practised ease of a card sharp, putting them in his front pocket once he was satisfied the amount was correct.

Marty then put a hand down the front of his jeans and pulled out a sizeable bag of off-white crystalline powder. He looked around Julia's bedsit, searching for a place to continue his work. He decided on the kitchen table, and Julia went over to sit with him while Geraldine stayed in front of the news, her anxiety sitting high in her chest. It didn't stop Geraldine turning to watch with curiosity the next stage of the ritual, though. Marty picked up a magazine from Julia's table.

'Is this okay?' he asked.

'Sure,' said Julia.

Marty felt the thickness of the magazine's cover and, once he was satisfied, he folded the glossy paper and then neatly tore off a square from its bottom quarter. He then folded the square in half diagonally and, taking the long edge of the triangle he'd created, folded it towards the point, leaving about one third at the top so it looked like a flattened paper boat. Marty finished his work by folding what were a moment ago the three points of a triangle in towards each other, making sure they would interlock before scoring the folds with his thumbnail. Satisfied, Marty reversed the process so that he was left with a flat square of paper in front of him.

'I don't need to weigh it, do I?' Marty asked Julia.

'No, that's okay,' said Julia.

Marty nodded and took out his wallet from the back pocket of his jeans, opened it and lifted a flap inside. He pulled out a Stanley knife blade and wiped it on the bottom of his t-shirt before laying it on the paper he'd just prepared. He then gingerly unknotted the bag that he'd pulled from his crotch, oh so gently as if it might explode. Once it was untied, he rolled back the top of the bag so it sat on Julia's kitchen table with its mouth open like a baby bird and used his blade to scoop out an amount of the powder which he transferred to the square of magazine paper. Marty did this twice and then looked at the small pile of powder and across to Julia. Neither said anything while Marty dipped back into his bag for one more speck of speed, which he deposited on top of the small mound he'd just created. He smoothed the mound into a flat rectangle with the edge of the blade so that it took up the space at the centre of the packet. Marty then wiped his blade clean with the finger and thumb of his left hand, making a show of licking them before putting the metal trapezium back in his wallet and replacing it in his back pocket. He refolded the package, carefully tucking in the edges, and handed it to Julia. She took it from him and held it hidden in the palm of her hand. The two of them sat in silence at the kitchen table. Geraldine wondered if now would be the right time to ask, but the ritual wasn't quite over yet.

'Do you want a line?' said Julia.

'I think I've got time,' said Marty.

Julia unfolded the packet Marty had given her a lengthy minute ago and left it sitting open on the table while she went over to the middle of her three kitchen drawers and, reaching into the back, returned to the table with a small mirror and her own Stanley blade. She scooped up a smidge of the powder from the packet with her blade, tapped it gently onto the mirror and chopped it up, working through the crystals until she was left with a rough circle of fresh white powder which she then separated into two halves, drawing each one into a line with the sharp corner of the dull steel. Marty had already rolled up one of the pound notes Julia had given him earlier and, when preparations were complete, he handed it to her and watched her lean over the mirror, the banknote held in her right nostril, her left hand holding back her hair, and noisily inhale a line of the powder. Julia raised her head and handed the note to Marty who snorted the remaining line of speed. Julia wiped the mirror with her thumb, licking it clean before putting mirror, blade and her newly acquired packet of speed away in the back recess of her middle kitchen drawer. Transaction over, Marty stood up.

'Right, I've got to go,' said Marty. 'I've got someone else waiting for me.'

'Wait,' said Julia. 'What about Geraldine?'

Marty looked over at Geraldine. He'd clearly forgotten she was there.

'Oh, yeah, that's right,' he said, 'I haven't been able to get what you need yet.'

'Oh,' said Geraldine. 'That's alright.'

'Will you be at the Queens on Saturday?' said Marty.

'Yes,' said Geraldine.

'I'll meet you there,' said Marty, and with that he was gone.

'I'm sorry, love,' said Julia, registering the disappointment on Geraldine's face.

'It's okay,' said Geraldine, getting up to leave.

'Can you put this in next door's bin on your way out?' said Julia, holding out the magazine with the mutilated cover.

Geraldine took it from her, and left.

42

Joe had just rung last orders when Marty arrived at the Queens on Saturday night, long after Geraldine had given up any faint hope she had brought with her. He wandered through the open door of the pub and looked around, spotting Geraldine almost instantly. He was carrying a small canvas satchel over his right shoulder, and as he sat down next to Geraldine he slipped it over his arm and let it come to rest on the curved bench seat between them. Marty patted the satchel.

'I think this is what you want,' he said.

'Okay,' said Geraldine, unsure whether she should thank him or say anything else.

'That'll be twenty quid,' Marty said. 'I don't think I know anyone else who'll be wanting it.'

Geraldine wanted to look inside Marty's bag but something told her she shouldn't. Instead she fished out four five-pound notes from her purse, taking them out inside her handbag so no-one could see what she was doing and folding them over so she could hand them to Marty palm to palm, just like she'd seen Julia do. Marty's hand was cold and dry, exactly the opposite of how Geraldine had imagined it might feel.

'Do you have something to put them in?' Marty asked her.

'No,' said Geraldine, totally unprepared.

'Keep this one,' said Marty, putting his hand back on the satchel. 'Give it back to me next time you see me.'

Geraldine smiled, and this time she thanked him. Marty smiled back, dropping the super aloof act for a moment.

'Good luck,' he said as he got up to leave, having a brief chat with Harry and Julia on his way out.

'What was that about?' said Harry when Marty had left.

'Nothing,' said Geraldine.

'Didn't look like nothing to me,' said Harry, eyeing the satchel still sitting next to Geraldine.

'No, it's nothing,' said Geraldine. 'It's okay.'

'Okay, then,' said Harry. 'I trust you, our kid. Just be careful, alright.'

'I am,' said Geraldine.

▪▫▪

When they made it home, instead of taking a right with Harry into the lounge room to finish off their night with a joint, Geraldine went straight upstairs to her room. Finally, she got to open Marty's satchel. Inside were nine blue-and-white boxes, each with the label *Estrace, 4mg, Prescription Only*. Geraldine counted the boxes again. Nine. Nine months supply of estrogen. Her heart was racing with simultaneous fear and joy. Geraldine took a deep breath and contemplated her options. She sat for a minute or two to calm her beating heart and decided to go downstairs and tell Harry. As she walked by the phone in the hallway, she wished she could ring Sasha and tell her the news, but it was way too late, Harry would have to do.

'You're back, our kid,' said Harry, holding out his joint for her as she came into the lounge room and sat next to him.

'Yeah,' said Geraldine, smiling as she exhaled, feeling the almost instant intensity of the high.

Geraldine told Harry what she'd been up to, how she'd been to the doctor, tried to do things the right way and then decided to resort to calling on Marty's services. The whole episode rushed from her, and Harry sat and listened in silence while he rolled another joint.

'I'm made up for you, our kid,' Harry said when Geraldine had run out of words. 'I was worried when I saw you with Marty tonight, especially with that bag. We don't need another dealer in the family.'

'What?' said Geraldine with surprise loud enough that Harry shushed her in case she woke Grace.

'Why do you think I used to ask you to carry my bags when we went back to school?' said Harry.

'You fucker!' said Geraldine beginning to laugh. 'You absolute fucker! You owe me!'

'You do alright, our kid,' said Harry.

'Yeah, I do,' said Geraldine, smiling again.

''Ere,' said Harry, 'chuck some water on the fire, will you?'

They dissolved into fits of giggles.

43

Frank returned to Weston-super-Mare at the end of November. After he'd been home for a few weeks the noise started again at St Austell, mostly after closing time. Geraldine would lie in her bed and listen, no longer afraid of what might happen with Frank and Grace, her attention divided between their histrionics and the laconic tones of John Peel on the radio she took to bed with her each weeknight. Peel's transmissions were more constant than Frank and Grace's and certainly made more sense. He brought new music to Geraldine, gave life to the words she'd read in *NME* and *Melody Maker*, and confirmed for her that the world she belonged to was anywhere but inside the walls of St Austell and the confines of whatever life Frank and Grace imagined she should be living. Emboldened by her recent successes, Geraldine began to branch out.

Next time Geraldine fetched up at John Stookes', she enquired casually if he'd like to smoke a joint.

'What?' said John, sitting up on his bed where he'd been, just a moment before, lying back listening to Deep Purple.

'I've got some hash,' said Geraldine. 'Do you want some?'

'Yeah, okay?' said John, not sounding too certain.

Geraldine rolled a joint, under the round-eyed gaze of her school friend.

'When did you learn how to do that?' said John.

'I don't know,' said Geraldine. 'A while ago.'

She lit the joint and got it going, then passed it over to John. He looked at Geraldine, her outstretched arm and the fat white joint between her index finger and thumb.

'Do you want it, or not?' said Geraldine, stretching her arm as far as it would reach.

John took it from her and took a tentative puff, inhaling and quickly exhaling. He waited for a moment and then repeated the action, handing the joint straight back to Geraldine on his second inhale. Geraldine kept smoking while John lay back on the bed. A minute or so later he sat upright so abruptly that Geraldine thought there was something wrong with him. His face was flushed and his eyes were closed.

'Give me some more of that!' said John, opening his eyes and reaching out his hand.

Geraldine passed the joint to him, laughing at his eagerness, quietly satisfied that she'd turned her friend on. John replaced *Made in Japan* with Hawkwind's *Warrior on the Edge of Time*. They listened in silence, not talking even when John sat up to turn the disc over to side two and the backward mastered beginning of 'Magnu'. This time it was Geraldine's turn to spring into life.

'Oh. Oh!' she said.

'What? What is it?' said John. 'Is my mum home?'

'What? I don't know,' said Geraldine. '"Is my mum home?"' she mimicked, falling on her side, laughing. When Geraldine sat up again, John was looking hurt. Geraldine decided not to make any more of it.

'No, no,' she said, 'Hawkwind are playing in London later this month. We should go.'

'We should?' said John.

'Well, I'm going to, anyway,' said Geraldine, not knowing if she'd be able to get tickets, how she'd get there or who she'd go with but, now she'd put it out there, she was determined to make it happen. 'Have you got this week's *NME*?'

John handed his copy to Geraldine, and she flicked through to the back pages and there it was, Hawkwind at the Lyceum Ballroom, tickets from the usual outlets.

'I wonder if Ken's got any?' said Geraldine.

'Who?' said John.

'Ken. Ken Exon,' said Geraldine and, when she realised John was none the wiser, 'You know, Exon's records.'

'Oh, yeah,' said John, looking like he knew he had a lot of catching up to do.

▪▫▪

The night was memorable as much for the journey as for the music. Geraldine and John hitched along the M4, finding their way to London in two rides, which Geraldine declared a world record despite having no idea. They found their way to the Underground and Hammersmith station, and from there were guided on the rest of their journey by the stream of people with long hair wearing double denim, or denim and leather. They could equally as well have followed the waft of hash smoke. As for the music, there were three things Geraldine took away from the night. The first was the existence of the all-female band Androids of Mu. Next for Geraldine were headliners Hawkwind, whose light and sound show mesmerised her but didn't quite reach her core the way the Jam had. Best of all for Geraldine was Inner City Unit. Fronted by ex-Hawkwind member Nik Turner, who, Geraldine had read, was kicked out of the band for taking too many drugs, Inner City Unit were guerrilla punks who did better versions of 'Master of the Universe' and 'Brainstorm' than Hawkwind did, transforming them from chugging stoner rock into spiky punk anthems. Geraldine liked that very much and so she put Inner City Unit on her list of bands she needed to know more about.

■□■

The weekend after she and John got back from London, Geraldine was in Bristol, thumbing through the racks of a record store in St Pauls. When she came across a copy of Inner City Unit's debut single on twelve-inch, she was tempted, but the two pounds fifty the record store wanted for it was a bit too much for Geraldine's liking. After long minutes spent holding the record, inspecting its sleeve, taking out the black grooved disc and minutely examining it, even reading the text that had been scratched into the run-out groove – *Poppa MM Mao Mao* – Geraldine put the record back on the shelf, tucking it away out of alphabetical order to make it harder to find in case she changed her mind.

Geraldine had turned to walk out of the shop when a flash of visual memory made her pivot and sort through the rack to find the record again. She lifted the cover to eye level. The four scrawled signatures on the front were blue while the rest of the cover was black and white. She ran her fingertips over the blue squiggles and could feel the faint indentations where pen had been steered across the thin card of the front cover. Geraldine knew all about errant pen strokes and making marks you didn't intend. The signatures were real. She took the record to the counter and held it out to the shopkeeper who by now was eyeing her suspiciously. He inspected Geraldine and then the record.

'That'll be two pound fifty,' he said.

Geraldine handed over the money and waited impatiently while he bagged it, folding down the opening of the bag and sticking it in place with sellotape. She mostly ran to Bristol Temple Meads station and on the train home looked over the cover of her new record again and again. Just before getting off at Weston, Geraldine registered that the band had put their address on the back cover. Up in her room, listening to 'Solitary Ashtray' and the B-side dub version on repeat, Geraldine wrote Nik Turner a letter. She described how she'd just seen them in London and gave a bit of background to herself and the dullness of life in Weston compared to how exciting she thought London must be, though she'd now been there a total of one time.

A couple of weeks later, as she was about to leave for school, the post plopped through the letterbox at St Austell. Geraldine didn't normally get letters, but she'd been checking when she saw it arrive in the last few weeks, just in case she got a reply from Mr Turner. She sorted through the envelopes that came through the door that morning and there, near the bottom of the pile, was one addressed to her, a plain white envelope with a stamp and no return address. Geraldine felt a rush of anticipation as she tore open the envelope. Inside were two sheets of stickers bearing Inner City Unit's logo in red on a white background. She checked and rechecked the envelope and between the sheets of stickers, but there was nothing else. Geraldine's excitement turned to disappointment. Having identified who it was from, she'd been hoping for a letter from the band, a literary insight into their life in London, but it wasn't to be. Geraldine took a file out of her schoolbag, intending to put one of the stickers on it so she could show Sasha, John and anyone else at school she thought might be even slightly interested. The stickers were in two rows of four and, as she was about to peel off the one from top left, she noticed something stuck into the middle of the sheet. It was a small square, dark green with a small black star in the middle. Geraldine studied it, sitting there held in place with sellotape. She'd never seen one before, only ever heard them talked about, but she was sure it was a blotter of acid. Geraldine's heart skipped. She looked around behind her in case Frank or Grace was watching, but she was on her own. She carefully peeled the sellotape from the backing paper and, when she had released the square of blotting paper, folded the sellotape back around it and stuck it down as tightly as she could. She then put the square in her pocket and the stickers in her schoolbag. Geraldine opened the door and left for school.

■□■

'Where've you been?' said John, waiting for her on the railway bridge.

'I got a letter,' said Geraldine.

'Oh,' said John. 'Everything alright?'

'Yes,' said Geraldine, giving him a little smile.

'Alright, let's go then,' said John.

'Wait,' said Geraldine. 'Do you want some acid?'

'Oh yer, sure,' said John, giving her his best Wurzel accent.

'No, no, I mean it,' said Geraldine.

She explained how she'd come about this morning's mail and then pulled the tiny square out of her pocket as proof.

'Here, look,' said Geraldine, opening her palm.

John leaned forward to look into Geraldine's hand and then at her.

'Yer, right,' he said, still heavy on the Somerset.

'No, it's true,' Geraldine said. 'I'm going to take it. Now.'

'Now?' said John.

'Yeah,' she said. 'Do you want some or not?'

John was still an unbeliever, but he also didn't want his friend to leave him behind.

'Alright, then, I'll have some.'

Geraldine rummaged in her bag for her pencil case, took out her scissors and cut the square in half. She offered half to John and held on to the other half while she put away her stationery.

'What do we do?' said John.

'I dunno,' said Geraldine. 'Chew it up and swallow it, I suppose.'

The schoolmates chewed and swallowed their halves at the same time and then turned to continue to their destination. By the time they reached the school gate Geraldine and, by the sound of him, John, were on the upswing of a fierce trip. They were giggling uncontrollably. Everything was funny and they didn't care one bit who knew about it. Geraldine's chest felt like liquid neon, sparking with electricity, though her head was surprisingly calm and peaceful except for the absolute requirement that she laugh at everything all the time. She tried to hold it in, but after a few moments the laughter came bursting out again. It was relentless and she could feel her cheeks beginning to ache and the corners of her mouth felt like they would tear apart from being stretched so tightly. Geraldine didn't care, she just needed to laugh. The two of them had enough sense left in them to turn around and leave school before they got swept up in the river of kids heading for their classrooms. Today had just been designated a non-school day for Geraldine and John. Instead, they spent the day wandering the streets of Weston-super-Mare doing their best to keep out of sight and not draw attention to themselves, a job made mighty difficult by all the laughter.

44

'How's it going?' said Sasha.

'It's going well,' said Geraldine, raising her head to look at Sasha.

It was Friday after school and they were lying together on the bed in the room where Harry still practised guitar most days. The room was next to the lounge where Grace and Frank, when he was home, spent most of their time, but it seemed to raise less interest for the pair to spend their time shut in here than in Geraldine's bedroom.

'No, I mean, how's it going,' said Sasha, looking down at Geraldine's chest.

Geraldine studied Sasha's eye makeup for a moment, the thick black eyeliner and pink eyeshadow blending into purple and black at the outside edge of her eyelids.

'Oh, how's that going, do you mean?' said Geraldine, looking Sasha in the eye. 'You mean, how's the estrogen going? Is that what you mean?'

Geraldine had decided that she needed to be matter-of-fact about her medical experiment. She didn't want any innuendo with the people close to her.

'Yes,' said Sasha, 'how's the estrogen going?'

'I really don't feel much different,' said Geraldine. 'But my nipples are sore and hard, and I think I can see my boobs growing.'

'Really?' said Sasha. 'Can I have a look?'

'Um, sure,' said Geraldine, sitting up to unbutton her school shirt.

Geraldine held her shirt open and Sasha looked intently at her chest.

'I think I can see something,' she said. 'I think I can see some growth.'

'I think so,' said Geraldine, looking down at herself. 'I don't know, it's early days yet.'

Geraldine had just started the third box of the pills she'd bought from Marty and, always one to plan ahead, was already beginning to wonder where she'd get her next supply from.

'Can I touch them?' said Sasha.

'Er, yes,' said Geraldine, feeling a rush of arousal.

Sasha reached out and touched Geraldine's right nipple, brushing her fingertips across it. She did the same with her left hand and then took each of Geraldine's nipples between her thumb and forefinger and gave them a tentative squeeze.

'How does that feel?' said Sasha.

'Oh, god, that feels good,' said Geraldine, her eyes closed as she sat in front of Sasha.

Sasha released her slight grip, bringing her arms to folded across her chest.

'I didn't mean that!' said Sasha.

'I'm sorry,' said Geraldine. 'It felt sore when you squeezed, but it just felt so good.'

Geraldine leaned in to kiss Sasha, but Sasha moved away.

'No. Not now,' she said. 'I didn't mean it to be like this.'

'I'm sorry,' said Geraldine again, buttoning up her shirt. 'I didn't either.'

■□■

Later that evening, freezing cold at their bus stop on the prom, the pair talked about earlier on the bed.

'I just didn't expect that,' said Sasha.

'Neither did I,' said Geraldine. 'It just happened. I didn't mean anything by it.'

'I know, but I don't want to,' said Sasha. 'I don't want to have sex yet.'

'It's okay,' said Geraldine, 'I don't want to, either.'

The two walked back to Sasha's house in silence, but hand in hand.

'Do you want to come in for a bit?' said Sasha, as they were standing at her front door, yellow light spilling on them from the glass that crowned the dark varnish and brass of the entry.

'No, it's alright,' said Geraldine. 'I'm going to get off home.'

Sasha leaned in to kiss Geraldine goodnight and the two parted as they always did: Geraldine's hands under Sasha's, and Geraldine backing away slowly until they could no longer hold each other's grip. Geraldine walked home and felt like things would be okay. In bed that night, she used one hand to touch her nipples while bringing herself to the most delicious orgasm.

Afterwards, she lay in bed and did a mental inventory of her body and how it was feeling, deciding that things did feel different but not being able to pinpoint quite how.

■□■

Christmas came and went in a flash. Frank announced that he'd be going back to Libya for another three months in the first week of the New Year, Geraldine marvelling to herself that he'd given the family so much notice this time. The best present of that Christmas was a copy of *Never Mind the Bollocks, Here's the Sex Pistols*. Somehow Geraldine still hadn't got around to buying a copy. She had the four singles, but the album was a most welcome addition to her growing record collection. Geraldine played it over and over while the rest of her family were trying to sleep off their Christmas lunch.

'Turn that fucking racket off,' Harry said to her, eventually, opening one eye where he was lying on the floor under the lounge-room window.

Geraldine looked at him, shocked, holding back a tear. She left the room with her record player, went upstairs and lay on her bed fuming in silence. Harry poked his head around her bedroom door over an hour later.

'You alright, our kid?' he said.

'Yeah, I'm okay,' said Geraldine, refusing to make eye contact.

'I didn't mean anything,' Harry said. 'It was just getting a bit much. Frank was giving me the look, you know?'

Geraldine looked up at Harry, still standing at her bedroom door.

'Yeah, okay,' she said as she sniffed back a tear.

'You alright?' said Harry again.

'Yeah, I'm okay,' repeated Geraldine.

'Come downstairs, then,' said Harry. 'We're going to have some more trifle. If you stay here, they won't save any for you.'

Geraldine followed Harry downstairs to rejoin the festivities. They were short-lived, Harry heading straight out after trifle, leaving Geraldine to what felt like an empty house.

45

Harry waited in the van while Geraldine knocked on Sasha's door. She was greeted by Margaret, Sasha's mum.

'You will look after my daughter, won't you?' said Margaret.

'Yes,' said Geraldine, 'Harry's with us as well,' she continued, glancing towards the Escort van stood on the road, motor running.

'Yes,' said Margaret, 'that's what I'm worried about. Why don't the two of you stay here with the other kids?'

Geraldine thought for a moment and decided on a change of strategy.

'If that's what Sasha wants to do,' she said.

Margaret looked hard at Geraldine.

'Fine, she can go, but you need to be back here by one.'

'We will,' said Geraldine.

■□■

New Year's at the Queens was a rowdy affair filled with music, booze, drugs and the occasional fight. Marty made an early appearance and the collective members of the Desk went out the back of the pub to where their cars were parked to prepare themselves for the long night ahead.

'Do you want some?' asked Harry as Geraldine watched him cut up some lines on the plastic covering of his map book.

Geraldine looked at Sasha. Sasha shook her head. 'Yes,' said Geraldine.

The powder tasted bitter in the back of Geraldine's throat. She could feel snot gathering in her nasal cavity and she didn't know whether to spit it out or swallow it down. Harry had been watching her and gave her a quick instruction.

'Swallow it.'

Geraldine hocked the rest of the powder from her nostril and swallowed with an exaggerated gulp.

'It'll be alright,' said Harry. 'No need to look so worried. You've only had a little bit. Here, have some of this, it'll help keep you calm until you start coming up.'

Harry handed Geraldine a joint and she took a few hungry tokes, enjoying the warmth of the hash as it found its way into her bloodstream. She passed the joint to Sasha and, feeling much better about the world, followed her girlfriend and the band back inside the pub.

Until that night, Geraldine had been an absolute wallflower when she was at the Queens with the Desk. This evening, she felt untouchable. She hadn't noticed until she found herself in the middle of an earnest conversation with a complete stranger about how crap Racey had become since they made it and how much bigger the Desk would be when they inevitably signed their own record deal. According to Geraldine, the difference was that the Desk wouldn't sell out and record music that wasn't them, they would stay true to their own music. The punter looked at her.

'And what do you have to do with them?' he asked.

Geraldine missed his sarcasm.

'They're mine,' she said. 'I manage them. They wouldn't be here if it wasn't for me.'

The bloke turned away; he'd already had enough. Geraldine realised she had an enormous thirst. She turned back to Sasha.

'Do you want a drink?' she asked.

'I'll have a lemon lime and bitters,' said Sasha.

'Nah, we're at the pub,' said Geraldine. 'Let's have a proper drink.'

'Really?' said Sasha.

'Yes! C'mon, let's go get a drink,' said Geraldine. 'What do you want?'

'I'll have a half of shandy,' said Sasha.

'Is that all?' said Geraldine. 'C'mon, have a proper drink.'

Sasha gave Geraldine a look that pierced her omnipotence for a moment.

'Well, I'm having a pint,' she said.

Geraldine headed to the bar and stood leaning up against its smooth wooden edge until she caught Joe's eye.

'Half of shandy and a pint of lager, please Joe,' she said. 'In a straight glass.'

Joe glared at her across the bar.

'Just this once,' he said, turning to get the glasses for her drinks. 'You be fucking careful,' Joe said as he put the drinks on the bar.

'I will!' said Geraldine, pushing her way through the crowd to get back to Sasha, more than one person giving her a glare as she elbowed her way across the room. Geraldine gulped down her pint and made to go back to the bar for another.

'I think that's enough for now,' said Sasha, her hand on Geraldine's arm as she rose from their bench seat.

Geraldine sat back down, banging her pint glass on the table with a dull clank. She sat and surveyed the room, itching to be in motion. Sasha kept her hand on Geraldine's arm.

■□■

Home in the early hours of the morning, Geraldine crashed hard, only waking from a dreamless sleep just before noon on what was still New Year's Day. She opened her eyes, irritated by the light that was breaking through her curtains. Geraldine's head felt scratchy, her limbs were heavy and delinquent, refusing to move when she wanted them to. Her mind was vacuous and unprepared to face the day. As she came to properly, the emptiness was filled with fears from the past and the probability that there would be fears in the future too. Geraldine was well aware of what caused her fears, but she generally kept those people, places and events hidden from her view. Now they were swarming her mind. She turned over to go back to sleep, but sleep would not return.

■□■

Early in the New Year, Geraldine bumped into Marty as she was walking up High Street.

'You going to Karl's Bar?' he asked.

'Er, no,' said Geraldine, 'Woolworths.' It was a destination she had almost reached.

'Ah, I see,' said Marty.

The two stood in silence until Geraldine acted on an impulse.

'Can you get me some speed?' she said.

'Here, come with me,' Marty said, looking around.

He turned and started walking back up High Street. Geraldine followed as they went past Woolies and found their way to the gardens at the top of the shopping mall. Marty took a left and sat on one of the stone seats set into the wall that divided the gardens in two. Geraldine sat next to him.

'How much do you want?'

Geraldine thought for a moment. She'd never made a transaction like this before, but she'd heard it talked about plenty of times now.

'Can I get a gram?' she asked, hoping she'd said the right thing.

'A gram?' said Marty. 'As much as that?'

Geraldine almost changed her mind, but she was very much one for sticking with things.

'Yes,' she said.

'Do you have the money? It's sixteen pounds.'

Geraldine did. She found three fivers and a one-pound note in her purse and folded them into her palm, holding out her hand to Marty who took the cash from her.

'Hold tight,' he said. 'I'll have it for you in a day or two.'

Geraldine raised her eyebrows in surprise.

'Okay, then,' she said.

Marty got up and continued his journey. Geraldine walked back down High Street with him for a while, walking past Woolies one more time. She no longer had enough with her for the records she'd planned on buying with the money her Grandma and Grandad had sent for Christmas. They parted ways at the bottom of High Street and Geraldine took herself home.

■□■

Weeks later Geraldine answered a knock at the door of St Austell, early one morning before school. There was Marty.

'Hello?' she said, surprised that he'd turned up on her doorstep, that he'd even turned up at all.

'Sorry,' said Marty, 'I've been away for a while. I got abducted by the mafia to Nicaragua.' Deadpan all the way.

Marty handed Geraldine her sixteen pounds in crisp one-pound notes and turned and walked away without saying another word. Geraldine watched him go, noting that Marty had a tan.

46

By spring term of 1981, school felt less and less relevant to Geraldine. She was busy doing other things, and her growing pursuit of the high life wasn't entirely compatible with getting up in the morning or spending time in class. It wasn't that Geraldine wasn't interested in learning – she most certainly was – it was just that she felt like she'd learned everything she could inside the gates of Westland Comprehensive. Geraldine spoke to Mr Potts about it at the end of English, just before half-term.

'Gerald, you're just about the smartest kid I've ever taught,' said Mr Potts.

'But I don't know if I want to be here,' said Geraldine, hedging, because she definitely knew she didn't.

'What would you do?' said Mr Potts. 'What sort of job could you get?'

'I want to work in music,' said Geraldine.

Mr Potts looked at her like he'd been here before.

'Ah, I see,' he said. 'You know you can't just get a job in music? What do you think you'd do?'

'I want to keep doing what I'm doing now,' said Geraldine. 'Working with bands and putting on shows.'

'You do that now?' said Mr Potts, his aspect changing.

'I do,' said Geraldine.

She gave Mr Potts a quick career outline and, as she took him through her business he raised his eyebrows more than once.

'This is all you, Gerald?' said Mr Potts. 'You do this yourself?'

'Yes, I do,' said Geraldine. 'And there's one more thing, my name is Geraldine.'

This was definitely news to Mr Potts. He looked at Geraldine and raised his eyebrows again. This was definitely not somewhere he'd been before.

'What do you mean?' he said.

'I'm a girl,' Geraldine stated, matter-of-factly, making sure to maintain eye contact with her teacher and not be the first to look away.

'Look, Gerald …'

'Geraldine,' she said.

'Yes, err, look, err, Geraldine,' said Mr Potts. 'I don't know what to do. This … I've never dealt with this before.'

'It's okay,' said Geraldine, 'I don't need you to do anything, I just wanted you to know.'

'Why?' said Mr Potts.

'Because it's important to me,' said Geraldine. 'And you've been good to me. I just wanted you to know.'

'Do you need to speak to anyone?' said Mr Potts.

'No, it's okay,' said Geraldine, 'I've been to see a doctor.'

Geraldine decided not to tell Mr Potts what a disaster that had been, she just didn't want him trying to help and ending up interfering.

'Well then,' said Mr Potts, 'thank you for telling me?'

Geraldine smiled at her teacher.

'That's okay,' she said.

'But I want you to stay in school as long as you can, Geraldine,' said Mr Potts. 'You're still quite young, you know. You could do anything.'

'I know what I want to do,' said Geraldine.

Geraldine decided she'd stay in school for a while longer.

■□■

Harry's departure from St Austell came as suddenly as one of Frank's announcements.

'I'll be back in the summer,' he told Geraldine. 'I'm heading over to Morocco for a while.'

'But what about the Desk?' said Geraldine.

'They don't need me,' said Harry. 'You'll be here to look after them, and Bopay can play all of my parts and his own. He usually does anyway. Now, you going to come out with us tonight for a few drinks?'

They met at Julia's, her windows and curtains still closed against the cold. the Desk and their close friends and partners crammed into Julia's bedsit, smoked joints, did lines and drank cider until they were ready to go to the pub. They walked into town, stopping at the chippy along the way. Geraldine couldn't decide if she was hungry, but she ate a bag of chips anyway, the hot grease making her stomach churn as she swallowed down each handful. At the Queens, Geraldine went to the bar to speak to Joe.

'No!' he said, as soon as he saw her.

'It's okay, Joe,' said Geraldine, 'I'm not after a drink.'

'Alright, what is it then?'

'Harry's going away for a bit …'

'He is, is he?' said Joe. 'They don't usually give you warning, you know.'

Geraldine gave him a confused look for a moment.

'No, not that,' said Geraldine. 'He's going to Morocco.'

'Oh yeah?' said Joe. 'And then straight back home for a long stretch?'

'No,' said Geraldine, pausing as she realised what Harry was most likely up to. Cold fear rose in her chest and just about brought the chips with it. 'No,' she said again, 'I just wanted to let you know he won't be here for a while, but Bopay will play his parts.'

'Oh, I see,' said Joe. 'That'll be fifty quid a night then, won't it?'

'No,' said Geraldine. 'It's still the same band playing the same songs. It's still sixty pounds.'

Joe glared at Geraldine.

'Make sure they don't let me down,' he said.

■□■

Harry returned from Morocco only briefly, spending two nights at St Austell in early June before leaving for the summer festival circuit. When he'd arrived unannounced at the front door, lateish, just as the light behind him was fading, Geraldine had looked him up and down before speaking. He was thin, his face gaunt and his eyes dark and hooded with worry.

'It's you,' said Geraldine.

'Yeah, our kid, it's me,' said Harry. 'Can I come in? I'm a bit tired.'

Geraldine stepped aside to let Harry in. She looked behind him as he stepped through the door sideways to get past her. His Escort van was parked on the road outside the house like he'd never been gone, but his return felt like another loss to Geraldine. Harry took the first right into the lounge room where Grace was sat in front of the telly. She looked up at him.

'You're back, Harry,' said Grace.

'Looks like it,' Harry said, sitting down.

'Are you staying long?' was Grace's only other question.

'I don't know, Mum,' said Harry as he slipped off his shoes and put his feet up on the pouffe in front of him.

'Phwoar! Harry!' said Grace. 'Your feet stink!'

'Yeah, I know,' said Harry. 'Sorry!' He laughed at her screwed-up face.

'Go and get yourself a bath,' said Grace.

'I will,' said Harry. 'Tomorrow.'

'Do you want something to eat?' said Geraldine, still standing at the door of the lounge.

'Yes, please,' said Harry.

■□■

Geraldine lay on the bed and listened to Harry play the guitar he'd left behind when he went on his trip. She'd decided against going to school that morning. Waiting downstairs, she'd decided against going to school that morning, whiling away the hours until Harry came down around midday. He was wearing the same clothes he'd arrived in the night before.

'Morning,' he said, when he saw Geraldine on the bed in the semi-darkness.

'Morning,' she said.

Harry lit a cigarette and stood for a while smoking it vigorously, each breath in deeper than the last, each exhalation like he was trying to expel something living inside him. Geraldine watched him, wondering if she should say something, but decided to keep her thoughts to herself. Harry stepped over and crushed out his cigarette in the ashtray on the small table at the side of the bed where Geraldine was. Satisfied it was out, he picked up his guitar, switched on his amp and, when it was warmed up and ready, started to play. Geraldine closed her eyes and listened.

'C'mon, let's go to the pub,' said Harry when he'd put down his guitar.

The siblings walked to the local, up and around the corner at the other end of Langport Road. There was some slight warmth in the air, but the stiff breeze from the Severn that chased the clouds across the sky suggested it wouldn't last long. Harry returned to the table, a pint of lager in his right hand and a lemon, lime and bitters for Geraldine in his left. He passed

Geraldine's drink to her as he sat down. He placed his glass carefully on a fresh beer mat and lit a cigarette, blowing out smoke as he picked up his glass and raised it to his mouth to take a long draught.

'So, how are you, our kid?' said Harry.

'I'm okay,' said Geraldine, looking at Harry, wanting him to spill first but realising that this was unlikely.

'Just okay?' said Harry, slipping into his rarely reprised role of big brother.

'Yeah, I'm okay,' said Geraldine. 'What about you?'

'I'm okay,' said Harry, taking another swallow from his pint.

Geraldine decided to take a risk.

'You don't look okay,' she said.

Harry looked at her. There was anger in his eyes for a moment. Geraldine saw his body tense as he leaned forward. She noticed the grey at his temples.

'I'm okay, Geraldine,' said Harry. 'I am.'

He rested back in his chair and finished up his pint.

'I've just got things I need to do,' Harry said as he stood up to get another drink.

Geraldine watched him go, his wide shoulders, hair now halfway down his back, waist pinched and his jeans and belt only just holding up on his hips. She knew he wasn't alright, but she also knew there was nothing she could do. Even so, Geraldine couldn't contain her curiosity.

'So, what're you going to do now?' said Geraldine when Harry returned to their table.

'I'm heading off tomorrow,' said Harry.

'Tomorrow?'

'It'll be alright, our kid,' said Harry. 'I've just got things to do. Come to Glastonbury. I'll meet you there. How about that?'

47

Geraldine and Sasha were sitting at their bus stop, the almost-summer evening still chilly, but there were no blue lips or chattering teeth tonight.

'I'm going to Glastonbury,' said Geraldine.

'You are?' said Sasha.

'Yeah,' said Geraldine. 'Come with me?'

'I don't know,' said Sasha. 'I'll have to ask my mum. Is your mum okay with you going?'

'I haven't told her yet,' said Geraldine.

It didn't occur to Geraldine that Frank wasn't the only one in the family who could delay important news to the last moment.

'Do you want me to come with you?' asked Sasha, with a tentative smile.

'I do,' said Geraldine. 'I'd really like that.'

Geraldine leaned into Sasha and they kissed, then sat until the sky was dark, Geraldine's head resting on Sasha's shoulder.

'You'll definitely ask your mum?' said Geraldine as she left Sasha at her doorstep.

■□■

Geraldine and Sasha set out for Glastonbury carrying the sleeping bags and a tent they'd borrowed from Sasha's mum. Geraldine had assured Margaret they were going with Harry, who would keep an eye on them over the weekend. As they stumbled onto the bus that would take them on the first part of their journey, the couple kept their heads low in case someone saw them. Standing in a layby at the side of the A370, her thumb begging a ride from passing cars, Geraldine assured Sasha that someone would definitely pick them up. They'd been waiting nearly two hours before Geraldine's assurances proved to have any substance. A purple Morris Marina slowed as it drove by them, the driver, an older man, looking curiously at the pair. He made to drive on and then must have thought the better of it, pulling into the side of the road and then reversing towards the pair as they jogged up the road. When they were alongside the car he wound down the passenger window. Geraldine stepped forward and rested her hands on the roof of the car as she looked in at the man.

'Are you two alright?' he said.

'Yes, we're fine, thank you,' said Geraldine. 'We're going to Glastonbury. Can you give us a lift?'

'I wasn't really ...' said the man. 'I just wanted to know if you're okay.'

'We are,' Geraldine confirmed.

'I'm only going to Brent Knoll,' said the man.

'That's okay,' said Geraldine, 'we can find another lift there.'

'Alright, get in,' said the man, sounding reluctant.

Geraldine opened the front passenger door, before he could change his mind, motioning for Sasha to get in the back. She settled with the tent and a sleeping bag on her knee and turned to make sure Sasha was in.

'Thank you,' Geraldine said, giving the man her best innocent smile.

He put the car in gear and pulled out with a look on his face that said he'd just been conned but didn't quite know how.

■□■

Their next ride was a young woman in a small bright yellow car.

'Are you two going to Glasto?' she said as she pulled up alongside them.

'We are,' said Geraldine.

'Hop in, then.'

She dropped them into the centre of town.

'You know the way from here?' she asked as she made to pull away.

'Yes, we do, thank you,' said Geraldine.

'Good luck, have fun,' said the woman as she drove away.

The couple walked through the town to the A361. Traffic was beginning to get heavy as cars converged on Pilton and Worthy Farm.

'We should walk,' said Geraldine, hitching the tent over her right shoulder and carrying a sleeping bag in her left hand. Sasha fell in behind her.

'How far is it from here?' she said.

'About eight miles.'

'Eight miles?!' said Sasha.

'We'll get a lift soon,' said Geraldine, as an increasingly heavy line of traffic went by.

Eventually, they did get a lift, but not before even Geraldine had begun to think their luck might have run out. The couple who picked them up were also going to Glastonbury.

'You can come in with us,' said the woman in the passenger seat. 'Save you walking any more. You both look tired.'

She looked to Geraldine to be in her early twenties, but she'd already taken on a motherly air about the young couple in the back seat of the tan Ford Cortina that belonged to her sales rep boyfriend. When they came to a halt in the line of traffic on the entry road to Worthy Farm, Geraldine spoke up.

'It's okay, we'll get out here,' she said. 'We can walk the rest of the way.'

'Are you sure?' said the woman, turning around to look at the pair in the back seat of the car with concern lining her brow.

'Yeah, we have to meet my brother,' said Geraldine, 'so this will be fine. Thank you.'

'Alright then,' said the woman, her worry slightly dissipated.

Geraldine and Sasha got out of the car on the passenger side and started walking alongside the line of cars.

'Here, come this way,' said Geraldine, when she saw a gate to their left.

'What?' said Sasha. 'Why?'

'Just come with me,' Geraldine said, holding out her hands for Sasha's sleeping bag, which she then dropped on the other side of the gate, quickly followed by the tent and the second sleeping bag. Geraldine climbed over and watched as Sasha followed her. She picked up a sleeping bag and handed it to Sasha, shouldering the tent again, the second bag in her other hand, and started to stride across the field away from the festival site.

'What're we doing, Geraldine?' said Sasha, when she caught up.

'We need to go around the back of the fields,' said Geraldine. 'Harry said we can get in for free if we go around.'

'Oh, okay,' said Sasha. 'Are you sure?'

'Yeah, yeah, it'll be okay,' said Geraldine, not at all sure.

An hour later, the couple climbed through a barbed-wire fence, Geraldine having first dropped their kit on the other side. They'd made it. They were at Glastonbury.

Tent pitched and sleeping bags laid out, the pair set off to explore the festival grounds. Their campsite was on a hill and below them was the pyramid stage, the last of the evening's sunlight glinting off its roof, the people working on it visible even from this distance. The couple walked down the hill, Sasha looking back constantly to make sure she had sight of where they'd pitched their tent, Geraldine with eyes only for the stage that loomed into larger view with every step. By the time they reached the bottom of the hill they could see people entering the festival grounds in a steady stream, vehicles being directed to the opposite side of the farm. The pyramid stage was flanked by smaller tents and marquees being set up to sell food and merchandise, and for other components of the festival including films, dance and live theatre. Geraldine was intrigued by the scale of the event. She walked Sasha towards the pyramid stage until they were standing right at the security barrier. This close, Geraldine had to look up to see what was happening in the mouth of the corrugated-iron structure. Roadies and technicians were setting up equipment, mostly wearing the required uniform of blue jeans and black t-shirt. Lights flicked on and off and there was the occasional intonation of 'One-two, check, check one-two' over the PA, sometimes accompanied by a squeal of feedback. Geraldine turned around and surveyed the field the pyramid stage faced with its initially gentle and then ever steepening rise. The top of the field was lined with more tents of various colours and camping grounds stood to either side of the field on the higher ground.

It was Thursday evening and there were relatively few people at the festival this early on. Geraldine and Sasha walked to the top of the field, past the sound desk occupying a steel and canvas structure about halfway up, and to the row of tents they had spied a few minutes ago. Some were still setting up, but others were already selling their wares.

'Shall we get some food?' said Geraldine.

They settled for a burger and chips and a can of lemonade, perching themselves on the grass not far from the tent where they'd bought their dinner so they could eat and watch people go by. As far as Geraldine could see, festivalgoers came in all varieties. There were groups of biker-looking types, always more men than women. There were young couples, some pushing babies in prams, or carrying toddlers too tired for any more walking today. There were old people, one couple who Geraldine thought must have been older than Bryn and Flora, her grandparents. She stared after them until they disappeared from view, wondering what they would be doing here at Worthy Farm. Mostly the people were young, late teens to early twenties. Geraldine kept a close watch for Harry, as she had the entire day, but despite some false sightings, he didn't make an appearance.

As the sun set behind the silver cowshed, Sasha nudged Geraldine.

'Let's head back to the tent,' she said. 'Otherwise it might be too dark.'

'Yeah, c'mon,' said Geraldine, 'let's go.'

She held out a hand to Sasha, bowing at the waist.

'Milady,' she said with a giggle, 'shall we repair to the boudoir?'

Sasha looked up at Geraldine as if she had suddenly become the world's least attractive teenager. She got up under her own steam and began walking along the line of merchandise tents towards where they were camped.

'If you think any of that's happening tonight or any other night,' said Sasha, 'you've got another thing coming.'

With that, she broke into a jog with Geraldine running behind her.

'But, Milady,' Geraldine said, 'I mean no ill will or misfortune to come to you.'

'Talk properly!' Sasha said, slowing to a walk as she looked around her to get her bearings.

Geraldine took Sasha's hand and they wandered back to their tent, stepping in between and around campsites that were already set up, some with fires and groups of people chatting, playing guitars, singing and smoking joints. As they moved into an area of greater darkness, hoping they were closer to their tent, Geraldine tripped on a guide rope, pulling a tent peg clean from the ground, resulting in the tent to their right ending up in a semi-collapse. They looked around in horror, but the tent's owners didn't seem to be in the vicinity and those who were didn't seem to notice or care what had happened. After that, they stepped with exaggerated care until they found their two-man tent right where they'd left it. Geraldine took one last look down the hill and breathed in the lights and sounds of Glastonbury before she joined Sasha in the tent. Zipped into their own sleeping bags, the pair kissed and then lay talking. Geraldine was quite deep into telling Sasha what she wanted to do tomorrow before she realised she was the only one of them still conscious. She smiled, yawned and turned over half on her front, half on her side, her head resting on a scrunched-up jumper. She didn't have long to regret not bringing a pillow before the chill of the Friday morning sunrise woke her.

48

Come midday Saturday, Geraldine was lying on her back, staring up at the sky. Clouds marshalled themselves into a stone table and Geraldine witnessed the hand of God chopping up bodies with an axe. As trips went, it should have been freaking Geraldine out, but she was at peace with the imagery, watching curiously without a care in the world – until someone stuck a camera in her face. Geraldine's immediate thought was that it was a press photographer. The idea of Grace seeing her on the front page of *The Sun* scared Geraldine far more than a vengeful god dismembering the bodies of the unfaithful. Geraldine had already made her peace with God, having long ago dispensed with any possibility of his existence. The possibility of making peace with Grace was, it seemed, far more distant. Geraldine covered her face with her hands, having some difficulty coordinating her movements.

'No,' she said, rolling from side to side on the ground to make herself more difficult to get into frame. 'No pictures.'

The cameraman laughed and kept following Geraldine's movements with his lens, determined to get the shot.

'No!' said Geraldine, more forcefully. 'No pictures.'

'It's okay, Geraldine, it's me,' said the cameraman.

Geraldine took her hands from her face and looked up to see a man looking down at her, his ginger locks hanging in his face. Behind him, God had finished his work and the clouds had returned to sitting above them in the sky, watchful.

'What the fuck?' said Geraldine. 'What the fuck are you doing?'

'It's okay,' said the man. 'I just wanted to get a picture, It's okay.'

Geraldine sat up and looked around her, realising the photographer was one of the Weston Bikers' Club. Earlier that morning, she and Sasha had found them camped just to stage right, as close to the pyramid stage as you could get without being in the middle of the crush. Geraldine didn't know them that well, mostly through times she'd come across them with Harry in various pubs and venues, but she'd always liked Jem Stone and, when he'd called them over as they were wandering aimlessly, Geraldine looking for Harry, and Sasha beginning to wonder how many more laps of the festival site they'd have to do, they were both relieved to be able to have a break. As well as the company, sitting still for a while brought other benefits. People stopped by selling all varieties of drugs.

When a young man from Amsterdam stopped by selling Green Spaceships, Geraldine was instantly interested. Jem Stone and his greasy mates looked the clean-cut young man over.

'You're not bacon, are you?' said one of them, getting a rise of laughter out of his friends.

'Erm, no?' said the man from Amsterdam, making to move off.

'Jonesy, don't be stupid,' said Jem. 'The pigs aren't allowed in here. It's cool. Just relax.'

There was general oinking and snorting from the leather-clad motorcycle enthusiasts, and much giggling. Sasha looked at Geraldine and made motions with her head to leave. Geraldine ignored her, keeping her eyes on the soap opera unfolding in front of them.

'It's alright,' said Jem, 'they're just being stupid. Come and show us what you've got.'

The young Dutchman stepped over and opened his palm.

'Best acid you'll ever have,' he said.

In his hand was a small translucent green star, looking like a tiny boiled sweet encased in sellotape.

'Four fifty a tab,' said the dealer. 'Keep you going all weekend.'

'Okay, give me one,' said Jem, fishing in his jeans pocket for some money.

'I'll have one, too,' said Geraldine. 'Sasha?'

Sasha shook her head, still motioning for them to go.

■□■

When the sun began to drop, Geraldine and Sasha were still with Jem and the other bikers.

'Come on, Geraldine, I want to go back to the tent for a while,' said Sasha.

'Okay.'

The couple got up and said goodbye to the hairy bikers, turning to walk back up the hill and then take a right to their campsite. After an hour of looking, they still were no closer to finding their tent. Geraldine wasn't that fussed about the search, but Sasha's growing distress broke through eventually.

'Hey, come here,' said Geraldine, holding out her hands for Sasha.

Sasha looked at her as if she was weighing up her options. Her first instinct right now certainly wasn't to find her way into Geraldine's arms. Eventually, Sasha closed the gap between them and allowed Geraldine to put her arm around her shoulder and pull her in close.

'It'll be okay,' said Geraldine. 'We'll find the tent, I promise.'

'You do?' said Sasha. 'How the fuck would you know anything? You're tripping out of your mind.'

'It's settled,' said Geraldine. 'I'm okay, I just feel …' Geraldine searched through the recesses of her body and mind, 'good!'

Sasha lifted her head from Geraldine's shoulder and looked her in the eye.

'I think I want to go home, Geraldine,' she said.

Geraldine hesitated. She had no resources to deal with what was happening. It was after dark and they had no transport, no shelter; they were stuck in a field with twenty thousand other human beings. Geraldine's stomach began to fill with that ticklish feeling, the one that was often followed by cramps, palpitations, shortness of breath and cold sweats. She breathed in deeply, feeling the air fill her lungs, seeing the colours swirl inside her as it flowed through her groin and into her legs. Breathing out again, Geraldine felt a wave of euphoria replace her breath. Having staved off her panic attack, she was ready to recreate the illusion of control.

'Okay,' said Geraldine, 'let's go home.'

Sasha smiled, her eyes welling up.

'But we can't go home now, we'll never get a ride,' said Geraldine. 'We'll go first thing tomorrow. Is that okay?'

'Yes,' said Sasha, 'that's okay.'

'Good,' said Geraldine. 'Now, shall we keep looking for the tent, or shall we go and see some bands?'

Geraldine's eyes were already fixed on the pyramid stage in the distance at the bottom of the hill.

'Yeah,' said Sasha, 'let's go and see some bands.'

■□■

New Order took to the pyramid stage to what sounded like the crescendoing thrum of a spaceship's engines. Geraldine stood front and centre and watched the ungainly silver cowshed lift off and rocket into the sky, propelled by the sound coming through the PA. When she looked down again there was New Order still on stage, working their way through their set. At one point Bernard Sumner tripped and ended up on his back still playing his guitar but unable to get back on his feet. It took two roadies to help him up. Geraldine took comfort from the knowledge that she was maybe not the highest person at Glastonbury and began to wonder if there might be any truth to the rumour that the members of New Order shared a house in Manchester, feeding their smack habits and burning the furniture and floorboards to keep warm. Hawkwind followed New Order, headlining Glastonbury as they still did most all of the summer festivals across the UK. Laser light streamed from the top of the pyramid stage, hogging all of Geraldine's attention. Afterwards, Bernie Sumner's fall and the liquid green of the lasers were all she remembered about the music.

When the lights went down, Geraldine and Sasha returned to their quest to find their tent. Eventually they stepped into the movie tent, a white marquee around halfway up the hill, where Sasha was sure they had pitched their own much less impressive accommodation. The two lay side by side on bean bags and Geraldine got caught up in a film study of a romance between a young man and a much older woman. The last two films Geraldine had seen were *Star Wars Episode IV* and *National Lampoon's Animal House*. She was unprepared for the gentle charm and outright quirkiness of *Harold and Maude*. Geraldine didn't want to like it, but she was drawn into the screen, her focus fuelled by LSD. When she woke, still in the bean bag, another film playing on the makeshift screen strung up along the length of the marquee and dawn beginning to light the fields of Worthy Farm, Geraldine was alone.

49

Geraldine spent hours on Sunday morning looking for Sasha and their tent, still keeping watch for Harry's arrival, faintly hoping that he would rescue her from this weekend. She walked up the hill, but was still unable to find their tent. She circled back down the hill to the side of the pyramid stage and surveyed the array of bodies that comprised the Weston-super-Mare bikers' club. Sasha wasn't among them and Geraldine didn't bother sticking her head into any tents: she knew she'd never find Sasha there. Around midmorning, Geraldine went to the first-aid tent and stood at the entry looking inside, hoping to see Sasha there.

'Are you alright, love?' said one of the uniformed volunteers.

'Er, yeah, I'm okay,' said Geraldine, feeling like she was anything but. 'I'm looking for my girlfriend.'

'What's her name?'

Geraldine hesitated, the uniform making her cautious. She kept looking into the tent, making sure Sasha wasn't in there.

'It's okay, I'll keep looking,' she said, turning and walking away.

Geraldine headed back up the hill to the spot where she knew their tent must be and where, when she finally found it, she was sure she would find Sasha as well. The continued absence of both the tent and Sasha pushed Geraldine's thoughts and nervous system into overdrive. Panic began to overwhelm her and she found a patch of grass to lie on before her legs started to give way. Hundreds of people walked by in the hour that Geraldine lay on the grass, forearm over her eyes to shield them from the sun and her fears from the world. When she sat up, they kept on streaming. Geraldine looked around her, hoping to see Sasha, or Harry, but she remained alone. She stood up and joined the stream of people heading towards the pyramid stage, but when the trail took a left to keep heading down the slope, Geraldine took a right towards the exit and kept walking until she found the road. She turned left again and walked, head down, along the side of the A361. Cars drove by, but Geraldine wasn't looking for a lift. As she was getting close to Glastonbury village a car pulled over and waited at the side of the road until she caught up. An older man, wearing a flat cap on top of his grey hair, wound down the passenger window.

'Where're you going?' he said.

'Weston,' said Geraldine.

'I can take you to Bleadon,' he said.

'Okay,' said Geraldine, already getting into the passenger seat.

After half an hour of her vague one-word answers the driver of the car made his play.

'I can drop you at a police station,' he said.

'Okay,' said Geraldine, beyond caring.

Not getting the answer he expected, the man drove on. When he finally dropped Geraldine at the top of Bleadon Hill she got out of the car without saying thank you or goodbye. She was relieved to be almost home and this helped her pick up her step. An hour later, Geraldine was letting herself in the front door of St Austell. She went straight upstairs to sleep, leaving it until that night to ring Sasha.

'Can I speak to Sasha, please?' Geraldine said to Margaret, skipping over asking if her daughter was home safe.

'I don't think Sasha wants to talk to you, Geraldine,' said Margaret.

'Can I call back later?'

'I don't think that's a good idea.'

The line went dead.

50

Harry's continued absence created a hash supply problem for the Desk, one that they turned to Geraldine to fix.

'I will ask around,' said Geraldine, when Julia outlined their problem at rehearsal.

'I wouldn't ask, love,' said Julia, 'but everyone is out at the moment.'

Geraldine had already arranged to meet with Marty to replenish her supply of estrogen, so when they were sitting across the table from each other, drinking tea in a booth at Connie's on Regent Street, she thought she'd take a chance.

'No, I only really do speed and pills, sometimes coke when it's available,' said Marty. 'And your pills now,' he added, smiling. 'How's that all going, anyway?'

'Yeah, good,' said Geraldine, ducking her head self-consciously.

'I can ask around for you,' said Marty. 'Do you want some speed?'

'Yeah, okay.'

'See you around', said Marty, when they'd finished their transaction.

■□■

This time Geraldine didn't have to wait too long. Marty came to the door of St Austell early the next Saturday evening. Grace answered the door.

'Is Geraldine here?' said Marty.

Grace paused, looking at the leather-jacketed man at the door, trying to work out where she'd seen him before.

'You're a friend of Harry's, aren't you?' she asked.

'Yes,' said Marty, shuffling his feet. 'Is Geraldine in?'

'Gerald?' said Grace.

'Yes, okay then,' said Marty.

'Just a minute,' said Grace, closing the door as she turned towards the stairs.

Marty and Geraldine found very little to say to each other as they walked over the railway bridge towards the Oldmixon estate. As they walked past Geraldine's school she almost stopped and told Marty she needed to go home, but Geraldine very rarely pulled out part way through something and tonight wasn't going to be the night she started. Marty pushed open a low gate and walked up the path to the door of a house midway along a terraced row one street into the estate. The door had faded, peeling dark-blue paint and a brass letterbox and knocker that were blackened with oxidation. Marty rapped the knocker twice and a face appeared at the curtain, a youngish man with a wispy beard. The door opened and they were invited directly into the lounge room. After introductions were made to the occupants, Tony with the wispy beard, and his girlfriend, Jan, Marty sat back with his cup of tea and let Geraldine take over, only she didn't really know what to say next. The couple whose house they were sitting in looked her over from their seats across from the television. *Hi-de-Hi!* was on. Eventually, someone spoke.

'How much are you looking for?' said Jan, her hand disappearing behind her ear and scratching inside the long, loosely tied blond hair.

'A quarter?' said Geraldine.

'We can do that,' said Jan. 'Tony, do you want to go and get it?'

Tony got up from his seat and disappeared into the back of the house. Geraldine thought she heard the back door being unlocked and opening and closing and, after what seemed like forever, opening and closing and being locked again. Tony resumed his seat after handing something to Jan.

'That's four pounds,' said Jan.

Geraldine fished the money out of her bag and stood up to hand it over to Jan. As she passed it over, Jan gave her a small cling-film-wrapped rectangle of hash. As was required, Geraldine rolled a joint, and the four of them sat and smoked it.

'You're Harry's brother, right?' said Jan, after the joint was finished.

'Sister,' said Geraldine.

'Okay, sister,' said Jan. 'Where's Harry?'

'I don't know,' said Geraldine.

'Hmmm,' said Jan, 'well, you know where to come next time now, don't you?'

'Yes, thank you,' said Geraldine.

She sat with the three of them for what she hoped was long enough and then announced her departure.

'I've got to go,' said Geraldine. 'The Desk will be at the Queens soon.'

'Might see you there later,' said Marty, staying in his seat.

Tony showed Geraldine to the door and she started her journey back out of the council estate, up the hill and over the railway bridge, only slowing her pace as she approached Langport Road. Instead of turning left for home, she continued on to the Queens.

'Here,' Geraldine said to Julia, as she handed her the cling-film parcel.

Julia opened her palm and looked down at it.

'Is that all?'

'Yes,' said Geraldine, 'for now.'

'I guess it'll have to do,' said Julia. 'At least you got something.'

51

Geraldine arrived in Australia in November 1981 with a habit and no supply. She'd hidden a handful of cannabis seeds in the patch on the leg of her jeans, but just before they landed in Kuala Lumpur she chickened out, visiting the toilet and digging out the small greenish-brown balls and swallowing them. She returned to her seat by the window, Grace sitting in the middle, Frank on the aisle, and looked out as the lights on the ground got larger with the plane's descent. She was worried about her estrogen. In the end she'd decided to bring only one packet with her, reasoning that she could explain it away if she was quizzed about it, but still worried whether, at seventeen, she could be tried as an adult if she was busted.

As was their way, Frank and Grace had given little notice of the move. Frank came home on a break from his contract work in Libya in early October and said he wasn't due to return until next year. This time around, his presence in the house did little to disturb Geraldine's life; she continued to come and go as she pleased, most evenings timing her return home for after she knew her parents would be in bed. This night she found Frank and Grace up late in the lounge room. Geraldine contemplated going straight up to her room but decided this would likely raise more questions than her dilated pupils and jittery legs, so she opened the sliding door to the lounge just enough to pop her head through.

'Night,' said Geraldine.

'Hang on,' said Frank, 'we need to talk to you.'

'Oh?' said Geraldine, opening the door just enough for her to slip through, adrenaline tugging at her shoulder joints on its way to her arms.

Geraldine stood just inside the doorway to the lounge room, having no intention of sitting down. Frank seemed to understand, so he turned and spoke to Geraldine from his lounge chair, head extended around its wing.

'We're going to Australia,' he said.

'Oh,' said Geraldine, relieved that this was all the news was. 'See you when you get back.'

'No,' said Frank, 'we're going there to live.'

'Oh?' said Geraldine. 'I'll see you sometime, then?'

Geraldine began calculating what life would be like without Frank and Grace. She'd have to find somewhere to live, but apart from that, she didn't think things would be much different.

'No,' said Frank, 'you're coming with us.'

Geraldine ceased her calculations.

'No, I'm not,' she fired back.

'You are,' said Frank. 'You're coming with us.'

'When are you going?' said Geraldine, not acknowledging that she was part of Frank and Grace's plans just yet.

'Two weeks,' said Frank.

No-one had been able to locate Harry before they left, so Frank left letters for him at St Austell, which was still up for sale when they moved, and at the newsagents along with a card in the window asking Harry to get in touch. To Geraldine it felt like less than enough, but there was no other way of getting in touch with her absent brother. Twenty-seven hours later, in the early hours of 11 November 1981, Frank, Grace and Geraldine arrived at Perth Airport. Once the Sturmers cleared customs and immigration, everything on the arrivals side was closed, just a group of sleepy, subdued people waiting to greet the passengers. Waiting for the Sturmers were Ada and George Williams, an English couple Frank and Grace had known in Zambia. Ada was a short oblong. George was tall with a long face and made up for his baldness by growing his hair over his jug ears. Geraldine saw them and remembered going for a sleepover at their house one night with their two boys, one younger and one older than her. Around eleven she'd insisted they call Frank and Grace to bring her home. Frank arrived drunk and angry, almost making Geraldine regret her decision, but not quite. On their way out of the terminal, Ada pointed out the black swans in the pond in the forecourt as they walked to the carpark. Geraldine was too busy coping with the heat and a new kind of sweating to notice one of Western Australia's greatest contributions to modern science.

'Belt up,' said Ada, as they settled into the Williamses' Kingswood wagon.

'What?' said Frank.

'Belt up!' Ada's voice reached an even higher pitch. 'You have to wear seatbelts here, it's the law.'

'Oh, belt up,' said Frank. 'Seatbelts. You have to wear them here?'

'Yes, it's the law,' Ada said again.

'We don't have to in England,' said Frank, as he buckled up.

'Fine and demerits, if you don't have them on here,' said Ada.

'What's demerits?' said Frank.

'Like a black mark on your licence,' said George.

'Oh,' said Frank.

They fell into silence as the big V8 pulled them through the airport carpark and onto Great Eastern Highway, although in the dark the Sturmers had no idea where they were.

■□■

As far as Geraldine was concerned, things weren't much better in the light. Over time, she had learned that coming down from speed was a life-sapping, twenty-four hours of ennui and sadness. On the comedown, every part of Geraldine's body ached, sometimes simultaneously, sometimes major limbs and organs taking turns as if to keep things interesting. Geraldine's eyes felt heavy, the lids almost permanently on the close, her head ached and no amount of paracetamol would ease it. Her thoughts became someone else's, stray ideas that stank of hopelessness, futility and, sometimes, death. Geraldine usually sat with these sensations, thoughts and feelings because she knew their possession of her was time-limited. Now, they were with her permanently, and Geraldine began to worry that she wouldn't be able to shake them. The only way she knew how was to do some more speed, and that was currently an impossibility.

During her first weeks in Perth, Geraldine retreated into sleep. Most days she would rise late and watch *The Mike Walsh Show* with Grace and Ada. The darkened lounge room, curtains shut tight against the relentless sun, suited

Geraldine. She could sit quietly, hardly noticed by the two other women. What she saw on the television confused her. The music sounded like it was stuck in a pre-Beatles version of the sixties and the comedy was mostly lowbrow, riding on anything but wit and timing. It all felt manufactured and sanitary to Geraldine – she didn't get it, but at least it was a distraction. Afterwards Geraldine would go back to the room she was sharing with the Williamses' youngest son, Kevin, and listen to records, read and nap until he came home from school. Each afternoon, Geraldine would badger Kevin for any leads on where she could get hold of some drugs. Every day the answer was the same: wait until Jack gets home from over East.

A few weeks in, Geraldine's body began to settle, but her mind remained on edge, keeping her bowels on standby for whatever disaster it imagined might take her down. When she first attempted a solo trip outside the blond brick walls of the Williamses' Maddington spread, Geraldine found herself in a wide, dry wasteland where everything from the heat to the flies to the dizzying height of the sky conspired against her. Geraldine returned, defeated by the crushing silence of the empty streets, having no idea how to transport herself elsewhere. When she got back to the house, she gave in for the first time to an invitation to swim in the backyard pool. She wore a borrowed pair of trunks, being corrected by Ada who told her they're called bathers in Australia, and a t-shirt to cover her breasts as best she could.

'That's good thinking, Gerald,' said Ada. 'The t-shirt'll keep the sun off your back.'

They have no fucking idea, Geraldine thought.

■□■

The Williamses' eldest son, Jack, came home the week before Christmas. Riding with him in the passenger seat of his mum's ancient, dun-coloured mini, Geraldine began to learn another way of life. First lesson was that the drugs of choice in 1980s Perth were, by dint of their availability, grass and, in the inner suburbs, heroin. Geraldine was up for the former, but had always been afraid of the latter.

'What about speed?' Geraldine asked, as they buzzed along Albany Highway.

'What?' said Jack.

'Speed. Amphetamines,' said Geraldine.

'No, I don't think so,' said Jack, obviously uncertain what she was on about.

Geraldine's heart sank. She sat back in her seat watching the lights and cars go by. They passed rows of houses, each sitting on its own patch of land. They drove by strings of shops, streets full of fast-food outlets with drive-throughs and massive carparks big enough to build housing estates on. They drove by shopping centres of the type and dimension that Geraldine imagined existed only in America, these with even bigger carparks. Albany Highway ribboned through the southern stretch of Perth and gave Geraldine a glimpse of all its flavours. She felt the sense of newness and distance acutely and began to wonder how she'd find her way in this city and the country it clung to the edge of. They were on their way to the Overflow to see Dave Warner's From the Suburbs, crossing the Swan River via the Narrows Bridge, the high-rise buildings of the city proper on their right and seemingly infinite empty blackness to their left.

'You'll love Dave Warner,' said Jack confidently.

'What sort of music does he play?' said Geraldine.

'Punk,' said Jack.

Geraldine's spirits lifted.

Jack and Geraldine paid the cover charge and shuffled into the room, a crush of punters in front of and behind them. When he'd said they were going to a pub, Geraldine had a picture in her mind that was vastly different to where she found herself. The Overflow was a glass-and-steel box that felt like it had been built yesterday. Geraldine looked around her at the growing crowd. People were dressed for summer, some looking like they'd come straight from the beach, shorts and skimpy tops being the prevailing fashion for both males and females. Geraldine was wearing her Docs, jeans and her favourite jacket over a white X-Ray Spex t-shirt. She noticed people glancing at her as they jostled by with jugs of amber beer in hand and began to feel uncomfortable. When Jack had finished at the bar, they took up a spot at the back of the room, drinks in hand, and Geraldine watched on as the evening unfolded. Everything was the same. The steady growth of the crowd, the noise rising as anticipation ratcheted up and up. The support bands that were largely ignored and, finally, the dimmed lights and silence over the PA that signalled the main event. Warner and his band played their set with manic energy, and the punters responded in kind. Everything was the same, except for Geraldine. Nothing about the music or the band's performance reached her. Geraldine couldn't pin where her feeling of detachment came from, it was like her body was there, but her mind was somewhere else. Warner sang songs about identity, but they had nothing to do with Geraldine's. It was as if they spoke the same language but all the words had different meanings.

On the way home they stopped off at Hungry Jack's, parking outside and walking into the fast-food outlet. Geraldine had no idea what to order, the massive backlit menus on each side of the counter overwhelming her. Jack looked at her and back to the girl standing at the microphone and gave their order.

'Two Whoppers with cheese, two large fries and two Cokes,' the girl repeated into the microphone.

In what seemed like only moments, their order was handed to them on a tray and they walked over to a booth to sit and eat. Geraldine unwrapped her burger, and her nose was filled with the smell of charred meat and tomato sauce. She picked up the warm bun and took a bite. It was just about the best thing she'd ever tasted, but she didn't say that to Jack.

'These aren't chips,' she said, holding up the cardboard pouch.

'No, that's right, they're fries,' said Jack.

'And this Coke is watery.'

'Next time ask for no ice,' said Jack. 'You get more that way, anyway. How's the Whopper?'

'Yeah, it's okay,' said Geraldine, giving nothing away.

'Did you like Dave Warner?' said Jack.

'Nah, not really,' said Geraldine.

52

Geraldine clung on to Jack because he had a supply of pot, but he wasn't exactly her type. He had curly blond hair, milky-blue eyes and a spoke with the prehistoric screech of a cockatoo on the wing. When he wasn't home for Christmas, he did something in the army over in Sydney. Geraldine didn't ask what and he never told her. The good thing was, he had a lot of friends all over Perth, and Geraldine rode with him as he paid them all a visit, the mini putting on the kilometres from Rockingham to Leederville, City Beach and Craigie. There was also the occasional party and, in between, they'd go to pubs to see bands. Geraldine hated them all equally.

Through Jack, Geraldine met Claire. She lived so close to the Williams family home that they walked there in minutes, taking the road up at the T-junction and the first right. Claire had hair so wiry that she had to tame it with combs either side and a scrunchy to keep it from springing forward into her face. She wore a denim Stuart Membery skirt that came down to her ankles, and completely covered her bottom half when she sat on the floor, which was something she did often. Her face was young, lightly tanned like her exposed shoulders, but her brown eyes were old. When she smiled, Geraldine felt like the world and everything in it would be okay.

'So, you're just here from England?' Claire said.

'Yes, we came a bit over a month ago,' said Geraldine.

'It must be hard leaving people behind?'

Geraldine hadn't thought about it much since she arrived, she'd been too wrapped up in herself. She wondered about Harry for a moment – she'd not heard from him since just before Glastonbury. She'd been hoping for a letter from him, but nothing had come so far.

'It is,' she said.

'Come here,' said Claire, holding out her arms.

She took Geraldine up in a hug. Geraldine leaned into her and felt the comfort of human contact. The last time she'd experienced anything close to this was when she and Sasha had sat at their bus stop, keeping each other warm against the wind. Geraldine's throat caught at the thought of Sasha. She hadn't spoken to her since Glastonbury and still felt bad about how things had turned out. Everything seemed to hinge on her trip to that festival. Geraldine sobbed silently, her chest heaving, hoping Jack wouldn't notice.

'I've got to go,' said Jack, eventually. 'You know the way home, don't you, Gerald?'

'Yes,' said Geraldine, 'and it's Geraldine.'

Jack didn't reply as he left Claire's room.

When Geraldine raised her head, her eyes were still red and she could see a damp spot on Claire's white top.

'I'm sorry,' said Geraldine, feeling ashamed.

'It's okay,' said Claire, 'we came here from Holland five years ago and I still miss home … everyone.'

Geraldine sat up, releasing herself from Claire's arms. The pair looked at each other for a while. Eventually Claire spoke tentatively.

'What did you mean, "Geraldine"?'

'That's who people know me as,' said Geraldine.

'Yes, okay, but what does that mean?' said Claire.

'That's just who I am.'

'What do you mean?' said Claire, 'You're going to have to give me more than that.'

'I'm a woman,' Geraldine said, 'like you.'

'A woman?' said Claire, looking at Geraldine all over again. 'Yes, yes, that makes sense, doesn't it? So, that's your name, then?'

'Yes, Geraldine,' said Geraldine.

'Oh, that's so delicious. Your parents almost got it right.'

'Yes,' said Geraldine, 'it's the closest they've ever come.'

'Do they know?'

'No,' said Geraldine. 'I mean they do, but they don't want to know.'

'So, am I the only one?'

'No, lots of people knew back in England. My brother, my girlfriend, friends. It wasn't exactly a secret. I just didn't go about shouting it from the rooftops.'

'Your girlfriend?'

'We're not together anymore.'

'Ah, I see,' said Claire. 'So I'm the first to know in Australia?'

'You are,' said Geraldine.

Claire seemed pleased with that news.

■□■

Claire took Geraldine to the Cat and Fiddle, all the way over in Mount Lawley.

'You want to see some punk music,' she said, 'we'll go and see some.'

Claire's car was old, massive and formerly silver, now mostly rust. It was automatic, the first one Geraldine had ever seen, and required some complicated-looking pushing of buttons and pulling of levers on the dashboard to select a gear. Once you were off, it rolled along the road like it could keep going forever.

'I'm a terrible driver,' Claire said once they were moving. 'I think that's why Dad got me such a big car – lots of protection.'

Geraldine didn't care. She was excited, and even the faint risk of death and injury at the hands of Claire's driving couldn't dampen her spirits. When they arrived, Geraldine remained encouraged. Along with its English-sounding name, Geraldine's assessment of the venue was that it looked like a proper pub from the outside. Inside it didn't do too badly either: a bar, a few tables and bare wooden floorboards. When Geraldine and Claire stepped across the threshold, they swelled the numbers in the room to five. From Geraldine's perspective the low audience numbers were equally promising. Maybe they might be onto something here. Geraldine was just thinking that when the music started. It was loud, it was abrasive, it was delivered with purpose and very little skill, but according to her narrow definition, punk music it was not. Geraldine sat through the first band feeling sour and watched as people filtered into the room. By the time the band had finished there were about twenty punters milling around in small groups, drinking, smoking and, as is required with live music, waiting. People kept coming in in ones and twos and, when the second band stepped up to do its thing, there were about thirty people there to witness them. Geraldine held her breath as they began and then let it go. They were equally shit.

'Hey, nice badge,' someone said as they wandered by Geraldine at the next break.

Geraldine held still, glaring back, expecting an insult or a punch.

'I'm Lucas,' the person said, holding out his hand.

'Oh, uh, Geraldine.'

They shook.

'Where did you get the badge?' said Lucas. 'You can't get them here.'

'I brought it with me,' said Geraldine. 'I've just come over from England.'

'Holiday, or to live?'

'To live,' said Geraldine.

'Bad luck,' said Lucas. 'There's nothing happening here.'

'Do you want it?' said Geraldine, taking the badge off her lapel.

'Really?' said Lucas.

'Yeah, I'm not going to be here long,' said Geraldine. 'I can get another one when I get home.'

'Wow! Thanks,' said Lucas, holding out his hand. 'Maybe see you again before you go?'

'Yeah, sure,' said Geraldine.

Lucas wandered off to the bar and as Geraldine watched him go, Claire elbowed her in the ribs.

'He totally liked you,' she said.

'What?' said Geraldine. 'He did not.'

'Trust me, I know these things. He was into you in a big way.'

Geraldine blushed and looked at Lucas standing at the bar.

'Come on, let's go,' Geraldine said. 'The music's shit here.'

■□■

Driving home, Claire said, 'So, what's your preference?'

'What do you mean?' said Geraldine.

'Do you like boys or girls?'

Geraldine leaned back in her seat and watched the road go by for a while. She observed Claire as she lit a cigarette using the lighter on the dashboard, inhaling and then exhaling the blue smoke.

'I don't know,' said Geraldine, eventually.

'Don't know what?' said Claire.

'If I prefer boys or girls.'

'Oh, still on that are we?' said Claire, turning to grin at Geraldine, looking away from the road for so long that Geraldine nearly squealed. 'Well, you should find out. If you'd played your cards right you could be in bed with Lucas right now.'

Geraldine sat back and thought some more.

'Is that the best place in Perth for punk bands?' Geraldine said after a while.

'Don't you go changing the subject!'

'What about you?' said Geraldine. 'What's your preference?'

'I don't know if you're ready to know just yet,' said Claire.

53

After Christmas, Frank made an announcement.

'We're moving to Dampier,' he said. 'I've got a job up there.'

'To where?' said Geraldine.

'Dampier,' said Frank. 'It's up north.'

Geraldine was still none the wiser. She was only just sorting out Perth's geography, first arriving at the understanding that Maddington was a shithole and that the further west you went, the less arid things were. Australia was a country with a geography so vast that it was incomprehensible to the uninitiated. Terms like up north, down south and over east meant something if you'd been there, otherwise they were just vague directions.

'Where exactly up north?' Geraldine asked, hoping it might be close to Leederville or Mount Lawley.

'About sixteen hundred kilometres,' said Frank.

'Oh, fuck! Really?' said Geraldine. 'That's not in Perth then, is it?'

'No,' said Frank, looking at her like she was slow.

'When are you going?' said Geraldine.

'End of January.'

'Okay,' said Geraldine, keeping the rest of her thoughts to herself.

Geraldine knew she was never going to Dampier, but she needed to work out how she was going to make that happen. Flat-out refusal hadn't worked out too well for her last time, so this time she needed a different approach.

Geraldine consulted Claire. They were sitting on the floor in her bedroom.

'I need somewhere to live,' she said.

'Why?' said Claire. 'What's happening?'

'My dad's got a job up north, in Dampier.'

'You don't want to go with them?'

'No,' said Geraldine. 'No, I can't.'

'Well, what are you going to do then?'

'I was hoping you'd tell me,' said Geraldine.

'Let me give it some thought,' said Claire.

Geraldine made her first solo outing to the Cat and Fiddle early in the New Year, telling herself across four bus trips and one train ride that she wasn't going just to see if Lucas would be there. As she walked up Beaufort Street, Geraldine was reminded again that Perth was a city built for cars; the only sign of foot traffic was the few people straggling into the Queens, a dark and uninviting looking establishment, and the obviously out-of-it young woman who asked her for a light as she walked past the church on the other side of the street.

She entered the Cat and Fiddle through the wooden corner door and asked for a cider at the bar. Taking her drink to a table at the back of the room, Geraldine watched the goings-on on the stage, taking in the familiar sight of amplifiers and instruments being pieced together. As people slowly filtered into the room, Geraldine smiled to herself, remembering the nights she'd kept the same vigil at events in Weston, except this time it didn't matter to her if anyone turned up – she wouldn't be the one paying the bills. Her thoughts created a familiar feeling in the pit of her stomach. Geraldine knew well the many guises of homesickness. In her early years it had been a simple yearning to be wherever her parents were; now it had evolved into something far more complex as Geraldine wrestled with the idea of home. Life in England hadn't exactly ended on a high note for her, but the graft with Australia wasn't taking and her urge to return to the familiar was strong.

The smile had long gone from Geraldine's face when she heard a voice.

'Tonight's not going to be that bad, is it?'

Geraldine looked up and saw Lucas. He was wearing a black t-shirt and white jeans that just reached the top of his Doc Martens. His hair was black and untidy, but it didn't look deliberate to Geraldine. His face formed around a nose that was slightly too big, overshadowing his plump lips. His eyes were quizzical, and Geraldine realised she'd been staring at him for too long without speaking.

'Uh, yeah, well I hope not,' she said.

'Can I sit down?' Lucas asked.

'Yeah, of course,' said Geraldine.

'Here on your own tonight? 'Where's your girlfriend?'

Geraldine looked at him. This time it was her turn to look quizzical.

'Oh, Claire,' she said. 'She's not my girlfriend.'

They concentrated on their drinks for a while as they both looked towards the stage where the obligatory refrain of 'Check, check one-two' indicated that a start to the evening's proceedings was imminent. Geraldine stayed until the end of the night, not for the music, but to see what would happen with Lucas. She settled in her seat, watching him work the room between sets, talking to the bands and nodding to the punters, giving some of them a greeting as he made his way up and down the dusty floorboards. When the last band was packing up their gear and the houselights were up, Lucas came and sat next to Geraldine again.

'You're still here,' he said.

'Yup,' said Geraldine.

'And, you're still here-*here*,' said Lucas. 'Last time you said you were in a hurry to get back to England.'

'Yeah, well, I thought I'd give this place one more go,' said Geraldine, giving him the faintest smile.

'Do you want to come back to my place?'

Lucas' flat was in a dark-brown brick building a short walk up Walcott Street. To Geraldine it looked like it could have once been some sort of gothic mansion, a place where the likes of Frankenstein's monster and other shunned and misunderstood characters had been dreamed up. When she saw where Lucas was headed, she hung back, wondering what she was getting herself into. The red cement stairs at the side of the building reminded Geraldine of Zambia and, for a moment, her head was a whirl of times, places and experiences. She felt dizzy and couldn't catch her breath. Lucas opened the gate at the side of the building and turned to Geraldine.

'Are you okay?' he asked.

'I might go home,' said Geraldine, barely finding enough breath to say the words.

'Where's home?' said Lucas. 'How did you get here?'

'Why do you want to know that?' she said, taking a step backwards.

'It's cool,' said Lucas, 'I don't need to know. I was just thinking, there might not be any buses now. Unless you drove?'

'No, I caught the bus,' said Geraldine, 'and a train.'

'And a train?' said Lucas. 'Where did you come from?'

'Maddington,' said Geraldine.

'Fuck!' said Lucas. 'That's a long way!'

'Yeah, I know,' said Geraldine, smiling faintly.

'Come on,' said Lucas. 'Come inside for a bit and we'll figure out what to do.'

Geraldine followed Lucas up the stairs to his flat. Inside it was old and run down, but it looked clean enough to Geraldine. The furnishings were an assortment, but things matched somehow, even if they were never intended to by whoever designed them.

'Here, sit down,' said Lucas, gesturing to an armchair sitting opposite the longest settee Geraldine had ever seen. 'I'll get you some water.'

He disappeared into the kitchen and, as she listened to the clink of glasses and running water Geraldine took in her surroundings. The lounge room was large enough, a dining table over towards the kitchen door that was spilling white light into the living area. There was a painting on the wall above the settee. It looked like an original to Geraldine, although she had no reference for this observation. In the dimly lit room she could see bold strokes of colour, but no discernible shapes of people or things. At the opposite end of the room was another doorway, ajar but emitting only darkness. Geraldine assumed this was a bedroom.

'Here,' said Lucas, making Geraldine start as he stood in front of her, holding out a glass of water. 'You look like you could do with this.'

The glass was tinted green and matched the one Lucas held in his other hand. Geraldine watched him sit down and take a sip before doing the same herself. The water was tepid, but it didn't matter to Geraldine. After the first sip she gulped down most of the rest of her drink, having to force herself to leave some in the bottom of her glass, not wanting to appear in some way impolite.

'Looks like I was right,' said Lucas.

He looked across the space between the two chairs and waited. Geraldine looked at him and then looked away, staring at the floor.

'You can stay if you like,' said Lucas. 'I'll sleep on the lounge, you can have the bed. You're never going to get home tonight, anyway.'

54

Geraldine opened her eyes, unable to ignore the sun streaming through the crack in the curtains any longer. She sat up and took stock, and put her clothes on, including her Docs, the events of last night still fresh in her mind. Geraldine put her head shyly around the bedroom door. The living room was empty, but she could hear sounds coming from the kitchen.

'Good morning,' said Lucas, rounding the door with a smile. 'Did you sleep okay?'

Geraldine thought for a moment.

'Yes, I did,' she said.

'You sound surprised,' said Lucas.

'I am a bit,' said Geraldine. 'I haven't slept properly for ages.'

'Are you off?' said Lucas.

Geraldine didn't know what he meant until she registered that she was fully dressed for the street, mostly an English winter street, her bag over her shoulder, and here was Lucas wearing a t-shirt and a pair of baggy shorts.

'Oh,' said Geraldine, 'no, not really. Just thought I'd get dressed.'

'So, you'll stay for a bit?'

'Um, yes?' said Geraldine.

'Tea? Toast?' said Lucas.

'Yes, please,' said Geraldine.

'Make yourself comfy,' Lucas said, disappearing back into the kitchen. 'Take off your boots.'

When he returned, Geraldine was sitting in the same lounge chair as last night, her feet under her, her boots on the floor where she'd pushed them off with her toes.

'That's better,' said Lucas, looking at Geraldine as he handed her a mug and put a plate of toast on the table in front of her.

'I don't like Vegemite,' she said, looking at the toast.

'Have you even tried it?'

'No.'

'Maybe give it a go before you decide, then?' said Lucas.

■□■

'He was lovely,' Geraldine told Claire when she finally made it back to Maddington late that afternoon.

'I'm jealous,' said Claire. 'Tell me what happened.'

'Nothing,' said Geraldine.

'Nothing?'

'That's right, nothing happened.'

'Are you mad?' said Claire. 'You stayed over at his place and nothing happened.'

'We just talked,' said Geraldine, smiling.

'For real? Are you telling me everything?'

'I am,' said Geraldine.

'Are you going to see him again?'

When Geraldine finally made it back to the Williamses' she was greeted with worry that felt like rage.

'Where have you been?' said Frank.

'I was out,' was all Geraldine would offer.

'Out where?'

'I went to see a friend and missed the last bus home, so I stayed at his place.'

'You need to tell us if you're not coming home, luv,' said Grace.

'I didn't know, Mum,' said Geraldine. 'I'm sorry.'

They left the conversation there, Geraldine more determined than ever that she wouldn't be going to Dampier.

■□■

The next time Geraldine set out for Mount Lawley she gave Frank and Grace advance notice that she wouldn't be home that night. They didn't look pleased but they didn't try to stop her either. Geraldine felt her heart race as she climbed the eighteen red steps to Lucas' flat. When she reached the landing, he was standing at the open door.

'You made it,' he said. 'Come on in.'

Geraldine stepped inside and sat on the lounge chair. In the afternoon light she could see it was covered in yellowy-green fabric, slightly worn, but deliciously deep and inviting. The settee was a lighter shade of green and strewn with mismatched cushions. The canvas above it was mostly green as well, as if it was meant to match the furniture.

'Oh, that,' said Lucas, as he followed Geraldine's gaze. 'I painted that to match the furniture.'

'You painted it?' said Geraldine.

'Yes.'

'You're a painter?'

'Of sorts,' he said.

Geraldine and Lucas spent the rest of the afternoon talking, not noticing the light dim until they were sitting almost in darkness. Lucas reached over and switched on the lamp sitting on the table next to the settee.

'That's better,' he said. 'I can see you again.'

Geraldine smiled, shifting in her chair.

'Are you hungry?' said Lucas.

'No, I don't think so,' said Geraldine.

'Would you like to go to bed, then?'

'Yes, please,' said Geraldine.

■□■

Geraldine checked in with Claire on her way back home.

'So, what happened?' said Claire.

'Nothing,' said Geraldine.

'You have got to be kidding me. I would have been all over him by now.'

'He's okay,' said Geraldine. 'Do you think he's okay?'

'He's just lovely, darling,' said Claire. 'Now, tell me, what happened.'

'We had sex,' said Geraldine.

'Oh, my love! You clever girl. How was it?'

'It was rather lovely, actually,' said Geraldine.

'Now, you did use protection like I told you, didn't you?' said Claire.

'Yes, Mum,' said Geraldine, chuckling.

'Don't be cheeky, darling. Your mum would never give you such good advice.'

Claire reached out her arms to Geraldine and the pair hugged.

'Thank you,' said Geraldine.

'What for?' said Claire. 'I haven't done anything yet. Although I do have some news for you, if you're interested.'

'Oh, yes, what's that, then?'

'I know someone who's looking for someone,' said Claire. 'I think I might have found you a job.'

'Really?'

'Yes, come with me and meet them tomorrow.'

■□■

Back at the Williamses', Geraldine lay on her bed trying to figure everything out. If she got a job, she'd have a reason to stay in Perth beyond the end of the month. She'd just need somewhere to live. Geraldine knew she'd need to have a job for a while before she could rent something. Even share houses asked for a bond and rent in advance, and she didn't have the money right now. As far as she could figure, she had a couple of options. She could ask Frank and Grace for the money or she could ask Ada and George if she could stay on at their house for a bit after Frank and Grace went to Dampier. Geraldine wanted to make a clean break so she decided to ask the Williamses, but she knew she'd have to clear the reason for staying with Frank and Grace first.

'Where would you stay?' said Grace, once she and Frank had digested the idea that Geraldine might stay in Perth to work.

'I thought I'd ask Ada and George if I could stay here for a while until I've saved some money.'

Frank and Grace looked at each other.

'I don't know if that's such a good idea,' said Grace.

'Why not?' said Geraldine.

'I don't know,' said Grace, looking to Frank. 'It just might not be such a good idea.'

'Well, I'm going to ask them anyway.'

'Right,' said Frank, 'but don't be disappointed if they say no.'

■□■

Geraldine took a breath and started the conversation after dinner. They were outside under the pergola, the two couples drinking wine and smoking, Kevin in the pool.

'Ada? George?' Geraldine said to get their attention.

Ada turned towards her.

'Yes?' said George.

'It looks like I've found a job,' said Geraldine.

'Oh, yes?' said George.

'I was wondering …' Geraldine paused. 'Would it be okay if I stayed with you for a while after Mum and Dad move to Dampier?'

Ada and George exchanged looks.

'Er, no, I don't think so,' said George.

'It would only be for a little while,' said Geraldine.

'No,' said Ada. 'You're not staying under our roof.'

'Why?' said Geraldine, wondering what was wrong.

'Leave it, Gerald,' said Frank.

Geraldine got up and left the table. Frank and Grace came into her room a few minutes later and sat side by side on the bed opposite Geraldine.

'You can't stay here,' said Frank.

Geraldine sat up and faced her parents.

'Why not?' she asked.

'You just can't,' said Frank. 'Ada and George don't want you staying here.'

'Why?' said Geraldine.

'They think you're a bad influence,' said Frank.

'A bad influence?'

'Yes,' said Grace, 'on Kevin. They don't want you sharing a room with him.'

'Why not?' said Geraldine.

'You know full well why not,' said Frank. 'You can't go around like you do without people noticing.'

'Go around like I do?' said Geraldine, the problem becoming clear to her.

'It's Ada and George's house,' said Frank. 'We're lucky they've let us stay this long.'

'Lucky?' said Geraldine.

'Aye,' said Frank, turning on the Yorkshire, 'lucky. Now, that's an end to it.'

'What if I find somewhere else?' said Geraldine.

'You can stay in Perth,' said Frank. 'If you find somewhere, you can stay.'

Geraldine picked herself up and left the room, Frank and Grace still sitting on the bed. She walked the distance to Claire's at a furious pace, her face dripping with sweat by the time she reached the blond-wood door. Once they were sitting on the floor in Claire's room, Geraldine spat out her words.

'They don't want me,' she said.

'Who?' said Claire. 'Who doesn't want you?'

'Them,' said Geraldine. 'Them. Everyone. No-one wants me.'

By now she was sobbing hard, her head hanging down in her lap. When the roaring began, Claire put a hand on Geraldine's shoulder.

'I want you,' she said.

Geraldine raised her head slowly.

'Really?' she said.

'Yes, really,' said Claire. 'Now let's sort all this out. Tell me what happened.'

55

Geraldine began working in Derek and Jill Coulter's Highgate warehouse in the summer of 1982, just before Frank and Grace departed for Dampier. She started out picking and packing orders for retailers across Perth and was soon fronting up to shops to get them to stock the latest items as well as finding new outlets. Boans and Aherns were among her best clients, and they became easy pickings for Geraldine once she realised that they spent a lot of time looking over each other's fences. Besides, she ploughed a fair bit of her wages back into the two department stores, buying the latest arrivals and showing them off for Lucas when she got them home. Once he'd seen enough, Lucas would end Geraldine's fashion parades with a shy instruction.

'Go put on my favourite outfit.'

Geraldine would disappear into the bedroom for a few moments, returning in all her naked glory.

■□■

Lucas worked in an abandoned shop down on the opposite side of Beaufort Street from the Queens. He painted in the display window for all the world to see, though not a single one of the few pedestrians walking by would have had a clue who he was. He spent most Fridays with artist colleagues from the Media Arts Collective, often getting home late buzzing with ideas and vitriol about and the politics of living in what he called one of the last colonial outposts.

'You know,' Lucas said one Friday night, 'meeting like we do in a public place is still illegal in Western Australia without a permit from the police.'

'Oh yeah?' said Geraldine, distracted by the glow of the TV.

'Yeah, it is!' said Lucas. 'Geraldine, listen. Listen to me. This is important stuff.'

Geraldine turned away from the film and looked at Lucas still standing, the glow of the kitchen light behind him.

'Did you get arrested tonight, or something?'

'No.'

'Did the cops come and move you on?'

'No.'

'What the fuck are you complaining about then?'

'You don't understand, Geraldine. We're not even free to gather in public places and share ideas in this state.'

'It must be Friday, hey.'

'What do you mean?'

'You're a part-time activist, Lucas. I never hear any of this shit from you any other day of the week. You're all talk and paintings.'

'You take that back!'

'Make me.'

Lucas launched himself at Geraldine and held her down on the couch where she'd been zoning out in front of the TV. He held his face close to hers, pinning her arms and using the weight of his body to keep her in place.

'Take that back.'

Geraldine could feel the movement of his breath on her lips. She extended her neck and kissed him.

'Make me,' she said.

Afterwards, Lucas cut up some grass and packed a cone, handing the bong to Geraldine. They sat in front of the TV until the station shut down, Lucas' activist fervour diluted by the sex and drugs. Geraldine closed her eyes and replayed all the times she'd been held down.

■□■

Though she saw plenty of it, Geraldine remained indifferent to what was being served up in Perth's music scene. Lucas was known in venues across the city and they rarely had to pay a cover charge. He, and increasingly Geraldine, would spend nights talking to musicians, getting to know who was doing what and where. Geraldine didn't consider it to be research of any kind, in her mind she was just being polite, but she had a turning point in a city nightclub late one night when she saw a cover band play a note-perfect version of 'Going Underground'. It was a song she'd never seen the Jam play live, her abrupt departure from England having limited to three the number of times she got to see them, but she knew they'd never have done it this way. Geraldine was so angered by the band's performance that she gave them two fingers, an act that would have seen her removed from the venue by the bouncers had it not been for Lucas' intervention.

'I want to go, anyway,' said Geraldine, once Lucas had smoothed things over. 'I'm fucking sick of this.'

In the car on the way home the words poured out of Geraldine. She railed against the copycat cover bands making money out of other people's art and the boring original bands who all sounded like they were stuck in another era or came from a different world entirely.

'I think that's the point, isn't it?' said Lucas, when Geraldine paused for breath.

'What?' said Geraldine. 'What do you mean?'

'Well, you are in a different world, remember?' said Lucas. 'This is Australia.'

Geraldine looked at him, her eyes narrowed.

'But it's second-rate,' she said.

'No,' said Lucas, 'it's Australia. Maybe you just don't get it?'

Geraldine looked away, watching the scenery passing by and hiding her tears. When he heard her breath settle, Lucas spoke again.

'You should do something about it,' he said.

'What do you mean?' she said, turning her head back to him.

'You know pretty much everyone in town now. Start something.'

■□■

In bed one evening, they were drifting off to sleep, bathed in the glow of their orgasms and the words just fell out of him.

'I know somewhere you can get waxed, if you like,' said Lucas.

'You fucking what?' said Geraldine.

'I know somewhere,' he repeated, turning back around towards her. 'It's not a big deal, is it? You're just getting a bit hairy.'

‘Fuck you!’ said Geraldine, getting out of bed and beginning to dress.

‘What?’ said Lucas. ‘What are you doing?’

‘I’m taking my fucking hairy crack and I’m leaving,’ she said, throwing the underpants she’d found mixed with her knickers at his head.

Geraldine ran down the stairs and down into the one a.m. stillness of Walcott Street. She headed away from Beaufort Street, and when she reached the end took a right up Charles Street, walking until she couldn’t. Geraldine sat down, still boiling with anger. When she realised there was nothing she could do she finally stood up and retraced her steps. Red light was breaking through the clouds when she opened the gate and climbed the stairs to the flat. Lucas was in bed asleep and Geraldine tried unsuccessfully not to wake him as she undressed and slipped back into her side.

‘Are you okay?’ Lucas asked, reaching out an arm for her.

Geraldine rested her head on the vee of Lucas’ armpit, smelling his sweat from another hot night.

‘No.’

‘What can I do?’

‘I don’t know,’ said Geraldine. ‘Nothing.’

‘I’m sorry.’

‘I know. It’s not your fault.’

‘What can I do?’ Lucas asked again.

‘I don’t know,’ Geraldine repeated. ‘Nothing.’

Geraldine told Lucas about her humiliating visit to the doctor in England and her black-marketeering.

‘Geez, Geraldine, you’re fucking amazing,’ he said.

‘What do you mean?’

‘Well, I don’t know anyone else who would do that,’ said Lucas. ‘I’m just, like … That’s just amazing is all.’

‘You think?’ said Geraldine.

‘Yeah! You’re an outlaw! But you’re fucking right, aren’t you? I mean you’ve just done what you needed to do.’

‘Yes,’ said Geraldine, ‘and now I need to do it again somehow.’

‘And there’s no way you’d try another doctor here?’

Geraldine shook her head.

'Are you sure?' said Lucas. 'They'd only need to take one look at you to know you're right.'

Geraldine raised her head to get a better look at Lucas.

'What do you mean?'

'Well,' said Lucas, 'which bit of you is male?'

'My fucking hairy crack, for starters,' said Geraldine, 'and this!' she continued, throwing aside the sheet and rolling onto her back.

Lucas looked at her.

'Geraldine,' he said, 'I've always seen you as female, since the first I saw you. What makes someone a woman or a man, anyway? We've talked about this at the collective. You're not the only one, you know.'

'You haven't been talking about me, have you?' Geraldine said, covering her body with the sheet.

'No,' said Lucas. 'No way. We talk about lots of stuff, but I'd never talk about you like that. But there are other transsexuals, right here in Perth.'

'But none of them are like me, are they?' said Geraldine.

'No,' said Lucas, 'there's no-one like you.'

They lay side by side for a while and Geraldine began to drift off to sleep.

'Do you have private health cover?' Lucas asked, just before she was gone.

'Do I have what?' said Geraldine, opening her eyes but not looking at Lucas.

'Private health cover. To help pay the doctor's bills.'

'I'm not going to the doctor,' she said, and closed her eyes.

56

Five years after her visit to the doctor with her mum in Weston-super-Mare, Geraldine chose to go to this first appointment on her own. The GP had been recommended by one of the members of Lucas' collective, and it took Geraldine three buses to get to her rooms in Subiaco. On the way, as well as reminding herself that she must learn to drive, Geraldine tried to think of anything but what she would say. The medical clinic was in a converted house on a suburban street. Geraldine pushed open the glossy white front door and walked down a short passageway to reception.

'Geraldine Sturmer to see Dr Higson,' Geraldine said to the woman in white behind the counter.

The woman checked her list of appointments and, satisfied that Geraldine was on it, handed her a clipboard.

'Fill this in, please, and bring it back when you're done.'

Geraldine sat down to fill in the form. She hesitated over the choices for Sex – Male/Female. Geraldine hovered the pen over the words and eventually circled 'Female'. Signing at the bottom of the form, Geraldine took the clipboard to reception and went back to her chair to wait, her heart racing.

Dr Higson was younger than Geraldine had expected her to be, her only previous experience with the medical profession being doctors who were old and male. Despite her youth, Dr Higson looked like a mother. Her skin was fresh and her eyes smiled no matter what the rest of her face was doing.

'Geraldine?' she said, looking around the waiting room.

Geraldine stood up and walked towards Dr Higson, who on seeing her turned and walked back towards the hallway.

'This way,' said Dr Higson, without looking back.

Geraldine had to do some very stern self-talk to stop herself from running past the doctor and out the front door.

'Now, what can I do for you?' said Dr Higson once they were seated and she'd read over Geraldine's form.

Geraldine took a breath in and out while Dr Higson looked at her intently.

'I'm a woman,' was all Geraldine could say to begin with.

Dr Higson continued looking at her without speaking.

'I'm a woman,' Geraldine said again. 'I need your help.'

For a moment, Geraldine thought the doctor was going to keep just looking at her. She shifted in her seat and looked away from the doctor's gaze.

'How long have you felt like this, Geraldine?' Dr Higson asked her eventually.

'All my life,' said Geraldine, making eye contact with the doctor again.

'Okay, so what are you hoping I can do for you?'

'I—' said Geraldine, 'I don't know. I went to see a doctor back in England and he told me not to waste his time.'

'And do you think you're wasting my time?' said the doctor.

'I don't know,' said Geraldine. 'No. I just try to be me.'

The doctor looked at Geraldine again.

'Well, I have to say, you're doing a pretty fine job,' she said smiling.

'Thank you,' said Geraldine, only just getting the words out before she started to cry.

Dr Higson handed her a tissue.

■□■

Geraldine walked out of Dr Higson's surgery and floated up the street feeling a deep sense of peace. As soon as she got home she picked up the phone to make an appointment with Dr Miller, the psychiatrist Dr Higson had referred her to. At first, when the doctor had told Geraldine that she would need to see a psychiatrist, she had stiffened with anger and hurt.

'But there's nothing wrong with me,' she said.

'I know,' said Dr Higson, 'but that's what we've got to do so you can get back on estrogen. Don't worry, it'll be okay, it's just what we have to do.'

Geraldine had quickly calmed down, trusting that Dr Higson was on her side and, feeling like things were finally running her way, looked forward to taking whatever next steps she needed to take. Her phone call to Dr Miller's number brought Geraldine back to earth with a mighty thud.

'What do you mean "there's a waiting list"?' she said into the phone.

Geraldine listened to the voice at the other end of the line.

'But I need to see him,' said Geraldine.

Geraldine listened some more.

'But, I can't wait, I need to see him now.'

Geraldine listened some more.

'My address?' she said. 'You're going to write me a letter? You can't even give me an appointment now?'

Geraldine listened some more. She recited her address into the mouthpiece then listened some more.

'A few weeks?' she said.

Geraldine listened some more.

'That's when I'll get the letter? The appointment might not be for six months?'

Geraldine listened some more. Then she smashed the phone down so hard she broke the dialler. She sat and looked at the broken plastic for a long time. Then she got up and rummaged through the bottom drawer in the kitchen, finding a tube of glue, and carefully stuck the dialler back together, hoping that when it set it would be strong enough to keep doing its job and that Lucas wouldn't notice. Afterwards, Geraldine went to bed and stayed there until Lucas returned home long after dark.

■□■

By the time the letter from Royal Perth Hospital arrived, Geraldine had just about expelled her rage. What surprised her was the sadness and lethargy that followed her spike of emotion, having been lifted up and then, in her eyes, so cruelly let down again by the medical system. She had difficulty concentrating, settling to her tasks at work, and found it hard to pretend that she was interested in the shop owners and department store workers who enabled her to make a living. Lucas took Geraldine to the ocean, but summer was gone and she didn't find the mess of foamy waves ruined by the south-westerly wind at all inviting. Geraldine tried more alcohol, more grass, but whatever was living inside her never properly went away. She slept and waited.

'Do you think you should go back and see the doctor?' Lucas asked, eventually.

'What for?' said Geraldine. 'It just shouldn't be this hard. I'm playing their game now and they make me wait and wait. Six months! How could it take six months to get to see a doctor?'

'Geraldine,' said Lucas, 'it's six months. You've been waiting your whole life so far. Can you not wait a little while longer?'

'I don't think it's the time, really,' said Geraldine. 'I think it's that they're making me wait. It's because they're the ones in control. That's what I can't get over.'

'I'm going to hate myself for saying this,' said Lucas.

'What?' said Geraldine.

'Do something about it,' he said.

Geraldine looked at Lucas across the bed and punched him hard on the shoulder.

'You're right, you should fucking hate yourself,' she said beginning to laugh.

Lucas held his shoulder, smiling back at her. 'That hurt,' he said.

'Oh, poor darling, do you want me to make it better?'

'Yes,' he said.

'Fuck off!' said Geraldine, getting out of bed, still laughing.

■□■

Geraldine sat opposite Claire at the cafe.

'You're looking tired,' Claire said.

'Yeah, no, I'm okay,' said Geraldine.

'Come on, Geraldine, who is it you are speaking with?'

Geraldine always knew Claire was properly serious when she slipped back into the formal English she'd learned when she came to live in Australia.

'I'm worried about you.' Claire said.

'Why?'

'Because I am. You know, because I care?'

Geraldine took a long pull of her Diet Coke.

'I don't know what's wrong, Claire. Sometimes I feel like I'm dying, like I've got some sort of horrible disease.'

'Then you should go see a doctor.'

'I can't. What if I'm right? I'm scared, Claire. Sometimes I don't know how I'm going to survive.'

'How's things with you and Lucas?'

'They're okay.'

'Just okay?'

Geraldine took another slug of her drink.

'Yeah, okay,' she said. 'No, better than okay. Lucas is lovely. He's kind. He gave me a place to stay.'

'Do you love him?'

'Remember when we were in the car that time, Claire, the first time you brought me here?' said Geraldine.

'What about it?'

'You never told me.'

'Never told you what?'

'Who you sleep with.'

'Well, I'm not sleeping with anyone at the moment.'

'You know that's not what I mean,' Geraldine said.

'I like variety, let's say that much,' said Claire. 'Now, back to you. Do you love him?'

As she walked back up Beaufort Street towards Lucas' flat, Geraldine's breath began to betray her. She slowed her steps to ward off the staggers, leaning her bum against the churchyard wall while she reoriented herself. Geraldine looked down Beaufort Street back to where she'd just been sitting with Claire and thought she saw the rusty glint of her car. Geraldine's breath quickened again and then stopped as an ancient faux-American sedan rolled past her. Not Claire. Claire was long gone.

57

In her time of waiting, Geraldine decided that motion was her best defence against the rising tide of whatever it was that assailed her. By the time her appointment with Dr Miller came around, Geraldine was working days and nights, still selling Glomesh and now booking musicians into venues across Perth, mostly solos and duos who stood in corners of pubs and played music while the patrons ignored them. She was perpetually tired, but Geraldine found that concentrating on work and returning to the craft she'd begun to learn in Weston-super-Mare kept the dissenting voices from the ascendancy in the chatter of her mind.

Geraldine's appointment began with the filling in of the forms, this time a questionnaire about how she was feeling tucked under the usual name, address and identity questions. Geraldine skimmed through the questionnaire, which asked her to think about herself over the last two weeks and answer questions like, 'I felt there was nothing good for me in the future' and 'I had difficulty concentrating on tasks'. This time she breezed through the gender question, not hesitating to circle 'Female', but the survey questions made her stop and think. In the end, Geraldine decided to lie.

Dr Miller was an older male with greying hair, a craggy face and a moustache. Geraldine took an instant dislike to him. She sat in the seat he'd gestured to and watched while he shuffled through his papers. Geraldine put her hand on her left knee to stop it jiggling, only to have the right one start up.

'So, Geraldine,' said Dr Miller after what felt like to her had been longer than forever, 'it seems you're in exceedingly good health.'

Geraldine didn't know if he was asking her a question, so she kept quiet.

'Yes,' said the doctor, looking across his desk at her, 'the blood tests show nothing out of the ordinary. Slightly low testosterone level, but within range.'

Again, Geraldine kept quiet.

'And the survey you just filled in,' said Dr Miller, 'I just scored it and it looks like your mood is good, too. Is it?'

Geraldine wondered if there was something in her responses that had given her away.

'Er, yes, I'm fine, thank you, doctor,' she said.

'So, why are you here, then?'

'Um, you have a letter from Dr Higson?' Geraldine began.

'Yes, I have the letter, Geraldine, but I was hoping you might tell me yourself,' said the doctor, just barely cracking a smile.

'Er, okay,' said Geraldine. 'I'm a woman, as you can see. I've known forever, but I have this other body …'

'Yes?' said the doctor.

'Well, it's not mine,' said Geraldine. 'It is, but it isn't, it's not female.'

'Are you not female?' said the doctor.

'No,' said Geraldine, 'I mean, yes, I am, I always have been, but my body is wrong. I need to change that.'

'So, if you had a pill that would make you your choice of either male or female and give you the body that matched your gender, would you take it?'

Geraldine considered the question, looking for loopholes and trickiness that might bring unexpected consequences with her choice of answer. Dr Miller watched her while she thought.

'Yes, in an instant,' she said.

'And, just to confirm, Geraldine, what would your choice be?'

'Female,' said Geraldine.

This seemed to satisfy Dr Miller. He spent the rest of their time talking about what could happen next. Toward the end of the appointment, Dr Miller invited Geraldine back into what had mostly been a one-sided conversation.

'Whatever you choose, Geraldine, it's up to you. None of this will change who you already are. It's not really you who needs to change, it's almost everyone else. I just want to make sure you're informed about the effects and potential risks. I think we start with estrogen and an anti-androgen to lower your testosterone, and we can talk about what next in six months or so. What do you say?'

'Yes,' said Geraldine, keeping her response short lest she sounded too greedy.

'Good,' said Dr Miller. 'I'll give you the prescriptions and you can make another appointment for six months' time on the way out. I'll also write to Dr Higson to let her know what we've decided.'

'Thank you,' said Geraldine.

'Any problems, give me a call,' said the doctor. 'And think about what I said.'

58

Geraldine first talked to Brent and Janine after a battle of the bands at the Cloverdale Hotel. The winner that night was a hair metal trio called Threesome, who were obviously going places. But they weren't what attracted Geraldine, who was taken with an outfit that called themselves Witless, fronted by a young singer with scruffy blond hair who, when he opened his mouth, had a voice that was all feisty sadness. He was sided by a dark-haired guitar player with a black leather jacket who drove their songs forward with deftness and dexterity, knowing exactly when to step back and play nothing and when to give it everything. The two shared a mic when they sang harmonies and, best of all in Geraldine's mind, they played an almost unrecognisable version of Television's 'Friction', collapsing it to a ragged halt after just a few minutes, the singer back announcing the song with, 'Fuck it, that's all we could be bothered to learn.'

'You two were great,' said Geraldine in the green room after the show.

'And the band?' said Janine.

'Oh, yeah, and the band,' said Geraldine.

They told her they'd call, but after a couple of weeks of not hearing from them, Geraldine decided to take a different tack. She turned up at their Leederville share house on a Saturday morning, not too early, and knocked on the door. The woman who answered, wearing a blue sarong and looking like she'd not yet been to bed, was neither Brent nor Janine. She stood at the half-open door, her hand holding its edge, and looked at Geraldine suspiciously without saying a word.

'Are Brent and Janine home?' said Geraldine.

'Uh, yeah, I'm not sure,' said the woman. 'I think so.'

She opened the door and turned to walk back into the entryway.

'Come, this way,' she said.

Geraldine could see the entry led to the kitchen and beyond that an open living area.

'It's that one,' the woman said, gesturing to a closed door on the right of the entryway while continuing her journey back to the kitchen.

Geraldine stood at the closed door while she thought about what to do next. In the end she figured she was already intruding so she may as well go all the way. She knocked on the cream wood. There was no answer. Geraldine knocked again, more urgently this time, with the same result. She stood in the hallway listening for any signs of life in the bedroom but heard nothing. Geraldine took a breath and turned towards the kitchen, where she found the woman who had let her in the house sitting in a papasan chair with a steaming mug in one hand and a cigarette in the other.

'Hi. I don't think we've been introduced.'

'I don't think we have,' said the woman, clearly surprised to see Geraldine at this end of the house.

'What's your name?' said Geraldine.

'Well, who wants to know?' said the woman, sweeping her hair out of her eyes with the hand holding the cigarette.

'I'm Geraldine. I met Brent and Janine a while ago. Their band played a show at the Cloverdale.'

'Oh, right,' said the woman, warming up ever so slightly. 'I'm Alexandra, but people call me Alex.'

'Nice to meet you, Alex,' said Geraldine. 'Do you mind if I sit down?'

'Nope,' said Alex, 'knock yourself out.'

Geraldine pulled out one of the chairs at the dining table and turned it half towards where Alex was sitting, the sun streaming in over her shoulder.

'I tried knocking on their door,' said Geraldine, gesturing down the passage with her head. 'Do you think they'll be up soon? Are they even home, do you know?'

'I'm sorry,' said Alex, 'I don't know. We were pretty wasted last night, but I think they're still home. Do you want a cup of coffee?'

'Do you have any tea?' said Geraldine.

'Yeah, over on the bench there, next to the kettle,' said Alex. 'Help yourself.'

Geraldine walked behind the kitchen bench and filled the kettle, putting it on the gas and then looked for a mug.

'Any of these?' she said to Alex, holding up a mug from the dish rack.

'Yeah, that'll do.'

Geraldine was pouring boiling water onto a teabag when she heard Brent's voice.

'What the fuck?' he said, looking at Geraldine. 'How did you get in here?'

Geraldine finished pouring and put the kettle back on the stove.

'Alex let me in,' she said. 'I tried knocking on your door, but …'

'Yeah, well, we were asleep,' said Brent. 'And I'm going for a shower.'

Brent's announcement explained his decision to wear just a towel around his waist. Geraldine's next guess might have been the beach, but Brent didn't seem like a beachy type to her and, besides, it was winter.

'I can wait, if that's okay,' said Geraldine.

Brent glared at her as he walked towards the bathroom at the back of the house. Geraldine decided to take his look as an invitation to stay at least long enough to drink her tea. She returned to her seat over by Alex.

'He's just lovely, isn't he?' Alex said to Geraldine, the lines around her eyes as she smiled giving away her age.

'Seems so,' said Geraldine.

Alex lit another cigarette while they sat and waited. When Brent had made the return journey from the shower, Janine repeated his steps, a towel wrapped around her chest. She eyed Geraldine as she walked by but gave her no other greeting or hint of recognition. Geraldine looked down, fiddled with her almost empty mug and considered taking a draught of the cold dregs to show Janine that she still had a reason to be in her dining area. Alex sat and watched, enjoying the show. When Janine returned from the bathroom, her wet hair leaving a trail of water behind her, Geraldine heard voices coming from their bedroom, muffled and indecipherable through the sturdy door and thick internal walls of the 1930s California bungalow. When they finally emerged from their room, Brent and Janine took up chairs on the opposite side of the table to Geraldine.

'Now,' said Brent, 'who the fuck are you?'

Geraldine hadn't expected this opening; she was used to people remembering her.

'Oh, er, um,' Geraldine fumbled. 'I'm Geraldine.'

Brent kept looking at her. Janine was looking over at the kitchen bench like she'd lost something.

'We met at the Cloverdale,' said Geraldine. 'I gave you my number.'

'Did we ring you?' said Brent.

'No,' said Geraldine.

'So, what are you doing here, then?' said Brent. 'How did you find out where we live?'

'Lucas gave me your address,' said Geraldine.

'Who's that?' said Brent.

By now Janine was over in the kitchen, kettle back on the stove and making coffee.

'You remember, Lucas,' said Janine. 'He's the painter. I think his daddy gives him money.'

Geraldine almost came to Lucas' defence, but she decided to let it go.

'Oh, him,' said Brent with a smirk.

He looked back at Geraldine.

'I'm Lucas' girlfriend,' she said.

Brent looked at her, inspected her.

'Well, alright then!' he said with a raised eyebrow. 'Good old Lucas.'

'Stop it,' said Janine, back at the table with two mugs of coffee. 'Leave the poor girl alone, she'll start to think we're being rude or something.'

'Sorry,' said Brent, 'we get all sorts here. It's hard keeping up sometimes. What do you want?'

Geraldine left her encounter with Brent and Janine wondering if she was wasting her time trying to work with them. They'd heard her out, Brent with a look of defiant indifference and Janine at best neutral. They told her they'd call and, when Geraldine asked, assured her they actually would this time. Geraldine wasn't convinced, but there wasn't much more she could do, so she left it at that. She walked up Woolwich Street towards the city, the quiet calm separating her from her thoughts.

On the bus home Geraldine closed her eyes and thought about the future.

'Hey, gay boy, get out of my seat.'

Geraldine opened her eyes with a start. The owner of the voice was in his mid-twenties and dressed all in black from his desert boots to his mullet, the only hint of colour the white AC/DC logo on his t-shirt. Standing behind him was a woman. Geraldine could see her green eyes looking around his shoulder.

She took a breath. 'Fuck off,' Geraldine said.

The bogan balled up his fists and opened his mouth. His companion tugged at his shoulder.

'Maybe leave him alone?' she said.

'No way,' he said and then looked back at Geraldine. 'Get out of my seat.'

'Make me,' said Geraldine, staring at him and leaning back against the window of the bus, stretching out her legs to take up the rest of the space on the seat.

'C'mon, let's go,' said the girl.

The man spat at Geraldine, his spittle landing on her cheek.

'C'mon, let's go,' he said, turning to his companion.

Geraldine wiped her face on her sleeve and stared at the couple as they moved closer to the back of the bus. She breathed in and out until her heart rate was back to normal. When the man turned to sit down and saw Geraldine staring, he looked away. The girl's face looked like an apology, a half smile and worried eyes. Geraldine shook her head at her and then broke contact. She leaned her forehead against the bus window and closed her eyes again, letting the vibrations and the sound of the diesel engine soothe with its mechanical lullaby.

59

The drug that killed Geraldine wasn't recreational, it had been prescribed for her by Dr Miller. Used to treat high blood pressure and heart disease, Dr Miller had explained to Geraldine that the spironolactone would lower her testosterone levels helping with the feminising effects of the estrogen. Geraldine had been feeling pressure in her chest for weeks, maybe a month or two before she died, but she wrote it off as anxiety, took a breath and carried on.

Geraldine opened her eyes on a sunny September Saturday morning to find herself alone in bed. Lucas would often get up early to paint, returning around lunchtime with chocolate brioche for their breakfast. Geraldine turned over to get another half hour and could almost smell the doughy bread and the sharp tang of the dark chocolate. When she woke again, Geraldine decided to get up and face the day, the sun now too bright to ignore any longer. She sat up and waited at the edge of the bed for a moment before standing naked, waiting another moment for the dizziness to dissipate. Geraldine's head didn't quite clear so she decided that movement was her best bet. She took the two steps to the foot of the bed, picked up the doona, one hand on each of its bottom corners and gave its cloudy whiteness a shake, watching it settle into place on the bed. Not quite satisfied with where it lay, Geraldine gave the doona another shake.

Geraldine came to on the rug at the foot of the bed, the doona, still gripped in each of her hands, partially covering her and the bottom quarter of the mattress. Bob was nestled between her neck and shoulder – she could feel his silky fur as he adjusted to curl himself into her and hear the urgency of his heartbeat. Geraldine felt tired, tireder than she had ever been. She let go of the doona and slept.

'Go away, you'll scare Bob,' said Geraldine. 'Leave me, I just need to sleep.'

'No, Geraldine,' said Lucas, 'you need to wake up.'

He was standing over her, a leg either side of her naked body, his face close to hers. Geraldine tried to raise her hands to protect herself, but she couldn't.

'Shhh,' said Lucas. 'Just look at me. I've called an ambulance.'

'An ambulance?' said Geraldine. 'I've just been sleeping. I'll be okay, I just need to wake up.'

'What's that?' said Lucas. 'I can't hear you. No, no, don't close your eyes, keep looking at me.'

Geraldine struggled to open her eyes. Lucas' face was framed with sunlight.

'Are you Jesus?' said Geraldine.

'What?' said Lucas. 'I can't hear you. Have you taken something, Geraldine? Did Brent give you something?'

Geraldine closed her eyes and went back to sleep, her breath so shallow that Lucas had to put his ear to her mouth to make sure she was still alive.

■□■

Geraldine woke the next morning in Royal Perth Hospital, a drip in her arm and Lucas in the chair by her side. Her mouth was so dry, her lips so cracked she could barely manipulate her tongue to speak.

'Lucas,' she said.

Lucas started in the chair, turned towards her. He looked down at Geraldine in the bed with a tear rolling down the right side of his face. He wiped it away.

'Geraldine,' he said. 'What? What did you say? You're awake.'

He tried to smile but his eyes gave him away.

'Lucas,' Geraldine said again.

'I can't understand what you're saying. Here, have a drink.'

Lucas filled a paper cup from a plastic jug and held it to Geraldine's mouth. She tried to drink, but her lips were like stone. Lucas tipped up the cup and watched as some water dribbled into Geraldine's mouth while the rest spilled down her front. Geraldine choked and opened her mouth painfully while she spluttered most of the water into Lucas' face.

'More,' she said.

Lucas held the cup to her lips, and this time Geraldine was able to drink without dribbling and spitting water like a toddler.

'Lucas,' Geraldine said again.

'Geraldine,' he said, 'I thought you were gone.'

'What happened?' she asked.

'The doctor in emergency said low sodium,' said Lucas. 'Your heart stopped in the ambulance, I thought you were going to die.'

'I think I did,' said Geraldine. 'Bob was with me. He only comes when I'm dying.'

'What?' said Lucas.

'Bob,' said Geraldine. 'Is he here?'

Lucas made a show of looking around the room that contained one bed, one chair and very little else.

'No, I don't think so,' he said. 'Who the fuck is Bob?'

'I don't know really,' said Geraldine, 'but he comes around sometimes when I'm thinking about leaving.'

'Leaving?' said Lucas, now more confused.

'It's okay,' said Geraldine, 'he's this little furry thing. He's no competition for you.'

■□■

The ward doctor came to see Geraldine later that morning. He introduced himself and then turned to Lucas.

'Who are you?'

'I'm Lucas.'

'Are you a relative?' said the doctor.

'Yes, um, no,' said Lucas. 'I'm Geraldine's boyfriend.'

'Geraldine?' said the doctor.

'Yes,' said Lucas, looking over at Geraldine, who was lying in her hospital bed watching the to and fro.

'Can you leave the room while we examine the patient, please?' the doctor said, framing it as a request when it was clearly a direction.

'I'd like him to stay,' said Geraldine.

'Don't worry,' said the doctor, looking at Geraldine for the first time, 'he can come back in when I've finished.'

Geraldine didn't have the strength to argue.

'Now, Gerald,' said the doctor, 'you've had a very serious episode. You could have died.'

'It's Geraldine.'

'Look, this is very serious,' said the doctor. 'I'm not about to indulge your little fantasy, I have more important things to do, so please don't waste my time.'

Geraldine looked at him. She was afraid of what might happen next; the heart rate monitor at the side of her bed showed an instant spike.

'Try to stay calm, please,' the doctor said, glancing at the display on the machine. 'I just have some questions for you.'

Geraldine nodded as she breathed in and tried to get a grip on her anxiety.

'Why are you taking spironolactone?' the doctor asked.

'I, er, Dr Miller gave it to me.'

'Yes, I can see that he's the prescribing doctor, but what is he treating you for?'

'Because I'm a woman,' Geraldine said quietly. 'He's helping me.'

The doctor looked at Geraldine.

'Well, clearly you're not, Gerald,' said the doctor. 'And that drug damned near killed you. You're staying here so we can keep an eye on you. I'll be back to check on you later today.'

Finished with his patient, the doctor scribbled some notes on Geraldine's chart and hung the clipboard at the foot of the bed, leaving the room without saying another word. When Lucas came back into her room Geraldine had sunk her head into the pillows, her face turned from the door.

'Are you okay?' said Lucas.

Geraldine didn't answer.

■□■

Dr Miller came to visit Geraldine late on Monday. He stood in the doorway of her room and she eyed him suspiciously from her hospital bed, unsure what it was he'd come to say.

'How are you, Geraldine?'

'I'm okay.'

'I hear you've been having a rough time.'

Geraldine took Dr Miller's cue and unleashed.

'That doctor,' she said, 'I don't even know what his name is, but I'm over people like him. If he calls me Gerald one more time, I'm going to get out of this bed and punch him in the face.'

Dr Miller smiled. 'I meant with your side effects from the spiro,' he said, 'but it sounds like you're recovering well.'

Dr Miller took a step to the chair next to Geraldine's bed and sat down.

'Oh, yeah, I'm feeling a bit better,' said Geraldine.

'Geraldine, why are you so angry about the doctor here?' said Dr Miller.

'Because he's been denying who I am,' said Geraldine. 'Deliberately.'

'Deliberately?' said Dr Miller.

'Oh, yes,' said Geraldine, 'absolutely.'

'Why do you think he'd do that?'

'It's obvious, isn't it?' said Geraldine.

'Is it?' said Dr Miller. 'Tell me.'

Geraldine paused to marshal her thoughts. She'd felt confident in her knowledge until Dr Miller had asked her to explain. When she thought about how to describe it, all she had was her certainty.

'I don't know,' said Geraldine slowly, 'I just know that it's deliberate. He wouldn't even let Lucas stay in the room while he was talking to me.'

'Well,' said Dr Miller, 'maybe you need to have a think about that and we can talk about it some more next time we meet. Looks like they'll be discharging you tomorrow. Why don't you give my receptionist a call to make an appointment to see me?'

'Okay,' said Geraldine.

Dr Miller stood up.

'I'll see you soon, Geraldine,' he said. 'Look after yourself. Meantime, stay off the spiro and we'll talk about that when I see you as well.'

■□■

There were messages for Geraldine when she got back to Lucas' flat, including one from Janine. Geraldine decided not to call back. Her post-hospital exhaustion made even the task of dialling the phone feel insurmountable. She sat on the chair she'd occupied the first time she'd come to Lucas' place and looked around her, eyes only half focused. For a moment she thought she saw Bob skittering behind the couch opposite her, but she knew he was long gone. The space around her felt unsettled.

60

Sitting on the other side of Dr Miller's desk a couple of weeks later, Geraldine was ready to explain what she'd been unable to articulate in the hospital.

'He denied my existence,' she said.

'What do you mean?' said Dr Miller.

'He wouldn't listen to me or recognise who I am. He used my birth name like it was a threat. And he wouldn't let Lucas be with me.'

'That's because it's illegal,' said Dr Miller.

'What do you mean?'

'I assume you and Lucas have a sexual relationship,' said Dr Miller.

'Yes,' said Geraldine.

'That's against the law here in Western Australia.'

Geraldine looked at Dr Miller, her frown hooding her eyes.

'Against the law?'

'Yes,' said Dr Miller, looking back at her and waiting for her reply, which was a long time coming.

'Fuck,' said Geraldine, quietly, mostly to herself. 'Fuck,' she said again, this time to Dr Miller. 'Fuck that and fuck him and fuck you.'

Geraldine stood up and made to leave.

'Geraldine!' Dr Miller's raised voice made Geraldine sit down again. 'Geraldine,' he said again, 'I'm on your side. I can understand that you're angry, but I'm on your side. Not everyone in the world is against you. You should remember that.'

Geraldine looked at Dr Miller and nodded without saying anything.

'You're right,' continued Dr Miller, 'there are people who don't believe, don't agree with you. Every day I have people telling me that what I do to help people like you is wrong, but that doesn't mean I'm wrong and it doesn't mean you are, either.'

Geraldine's eyebrows released her frown as they pushed up in surprise.

'But you,' she said, 'you're a doctor. What do you mean – people tell you you're wrong?'

'What I do is highly contested, Geraldine. We're pushing the envelope here and not everyone agrees. In fact, hardly anyone does.'

'So, why do you do it?' said Geraldine.

'Because of people like you,' said Dr Miller. 'So I can help you to be who you are.'

Dr Miller handed her a tissue across the expanse of his desk.

Geraldine snorted with tears and laughter.

'That'd be good,' she said.

■□■

Geraldine left Dr Miller with a prescription for cyproterone, his explanation of the long list of potential side effects zinging through her mind.

'We're going to start on a really low dose,' Dr Miller had said, 'and see what that does for you. You shouldn't have any trouble with it that way.'

Geraldine was filled with fear. She didn't want to experience death again and even more she didn't want to end up back in hospital.

■□■

Claire came to see Geraldine the day after her appointment with Dr Miller. Looking at her across the lounge room from her position in still-sick repose on the couch, Geraldine realised this was the first time Claire had come to visit her at Lucas' flat.

'You don't really like Lucas, do you?' said Geraldine, mostly as a confirmation of her own realisation.

'I do,' said Claire. 'He's fine. I just don't like him for you.'

'Oh?' said Geraldine. 'And who do you like for me, then?'

'No-one in particular. I just think you can do better.'

Geraldine studied her friend and, though she wouldn't say it right now, knew that Claire was right. She held her tongue while she gathered her thoughts.

'Did you know that we're illegal?' she said.

'What on earth do you mean, Geraldine?'

'It's against the law for us to have sex in Western Australia. Me and Lucas,'

Geraldine confirmed. 'Me and you would be okay.'

'Oh that. Yeah, I did,' said Claire. 'And, as for us having sex, I love you, babe, but not like that.'

'I know, but it's fun to think about sometimes. I reckon you'd be a wild ride.'

'Oh, you don't know that half of it,' said Claire. 'If you and Lucas are against the law, I ought to be in jail by now.'

Claire's smile turned into a throaty laugh. She lit a cigarette and Geraldine watched her, wondering.

'What do you mean, Claire?'

'I'm a sex worker, Geraldine.'

'Oh. You told me you worked in a call centre.'

'Yeah, call girl. Get it?'

Geraldine laughed even while she was stung by her friend's secrecy. She decided to get over it and say nothing. Claire's news about Lucas was a greater concern for her.

61

Eventually, Geraldine made the call to Janine. They met at the Rosemount Hotel in North Perth. Geraldine got the drinks: beer for Janine and cider for herself. She sat down opposite Janine and passed over her glass. It was early on a Monday evening and quiet, no live music on the menu tonight. Geraldine looked at Janine across the table as they settled with their drinks. Her black mullet reminded Geraldine of the bogan she'd had the run-in with on the bus, but everything else about her was completely different, from her wide brown eyes to her deliciously pink lips, the silver and jade necklace and her hands with their long slender fingers, each one adorned with a silver ring, some of them simple bands, others more ornate and bearing stones of various colours. On her right ring finger was a snake's head, rising from its silver base, mouth open as if ready to strike. She even had a ring on her right thumb.

'I'd like to play here some time,' said Janine.

'What?' said Geraldine, dragging herself back to the present.

'Here,' said Janine. 'I want to play here. Can you make that happen?'

'Sure,' said Geraldine, having no idea.

'You can?' said Janine.

'Yeah, of course,' said Geraldine, with so much confidence that she even believed herself.

'You know Brent's not keen, right?' said Janine.

Geraldine didn't know this. She'd suspected that neither of them was keen, as Janine put it, so she'd come tonight wondering what Janine might have to say for herself.

'I thought so,' said Geraldine.

They paused and took a sip of their drinks. Geraldine decided to take the lead and see what happened.

'What else would you like to do?' she said.

'What do you mean?' said Janine.

'Well, you said you want to play here,' said Geraldine. 'What else do you want to do?'

'I don't know, I guess I just want to see what happens.'

'You don't have a plan?' said Geraldine.

'No,' said Janine, looking across the table at Geraldine like she'd just teleported in from another planet.

'Would you like to have a plan?' said Geraldine. 'And someone to help you make it happen.'

'What about Brent?' said Janine.

'Do you really need him?'

■□■

Janine ended up staying with Geraldine at Lucas' flat for a while, sleeping on the long luxurious green couch that took up the wall underneath Lucas' painting. When Janine had told Brent she wanted to work on her own music he'd kicked her out of Witless and the house on Woolwich Street. When Geraldine got Janine's call it took her a while to help Janine settle back into coherent speech. Once she had a grip on what had happened, she told Janine to stay where she was and she'd be over to pick her up. Lucas drove Geraldine to West Leederville.

'What are we getting into here, Geraldine?' he said, looking at her from the driver's seat.

'We're just helping a friend, Lucas,' said Geraldine.

'But we hardly know these people,' said Lucas. 'Brent's a junkie, you know? Janine, too, probably.'

What Lucas said made sense, but it didn't deter Geraldine.

'I'm pretty sure Janine is okay,' she said.

'I fucking hope so,' said Lucas. 'I don't want to get in the middle of any of that sort of shit.'

'It'll be okay,' Geraldine said, hoping to reassure him but wondering now what she was getting herself into.

When they pulled up outside the deli, Janine rushed to the back door and jumped in.

‘Quick,’ she said, ‘we need to go.’

Lucas pulled the car away from the kerb.

‘What’s the hurry?’ said Geraldine.

‘I don’t know,’ said Janine, ‘I’m scared. Of what he might do.’

‘He hasn’t done anything to you, has he?’ said Geraldine. ‘He hasn’t hurt you?’

‘No,’ said Janine.

‘Okay,’ said Geraldine.

It wasn’t until they were upstairs in Lucas’ flat that Geraldine realised Janine had nothing with her.

‘Where’s all your stuff?’ she said.

‘Back at the house.’

‘Okay,’ said Geraldine, ‘we’ll go back and get it tomorrow. Do you still have a key?’

Janine searched in her bag.

‘Yes, I do,’ she said, holding it up as proof.

62

When Geraldine suggested to Lucas that they look for a rental over on the west side of the city he was reluctant.

'We could even buy a place,' said Geraldine.

They got into one of their long discussions, roaming all over the issue but never quite addressing what was between the two of them. When Lucas accused Geraldine of wanting to be a suburban housewife she was livid.

'What did you say?' said Geraldine.

'You heard me,' said Lucas.

'Go fuck yourself, you arsehole.'

'Well, tell me I'm wrong.'

Instead, Geraldine took another line.

'Well, at least my daddy doesn't pay for everything,' she said.

Geraldine could see the hurt and fear in Lucas' eyes. He sank back into the couch and looked at Geraldine like he was ready to cry.

'It doesn't seem to have done you any harm,' Lucas said eventually.

'What do you mean?' said Geraldine.

'You live here, too, you know,' said Lucas.

'Not for much longer if this keeps up.'

■□■

While Lucas slept, Geraldine struggled for calm and stillness. When she knew she wouldn't turn to Lucas, she got up and sat at the end of the couch where Janine was sleeping. She slid her hands under the blanket so she could rub Janine's feet, gently waking her. The two women talked into the early hours of the morning and, when they'd decided what to do, Geraldine crept back to the bedroom and climbed into the bed next to Lucas. He stirred but didn't wake. Geraldine lay next to him on her back, her mind throwing up thought after thought. She was still awake when Lucas planted a kiss on her cheek.

'Good morning,' he said, his breath like sour milk.

Geraldine turned on her side to face Lucas.

'Good morning,' she said, her eyes searching his, but finding nothing.

63

Geraldine, Claire and Janine moved to Rupert Street, Subiaco, just after Geraldine's twenty-first birthday in 1985. The house was at the Rokeby Road end of the street and looked like it hadn't been lived in for a while, its white facade tending more towards grey and the rose bushes in the front garden overgrown and strangled with grass. Inside were two front bedrooms either side of the passageway that led to the living area, kitchen and, at the back of the house, a sleep-out framed with louvred windows that opened onto the back garden, a path dividing two portions of overgrown couch edged by patches of dirt that may once have been flowerbeds. Geraldine and Janine had fallen for the place the moment they'd seen it, and when Geraldine had called Claire to tell her the news, she'd asked if there was room for her.

'Sure, you can have the sleep-out,' said Geraldine, not thinking to ask Janine.

When she told Janine, her friend's response was the wrong sort of chilled.

'Who is Claire?' she said.

'She's a friend of mine,' said Geraldine. 'She's one of the first people I met when I came over here.'

'Yeah, but I haven't met her,' said Janine, her eyes steel under her blunt fringe. 'You should have asked me.'

Geraldine's first impulse was to remind Janine how she'd rescued her and that she owed her. She opened her mouth to say the words, but something arrested her breath. It had a lot to do with Janine's folded arms. Geraldine had never seen her quite like this before and she was confused and, fortunately for her, the confusion made her wary.

'I'm sorry,' she said, 'I didn't think. I told her she'd have to have the sleep-out,' she said, thinking this would appease Janine.

'The sleep-out?' said Janine. 'I was going to have that, it's got room for my gear and I can practise in there.'

'Oh,' said Geraldine, 'of course. Well, have it then, it's your choice.'

'Thanks,' said Janine, 'but don't do that again.'

■□■

Telling Lucas what she'd decided was even trickier. It blew up into a blazing row and never recovered from there.

'So you're just going to fuck off and live with your girlfriends?' said Lucas.

Geraldine could hardly miss the sarcasm, but she asked anyway.

'What do you mean?' she said.

'You know what I fucking mean,' said Lucas.

'No, I don't think I do,' said Geraldine, knowing exactly what he meant, but wanting him to say it.

Lucas refused to oblige her, instead shifting the focus of his attention.

'Did you ever love me?' he said.

Geraldine thought for a long time, looking at Lucas across his coffee table from the chair where she'd first sat when she came up the red concrete stairs to his flat.

■□■

While Claire spent evenings and weekends restoring the gardens, humming gently as she tamed the rose bushes and pulled up weeds and grass roots, Janine spent most of her time at home in the sleep-out with her guitar. Around a month after they'd moved in, Janine walked into the lounge room where Geraldine and Claire were chortling archly at the inane script and wooden acting of *Cop Shop*.

'Do you two want to hear a song?'

Geraldine looked away from the TV, surprised at her annoyance at being interrupted. Janine was standing in the doorway to the kitchen, holding her acoustic guitar.

'Yeah, I'd love to,' said Claire, getting up to turn down the sound.

Janine pulled out a chair from the dining table and sat down, taking a breath before starting to play. When she finished, there was dead silence in the room.

'Did you like it?' said Janine, shifting in her chair.

'That was fucking spectacular,' said Geraldine.

'I agree,' said Claire. 'What she said.'

Janine smiled tentatively. 'Want to hear another one?'

Geraldine and Claire sat forward in their seats while they listened. Janine's voice was clear and bell-like, full and round. Geraldine had never heard anything like it before and her heart instantly fell for its beauty and warmth while her mind calculated the impact it would have on audiences. In all, Janine played six songs that night. When she'd finished, Geraldine followed her through to the sleep-out while Claire turned up the volume to watch *A Country Practice*.

'I didn't know,' said Geraldine, sitting next to Janine on the edge of her bed.

'Didn't know what?' said Janine.

'I didn't know you could sing like that,' said Geraldine. 'I knew you could play guitar, but that voice!'

'You like it?' said Janine.

'Like it?' said Geraldine. 'I love it, darling, and so will the rest of the world.'

'You think?' said Janine.

'I know,' said Geraldine.

She'd never been more certain of anything.

'I know we've talked about working together,' said Geraldine, 'but I don't know if I'm good enough for you.'

'What do you mean?' said Janine.

'I don't know if I can take you where you're going,' said Geraldine. 'You need someone proper, someone who knows the industry better than I do.'

'We'll see about that, shall we?' said Janine. 'You'll do me for now.'

'Okay,' said Geraldine, relieved. 'How about we work on putting a band together?'

'Yeah, we can do that,' said Janine, 'but I'd like to try out the songs a bit more. Can you get me a solo spot?'

'Too fucking right I can,' said Geraldine.

64

Her first Friday night at the Subi Hotel, Geraldine watched Janine get an early taste of her power as a performer. Right on Rokeby Road, the hotel's front bar was a magnet for workers and smart-suited businessmen catching a few drinks before heading home at the end of the working week, and a first stop for nightclubbers getting themselves prepped for a big night on the town. By six the place was usually heaving, the chatter turned into a wall of noise as alcohol and other substances kicked in. It was an intimidating place for a muso to play, squeezed up against the wall at the far end of the room under the TV where Friday night football was the main order of the day. Most people stood with their backs to you or, at best, side on at the bar, those facing in your direction showed the underside of their chins as they looked up at the TV.

Janine played her first song to absolute indifference. Geraldine watched from the side of the room as her friend sang her heart out and played with fire and skill that none of these ignorant fuckers would ever have seen before, if only they'd take a moment to look. Janine finished the song and looked over at Geraldine, dismay clouding her eyes. Geraldine clapped as loudly as she could, a couple of blokes at the bar looking around at her as if she was mad without registering why she was applauding. Janine dived into the next song with the same result. She looked over at Geraldine and shook her head. Geraldine gestured to her with her hand like a sock puppet mouthing, 'Talk to them.' Janine paused to tune her already in-tune guitar, head down. When she'd finished, she raised her face to the crowd, flicked back her hair and opened her mouth to let out a wail that cut through the unison of voices. A few heads turned towards her as she began to play the perseverative blues shuffle of Muddy Waters' 'Mannish Boy'.

'C'mon, men, sing this one with me,' Janine yelled into the microphone before breaking into the vocals.

By the time she got to the first refrain, enough people were singing the words with her that it began to quell the talk in the room, more heads turning to look at what was happening under the TV. By the time Janine reached the end the whole room was yelling the chorus back to her, confirming their manhood to the woman at the back of the room. Janine kept them repeating it over and over. People walking by on their way to somewhere else stepped into the bar to see what was happening, and by the time the noise had died down, the already full venue was rammed.

'Now I've got your attention,' said Janine to the crowd, 'how's about an original from yours truly. Are you up for that?'

The roar of the crowd carried Janine into her next song and when she'd finished her set they clapped and stamped their feet for more, those lining the pub's long wood-and-brass bar banging their hands on it to show their approval.

'Sorry, I don't have any more. You'll just have to come back next week,' Janine said with a grin as she started to pack her gear away.

A group of mostly males stayed by the tiny stage under the TV as the crowd behind them started to thin, people deciding that now was a good time to head to their next destinations. Janine spoke to each of them, shaking hands and telling those who asked that the Subi was the only place they could see her play. Geraldine slipped away to find the bar manager. When she'd come down a few weeks earlier to introduce herself and see if she could book a spot for Janine, Geraldine had been surprised to meet a woman.

'Well, you're a fucking woman, too,' Edie had said. 'Aren't you?'

'Yeah,' said Geraldine. 'Yes, I am.'

'Should be more of it, I reckon,' said Edie. 'Now, whaddaya want?'

Speaking to Edie now, Geraldine addressed Janine's 'See you next Friday' comment.

'Yeah, I reckon that'll be alright,' said Edie, watching the punters flow out of the bar.

'Two sets?' said Geraldine.

'Yep, that'll do for me,' said Edie.

'That'll be double, then,' said Geraldine.

'Yeah, alright then,' said Edie, 'but don't get too fucking cocky and wear out your welcome already. We'll see how next week goes, then we can talk some more.'

■□■

Next week there were people standing in the street looking in through the windows of the bar. Janine made them wait until the end of her second set before she played 'Mannish Boy', and this time it felt like the whole street was yelling the words back at her.

'I'm Janine McArdle,' said Janine as she played the final shuffle, hanging on the E, 'and don't you fucking forget it!'

■□■

'You've fucking got it!' Geraldine said to Janine as they left the Subi to walk home.

'Got what?' said Janine, with the archest of arch coyness.

'I don't know,' said Geraldine, 'but whatever the fuck it is, you've got it.'

The pair were still giggling at their conceit and everything the future might hold as Janine pushed open their gate. They sat in the lounge room and took the edge off their hubris with a few cones. Geraldine withdrew into her high and, looking at her surroundings, was transported for a moment back to St Austell, Langport Road. She looked to her left, expecting to see Harry, wanting to reach out and talk to him.

65

'So, you're well, Geraldine?' Dr Miller asked as a starter at her six-month follow-up.

Geraldine stopped to think about the question. She'd come to trust this old male a bit more since their last meeting.

'Yeah, I think I am,' she said.

'And the cyproterone, is it causing you any problems?'

'No, I feel fine on it. No worse than usual, anyway.'

'That's good. it's certainly had an impact on your testosterone level. It's lower than most females would be.'

Geraldine took in this news quietly.

'Wait, you said no worse?' said Dr Miller. 'What do you mean?'

'I mean I'm going fine. Things have changed a bit since I saw you last.'

'Oh?' said the doctor.

'Yes. Lucas and I aren't together anymore. I've moved into a house with a couple of girlfriends.'

'Do you have another partner?'

'No, not at the moment.'

'How are you feeling about all that?'

'I'm feeling like me. Properly me. Probably for the first time in my life.'

'That's good,' said Dr Miller.

They sat in silence while he looked at Geraldine across his desk.

'So, where to next, Geraldine?'

'What do you mean?'

'Well, if you don't mind me saying so, my observation is that you're a bit of a fighter.'

Geraldine was back on guard again.

'I don't mean anything negative by that,' Dr Miller said. 'I think you're a strong woman. I'm just wondering what you're planning to do with your strength.'

'What, besides everything I've already done?' said Geraldine.

'Yes, as well as that,' said the doctor.

66

'What do you mean?' said Geraldine, when the keys player in one of Perth's rising bands told her backstage that it was she who had inspired him.

'You're a fucking icon, Geraldine,' he said, 'You make it possible for people like me to exist.'

Geraldine looked at him quizzically.

'Nah, I'm nothing like that,' she said, 'I'm just the me I've always been.'

'But that's it,' he said. 'You just fucking rock who you are and people take notice of that. Your existence means there might be a place for others, too.'

Geraldine brushed off the compliment with laughter. Thinking about it afterwards, she had a moment of self-hate at what she'd done. She tracked down Gavin's number, gave him a call and arranged to meet.

■□■

'I'm sorry, Gavin,' Geraldine said, once they were seated.

'What?' said Gavin, 'what do you mean?'

'I blew you off the other night,' said Geraldine. 'I think you were telling me something important and I completely blanked you.'

'It's okay,' said Gavin. 'I shouldn't have just come out with it like that, but I didn't know when I'd get to see you again and I wanted to let you know.'

'Yeah, that's what I didn't get,' said Geraldine. 'What did you want to let me know?'

Gavin looked around the tables and booths of the Hungry Jack's they were sitting in. They were both drinking Diet Cokes, Geraldine's with no ice. She watched him look over the mostly empty fast-food joint, wondering what he was doing.

'What's the go, Gavin?' said Geraldine. 'I feel like I'm in some James Bond movie or something.'

'I want to make sure no-one can hear me,' said Gavin.

Geraldine looked at Gavin as she slurped up some Diet Coke through a fat yellow straw. She was beginning to lose patience with this whole thing.

'This is hard,' said Gavin. 'I've never really spoken to anyone else about this.'

Geraldine kept her eyes on Gavin, hoping she was managing to look sympathetic.

'I, uh, since I was a kid,' said Gavin, 'I've liked to wear women's clothes.'

'So?' said Geraldine.

'So, it's hard,' said Gavin. 'I started with my mum's things, bra and knickers, some lipstick and it would make me …'

Geraldine waited until she knew Gavin wasn't going to say any more without being nudged.

'Make you what?' she said. Then added, 'It's okay,' hoping to be reassuring.

This time Geraldine found herself looking around the room. HJ's hadn't changed much in the five years since she'd arrived in Perth.

'It would make me so horny,' Gavin finally said.

'Oh,' said Geraldine, hoping she'd managed to hide her surprise. 'So?'

'So, then afterwards, I'd feel so fucking stupid,' said Gavin. 'I'd just have to get everything off and … and I'd feel, I don't know, ashamed.'

'Right,' said Geraldine, beginning to feel properly out of her depth.

Gavin took a drink from his waxed paper cup, and Geraldine drank from hers. They sat across from each other and didn't say anything for a long while. A fly buzzed lazily across the space between them, landing next to a splatter of tomato sauce. Geraldine wondered for a moment what the previous occupants of the booth had talked about, concluding that it couldn't have been anywhere near as excruciating as this.

'Have you ever felt like that?' said Gavin, after he'd noisily finished his drink, shaking his cup to string it out by hurrying along the melting of the ice that still filled most of its volume.

'Er, no, I haven't really.' Geraldine took a breath and continued speaking. 'But, you know what, Gavin, that doesn't mean anything except that we're different. Everyone's different, you know. Do you still wear women's clothes?'

'Yeah, I do, but only in private, at home.'

'And how's that working for you?'

'I dunno,' said Gavin. 'It's less intense now, less … sexual. It just feels right.'

'Do you know why?' said Geraldine.

'I, no, not really,' said Gavin.

'So, why did you talk to me the other night?' said Geraldine.

'Well,' said Gavin, 'you're out there. People know you, respect you. No-one ever gives you a hard time.'

'That's not quite true,' said Geraldine.

'What do you mean?' said Gavin.

'I cop plenty,' said Geraldine. 'Random strangers, doctors, family.'

'Really?'

'Yep,' said Geraldine.

'So, how do you deal with it?' said Gavin. 'You go around like nothing could ever get to you.'s

'It's a good act, isn't it?' said Geraldine. 'Mostly these days, I just stand and face them. Sometimes I keep my head down, sometimes I run away, but mostly I stare those fuckers down.'

'I don't know if I could do that,' said Gavin.

'Maybe you don't have to,' said Geraldine. 'Maybe you just need to figure out how to do you first.'

'Yeah, maybe,' said Gavin. 'I dunno, it's hard.'

'It is,' said Geraldine, 'but after a while, it gets even harder hiding. You can't hide forever. Speaking of hiding, what would you like me to call you?'

'I have a name,' said Gavin, 'but I don't use it in public yet.'

'Do you want to tell me what it is? No pressure.'

'Kym. That's who I am,' she said, a smile breaking across her face.

'Would you like me to call you Kym?'

'Can we keep this between us?'

'Of course. You'll let me know when you're ready, right? In the meantime, that's who I'll always know you to be,' Geraldine said.

■□■

Geraldine took her idea first to Edie at the Subi Hotel. It was a Friday morning before opening and they sat on tall stools at the empty front bar drinking beer and huffing the smell of disinfectant that didn't quite mask last night's vomit.

'You want to bring Janine back to play a few more Fridays for us?' Edie said hopefully.

'Yeah, no, I don't think so,' said Geraldine, cursing herself for not being quick enough to take the lead.

'What then?' said Edie.

'I want to put on some events and I'm looking for the right venue,' said Geraldine.

'What sort of events?'

'I want to put on music in places that are safe for queer people, and trans people.'

Edie looked at Geraldine and took a sip of her drink.

'That can't happen here,' she said.

'What?' said Geraldine. 'Why?'

'Look, you know I'm a dyke, so I guess that's why you've come to me,' said Edie, 'but I'm running a bar. That'll lose us customers.'

Geraldine was gobsmacked. She'd expected a sympathetic hearing from Edie for exactly the reason Edie had just stated. What she got was a lesson in queer politics.

'People are scared,' said Edie. 'AIDS is dropping gay men like flies and scaring the shit out of all the heteros. It just won't work. We'd have people protesting in the street and no-one would come, not even the queer folk. It'd be a fucking disaster.'

'Do you really think so?' said Geraldine. 'It'd be that bad?'

'Yes,' said Edie. 'Worse probably.'

'Hmmm,' said Geraldine, 'well, okay, thank you.'

Geraldine made to finish her beer and head off.

'Just wait a minute,' said Edie, 'hear me out.'

Geraldine swivelled back on her stool to face Edie.

'I'm just telling it to you straight, no fucking pun intended,' said Edie. 'What about the Red Lion or Connections? Have you thought about those?'

'I have,' said Geraldine, 'but I want to use other venues. It's time we hit the mainstream.'

'I know what you mean,' said Edie, 'but I don't think it's the right time and I'm not doing anything like that here. I'd lose my job.'

'Maybe some things are worth losing your job over?' said Geraldine, getting up to leave.

■□■

It didn't matter whether the proprietors, owners, bookers, venue managers, whatever, were male or female, gay or straight, Geraldine kept getting the same knockback for pretty much the same reason. Everyone was scared and, apart from the few established gay venues in Perth, no-one was willing to be the first to step out of line. But every knockback made Geraldine more determined. After her seventh less-than-polite rejection, she stopped asking at established venues and turned her mind to alternatives. Geraldine also turned her mind to how she could create maximum impact. When she had it figured out, she talked it through with Janine.

'You're going to do what?' was Janine's initial reaction.

'You heard me,' said Geraldine.

'Are you sure?'

'I've never been more sure,' said Geraldine.

'Well, okay, then, I'm in,' said Janine. 'This is going to be a hoot!'

67

It wasn't hard to get the other bands on board once they knew Janine and her new band, Snake Oil, would be headlining, but Geraldine knew she needed to let them know what they were in for before she went ahead with the rest of her plan. She gathered them together in the back bar of the Charles, just after the skimpies had finished and the tradies had emptied the pub's carpark of their utes and topped up the roads with another hundred drunk drivers. Just another Friday night in Perth. When Geraldine told the bands what she had planned, there were questions, plenty of them, and Geraldine found herself standing up in front of an audience instead of at the back of the room, which was by far her preference. At the end of an hour she'd convinced the bands' members that what she had planned would give them more publicity than a front page in the local street press and a feature in the *West Australian* combined. That was the clincher for them. Geraldine had learned a long time ago that musicians will do pretty much anything for a bit of publicity.

■□■

When the production crew arrived at the back of the church at lunchtime on the Saturday of the show, their white-sided van was greeted by the parish priest.

'You will be careful, won't you?' was his first request.

'Yeah, mate,' said the black t-shirted muscle man who'd hopped out of the driver's side of the van. 'We know what we're doing.'

'Well, I'll leave you to it.'

In the week leading up to the show, Geraldine and the bands on the line-up had been flyering the Red Lion and Connections, handing over each 'Reclaim the Church' handbill with a word of encouragement and an exhortation to spread the word. When Edie called Geraldine on the Thursday before the show to warn her to be careful, she knew that word must be getting around. When she suggested Geraldine bring some flyers down to the Subi, Geraldine almost told her to fuck off, but instead she took some down, handing them to Edie and thanking her for her support.

'See you there, will we?' said Geraldine as she turned to leave the bar.

'I dunno,' said Edie. 'I might be busy.'

'Yeah, whatever,' said Geraldine.

■□■

On the Friday before the show, Geraldine dropped into Derek and Jill's Glomesh warehouse. It had been a few months since she'd quit selling fashion to concentrate on selling rock-and-roll full time.

'To what do we owe the honour?' said Derek, apparently still unhappy about losing his best saleswoman.

'It's alright, love,' said Jill to Geraldine. 'He just misses you is all. Do you want a cuppa?'

Geraldine accepted Jill's offer and they sat for a while in the break room mostly in silence, not always completely awkward. Finally, Derek moved things along.

'Some of us have to get to work,' he said, standing up. 'Is there anything we can do for you, Geraldine?'

'Can I use your fax machine?'

Derek looked at Jill.

'Of course you can, love,' said Jill. 'What're you sending?'

'Media releases,' said Geraldine. 'I'm trying to promote a show.'

'Oh, well,' said Jill, 'go ahead and good luck to you.'

Geraldine sent faxes to the *West Australian*, the *Sunday Times*, Channel 7, Channel 9, the ABC, 96FM and 6PR. Under the heading 'Queer Perth Reclaims the Church', the flyers announced that some of Perth's best musicians were due to play a show in Subiaco Church of Christ the next day and that the entire queer community of Perth – lesbian, gay, bisexual and trans – was invited. Geraldine had included her phone number for media contact. She went straight home after sending the faxes to wait for the calls.

■□■

There were no calls on Friday night. Geraldine went to bed disappointed and spent a sleepless night wondering at the wisdom of what she had started. The phone calls started the next morning before she'd properly woken up. Worse than that, she hadn't anticipated being asked to do live radio first thing in the morning. She was completely unprepared. By the time she arrived at the church, just after one in the afternoon, the priest was walking up and down the nave between the rows of pews looking agitated. The PA was in the final stages of set up and the bands would be arriving to soundcheck in about an hour. When the priest saw Geraldine framed with sunlight as she opened the front door of his church, he rushed towards her.

'Geraldine!' he shouted when he'd only just covered half the distance between them, his voice reverberating off the church's high ceilings.

Geraldine hurried her step to meet him.

'What is it?' she said. 'Is everything okay?'

'Yes, no, I don't know,' said the priest. 'I've had some calls about tonight, from the radio and the television. They're saying it will involve, er, homosexuals.'

Geraldine noted with satisfaction that TV stations were showing an interest.

'I don't know,' said Geraldine, sounding surprised. 'I guess some might come. That would be okay, wouldn't it?'

'Er, yes?' said the priest.

'So, it'll be okay, then?' said Geraldine.

The priest looked at Geraldine like he'd missed moving a critical piece on the chess board they'd been playing on since Geraldine had first come to meet him months ago.

'And the church will still get a nice donation,' added Geraldine.

The priest nodded and looked like he wanted to say more but didn't.

■□■

Geraldine had timed the start of the event for four in the afternoon, telling the priest that they would be finished by eight, a very respectable hour. As people started to drift towards the church entrance from three, Geraldine kept the front doors closed so that by the time four came around there was a sizeable crowd milling around in front of the church doors standing under the large rainbow flag Geraldine had persuaded Lucas to paint for the occasion. There were two TV crews filming, cameramen pointing at anything that moved and reporters holding microphones looking for a story to tell. When the police arrived, Geraldine was standing in front of the crowd on the top stair outside the church. A uniformed officer with a megaphone jumped out of the passenger door of the first cop car and began to address the people on the church steps.

'Disperse now, this is an illegal public gathering.'

The crowd at the top of the church steps quietened and shrank towards Geraldine. She moved to the other side of them to stand closest to the street and the cops.

'We've booked this church for an event and we're going inside to enjoy some music,' Geraldine shouted across to the police, who were advancing towards the church steps. Geraldine turned and yelled, 'Open the door!'

When the doors opened, the crowd stumbled inside the church, milling in the nave, but not yet taking seats. They were looking back at Geraldine standing in the doorway, the police advancing up the steps.

'Disperse now, this is an illegal public gathering,' the officer with the megaphone said again, so close that Geraldine felt her ears compress.

Geraldine stood her ground. 'We are here for a legal event organised by the church.'

The officers paused for a moment and Geraldine called on some of her expensive public schoolbook learning.

'I claim sanctuary for myself and my, er, colleagues,' said Geraldine. 'You cannot remove us from this church.'

68

Geraldine spent the evening of Saturday 29 March 1986 in a cell in the East Perth lock-up so she didn't see the news. When Claire came to pick her up the next morning she was moving stiffly, obviously in pain, bruising across her left cheek.

'What the fuck did they do to you?' said Claire, in the foyer of the police station.

'Nothing, let's just go,' said Geraldine.

'What the fuck did they do to you?' repeated Claire when they were sitting at home with a cup of tea.

'Nothing,' said Geraldine. 'Nothing. Where's Janine? Is she okay?'

'Yes, she was home by about five last night,' said Claire. 'We watched the whole thing on the news. Once the police arrested you it was pretty much all over.'

'Well, okay, then,' said Geraldine. 'I'm going to bed. Thanks for coming to get me.'

Geraldine would have given her best friend a smile, but her face hurt too much.

■□■

Geraldine woke to find Janine sitting on her bed, the room dark.

'What time is it?' said Geraldine.

'It's around eight,' said Janine.

Geraldine elbowed her way into a sitting position, expelling an *ungh* with every movement.

'Here, put some pillows behind me,' said Geraldine when she was L-shaped.

Janine leaned forward and stuffed pillows behind Geraldine's back. Geraldine gingerly eased back into them.

'What the fuck did they do to you?' said Janine.

'I don't think I really want to talk about it,' said Geraldine, flinching as Janine reached out her hand to touch the swollen bruise on Geraldine's cheek.

'Can you do me a favour?' said Geraldine.

'Yeah, sure, anything.'

'Pack me a cone, would you?'

Janine returned with a bowl of mull and the bong. They took turns to pull cones. By her third, Geraldine let herself slump against the pillows, her face beginning to relax.

'You want to know what happened?' said Geraldine.

'Yeah,' said Janine, 'but only if you want to tell me.'

'I have to tell someone,' said Geraldine. 'In the end, I think I have to tell everyone what happened, so I may as well start with you. Is Claire still home?'

'Yeah, she is,' said Janine.

'Claire,' Geraldine called out.

Claire came to Geraldine's door and stood part in the hallway, part in the bedroom.

'What is it?' she said.

'Come in,' said Geraldine. 'I'm just about to tell Janine what happened last night and I thought you might like to be first to hear it, too.'

Claire came in and sat down on the other side of Geraldine's bed.

'The two of you,' said Geraldine, 'you're my dearest friends. And, you know, what happened yesterday, what I did was really stupid. I didn't think about it. I didn't realise what could happen, but I ended up putting a lot of people at risk. Did everyone get home okay?'

'Oh, yeah,' said Janine. 'Once the cops took you away, everyone left the church pretty quickly and just went home. I mean, the bands and production crew had to stick around to load out, but I've never seen a quicker load-out than yesterday.' Janine's eyes crinkled as she thought about everyone rushing from the church. 'We were like naughty schoolkids cleaning up after muck-up day at school.'

'Yeah?' said Geraldine. 'I wouldn't know about that, I didn't finish school.'

'Oh, well anyway, it was pretty bloody funny,' said Janine. 'But we were worried about you.'

'I went to the lock-up straight away,' said Claire, 'but the police told me to go home and wait for you to call.'

'So, I was the only one arrested?'

'Yeah,' said Janine, 'I think it was that bit you did about sanctuary, it confused them.'

'I can tell you, they weren't confused when they got me in a cell,' said Geraldine. 'Two of them took me into a cell and told me to strip. I told them I wouldn't, that I wanted to speak to someone first. That's when one of them punched me in the face.'

Geraldine held her hand to her cheek, a reflex, and sucked in breath at the sting caused by the merest brush of her fingertips.

'I almost fell over backwards,' said Geraldine. 'I don't know how I managed to stay on my feet. The other one yelled at me again to strip and I just stood there. I went to turn around so I could at least have some privacy, and the one who punched me grabbed me by the shoulder and forced me to turn back towards them. I took off my top and bra first and I could see them looking at me like I was some kind of circus animal. Then I bent over and unlaced my boots, took them off and pulled off my jeans and knickers. I stood there in front of them with one hand over my cock, the other over my breasts and my socks on.'

Geraldine paused while she thought about how to tell the next part.

'I can still hear their voices,' she continued, 'their exact words, even though I don't know their names. Those fucking cunts never even told me their names. The one who hadn't punched me took a step towards me and put his face right in mine. "What the fuck sort of fucking freak are you?" he said. I could smell the coffee on his breath. I didn't say anything. I knew things would get bad and I didn't want to make them worse so I decided to just shut up. He kept his face in mine and I felt him grab me and squeeze. "Let's see if we can get you to make a noise, shall we?" he said as he kept squeezing. I almost fainted, I thought he was going to rip my bits off, but I didn't dare make a sound. I remember thinking how nice the cool of the cement floor was and there's not much else I can remember after that. Feels like they gave me a proper bashing.'

'Fuck, Geraldine,' said Janine. 'I'm so sorry.'

On the other side of the bed, Claire held Geraldine's hand and sobbed.

'What are we going to do?' said Janine.

'Nothing,' said Geraldine. 'Not yet.'

69

The phone started ringing on Monday morning, venues and musos telling Geraldine they wouldn't be working with her any longer. Midmorning, Frank was on the phone.

He opened with, 'We saw you on the news on Saturday. What were you thinking? What's going on?'

'Yeah, thanks Frank,' said Geraldine. 'I'm going well. How are you?'

'Don't play games with me,' said Frank. 'I'm still your father no matter what. We're worried about you.'

'Worried about me?'

Geraldine drew breath while she thought of all the things she could say in response to Frank. While she thought, she listened to the silence at the other end of the line, swore she could hear Frank lighting up a cigarette and inhaling while he waited for her to speak. She heard Grace's voice in the background, could see Frank with his hand over the mouthpiece while her parents talked about her. It had always been about her, never to her. Geraldine hung up the phone.

The next call was from Lucas.

'Have you seen today's paper?' he said.

'No,' said Geraldine. 'I've been on the phone all morning, haven't left the house yet.'

'You should go get a copy.'

'Is it bad?'

Bad enough,' said Lucas.

Geraldine hurried into some clothes and walked over Rokeby Road to the deli. She eyed the stack of the *West Australian* on a stand outside the shop, saved from being distributed on the wind by half a brick. She slid out the top copy and looked at the front page, which was taken up with the headline *CASINO OPENS*, no sign of Saturday's events. Geraldine went inside and put twenty cents on the counter and decided to look inside the paper once she was back home. She plonked the newspaper on the dining table and went to the kitchen to make tea. Sitting down with her steaming mug, Geraldine opened the paper and was greeted with the headline on page three: *TRANSSEXUAL TAKES ON CHURCH.*

Under the headline Geraldine saw a photo of herself in front of Subiaco Church's open doors, a uniformed man holding her by each arm, her face an ugly rictus, mouth open, eyes closed. In the darkness of the church Geraldine could make out people looking on from behind her. At the top of the photo, Lucas' rainbow flag was just in shot. Geraldine read the story, taking in the comments from the parish priest that at no time had Geraldine revealed to him that she was transsexual and that, if he'd known, he would have had a different view about the appropriateness of his event for the church. 'As father of my flock,' the priest was quoted as saying, 'I have a duty to protect. We can't have these sorts of people, transsexuals and homosexuals, disturbing our peace.' The police continued to run the line that the gathering was illegal, a spokesman quoted as saying that, '... one person, Gerald Sturmer, was arrested for obstructing police and was later released without charge. The rest of the crowd dispersed without incident.'.

Geraldine closed the paper and sat at the table with her tea. She drank, feeling the warmth of the liquid fill her chest. She heard the phone ringing in the hallway and decided not to answer it. She closed her eyes and enjoyed the absence of anything. When they returned, Geraldine's thoughts were a kaleidoscope interrupted by flashes of the events of the last few days and the physical pain that resulted. When her eyes popped open, Geraldine was surprised to find herself still sitting at the table. She listened to the shortness of her breath and knew that she couldn't stay where she was. She picked up her keys from next to the still-ringing phone and closed the peeling white front door behind her. She walked up the hill and negotiated the traffic on Thomas Street, making her way into the relative peace of Kings Park. Geraldine kept walking until she found herself at the war memorial that overlooked the Swan River and the construction site that was Perth's central business district. She leaned on the silver railings and looked out over the river, trying to keep her breath even. The sun was still making an arc through the cloudless sky over the hills in the east and Geraldine looked up to let it warm her face.

'I'm a woman,' Geraldine said to the sky and the river.

'I'm a woman,' she repeated a little bit louder for the straggle of tourists and locals visiting the war memorial on a Monday morning.

'I'm a woman!' Geraldine yelled to the entire world, this time turning heads.

As Geraldine closed her mouth she could hear her voice echoing back to her from the hills in the distance, see its volume ruffling the surface of the river, hear it repeated in the screeching of the white cockatoos.

'I'm a woman,' Geraldine said to herself as she pushed herself upright and turned to begin the journey home.

When Geraldine arrived home, Janine and Claire were sitting at the dining table with the paper open in front of them. The phone was still ringing. Geraldine ignored it as she dropped her keys on the hall table and ambled into the lounge. Her friends looked up when she came into view.

'We've been worried about you,' said Claire. 'Where've you been?'

'I decided I needed a walk,' said Geraldine. 'I went over to Kings Park.'

'Kings Park?' said Janine. 'You've never been there before in your fucking life.'

'I know,' said Geraldine, grinning. 'It's pretty nice. We should go there for a picnic one day.'

The three of them laughed.

'But, you're okay?' said Claire.

'Um, yeah, no, not really,' said Geraldine, 'but I think I will be. Just got a few things to figure out is all.'

'Like what?' said Janine, her eyes a mixture of curiosity and concern.

'Well, you've both read the paper,' said Geraldine.

■□■

Geraldine sat in the papasan chair, taking in the sun. She needed a moment to think. All her life, Geraldine had been herself. People had seen her as Gerald, particularly in her early days, but that hadn't mattered to her at all; she had an internal life that had no connection with theirs. When she started to let people into her world, no-one had ever questioned her, unless they were authority figures: the doctor in Weston-super-Mare, her parents, the Williamses, the doctor at Royal Perth, the police. There were the randoms, as well, like the bogan on the bus, but there'd always be randoms. As far as Geraldine was concerned, her truth was unremarkable – she was female and, at this stage of her life, very much a woman. But a transsexual? Geraldine understood the concept, she'd done the reading, but it was never a label she'd applied to herself. After reading this morning's paper, Geraldine felt like she needed to figure out why, because she knew that from now on, people were going to start asking her. And, after the summit with Kym that was part of the catalyst for all this, Geraldine knew there was work to be done.

70

Geraldine started picking up the phone. Its persistent ringing was beginning to annoy the shit out of her. Most of the calls were more musos and venues advising her they were taking their business elsewhere. By the end of the week Geraldine estimated that her business had been cut by about half. *Fuck 'em*, Geraldine thought, leaving the worry about what it would mean for her income for another time. Late in the afternoon, she received another call.

'Can I speak to Geraldine Sturmer, please?'

'Speaking,' said Geraldine.

'Geraldine, my name is Naomi Jones. I'm a journalist at the *Sunday Times*.'

'Oh?' said Geraldine.

'I was hoping we could meet,' the journalist said.

'What for?'

'I thought you might like to tell your side of the story.'

When Geraldine hung up the phone she found Claire in the back garden and asked if she had any film in her camera. Claire took the photos outside with Geraldine standing against the white wall at the back of the house, judging that natural light would be better than using a flash.

'Oh, babe,' said Claire, as she looked at Geraldine through her camera lens.

'Don't worry about it,' said Geraldine, 'just take the photos.'

Claire finished her work in silence and handed the black film canister to Geraldine for her to take for processing.

'What are you doing?' said Claire. 'What will you use the photos for?'

'I don't know, yet,' said Geraldine, knowing her plans exactly. 'I just thought it might be good to have them.'

■□■

When the journalist arrived she was wearing a dark suit, trousers, jacket, cream satin top and black brogues. Geraldine watched as the woman approached her table, feeling instantly inadequate in her Docs, jeans and Snake Oil t-shirt. The woman had a wide, almost flat face. Her hair was natural blond and just reached the collar of her jacket.

'Can I sit?' she said, as she approached the table in the cafe on James Street where they'd agreed to meet.

'Sure,' said Geraldine, half standing up.

The woman reached out her hand as she pulled out a chair.

'I'm Naomi, Nomes,' she said, as they shook hands. 'And you're Geraldine, of course.'

Geraldine looked up at Nomes, keeping her face neutral. She had no idea where this was going to end up.

'Do you want a coffee?' Nomes asked.

'Tea, please.'

The journalist went to the counter and placed their order.

'They'll bring it over,' she said, as she returned to her seat.

Geraldine said nothing, and the two women didn't speak again until their drinks had arrived. Geraldine poured her tea, liquid dribbling onto the table as she tipped up the stainless-steel teapot. She felt embarrassed and out of her depth, which was a new sensation for Geraldine. She decided to try going on the offensive.

'How did you get my number?' she said.

'It's not exactly a secret, is it?' said the journalist. 'From what I can gather most people in the music industry have it. I didn't have to do too much asking. By the way, love the band,' she said, looking at Geraldine's shirt.

Janine and her band were quite the thing in Perth these days. Geraldine folded her arms across her chest.

'Yeah, they're alright,' she said.

The journalist looked at Geraldine across the table, her hazel eyes unwavering.

'You look worried, Geraldine,' said the journalist. 'I can understand that.'

'No, I'm fine,' said Geraldine.

'Listen,' said the journalist. 'I want to give you a chance to tell your side of the story. Will you let me do that?'

■□■

Geraldine started by showing Nomes the photos Claire had taken a few days after she'd been released from the East Perth lock-up.

'We can't make that part of the story,' said Nomes.

'Why not?' said Geraldine, getting ready to leave.

'No, hang on, sit down,' said Nomes. 'Hear me out.'

Geraldine parked herself and looked across the table at Nomes, wanting to hate her.

'We can't use that right now,' said Nomes. 'I'm not saying it didn't happen, it happens all the time, but now is not the time. We need to get you out from under that and let people see how bloody ordinary you are.'

'Ordinary?' said Geraldine.

'Yes, ordinary. People need to know you're like them.'

Geraldine looked across the table at Nomes, her chest pumping with emotion.

'You think I'm ordinary?' she said.

'Yes,' said Nomes.

'You know, that's all I've ever wanted,' said Geraldine.

■□■

As with the article in the *West*, the phone had rung for days after the piece in the *Sunday Times*. Monday morning, Geraldine did radio on the ABC, the presenter giving her an opportunity to continue the 'I'm an ordinary woman' line. On 6PR, the shock jock took a different approach, and when he put it to Geraldine that she was just a chick with a dick, her first instinct was to hang up. She left so much dead air that the man in the studio was forced to fill it.

'Geraldine? Are you still on the line?'

'I am,' said Geraldine.

'So, what do you have to say to that?' said the presenter.

'I'm who I've always been,' said Geraldine. 'I'm a woman and if you can't deal with that, if you have to resort to childish insults to get your head around it, I'd suggest that you're the problem not me.'

'I think a lot of people would see it the same way as me,' said the presenter.

'I know they do,' said Geraldine, 'but they're wrong. My existence harms no-one and if you or other people want to harm me because of it, you're the problem.'

This time the dead air came from the presenter's side.

'That was transsexual, Geraldine Sturmer,' the presenter said eventually. 'The time is now ...'

Geraldine went to interject but realised she was no longer on air. She didn't bother to turn on the radio to listen to the talkback.

Towards the end of the week after the *Sunday Times* piece Geraldine answered the phone to hear Nomes' voice.

'So, what did you think?' said Nomes. 'Did I do good, or what?'

'You did good,' said Geraldine, 'thank you.'

'We should catch up. Talk about what next.'

'What next?' said Geraldine.

'Yeah, we can't just leave it there. What're you doing tonight?'

'Tonight? Ah, nothing.'

'Good,' said Nomes. 'Meet me at the Subi at eight.'

When Geraldine arrived, the pub was already swollen with noise, some poor bloke with a thin voice and an acoustic guitar trying to cut through the voices. Nomes stood up and walked through the crowd when she saw Geraldine, putting an arm around her shoulder and steering her back towards the door.

'Let's go somewhere quieter,' said Nomes, once they were on the street.

Sitting in a booth in a bar at the south end of Rokeby Road, just barely on the edge of the entertainment strip, Geraldine sipped her cider and wondered where things were going with Nomes. Nomes had got the first round in and came back with a white wine for her, the bulbous glass occasionally reflecting the minimalistic lighting as she constantly turned it with her fingers on its stem.

'So?' said Geraldine, eventually.

'Yes?' said Nomes, studying her glass as she smiled.

Geraldine decided she wasn't going to make it easy for Nomes.

'You called the meeting,' she said. 'What's on your mind?'

Nomes looked at Geraldine. 'You must have some idea,' she said.

Geraldine did. 'Um, no, I don't think so,' she said, smirking.

'Fuck off!' said Nomes. 'You know I like you.'

'Yes,' said Geraldine, looking away from her.

'So, that only leaves one item on the agenda,' said Nomes. 'Do you like me?'

■□■

'But, we do really need to talk about what next,' said Nomes.

It was morning and Geraldine was just coming to, stretching and assessing the size of her headache. Nomes was on her side looking at Geraldine, her chin resting on her hand. Geraldine brought her into focus and said the most intelligent thing she could think of.

'What?'

'We need to talk about what next,' said Nomes.

'Fuck off, I'm sleeping,' Geraldine said, as she put her pillow over her head.

When Geraldine finally woke up and headed towards the sunlight at the back of the house she found Nomes sitting at the dining table with Janine, drinking coffee and deep in conversation.

'See, Janine gets it,' said Nomes, looking up at Geraldine.

'Gets what?' said Geraldine, feeling her anger begin to rise.

'That it would be good to have a journalist in tow,' said Nomes.

Geraldine sat down at the table opposite Nomes and Janine and looked them over. They both smiled at her, sickly sweet, and rubbed shoulders like they'd been best friends forever. Geraldine was beginning to feel uncomfortable, but she wasn't sure why.

'I guess,' she said.

'You guess?' said Nomes.

'Yeah, I guess,' said Geraldine. 'Let's leave it at that.'

'Gotta go,' said Janine, as she stood up. 'It was nice to meet you, Nomes. Hope I see you again soon,' she said looking at Geraldine.

'I need tea,' said Geraldine, heading for the kitchen.

Nomes was still sitting at the table when Geraldine came back with her mug.

'Did I do something wrong?' said Nomes.

'Um, no?' said Geraldine.

'Then what's up?

'I don't know,' said Geraldine. 'Nothing.'

'Mmm, yes, well, I've got to go as well,' said Nomes. 'Give me a call sometime.'

Geraldine watched as Nomes walked up the passageway, listening to the front door latch as she left.

71

Geraldine waited a week before she called Nomes.

'I didn't think I'd hear from you again,' said Nomes, the line crackling like she was a long way from home.

Geraldine heard the interference and for a moment her heart dropped at the prospect that Nomes was somewhere else.

'Are you in Perth?' said Geraldine. 'Maybe we could catch up.'

'Are you sure?' said Nomes.

'Yes,' said Geraldine, 'I am. Sorry.'

'What for?'

'For being such a fucking bitch the other day,' said Geraldine. 'I've missed you.'

'Missed me, have you?' said Nomes. 'We'd better put that to rights, then. Do you know The Witch's Cauldron?'

'I've heard of it,' said Geraldine.

'Tomorrow at seven?' said Nomes.

'Okay.'

■□■

That gave Geraldine nearly twenty-four hours to decide what to wear. She searched her memory banks but she couldn't remember ever having been to an actual restaurant before. She'd been to plenty of fast-food joints, pubs and cafes, but not one single restaurant. In the end, Geraldine settled on basic black, a simple V-necked dress, just above the knees, black tights and her black Docs. Hair up? Hair down? She had no idea until Claire came to her rescue as she was pacing up and down the hallway outside their bedrooms, muttering to herself.

'Hair up, darling,' said Claire, 'and these. Here, turn around.'

She laced a string of pearls around Geraldine's neck. 'Are you sure you want to wear those boots?'

'Yes, now fuck off,' said Geraldine. 'Leave me alone.'

'Manners,' said Claire with a crumpled smile.

'Sorry,' said Geraldine, 'bit nervous.'

■□■

By the time Geraldine got to the restaurant, she had let her hair down. Nomes was waiting inside for her and stood up and waved as she approached the maître d's station. Geraldine paused for a moment, looking into the room of tables, still only half full at this early hour, and considered leaving. She took a deep breath and the first step towards Nomes, her legs feeling like they would give way under her. When she reached their table, Nomes stood up again.

'Hello Geraldine,' she said. 'I love your pearls.'

'They're not mine,' said Geraldine.

'Well, they suit you, anyway.'

Geraldine had never drunk champagne before. It went down a treat and by the time they were thinking about dessert, Geraldine was halfway between tipsy and completely smashed. Whenever they talked about the night afterwards, Geraldine would always ask if they'd had dessert and Nomes would say, 'Fucked if I know,' at which they would laugh like a pair of September magpies.

■□■

The morning after The Witch's Cauldron, bleary-eyed and hungover, Nomes suggested a trip to the beach. They'd woken up at Nomes' Osborne Park apartment, Geraldine having to think hard before she realised where she was and who she was with.

'C'mon, let's go for a swim,' said Nomes.

'No thanks,' said Geraldine, turning over to get some more sleep.

Geraldine ignored Nomes' finger as it ran across the top of her shoulders and then down the curve of her spine. She ignored it as it rounded her hip and the curve of her buttock. She ignored it as it made its way oh so gently down her arse crack. She tried hard to ignore it as it made its way across her perineum.

'Hey! No fair!' said Geraldine, as she rolled back towards Nomes.

'C'mon, let's go to the beach,' said Nomes, her face up close to Geraldine's, her breath smelling like the bottom of a cocky's cage.

'Fuck! Alright,' said Geraldine, beginning to learn that Nomes wasn't easily denied. 'Oh, wait, I don't have any bathers, or any other clothes at all,' said Geraldine.

'You can borrow some of mine,' said Nomes.

Down in the apartment complex carpark, Nomes handed Geraldine the keys to her blue Alfa Sud.

'Here, you drive, I think I might still be a bit pissed,' said Nomes.

'I can't,' said Geraldine. 'Besides, you drove home last night.'

'What do you mean, you can't?' said Nomes.

'I don't have my licence,' said Geraldine.

'Why not?'

'Because.'

'Because what?'

Geraldine handed the keys back to Nomes.

'I just don't,' she said.

■□■

A few days later, heads clearer and wrapped around each other in Geraldine's bed, Nomes raised the issue again.

'It's my name,' Geraldine said eventually.

'What do you mean?' said Nomes.

'I need to change my name before I get my driver's licence,' said Geraldine.

'So, do it,' said Nomes.

'Yeah, I should,' said Geraldine, 'but it's not enough.'

'What do you mean?' said Nomes.

'I can't change my gender,' said Geraldine. 'I can change my name, but I'll still be recorded as male on everything.'

'Fuck,' said Nomes.

'Yeah, I know,' said Geraldine.

'But you can't let that stop you from driving.'

'Yeah, I know,' said Geraldine, 'but I don't want to be caught halfway. There's my passport, everything. It's all male and there's no way to change it.'

'We need to get something happening here.'

'Like what?' said Geraldine.

'Well, for starters, we need to start writing to people, politicians, get it changed.'

'Okay,' said Geraldine, uncertainly.

'And you need to start being more visible,' said Nomes.

'Like how,' said Geraldine. 'Why?'

'You need to be the face of this,' said Nomes. 'I can help you. But first, you're going to change your name and learn how to drive.'

72

Geraldine was wary when she met the *West Australian*'s arts editor. Last time she'd had anything to do with the paper she'd not come out of it well. Nomes reassured her that it would be okay.

'He's a good bloke, Michael,' she said.

'I don't know if there's any such thing,' said Geraldine.

Michael Paulson was short and slight. He had red hair and was the exact opposite of what Geraldine had been expecting. They talked over coffee – tea for Geraldine; this time she made sure there was no spillage from the stainless-steel pot – in the same Northbridge cafe where she'd first met Nomes.

'Yeah, I remember that story,' Michael said when Geraldine mentioned her first foray into print. 'Nomes said the cops beat you up. Is that right?'

'Yes,' said Geraldine.

'Not the first time,' said Michael, 'and it won't be the last.'

'I still have the photos, if you want them,' said Geraldine.

'Nah,' said Michael, 'that's not my area.'

'What is it with you journalists?' said Geraldine. 'Why are you so shy of the police?'

'Where do you think the paper gets most of its stories?' said Michael, looking directly at Geraldine across the formica table.

'You are fucking kidding me,' said Geraldine.

'Nope,' said Michael. 'We rock the boat and we get cut off, and they give stuff to the *Sunday Times* instead. Doesn't matter to them.'

'Fuck,' said Geraldine, the connections beginning to dawn on her.

'Anyway, Snake Oil,' said Michael.

'Yeah,' said Geraldine, ungluing herself from her thoughts, 'are you interested?'

'I am,' said Michael, 'but I want to do something a bit different.'

'Like what?' said Geraldine.

'I want you to be part of the story,' said Michael.

'Oh, no,' said Geraldine, 'this is Janine's thing, I don't do front of house.'

'Hear me out,' said Michael. 'That thing with the church, that was you trying to open up more spaces where gays and lesbians can be safe, right?'

'And trans people,' said Geraldine.

'Oh, yes, right, of course,' said Michael. 'Well, listen. If we do a feature on the band and the relationship between you and Janine, we have that as part of the story.'

'How would it work?' said Geraldine.

'The paper's starting a series on partnerships in different lines of work,' said Michael, 'I want to pitch you and Janine for one of those.'

The piece came out in the *West Australian*'s weekend magazine, Janine and Geraldine looking out from the glossy front cover under the headline *BEHIND THE FRONT*. When Geraldine read the article, she couldn't remember if it was her or the journo who'd come up with the term 'dance rock' to describe Janine's music. It wasn't original, but it fitted the bill and there weren't too many bands in Australia doing what Snake Oil were doing. Geraldine cringed when she read that she was a mover in the Perth music industry. Apparently she'd established a thriving booking agency, starting out in her teens, and was also a crusader – the journalist's words, not hers – for gay rights.

73

Geraldine first walked up the steps of the sandstone building that overlooked the Mitchell Freeway and not much else in 1988. Nomes had schooled her in state politics and helped her get into the rhythm of writing letters to the elected members. For years, every reply Geraldine received was a polite *fuck-off, don't call us, we'll call you*. It was so much like the music business that Geraldine would have smiled at the irony if she hadn't died inside a little bit more when she received each epistle. She was surprised that the invitation to meet finally came from a Liberal member.

'I guess I'm hardwired working class,' Geraldine said when she showed Nomes the letter.

'Yeah, well it's not really the same here,' said Nomes, reminding Geraldine again that she was at home in a foreign country.

The meeting at Parliament House with newly elected member Kate Deans was brisk and brief. The politician did mention to Geraldine that she'd been to see Snake Oil once at the Warwick Hotel, but that was it for the small talk. Mostly she listened while Geraldine told her what it was she was trying to achieve. The politician invited Geraldine to join a reference group she was establishing, telling her to give her number to her adviser and they'd be in touch about a meeting.

'That was just another way of blowing me off, wasn't it?' said Geraldine as they walked down the wide beach-coloured steps on the way back to her car.

'I don't know,' said Nomes. 'I don't think so. Sit tight and see what happens.'

■□■

The invitation came about six months later, by mail, not by phone. Geraldine drove herself north to Kate Deans' electoral office, thinking it was the first time she'd seen these suburbs in daylight. Everything looked different and she had to pull over a couple of times to consult her UBD before she arrived at

Warwick shops. Geraldine pulled up, confused for a moment, not expecting to find a politician in a shopping centre outside of an election campaign. Of course, the woman herself wasn't there, it was the same adviser who'd been at the meeting at Parliament House, looking very young and nervous as he greeted people, fiddling with his tie and sweating. Geraldine sat back with a cup of tea and watched for most of the meeting Deans' LGBT Law Reform Reference Group. By the end, she wasn't convinced that anything but polite chat was the order of the day.

'Any questions?' said the adviser as he brought the meeting to a close, his tie still troubling him.

Geraldine put up her hand, feeling like she was back in school. It wasn't the only reason she felt uncomfortable. The other six people in the room were obviously more seasoned than she was, they had their lines ready and they knew what they wanted, which was for homosexuality to be legalised. It also didn't help Geraldine that they were all men. As the meeting had progressed, she got the distinct feeling that she'd been invited to the wrong show, and the polite indifference of the males in the room did nothing to quell her fears.

'Yes?' said the adviser.

'I, um, I wonder,' said Geraldine, 'if we're thinking widely enough?'

People who had been shuffling in their seats, preparing to head off, snapped their attention to her.

'What do you mean?' said one of them, an older man who'd held the floor for much of the meeting, prefacing most of his comments with, 'Speaking as an academic …'

'Well, I'm all for it to be legal for me to have sex,' said Geraldine, 'but I want more.'

'More?' said the academic.

In that moment he reminded Geraldine of Mr Gradgrind. She knew she was mixing her Dickens, but the thought made her smile and gave her courage.

'Yes, more,' she said. 'Trans people need to have their identities recognised.'

'Well, I don't know,' said the academic. 'One step at a time, maybe?'

■□■

'You do know you're a sanctimonious little prick?' said Geraldine.

Professor Roger Cartwright's office was a small deal in an impressive sandstone building, barely enough room for a desk and a bookcase. Geraldine sat opposite him, wondering why she'd bothered to take up his invitation to meet after the most recent meeting in Kate Deans' electoral office.

'And you, my dear, are a Johnny-come-lately who's going to set our cause back by years if you don't learn how to behave in polite company,' said Cartwright.

It was true, the last meeting of Deans' LGBT Reference Group had ended somewhat in disarray when Geraldine, feeling less intimidated a few meetings in, refused to budge on her proposal to combine reform of the laws that made homosexuality a criminal offence with legislation to enable transsexual people to have their genders legally recognised. Someone, she didn't know who, had said during the verbal melee that followed, 'Told you we shouldn't have let the trannies have a seat at the table.' There had been a brief silence.

'Which of you fuckers said that?' asked Geraldine.

More silence until the adviser, the one with the troublesome tie, stepped in and closed the meeting, wiping the sweat from his face.

Cartwright had followed Geraldine across the darkness of the shopping centre carpark and stood as she opened her car door. He reached her shoulder, just, but his presence was still imposing enough to cut through her stink and make her listen for a while. They agreed to meet in his office in the School of Arts at the University of Western Australia. Which was how they came to be sitting across a desk from each other trading insults.

'Our cause?' said Geraldine. 'Tell me, Professor, how it's our cause?'

'Gay men have been campaigning for equality since the sixties. It's been a long, hard fight and I haven't seen too many, what is it again, gender-diverse people coming along with us for the ride.'

Geraldine sucked in her breath, stood up, turned for the door and then turned back around and sat down again.

'First,' she said, 'I'm no Johnny-come-lately – it's Janet, if you must. Second, we've always been here. We've been on the marches, we've been at the barricades, you've just had your head so far up your arse that you haven't noticed us. I can show you the photos if you like.'

'What do you mean, "photos"?'

Geraldine gave Cartwright a quick overview of her church takeover and subsequent treatment in the East Perth lock-up.

'That was you?' said Cartwright. 'I remember seeing it on the news. The cops really did you over?'

'Yes, they did.'

'Fuck.'

'And, Janet? Really?'

'Yes, you transphobic fucker. Don't go misgendering me again.'

'Maybe you shouldn't be so liberal about the capacity of my arse, then?'

Geraldine couldn't remember who started first, but a full five minutes later they were still laughing, tears rolling down their faces. Every time one of them went to talk, the laughter started again. There was a knock at the door of Cartwright's office.

'Everything alright, Roger?' said the man who stuck his head around the door.

'Yes, yes, fine thank you,' said Cartwright while Geraldine kept her head down, not daring to look at whoever had interrupted them.

'Now, where were we?' said Cartwright once the door was closed again.

That started the giggling, which led to the laughter. When they could finally speak, they hammered out a deal.

'You should enrol here to study,' said Cartwright as Geraldine made to leave.

■□■

Geraldine sat next to Roger Cartwright in the public gallery as the legislation to decriminalise homosexuality passed through the Western Australian parliament at the end of 1989.

'You next,' said Roger as he put his arm around Geraldine, pulled her in and gave her a kiss on the cheek.

'Don't go being nice to me now, Cartwright,' she said, 'you'll make me get all emotional.'

The pair smiled at each other.

'You going to go out and have sex tonight, Roger?' said Geraldine.

'I wish.'

74

Geraldine sat in the backstage area at Perth Oval and watched the world go by. It was more like a small village than a green room, and she was currently sitting on a lounge chair, one of many pieces of soft furnishing that provided waystations for artists and hangers-on as they navigated their way from their dressing rooms to the performance areas and back, some better for wear than others. It was midafternoon and Snake Oil were due to play one of the smaller stages, their biggest break yet. Janine and the band were in their donga getting themselves ready, working on finding just the right side of high. Geraldine had left them to it. There was nothing more she could contribute at this stage, it was all up to Janine and the band, everything riding on a single thirty-minute set.

Geraldine watched as Kim Gordon wandered by. She wanted to wave and say hello but decided that reserve should be the order of her day. Tim Rogers and Tex Perkins stumbled on through behind Kim Gordon, each with a drink in hand and a durrie on the go. Tim turned to look at Geraldine, peered at her like he thought he should know who she was, but couldn't figure out if she was important enough to talk to. He turned to walk on and then turned back.

'I'm Tim,' he said, holding out a hand, durrie between his lips.

Geraldine sat up and leaned forward, slipping her hand into his.

'I feel like I should know you,' said Tim.

'I don't think so,' said Geraldine, leaning back in her chair, shielding her eyes from the sun. 'I look after Snake Oil, they're just about to go on.'

'Snake Oil?' said Tim. 'That's Janine McArdle, isn't it?'

'Yep,' said Geraldine, trying not to look smug.

'And you look after her?' said Tim. 'Why don't you ask her if she wants to come and play some guitar with us later?'

'What, Janine?' said Geraldine.

'Yes, Janine,' said Tim, laughing. 'Don't worry, you're alright! Now I think about it, I know who you are, too. I think everyone does. Come and see us before our set. If I tell you I don't remember, hit me.'

Tim and Tex wandered off and Geraldine watched them go. Geraldine closed her eyes. Inside she was fizzing with anticipation, outside she held herself as still as she could.

'Oy!'

It was Janine.

'What's up?' said Janine.

'Oh, not much,' said Geraldine, doing her best to hold back a smile.

'There's something,' said Janine. 'I know you. I can see you've been up to something. C'mon, spill.'

'No,' said Geraldine, 'play your set first and then I'll tell you.'

'Nope,' said Janine, 'you have to tell me now or I won't go on.'

Geraldine knew Janine would never pull a stunt like that. She was a muso through and through, but she'd never be anyone's rock-and-roll cliché.

'It's no big deal,' said Geraldine. 'I was just talking to Tim Rogers.'

'Tim Rogers! Ooh la la,' said Janine.

'Anyway, missy,' said Geraldine, 'he wants you to step up and play some guitar with You Am I later tonight. No biggie.'

'He what?' said Geraldine. 'No biggie? Why did you tell me that? I'll never be able to concentrate now.'

'Oh, shoosh,' said Geraldine. 'Go have another shot, it looks like you have room for it.'

'Yeah, good call,' said Janine.

She turned and wandered back the way she'd come, and next time Geraldine saw Janine, she had the rest of the band in tow. Geraldine got out of her comfy chair and stood up to follow them, wondering whether she should have put on some suncream.

Geraldine watched side of stage while Snake Oil played their first and only Big Day Out. The crowd was thin, but they were well up for it, sweating in the January heat while Janine and her band did their thing. Their music was loose and elastic, barely held together by the rhythm section, but just enough to give it that swing that had Snake Oil crossing genres and making each one sound like their own. Early in Snake Oil's sets, it was Janine's voice that drew the punters close to the stage and it was her guitar and the just-behind-the-beat drums and funked-up bass that kept them there. Snake Oil closed out their time with the massive sing along of 'Mannish Boy', Janine introducing it with, 'This one's for all the coke heads at the Subi Hotel.' The only downside to their moment was the black look Geraldine got from the stage manager as he pointed to the clock at the side of stage.

'Not cool,' he said to Geraldine.

Geraldine ignored him as she greeted Janine with a hug.

'Best yet,' she whispered into Janine's ear. 'Now, you'd better go learn some You Am I songs.'

Geraldine watched on as Janine mixed it with Tim Rogers after playing lead on their set closer, a pre-release version of 'Adam's Ribs'. Rogers had yelled Janine's name as he and his band left the stage, the crowd yelling for one more song. Tim, his arm around Janine, introduced her to the milling group of Aussie and overseas artists and industry types. Everyone was pleased to see Janine, but no-one really knew who the fuck she was, except the person who took a seat at the other end of Geraldine's couch. Geraldine glanced at him as he sat down, taking in his short but unruly dark hair and tanned face. He looked like he'd spent as much time in the sun today as she had. She looked away, eyes back on Janine.

'You know, maybe it's time you and Janine came to Melbourne,' the man said from his end of the couch.

Geraldine turned towards him.

'Do you think?'

'She's ready,' said the man.

'I don't know if I am,' said Geraldine.

'In the end, that doesn't matter, Geraldine,' said the man. 'Talk to her, and give me a call,' he said, handing her a scrap of paper, having written only his number on it, nothing else.

He got up and walked into the throng of musicians who greeted him like the oldest of friends. Janine came over and sat next to Geraldine, put her arm around her, gave her a kiss on the cheek and then nuzzled into the crook of her neck.

'This has been quite the day,' she said.

'It has,' said Geraldine, her eyes still on the milling cattle market in front of her.

'Who was that, just now?' said Janine.

'That,' said Geraldine, 'was Ken West.'

'Should I know who he is?' said Janine.

'He knows who you are,' said Geraldine. 'That's all that matters.'

75

Geraldine drove Janine to the airport, waiting with her while she checked in her guitars at the oversized luggage counter. She'd delayed until well after the year's run of Big Day Out shows was over before pulling the scrap of paper out of her bag and calling Ken West. When he finally came to the phone Geraldine was surprised that he remembered her. When she'd talked to Janine, Geraldine had reminded her of the conversation they'd had nearly a decade ago, that their arrangement was only ever until someone else came along who could help Janine with the next stage of her career.

'Just don't forget to namecheck me when you win your first ARIA,' said Geraldine.

'Yeah, right,' said Janine. 'Don't worry I'll be home in six months and you'll have to put me back in the Subi.'

'Not you,' said Geraldine.

Geraldine went through security with Janine, and they sat upstairs drinking in the bar while they waited for her flight to be called. She let go of Janine's hand as she showed her boarding pass at the gate and then stood at the windows and watched while the plane was towed away from the jet bridge. As the Qantas jet turned towards the runway, Geraldine turned from the window and made her way downstairs and outside to the carpark. She felt like she'd been punched in the guts.

■□■

Her first week in Melbourne, Janine called Geraldine every night and ran through the day's events, which mostly seemed to involve meeting people, watching people play and watching people record.

'They're going to get me in the studio soon,' said Janine.

'How soon?' said Geraldine.

'I don't know,' said Janine, 'I'll let you know.'

After that first week, Janine's calls were more sporadic until, after around three months, they stopped all together. Geraldine had Janine's mobile number, but she decided not to call, figuring Janine would reach out if she needed anything.

■□■

Geraldine picked up the phone on a Friday night. It was Janine.

'Turn on the TV tomorrow morning if you want a surprise,' said Janine.

'Whaddya mean?' said Geraldine, her heart quickening.

'I'm gonna be on *Breakfast Blast*,' said Janine.

'No fucking way!'

'Yes fucking way!' said Janine. 'Make sure you watch me?'

Geraldine heard the inflection in Janine's voice and she was flushed with love.

'Are you okay over there, Janine?' she said.

'Yeah, I'm okay,' said Janine, 'but I miss you.'

Geraldine and Claire watched *Breakfast Blast* together the next morning. When the show started, Geraldine leaned forward to get a better view. When presenter Dionne Lees announced, 'The latest and greatest from Melbourne, Ignition!' Geraldine didn't realise for a moment that she was looking at Janine gurning down the camera at her. She leaned even further forward, her hands resting on the coffee table. Janine was backed by a new band, same configuration, but not a single face that Geraldine recognised except her friend's. The music had the same swing and swagger, but Geraldine had never heard the song before.

Janine called Geraldine later that Saturday.

'Did you see me?' she said.

'Of course I fucking did,' said Geraldine. 'You were brilliant.'

'God, I was so nervous,' said Janine. 'Did I look good? Did you like the new song?'

'You looked fabulous and the new song sounded great,' said Geraldine. 'You're a fucking rockstar. I told you, didn't I?'

'Yeah, you did,' said Janine. 'I didn't believe you, but you believed in me.'

'That's okay,' said Geraldine, 'just telling it like it is.' Geraldine's face hurt from smiling. 'What's next?'

'We're recording an album and then they're talking about a tour.'

'You won't forget me, will you?' said Geraldine.

76

'I got a new job,' said Nomes, her legs wrapped around Geraldine's in the front bedroom at Rupert Street.

Since Janine had moved to Melbourne, Nomes had spent most nights at Geraldine's. They'd talked about moving in together, but nothing had come of it. Both were satisfied with their current arrangements.

'Oh, Nomes, congratulations!' said Geraldine, rousing herself from her almost sleep. 'What's the job?'

'It's a political editor position with the ABC. I'll get to do radio and maybe even some TV as well.'

'That's amazing, Nomes. I can't wait to see your beautiful face on my TV. When do you start?'

'End of next month, I have to be there.'

'They're in Perth, aren't they, the CBD?'

'Yeah, they are, but this job's in Darwin.'

'Darwin?'

'Yes.'

'So you'll be moving to Darwin at the end of next month and this is the first time you're telling me?'

'Yes.'

Geraldine sat up in the bed, disentangling herself from Nomes.

'I need a cup of tea,' she said. 'Do you want anything?'

'No, I'm right.'

When Geraldine returned to her bedroom, mug in hand, she sat in the chair at the foot of the bed. Nomes was sitting up against the headboard, her arms across her chest. Geraldine took three sips of her hot tea before she spoke again.

'You must've known about this for a while?'

'They told me just last week, but I applied for the job about two months ago.'

'And you didn't want to tell me?'

'I did, Geraldine, but I knew we'd never figure it out. It was just easier this way.'

'For who?'

'For me, of course, but for you as well.'

Geraldine digested Nomes' words. Her first instinct was to be angry, but she knew that Nomes was right.

'I'm really pleased for you, darling,' she said. 'You deserve this break.'

'Here, come back to bed.'

Geraldine set down her tea and climbed in next to Nomes. They spent the rest of the night talking, faces close together.

77

It was more than two years after they last spoke before Janine and Ignition made it to Perth. Their self-titled debut had topped the ARIA charts for a whole week in 1995 before being knocked off the top spot by the Beatles' *Anthology 1*.

'Men can screw you over even from beyond the grave,' Geraldine said to Janine when they talked about it at soundcheck in Fremantle's Metropolis nightclub.

The two had hugged ferociously when they first saw each other, Janine leaping down from the stage mid-song as she clocked Geraldine walking across the dancefloor, leaving her guitar on its back wailing like a screaming child.

The night was sold out, and as Geraldine watched Ignition's set she felt a sense of pride that confounded her. The closest she could get was that this was how a mother would feel. Geraldine dismissed the idea, banishing it and abandoning herself to the music. Janine finished the band's second encore with 'Mannish Boy', saying, 'We've run out of songs. This one's for all you Perth freaks, thanks for helping us get here.'

■□■

Ignition won the ARIA award for Best New Talent the year their debut album was released. Janine had invited Geraldine to come over for the awards ceremony, but she watched it at home on TV instead.

'But I'll be watching you, Janine,' she said.

'Yeah, I know,' said Janine.

When Janine stepped up to the podium to take the award, the other members of Ignition straggling along behind her, Geraldine watched her intently. Janine pushed her fringe back and used her forearm to shade her eyes from the lights in the venue as she looked across the people gathered at the ocean of tables in the Sydney Convention Centre.

'There's a lot of people here I should be thanking tonight,' said Janine, 'but only one I'm going to mention. Geraldine, I wouldn't be here if it wasn't for you. I know why you couldn't be here tonight. You wouldn't tell me, but I fucking know you, babe. I hope you don't have to fight much longer. I love you. Don't you ever stop being who you are.'

'Thank you, darling,' Geraldine said, through her tears.

■□■

When the media asked Janine about her acceptance speech she didn't hold back. The headlines ranged from *RISING STAR'S SNUB*, taking the line that Janine should have been more forthright in her praise and thanks for the people who made her and were actually at the awards ceremony to *MUSO THANKS TRANSSEXUAL MENTOR*, pushing the idea that there was something sleazy about Janine's past because of her association with Geraldine. And, of course, Geraldine's phone started to ring all over again. This time she brushed off the media's attention, declining all interviews and reeling off 'No comment' what felt like hundreds of times.

78

When Parliament passed the *Gender Reassignment Act* in the year 2000, allowing trans people to apply to have their genders legally recognised, Geraldine and Cartwright were there in the public gallery. They re-enacted their celebration from eleven years earlier.

'You going out to have sex tonight?' Cartwright asked Geraldine while they were still hugging.

'Fat fucking chance, darling. Maybe you and I should hook up?'

They started laughing but stifled themselves when Attorney General Deans, still on her feet, looked up in their direction.

▪▫▪

'So, how you feeling, hon?' Claire asked that night, looking down towards Geraldine's end of the couch.

They were sitting in their Yokine townhouse, the TV flickering silently on the other side of the lounge room.

'I don't know. I should be feeling good, shouldn't I? But I don't know. Mostly I just feel tired.'

'Well, that's not surprising. This has all been a long time coming. We should go out to celebrate.'

'Yeah, we should,' said Geraldine, 'but I don't know what we'd be celebrating. I think I might have fucked up.'

'What do you mean?'

'I don't know if it's enough. They still have all the control.'

'But it's progress, right?' said Claire.

'I don't know. I guess I'll find out.'

▪▫▪

Through all the many changes of partners, friends, psychiatrists and counsellors, Dr Higson had been a constant in Geraldine's life for nearly twenty years.

Today, when Geraldine went to see her, a week after the *Gender Reassignment Act* had become law, she had a lot of questions for Geraldine.

'So, you're planning on making an application?' asked Dr Higson.

'I am. It's going to take them a while to put everything together at their end. They've got to appoint a board and figure out what the application process will look like.'

'So, you've got a bit of time to prepare, then?'

'Yes, but I'd rather get going now. I've already waited too long for this.'

'Maybe it's a good thing you have some time? I think you have some things to consider before you make an application.'

'Like what?' said Geraldine, already having a fair idea of what she was about to hear.

'Are you thinking about surgery?'

Geraldine had. She'd talked it through with Dr Miller years ago and, as always, had done her homework. She'd also had some interesting conversations about sex reassignment surgery with Cartwright over the years. He'd suggested it would be a good research topic for Geraldine.

'So, I should have surgery so I can become the ideal woman?' said Geraldine.

'That's not what I'm saying,' said Dr Higson, 'but you know as well as I do that sex reassignment surgery is an option and, from what you've told me about how the new law was put together, it may make the difference for you.'

'Yes, it's an option,' said Geraldine, 'but not for me. I know it is for some people, but I don't need it and the government shouldn't force it on me.'

■□■

Geraldine was among the first to make an application to the Gender Reassignment Board and among the first to be rejected on the grounds that she didn't have the characteristics of a person of the gender to which she had applied to be reassigned.

'It's because I've still got a dick, isn't it?' Geraldine said to Dr Higson after receiving the letter from the Board.

'I did tell you not to get your hopes up, Geraldine,' said Dr Higson.

'Well, fuck those people,' said Geraldine. 'I'm not stopping now.'

79

'You look tired, chick,' Claire said to Geraldine from her end of the sofa. They were home on a Monday night, watching *The Mole*.

'Yeah, I'm alright,' said Geraldine. 'Just got a bit on my mind.'

'Mmm, okay, then,' said Claire. 'You're not losing weight are you?'

'Hey?' said Geraldine, distracted by the TV.

'You're not losing weight?'

'I don't think so. Look, don't worry about me, I'm okay.'

'Well, if you say so,' said Claire, turning back to the TV.

Geraldine watched the light flicker across Claire's face for a few moments.

'Do you think he's the mole?' she said.

'I dunno,' said Claire. 'He looks shifty, doesn't he?'

The two women turned their focus back to the TV lest they miss a vital clue.

■□■

Geraldine didn't notice she'd stopped eating. She'd wake up in the mornings, her stomach tight and her thoughts an unruly mob fighting for bandwidth inside her head. Geraldine convinced herself it was okay to skip breakfast, she'd eat something at lunchtime. When lunchtime came and her stomach was no more open for business than it had been when she woke, she deferred to teatime. Avoiding food when Claire was home was a bit more difficult, but Geraldine had become an expert in small portions and distributing leftovers around her plate at boarding school and this technique served her well now, meaning she could join in the evening meal with Claire while eating very little.

When she noticed that her jeans were baggy at the waist and in danger of slipping off her still narrow hips, Geraldine concluded that exercise might be a good antidote for whatever was consuming her. She decided to start her days with a walk, heading down Villiers Street with the goal of making it to the open space down towards Mount Lawley. The going on the first morning was tough and her legs felt like they might fold under her.

'There's nothing wrong with me,' Geraldine repeated to herself under her increasingly shallow breath as she forced herself to take each step.

By the time Geraldine reached the end of Villiers Street she decided she'd had enough.

'I really need to work on my fitness,' she said to herself.

Geraldine returned home, planning to push herself a little bit further the next day and the next until she reached her goal. The next morning she made it to the bottom of Villiers Street and took a right down Flinders. The sight and sound of the cars travelling up and down Flinders Street disoriented Geraldine. She looked up to the sky, and the gentle flight of the few remaining clouds made her head spin. She felt like she was about to hit the ground. Geraldine struggled for breath, certain she was suffocating. She stood as still as she could on the gelatinous pavement, hoping that the world wouldn't notice her. When she felt steadier, she wiped the sweat from her face with a clammy hand and turned around to make what felt like an impossible return journey. Geraldine didn't say the words out loud, but her mind played them for her over and over as she staggered home like last night's drunk: 'There's something wrong with you.' Geraldine made it to the papasan chair and curled into a ball. She was still there when Claire came home from work.

Giving up on exercise, Geraldine spent her mornings in the chair, letting the phone go through to the answering machine and trying to order her thoughts. Geraldine began to sleep as a means of escaping the assault of her mind. When lunchtime came, she made herself go to the kitchen to think about eating, looking in the fridge and the cupboards but was never quite able to make a decision. Every day her stomach's answer was the same and she returned to the chair to sit and sleep some more. Geraldine woke from her sleep with a sense that she was barely awake, that wherever, whatever it was that she visited was trying to suck her back down into the spiky blackness. Her sleep was a flood-swollen river filled with snags, rocks, silky silt that made her flesh feel impossibly dry, and large, fast-moving objects that she never saw, though she could feel their gravity as they spun past her.

80

Having spent her entire life standing alone, Geraldine began to feel the creep of loneliness for the first time. She wanted someone to talk to, someone who knew who she was, and every time she searched for that person she could list only one name – Harry. Over the years, Geraldine had maintained infrequent contact with her parents, who had become increasingly convinced that Harry was dead. Best Grace and Frank knew, he had last been living in Spain. Around ten years ago Harry had dropped completely out of sight.

Ruminating on those conversations, Geraldine decided she needed to find out what had happened to Harry. She turned on her computer and dialled up a connection to the internet, the squelching sound of the modem drilling between the lobes of her brain. She decided not to check the emails that were beginning to pile up unopened in her inbox, instead spooling up Netscape and opening the Google search page. When she'd figured out that her best option was to seek help from the Red Cross, Geraldine opened Mail and, without looking at the seemingly never-ending string of unreads, sent a message providing as much information as she could. The automatic reply told Geraldine that a search could take up to six months and that someone would be in touch if they needed further information before then. Geraldine read the message and shut down the computer, returning to her spot on the chair.

Geraldine's daydreams continued to be variations on the theme of drowning. By night, Harry began to visit her. He was close but not close enough to touch, and she couldn't tell if he'd aged in the years since she'd last seen him. He never spoke, and Geraldine could find no way of communicating with him. She didn't know if he was aware of her presence. Geraldine sometimes woke expecting to see Harry in her bedroom at the front of the townhouse. She would open her eyes and search the room. Some mornings she would open the sliding door and step out onto the balcony in case he was standing in the street looking up at her, or on the speck of grass that passed for a front garden. Geraldine began to stay longer in bed, hoping to see Harry again and avoiding the relentless suck of her daytime dreaming.

The email from the Red Cross came after four months. Geraldine trembled as she hovered the mouse pointer over the bold subject line and hesitated before double clicking. The text of the email was businesslike and perfunctory. She read it once and shut down her computer. She returned to the chair and, on waking late in the afternoon, decided to read the email again to make sure she hadn't missed anything. Her second reading confirmed that Harry was nowhere to be found.

Geraldine refused to process the information, but the blankness of her dreams that night confirmed the news. The next morning, instead of going straight to the papasan, Geraldine sat at the dining table with a cup of tea and forced herself to plan her day. Her business had kept ticking over, but it had been a good while since Geraldine had left the house to meet with venue owners and bookers, catch up with musos and work on growing her agency. She set herself the task for the day of clearing her inbox and returning calls that had slipped through to the answering machine. Geraldine was surprised at how quickly she dealt with her emails and gave herself a smile for getting back in the saddle with such ease. She was so pleased with herself that when she wrestled with the idea of picking up the phone and returning calls she decided to give herself the rest of the day off.

'Tomorrow will be soon enough,' Geraldine told herself.

■□■

It was another week before Geraldine checked her inbox again. Phone calls still went unanswered. Geraldine made a deal with herself that she would check her emails on Mondays, Wednesdays and Fridays, reasoning that she needed the rest of the week to herself. Often, by the time Friday came, Geraldine would convince herself that it was close enough to the weekend, and Monday would do.

81

The knocking started just after lunchtime on a Saturday. They didn't often get visitors, and Geraldine considered just sitting quietly and letting whoever it was move on. The knocking came again, louder, more insistent. Geraldine continued to sit. It wasn't until the third time, when Geraldine thought that whoever it was would break the front door's stained glass, that she got up to answer it.

'Oh, you are home,' said Edie when Geraldine cracked the door.

'Yes?' said Geraldine.

'Well, are you gonna let me in?'

'Yes?'

'Well, open the door, then.'

Geraldine stood back and Edie stepped inside and followed Geraldine to the dining table, where they sat across from each other.

'What the fuck's going on, Geraldine?'

'What do you mean?' said Geraldine, genuinely confused by Edie's anger and more than a little bit frightened.

'Damien didn't turn up for his set last night. You left me with no-one. Not that anyone really cared, but you let me down. No phone call, no email. What the fuck's going on, Geraldine?'

Geraldine stared at the woman across the table from her.

'Are you still in business?' said Edie. 'There's lots of talk around the traps. People are starting to get pissed off.'

'What do you mean?' said Geraldine.

'You don't know?' said Edie, her voice lowering a few decibels. 'You really don't know?'

'No,' said Geraldine, 'I've had a bit going on.'

'When was the last time you went to one of your venues? I haven't seen you out for ages. What's happening, Geraldine? Are you okay?'

Geraldine felt like there were too many of Edie's words for her to process.

'Yeah, I'm okay,' she said.

'Well, you'd better get your fucking shit together.'

Geraldine stood at the open door of her townhouse, making nice as she watched Edie get into her car, giving her a little wave as she drove away. She felt the acid burn of hatred rising in her chest and stood holding the edge of her front door as the feeling sank back inside her. Geraldine's feet wavered as she made her way back to the refuge of the chair.

'I'd better get my fucking shit together,' Geraldine said to herself as she drifted away into sleep.

82

Geraldine didn't know how long she'd taken to think it through, but once she'd made up her mind, she was immobilised by the idea of what she needed to do next. It could have been moments, minutes, hours, days, weeks, months, years, before she acted on her decision, time had lost all meaning for her. In that infinity of inaction, Geraldine checked and rechecked her logic, and every time the equations ground out the same answer. She thought about Mr Alcock and how pleased he would be that she had carried through the scientific method he had impregnated in her. Part of Geraldine still wanted his approval, was still enthralled by his mystery and promise. Part of her knew that what she'd decided was the only way to heal the gashes he'd made in her existence.

Geraldine couldn't remember the last time she'd driven her car. The silver Mazda hatchback was waiting faithfully when she opened the door to the garage, the space next to it empty. Claire was out for the night, not due to return home until tomorrow. Geraldine sat in the driver's seat and slipped the key into the ignition. She started the motor, the sound of it coming to life making her chest tremble. Her arms felt like the marrow in her bones had turned to lead as she held on to the steering wheel, hands at ten and two. Geraldine sat and breathed deeply as the motor settled into an idle. When she was ready, she opened the car's centre console and used the clicker to activate the garage door. She backed out into the driveway and clicked the blue button one more time, watching carefully until the garage was fully closed before pulling out onto Villiers Street.

The further east she got, the more Geraldine's anxiety made the task of continuing to drive impossible. Her mind was conflicted with thoughts, some her own and some belonging to the unbidden voice that had delivered to her an array of information throughout her life.

'You're going to die,' the voice told her. 'Pull over and stop the car, you're going to die.'

Geraldine and her voice were rarely in step. This time they had a shared narrative, but they were coming at the problem from different perspectives, seeking different outcomes. Geraldine's voice used the threat of death as a way of stoking her anxiety. It didn't want her dead, that would end the fun. Tonight, Geraldine's purpose was to end that fun definitively.

'Yes, I am,' she said as she kept on driving.

Greenmount Hill levelled out into Great Eastern Highway and, as Geraldine and her silver Mazda left behind the last driveway and roadside shack, she began her search proper. She kept her lights on high beam, ignoring the flashes and horns from the occasional trucks and cars coming the other way. Geraldine's eyes were fixed on the farthest point she could see in the distance. She lost count of the number of times she saw what she was looking for only to find herself keeping on driving.

Geraldine was shocked by the bite of the gravel as she steered the Mazda off the road. It almost yanked the steering wheel out of her hands and had her veering too far to the left. She pulled hard to the right and found herself swinging back towards the road, two wheels on the gravel, two on the bitumen, her car bucking and fighting as it tried to find the path of least resistance. The enormous whiteness of the tree veered in and out of view as the Mazda's headlights swept across it multiple times. When she finally managed to wrestle the car fully onto the gravel, its nose swung violently to the right leaving Geraldine approaching the tree side on, the Mazda's high beams lighting up the stand of ghost gums watching on from the other side of the road.

■□■

Geraldine didn't remember the moment of impact, but she was awake when someone opened her door.

'What's your name?' the person said, shining a torch in Geraldine's eyes.

Geraldine shielded her face from the sudden brightness.

'What's your name?' the person said with more urgency.

'Geraldine.'

'You've had a crash, Geraldine. Are you in pain? Do you remember what happened?'

Geraldine did some checking. Her chest felt like she'd been kicked repeatedly. Her right shoulder felt like someone had tried to wrench it from its socket. Her left thigh throbbed. She moved her head to talk to the person at her door and almost fainted with the sharpness of the pain.

'Are you okay? Stay with me.'

'Yes, I'm okay, I think.'

'Geraldine, I'm a paramedic. The first thing I want to do is put a brace on your neck. Sit tight, I'll be back in a moment.'

Geraldine stayed looking straight ahead while he disappeared back to the ambulance, his offsider keeping a quiet watch over her.

■□■

Geraldine was admitted to Midland hospital overnight. She had bruising on her chest and shoulder from the wrestle between the seatbelt, her body and inertia. She had what the doctor described as a corky on her left thigh from the impact with the Mazda's centre console, and she had mild whiplash and likely concussion, which was the main reason they were keeping Geraldine.

'What happened?' the doctor asked her.

'I don't really know, it's a bit of a blur.'

'What were you doing?'

'Just going for a drive.'

'Mm-hmm,' said the doctor, looking at Geraldine lying on the gurney.

'Do you need to speak to someone?' he asked.

'No, I don't think so,' said Geraldine. 'What for?'

'Sometimes people drive into trees deliberately,' said the doctor.

Geraldine looked up at him, held his gaze.

'Not me,' she said.

■□■

Up in her hospital room, the police asked much the same questions as the doctor, and Geraldine gave much the same answers. When they asked what she'd been doing, Geraldine began to lose her cool.

'I was going for a drive,' she said. 'It's still a free country, isn't it?'

'There's no need for that, Mr Sturmer,' said the man in khaki standing closest to her.

'Fuck off!' said Geraldine.

'Any more of that and I'll arrest you,' the copper said.

'Just try it,' said Geraldine, pressing the call button above her head.

A nurse arrived and briskly suggested to the two police officers that they step outside.

'Are you okay, Geraldine?' she said.

'Do you have anything for my pain?'

'Of course. I'll go and get something for you,' said the nurse who, as she turned to leave the room, said to the two policemen, 'It's time for you to go.'

'We'll come back tomorrow,' said the one standing closest to Geraldine.

When the nurse returned to Geraldine's room, she sat in the chair next to her bed and handed her a tiny paper cup with two pills in it and a slightly larger cup holding water.

'Here, take these, they'll help you sleep, too.'

The nurse sat and watched as Geraldine swallowed down the pills. For a while there was silence in the hospital room.

'Are you okay, love?' the nurse asked Geraldine.

'Yes, I'll be fine,' Geraldine tried to say, but the catch in her throat stole her breath and she couldn't form the last few words.

Geraldine swallowed and felt the crackle in her throat. She took a breath.

'Yes, I'll be okay,' she said, this time managing to make all her words audible.

The nurse reached out her hand and held it gently on top of Geraldine's. Geraldine remembered Harry holding her hand in the hospital in Weston after she'd been beaten up by Patrick Burges and the knowledge in his touch that everything would be okay. For a moment she felt safe again and then she looked at the nurse, a complete stranger, and knew that nothing could be okay ever again. She pulled her hand away from the nurse's.

'Promise me something, Geraldine,' said the nurse.

'What.'

'When you get out of here tomorrow, go talk to someone?'

83

A year on and Geraldine was still talking to someone. It had started the day she was discharged from Midland hospital, Claire guiding Geraldine across the carpark to her blue Corolla in the glare of the midmorning sun.

'Looks like summer's on the way,' Geraldine said as they pulled onto Great Eastern Highway, this time heading west back towards the city.

'Are we really talking about the weather, Geraldine?'

'Look, it's okay,' said Geraldine. 'Bob didn't even bother turning up this time. Cheeky little fucker.'

'What?' said Claire. 'What the hell are you on about?'

There was a long silence in the car as the two women looked straight ahead. After it had gone on a moment too long, Claire decided she'd had enough.

'I'm taking you to see Dr Higson,' she said.

'What? When?'

'Now.'

'No, Claire, I don't need that. I just need to go home and get some sleep.'

'Sleep is the last thing you need, Geraldine. You need some help and I'm going to make sure you get it. I'm so sorry, Geraldine, I've stood by and let this all happen, but I can't anymore.'

'What do you mean?' said Geraldine, her voice beginning to soften at her friend's apology. 'This isn't your fault.'

'You'll let me take you?'

'Yes, yes, okay.'

Claire sat in on the appointment with Geraldine.

'This is my friend, Claire,' Geraldine said before Dr Higson could ask.

'Hello,' said Dr Higson. 'What brings you here today?'

'I crashed my car,' said Geraldine.

'She spent last night in Midland hospital,' said Claire.

'Oh?' said Dr Higson. 'Are you okay? How did it happen?'

'I hit a tree,' said Geraldine.

'Did you?' said Dr Higson. 'Deliberately?'

Geraldine thought about lying again.

'Kind of?' said Geraldine, attempting a smile. 'But by the time I hit it I don't think I was really in control of the car.'

'Right,' said Dr Higson.

Later that afternoon, Geraldine and her overnight bag walked through the gates of a clinic that hid in plain sight at the Parliament end of the city, Claire at her side. She spent a month there relearning how to maintain her daily routines – waking, showering, eating, sleeping, with hourly checks for proof of life – and she talked, at first reluctantly and, in the end, because her life depended on it. A year later, with work humming again, Geraldine was still talking, this time with the counsellor who debriefed her on her weekly group therapy sessions.

'I hated the idea of group therapy at first,' said Geraldine.

'I know you did,' said Shelley, chuckling as she recalled Geraldine's resistance to almost everything to do with therapy.

'I didn't want to be spilling my guts to a group of strangers.'

'And you thought you were better than them, didn't you?'

'Yes, a little bit,' said Geraldine.

'And now?'

'It's just good to know that I'm not the only one. I felt so isolated, like no-one could be feeling the way I was. I didn't feel like I had any choices left. It all hurt too much.'

'Yes, choices,' said Shelley. 'What do you think you're going to do next?'

'I don't know,' said Geraldine. 'I can keep fighting or I can just take the easy path. I really don't know what to do.'

She looked at Shelley.

'Well, you'll just have to figure that out, won't you?' said Shelley.

84

Geraldine sat looking at Cartwright across his messy desk. It was late summer 2003 and, though he'd been to visit her once in the clinic, they hadn't seen each other since then.

'What brings you here, Geraldine?' said Cartwright.

Geraldine studied her friend and decided he was looking old.

'Were you serious?' she said.

'About what?'

'All those times you said I should come here and study. Were you serious?'

'Oh, that,' said Cartwright.

He paused and Geraldine and prepared herself for the blow.

'Yes, absolutely. You're the smartest person I've met in a long time.'

It was Geraldine's turn to hesitate. 'Thank you?'

'That's okay, Geraldine, I mean it. You'll have to do an undergrad degree first, but after that you can choose your own adventure. You will be nice to the other students, won't you? They're only children.'

'Fuck off, Roger! You know I always play nicely.'

They laughed but kept it down this time so as not to create another disturbance of mirth in the vaunted halls of Cartwright's building.

'There is one more thing, Geraldine,' said Cartwright. 'You may not know, because you've been out of the loop for a bit and it hasn't exactly made the news, of course.'

'What?'

'There are a couple of trans men who had their applications to the Gender Reassignment Board rejected, for the same reason as you – wrong reproductive bits. They appealed to the State Administrative Tribunal and the decision was overturned, but the Court of Appeal reinstated it, so now they're going to the High Court.'

'Fuck! You're kidding me.'

Geraldine had ridden Cartwright's precis of the case through a slam dance of emotions – anger, triumph, rage, faint hope.

'Nope, not kidding at all.'

85

Geraldine met Stephanie at the fundraiser. An outdoor concert at Langley Park, it was by far the biggest event Geraldine had put on, and she'd called in every favour and leaned on everyone she knew to put together the permits, the staging and the line-up. Since the early days of the Desk when Julia had taught Geraldine that people in the music industry should get paid for their work, she'd never asked anyone to give it away, until now.

'This isn't going to be like that show in the church, is it?' Ken West asked her when she called him to talk about Ignition headlining.

'Janine told you about that, did she?'

'She sure did. That was a ballsy move, Geraldine, but we can't have that sort of thing happening now. This is business, right?'

'Yes, business all the way.'

'What if I can get someone with more pull than Ignition to headline for you?'

In Geraldine's mind there was no-one bigger than Ignition. She ran through her protocols.

'Thank you,' said Geraldine.

■□■

Geraldine and Stephanie were introduced by a mutual friend, a photographer who worked schools by day and shot musicians evenings and weekends. They were in the VIP area, front of stage, and Stephanie asked Geraldine what the lanyard around her neck was for.

'So you could go backstage and meet Jimmy Barnes?' Stephanie said once Geraldine had explained.

'I could,' said Geraldine.

'I'd love to meet Barnesy,' said Stephanie. 'He's my favourite of all time.'

Geraldine took in the woman standing in front of her. They had their heads together so they could hear each other over local punk icons, Jebediah, so she had to take half a step back to get a proper look. Stephanie was wearing a dress and heels to an outdoor concert. She looked totally out of place, but Geraldine appreciated that she was doing her own thing when everyone around them was intent on fitting in. It was the first thing that attracted Geraldine to her.

'Here, have my pass,' said Geraldine, hanging the lanyard around Stephanie's neck.

Stephanie looked down at the laminate.

'Oh, no, I couldn't,' said Stephanie, making to take it off.

Geraldine reached out a hand and held Stephanie's in place.

'Take it, go meet Barnesy,' she said. 'They'll have no idea back there. As long as you've got that on no-one will care.'

'Really?' said Stephanie.

'Yep,' said Geraldine. 'See that person over there? Just go flash it to him. He'll let you through.'

Stephanie walked over towards the security barrier and the man dressed all in black. She looked around to Geraldine a few times before she made the distance, Geraldine waving her on. One last look and Stephanie was let through the barrier and then disappeared into the backstage area. She was back after five minutes.

'Did you see him?' Geraldine asked.

'No,' said Stephanie.

'You didn't? What were you doing back there, then?'

'I couldn't,' said Stephanie, handing the lanyard back to Geraldine.

'Don't worry,' said Geraldine, 'how about I introduce you after the show?'

'Really? Do you know him?'

'A little bit. Not really, but it'll be right.'

They stood together for the rest of the night and afterwards, when Stephanie was still high from her five seconds with Barnesy, Geraldine asked for her number.

86

Geraldine was nervous about meeting the two trans men at the centre of the High Court appeal. She'd only communicated with Brandon and Paul via email until now. She was envious because she wouldn't be standing up in court with them and felt the sting of shame that her own journey had denied her the strength to be front and centre at this most critical moment. She also felt guilty for the part she'd played in advising on what became the *Gender Reassignment Act*. It took all her learning from therapy not to conclude that she was a coward and a fraud.

'I'm so sorry,' said Geraldine, when the four of them were seated in a tutorial room down the hall from Cartwright's office.

'What do you mean?' said Brandon.

'I feel like what's happening to you is my fault. I was on Kate Deans' reference group.'

'Hang on a second, Geraldine,' said Cartwright. 'If I remember rightly, if it wasn't for you the government would never have even thought about recognition for trans people.'

'Maybe I should have just kept my big mouth shut?' said Geraldine.

'It doesn't matter,' said Paul. 'All that counts is that we win this, and the money you've raised is amazing. It means we can pay our legal bills.'

'I just don't feel like it's enough,' said Geraldine.

'For you, nothing is ever enough,' said Cartwright.

■□■

Geraldine took Steph with her to the celebration after the High Court ruled in favour of Brandon and Paul. She kept a low profile and made sure she was way at the back of the room upstairs at the Court Hotel when Brandon namechecked her for raising funds on their behalf. On their way out, Geraldine noticed a familiar figure on the dancefloor downstairs.

'Kym!' she called out as she nudged her way through the bodies.

The person looked over at Geraldine, confusion at first and then a smile of recognition on their face.

'Geraldine! It's been a while, hasn't it?' said Kym.

'It certainly has,' said Geraldine. 'When I saw you, I felt like it would be okay to call you by your name. I hope I didn't get that wrong.

'No, not at all,' said Kym, smiling.

'How fucking fabulous,' said Geraldine.

'It is,' said Kym. 'And it's so good to see you.'

■□■

'So, what happens now?' said Steph when they were in the car heading back to Geraldine's.

'What do you mean?'

'Are you going to go back and apply again?'

'What for?'

'To the Gender Reassignment Board.'

'Oh, that. I don't know,' said Geraldine. 'I don't know if I have it in me anymore. What if they refuse me again? I don't know if I could survive that.'

■□■

'I'll go with you,' said Steph when they were having breakfast the next morning.

'What?' said Geraldine, 'Where?'

'To the Board, when you reapply.'

'Are we still on this?' said Geraldine.

'Yes, we are,' said Steph. 'I think you need to do this, otherwise you're stuck. And I want to travel, Geraldine, with you. I want to spend the rest of my life with you.'

Geraldine looked at Steph, her mind racing at light speed.

'You want to spend the rest of your life with me?' she said.

'Don't go changing the subject now,' said Steph, 'that's not what we're talking about.'

'I think it is. I think you just changed the whole subject.'

'Uh-uh, no I didn't.'

'Oh, yes you did,' said Geraldine.

'So what if I did? So what if I just want to live a boring, ordinary life with you?'

'We can just be a pair of ordinary women the rest of our lives,' said Geraldine. 'That's perfectly fine with me.'

AUTHOR'S NOTE AND ACKNOWLEDGEMENTS

Geraldine is a work of fiction that includes references to some significant events in LGBTQIA+ rights and law reform in Western Australia.

In the story, Geraldine sits on an LGBT (there was no + at the time) community reference group that has input into what became the state of Western Australia's *Law Reform (Decriminalisation of Sodomy) Act 1989.*[1] As the name suggests, the Act decriminalised anal sex, but the parliamentarians who were party to drafting this legislation went out of their way to ensure that the general population could not mistake this legislation as in any way supporting same-sex relationships. The act prohibited encouragement of homosexual behaviour and made it unlawful to promote homosexuality in schools. The Act also stated on page one that 'the Parliament disapproves of sexual relations between persons of the same sex.'

While a step forward, the *Law Reform (Decriminalisation of Sodomy) Act 1989* was an exercise of the power of state government over the lives of ordinary Western Australian citizens, demonising their diversity and sexualities and giving assurances to the cisgender, heterosexual (cishet) majority that the queers wouldn't be coming after their children.

The *Law Reform (Decriminalisation of Sodomy) Act 1989* was repealed in 2002 and replaced with the *Acts Amendment (Lesbian and Gay Law Reform)*

---

1 *Law Reform (Decriminalization of Sodomy) Act 1989* https://www.legislation.wa.gov.au/legislation/prod/filestore.nsf/FileURL/mrdoc_1249.pdf/$FILE/Law%20Reform%20(Decriminalization%20of%20Sodomy)%20Act%201989%20-%20%5B01-b0-05%5D.pdf?OpenElement

Act 2002,[2] which updated a range of legislation to give LGBTQIA+ people greater equity.

In 2000 the Western Australian Parliament passed the *Gender Reassignment Act 2000*,[3] which established a Gender Reassignment Board with the power to issue gender recognition certificates, providing gender-diverse Western Australians with a way to have their genders legally recognised. This Act was problematic because it empowered the Gender Reassignment Board to make decisions about the lives and identities of gender-diverse people, and privileged evidence from medical practitioners, psychologists, family, friends, employers – anyone but the person making an application to have their gender recognised. Applicants were not required to submit their own evidence, but could do so if they chose, and were not required to attend meetings where the Board deliberated on their applications.

A little more than a decade ago, the Gender Reassignment Board attempted to use the *Gender Reassignment Act 2000* to force two transgender men to have hysterectomies before they could have their genders legally recognised. The two applicants, known only as A.B. and A.H., appealed the decision,[4] which was subsequently overturned by the High Court of Australia. *The Gender Reassignment Act 2000* was passed into legislation ostensibly to support gender-diverse people. At the time of this case, the members of the Gender Reassignment Board included leading practitioners in transgender medicine, and yet this Board interpreted the Act as enabling the imposition of state-sanctioned surgical mutilation on gender-diverse individuals. This Act is another example of how the Parliament and so-

---

2 *Acts Amendment (Lesbian and Gay Law Reform) Act 2002* https://www.legislation.wa.gov.au/legislation/statutes.nsf/main_mrtitle_2249_homepage.html

3 *Gender Reassignment Act 2000* https://www.legislation.wa.gov.au/legislation/statutes.nsf/law_a1986.html

4 *AB v Western Australia* https://humanrights.gov.au/sites/default/files/document/publication/AB_and_AH_article.pdf

called experts – the cishet majority – continue to exercise power over the lives of gender-diverse people.

The two trans men who fought the Gender Reassignment Board and won are heroes of Western Australia's transgender history. The inclusion of characters like them in the narrative of *Geraldine* is an entirely fictional recount of how their lives intersected with the life of the title character, because to write this story without reference to them would be impossible. It is my hope that, someday, their story can be told more fully and accurately. Without these two men, Geraldine would not exist, and neither would I.

Having been through the Gender Reassignment Board's process, I can attest that it is an exercise in ritual humiliation that is both cruel and unnecessary.

On 16 April 2024, the WA government announced that it would repeal the *Gender Reassignment Act*. At the media conference, the Attorney-General made comments connecting gender-diverse women to male sex criminals as justification for forcing people applying to have their genders legally recognised to undergo 'appropriate clinical treatment'. It is clear that, with repeal of the *Gender Reassignment Act*, the government intends to continue to treat gender-diverse people differently to cisgender people and to impose barriers on our existences that are unnecessary and designed to continue to oppress us.

I reject the label 'transgender' as it is just one more expression of the cishet majority's power over the lives of a small and highly marginalised group of people. For now, I prefer the term 'gender diverse'. I am a woman and, as long as I have breath in me, I will write and fight for a post-gender society where no-one has to apply to the government to have their gender recognised and no-one is treated as less because they don't conform to the male/female gender binary and are not part of the cishet majority.

The fight for LGBTQIA+ equity continues today.

■□■

If you've read this far, you've probably noticed that, in places, I have been loose with the timeline of real events to get them to fit Geraldine's narrative. I lived through the seventies, so chronology isn't my strong suit, but I do enjoy the idea of the wiki entries discussing what I've got wrong.

I would like to thank the editor of this book, Seth Malacari. In the early drafts of *Geraldine* I deliberately referenced some ideas about the experience of being gender diverse that I knew would be controversial and provoke strong responses. Seth's wise and deft editing saved me from miring *Geraldine* in debates that are better saved for other contexts and, for that, I thank him.

I also would like to thank Georgia Richter, publisher at Fremantle Press, for her encouragement and support during the early drafting of *Geraldine* and for telling me, when I first spoke with her, that I 'have a way with words'. Georgia's kindness and support was a big part of what enabled me to climb the mountain that is writing a novel.

Finally, I would like to acknowledge my family to whom this book is dedicated and my chosen family who continue to be an inspiration in my life. For LGBTQIA+ people, chosen family are often the difference between life and death, and I love the warm embrace of those who recognise me for who I am without question or need for explanation.

Also available

Some people are born into bad situations, some people have bad situations thrust upon them, and some people find bad situations through their dodgy choices, lack of information and personal idiosyncrasies. Julia's life sits at the intersection of all three.

From domestic dysfunction to extraordinary bad luck, Julia Lawrinson reflects on an intriguing, eventful and sometimes downright disastrous life with disarming honesty and wit.

From high school dropout on a psych ward to card-carrying lesbian on a motorbike, from enduring a controlling relationship with her ex-lover's brother to being chased by a media scrum outside a Perth court, the life of beloved children's author Julia Lawrinson is stranger than fiction – and she draws on all her power as a storyteller to turn a life of intense headlines into a wild, marvellous tale.

at fremantlepress.com.au